FriesenPress

Suite 300 - 990 Fort St
Victoria, BC, V8V 3K2
Canada

www.friesenpress.com

ISBN
978-1-5255-6703-2 (Hardcover)
978-1-5255-6704-9 (Paperback)
978-1-5255-6705-6 (eBook)

1. YOUNG ADULT FICTION, FANTASY

Distributed to the trade by The Ingram Book Company

FROM

OUT OF THE

SHADOWS

Book 1 of
THE AETERNIUM CYCLE

A.G.V. McPherson

For the dreamers.

FAERYLN

Snowy Lake

Waterdown

Syrvyad

Smallwood

Simarus Tower

★Argenrros Yad

Silvalta

Isyladar

Icewater

Bal algard

Selgus

Arturius

Elven Bay

LOCHADIA

THELEGARD

VIA

Mylos

Ilous Lake

Longwater

Boar Lake

SYLVARE

Sylvan Forest

★Arnya Elega

Rythesta

Bharghul

Stag Lake

★Lakedale

Brekshan

Longwood

PYRADIA

Fields

N

Glacial Ocean

Frozen Sea

METERNERRAS

HELVARK

Borhamm   Icevein   ★ Holmgard

Northguard Mountains

Mara's   Needlewood
Village

Pineshire   Rekram

ESRALAND   Snowy   ■ Waterdown
Lake

FAERYLN

Muthwing   Syrvyad
Forest
Everburrow   Smallwood   Dorn
★   Simarus   ★ Argenrros
Tower
BRYLAND   Savelta   Bali-   Therelissa
Gulfhollow   Isylalar   Treewater   salgari
Esnian   MARRELNIA
Gulf
Archurius   Selgus   Starwood

The Great Ocean

ESNIA   LOCHADIA   Elven
Bay
Mylas   THELEGARD   Andorei
Nedaryll   Ibas Lake   Longwater
Boar Lake   ISLAND
SYLVARE   OF
Sylvan Forest   ★ Arnva   Pharghul   BANISHMENT
Rylness   Elega
Nareda   Skog Lake   Brekshan   ★ Lakedale
NORTH   Longwood
HYNAR   Lindon
T'nel   PYRADIA   Fields
of Flame   Forest
Fire Mountains
Murnak   Phyrim   Ghielhard   Fort Vanguard
SOUTH   Yallum   Volhad
HYNAR   THE FELL   Forest of Ash
★ Shekai   LANDS   VANARIA
Bhat
The Black Sea

The Western Ocean

Esnian Sea

Stormy Sea

The Elven Sea

The Lost Ocean

0   60   180   300 DECIUMS

TABLE OF CONTENTS

Frozen Sea
HELVARK
Holmgard
Icevein
Borhamn
Northguard Mountains
Mara's Village
Needlewood
Pineshire
Rekram
Snowy Lake
Waterdown
FAERYLN
Mushroom Forest
Everburrow
Smallwood
Elmanus' Tower
Argenrros
Sylvenglad
Silvalta
Isyladar
Gulfhollow
Arcturius

PROLOGUE

"THEY FOUND US."

The girl's face blanched beneath her black cowl, heart pounding in her ears, pulse racing. Three simple words, and they had stolen the very breath from her lungs.

"What do we do?" she whispered back once her voice had unglued itself from her throat.

The man turned toward the girl, his face barely visible under his hood in the black of night. "We run," he answered simply.

Immediately, both man and girl sprinted across the moonlit forest floor. Instincts alone saved them from tripping over the many rocks and roots littering the mossy ground. The girl knew that so much as a stumble could spell death.

Arrows rattled in their quivers as the girl ran, sword thumping against her leg, bow bouncing in her hand. For a moment, she considered stopping, turning around, and firing at her assailants. But she knew it was foolish. How could one shoot something they couldn't see?

A branch whipped the girl in the face and she nearly stumbled, the sharp pain threatening to slow her down, to throw her off balance. She maintained control, however, only wincing as the sharp branch scratched her cheek. She felt moisture there but couldn't tell if it was sweat or blood.

For a moment, the girl's heart felt as though it had been pierced by ice, a spike of panic so intense, it nearly stole every last drop of strength from her burning muscles. At first, she wasn't sure what had caused the sudden lash of fear. An instant later, however, she heard a noise, a very faint thud just to her left, and she knew.

The man must have heard it too. "Go!" he yelled. "Run! Faster!"

The girl felt her stomach twist with fear and pumped her legs faster, thundering across the soft earth as quickly as she could. More thuds surrounded her, spraying little bits of soil into the air.

The girl was getting closer. If they could reach the outpost walls, they would be safe, or at least, safer. Already, she could see the gentle orange glow of the torches bleeding through the branches of the trees. So close.

Despite all common sense screaming at her not to, the girl risked a glance over her shoulder. Just long enough to catch a glimpse of a shadowy figure flit between two ash trees.

Just long enough for that figure to take aim and fire.

The girl froze. This time, she knew, the next thud would not come from the ground. It would be the thud of an arrow in her chest, streaking through mail and flesh to pierce her heart.

Just before the arrow struck her, something heavy slammed into the girl's side, smashing her into the dirt. She heard the *thrum* of a bow firing and the shadowy figure dropped to the ground.

She heard the thud of an arrow piercing flesh. But not her flesh.

The man groaned, breathing short and heavy as he lay splayed out across the moss. The silhouette of an arrow jutted out of his midsection, its black fletching glowing evilly in the moonlight. Something dark and twinkling was spilling out of the wound, seeping into the moss as it flowed down the man's sides.

Tears welled up in the girl's eyes as she crawled over to the man. Cradling his head in her arms, she could see pain in his eyes, as burning and fierce as the poison from the arrow spreading through his system.

"Father," she croaked, the only word she could get past the lump in her throat.

Her father reached up with a shaking hand to touch her cheek, leaving a smear of blood across it. "I am sorry," he said softly. "So sorry."

"Don't talk like that," the girl protested through her tears. "You're going to be ok. We're almost there. Just get up. Please."

"It's too late for me," the man replied. In her heart, the girl knew it was true, but she didn't want to accept it. Couldn't accept it. "There is no time. Quickly, take these," the man instructed, handing her a bundle of papers.

Hurriedly, the girl stuffed them into her belt, crying silently as she did. "I won't leave you," she sobbed.

"You must," the man insisted, as fiercely as he could. "And take these. I cannot bear to see them fall into their hands." He pushed a few items toward the girl. She couldn't see them clearly, but she knew what they were.

"Father, I can't," she whispered.

"You must," he said again. With his last breath, he looked deep into the girl's eyes and smiled. "Your mother would be so proud."

Then his chest fell for the last time and his head lolled over.

Had not another arrow landed by her feet, the girl would have stayed there, hunched over the body of her dead father, watering the ground with her grief. But the urgency of her situation snapped something in the girl's mind, severing her emotions just long enough for her to jump to her feet and run, though not before closing her father's eyes.

The girl ran harder and faster this time, feeling as though her heart would pound its way out of her chest. Her lungs heaved and burned with each breath, the pain of losing her father creeping back and sapping strength from her.

The girl steeled her mind to it, turned sadness into rage, anguish into fury, fuelled her tiring legs with the pain that burned within her. More arrows flew by her, some slamming into trees or glancing off rocks, others whizzing over her shoulder barely a hair's width from her throat.

Still the girl ran, clutching tightly to the gifts her father gave her. She couldn't let them go, couldn't lose the last part of him that she still had.

She was close now, so very close. She could see the end of the tree line, could hear the shouts of soldiers and see the wooden gates start to open, beckoning her to the safety of its interior. It was close, so close, just there across a small stretch of grass.

The girl cried out suddenly, fierce pain darting up her ankle as the tip of her boot snagged on a gnarled root. She skidded into the grassy stretch, dirt flying into her mouth as she landed.

She could hear voices yelling, urging her to get up and run. She heard the sound of longbows firing into the trees, trying to distract her pursuers. She heard her father's voice in her head, telling her to fight, to stand, to live.

Scrambling against the panic, the girl leapt to her feet, trying to ignore the pain in her ankle. She hurriedly scooped up her father's gifts, remembering his dying wish to keep them safe, and took off across the grass. Arrows continued to rain around her, although some were now flying at the archers on the outpost palisades.

Instinct told her to dive so she did, springing off the ground and flinging herself into the gateway of the outpost. An arrow thudded into the ground right where she had been. Several men clad in mail began immediately hauling the gate closed, and a grizzled old soldier rushed over to her.

The girl's face scraped against the dirt entrance, but she pushed away that pain, too. It didn't matter. She had completed the mission. She had the plans. As the soldier helped her to her feet, she reached down to her belt to grab them and hand them off to the man.

Her fingers grasped thin air.

A new form of panic set in as the girl began groping desperately at her belt, trying to find the papers. They weren't there.

Eyes wild, she cast a glance out of the gateway, which was rapidly closing. Her heart dropped. There they were, highlighted in the torchlight and strewn across the grass where she had fallen. The girl only saw them for an instant before a thin, pale hand scooped them up and stole them away into the blackness.

The girl sank to her knees as the heavy wooden gate slammed shut. There was no emotion to describe how she felt now, no word to fit the grief and loss and defeat that sat upon her shoulders, dragging her lower and lower into the earth like chains.

Her father had died for those plans. He had given his life so that she could complete the mission. And she had failed.

Her father had died in vain.

The girl didn't know what happened next, although she vaguely remembered being carried away by strong arms. She was broken, so utterly broken, her spirit shattered by the weight of her failure and her loss. Reality seemed to twist and fade, melding into a black cloud that filled her mind and choked her heart.

Eventually, her grief passed, and consciousness returned to her. She found herself lying in a simple bed, dressed in a plain white nightgown. She wasn't sure how much time had passed.

She was sure of one thing, however. There was much still to be done. She knew what her father would want of her, knew he would want for her to carry on and continue to fight the darkness.

And she knew that the darkness would come for her next.

CHAPTER I:
MAGIC, MISHAPS, AND MERCHANTS

A TALL, WHITE TOWER ROSE OUT OF ONE OF THE MANY hills overlooking the beautiful valley, where the High Elves of Faeryln dwelt. The tower's curved sides sloped gracefully into the air in a fashion typical of elvish architecture. A cuboidal room sat atop the tower's body, giving way to a tall, pointed roof made of blue slate that pierced the endless skies above it. Stained glass windows lined its walls, each surrounded by intricate carvings and overlooking a thin, elegant windowsill.

Without warning, the windows exploded into a rain of glass and fire.

Inside the tower, Silmanus cursed under his breath. The elf had barely activated a shielding spell in time and some of his long black hair had been singed, a sulphurous odour filling the air and causing Silmanus to wrinkle his nose. Black soot caked his normally gleaming, silvery skin, and his green and silver robes were dotted with burn marks.

Sighing heavily, the wizard waggled his fingers and muttered some arcane words, and the jewel atop his oaken staff flared bright green.

Slowly at first, but picking up speed as the spell worked, the room, utterly destroyed, began pulling itself back together. Any fires were extinguished, furniture repaired and righted itself, and scorch marks were cleaned from the walls. The shards of glass lying on the grass below flew up to the tower's top, reassembling themselves into the windows they once were.

In just about thirty seconds, the entire tower was back to normal, with not a trace of mishap, save Silmanus' sour face. He had come so close to stabilizing his latest magical development, a potion that, in theory, would be able to cure any poison or disease known to the world. However, Silmanus just couldn't get the potion's components to properly combine and each attempt he made ended in the same ball of fiery destruction.

The slender elf let out another sigh, slumping his narrow shoulders. The potion required an herb native only to the human kingdom of Eiraland, called frostpetal, making it an expensive product on the markets. It was also almost constantly sold out in herbalist shops throughout Faeryln, the High Elf kingdom where Silmanus dwelt. Without ordering it in advance, frostpetal was nearly impossible to acquire and Silmanus had foolishly assumed that he already had enough to complete his experiment.

That left Silmanus with two options: either make a gruelling journey north and harvest the frostpetal for himself or travel to Argenrros, the capital of Faeryln, and try to find the herb there.

Silmanus highly doubted that he would even find a single leaf of frostpetal anywhere in Argenrros but it was worth a try. He'd kick himself for a month if he went to all the trouble of travelling to Eiraland when he could have just found what he needed in a much nearer location; Eiraland was roughly 360 deciums north, as the crow flies.

There was something of an amusing story behind the decium. It was the distance a person could walk in ten minutes, and had been established thousands of years ago because of a silly argument between a dwarf and an elf about who could run better while drunk. In order to settle the dispute, a man made a racing lane by walking for ten minutes and then stopping, calling the distance a decium.

The amusing part was that, according to the tale, nobody actually won that race; both the elf and the dwarf were far too heavily intoxicated and doubled over vomiting before they even made it halfway.

While the debate may not have been settled, a new system of measurement was, and the decium became universally accepted. It was very handy for travelling, as approximate travel time could be worked out through a very simple conversion. If you could travel one decium in ten minutes, you could travel six in an hour, and that meant that Silmanus' journey of three-hundred sixty deciums would take sixty hours.

To make that considerable length of time even worse, Silmanus could really only travel for ten hours a day, and the journey to Needlewood by land wasn't straight and true, so it would take him over a week to get there without magic. Silmanus did have a magical loophole around that massive travel time, but it was very expensive and he didn't want to use it unless he had to, so trying Argenrros first was definitely the better option.

That in mind, Silmanus made his way to his room. It was simple yet comfortable. A white bed, uncomplicated in design but ornately carved in leaves and vines, sat along the wall beside the door. A polished oak desk rested against the wall perpendicular to the bed, and a large chest, made of wood and braced with iron, was placed beside it. Two windows overlooked the world below, alongside a candle holder containing magical candles that would light or extinguish on command.

Snapping his fingers to break the magical lock on his chest, Silmanus reached inside and fumbled through the large extradimensional space for the items he was looking for: a leather satchel with some basic provisions, a waterskin, a change of clothes, and a heavy coin purse jingling with money. Silmanus tugged on the leather string of his purse, spilling its contents into one of his outstretched palms to count his money. Golden Castles, silver Shields, and copper Helms glittered in his hand, each worth ten times as much as the next.

Satisfied that he had enough, Silmanus tied the purse to his belt and slung his satchel over his shoulder. He placed a hand atop the lid of the chest, about to close it, but hesitated, his heart yearning for him to produce one last item from the chest.

Against his own better judgement, Silmanus slowly reached back into the chest, pulling out the object—or rather, objects—causing so much conflict in him. In his slender hand was a belt, with two magnificent swords sheathed from it. Their glistening blades were long enough to be effective, but short enough that they weren't too heavy or awkward for the wizard to use. Their blades curved up at the ends in typical elvish fashion, matching the comfortable bends of the wooden hilts. Brilliant swirls of shining green adorned the blades, sweeping along them like vines. Forged by elven smiths, they were impeccably balanced and impossibly light, yet also stronger than any blade a human could craft. Elvish metalcraft was second only to that of the dwarves, a fact that infuriated the prideful sylvan race.

The sheaths themselves were no less extraordinary. Made of stiffened leather, they were shaped exclusively for Silmanus' swords and fit them perfectly. Intricate leaves had been stamped into them, as well as a sun at the bottom of one sheath and a moon at the bottom of the other.

Silmanus' heart began aching as though being torn apart at the sight of the weapons. A different kind of yearning rose up in his chest, a desperate longing for…

No. Silmanus hurriedly dropped the swords back into the chest, slamming shut the trunk's lid with a startling bang. The wizard blinked away the drops of moisture that had gathered in his eyes, forcing away the painful memories that haunted those elegant weapons.

Running a quick mental checklist to ensure he wasn't forgetting anything, Silmanus nodded to himself and exited his room, racing down the spiral stairs of his tower, his leather boots tapping against each of the steps.

Silmanus took a quick moment to admire his surroundings. His tower was perched on one of the many hills beside the Elf Valley, a beautiful dip in the land filled with lush forests and elven villages, as well as a long, shimmering river. Birds fluttered about in the valley forest, singing their admiration of the beautiful, cloudless spring morning, and Silmanus could hear the echoes of beautiful elven tunes from Argenrros, the Silver City, pride of the High Elf kingdom Faeryln. Its soaring silver towers glistened in the distance, tiny slivers of shimmering light from where Silmanus stood.

Beyond the hills on both sides of the valley were vast forests, full of oak and birch and other blooming deciduous trees. In the west, Smallwood, separating the valley from Gryzland, the gnome kingdom. In the east, Sylvyad, an enchanted forest stretching all the way to the distant Iron Mountains, where the dwarven kingdom of Thelegard laid.

A slight breeze rustled Silmanus' long hair, exposing his pointed ears, which twitched at the sound of a horse's whinny. Silmanus walked over to a small stable at the base of his tower, smiling at the gorgeous horse inside. Powerful muscles rippled beneath soft white fur as the horse tossed its flowing white mane, pawing impatiently at the soft ground. Deep, intelligent eyes bored into Silmanus', seeming to say, "What in Gods' names took you so long?"

"Alright, alright," Silmanus chuckled, undoing the latch on his horse's stable. Blizzard was not a patient creature. "Hold your horses, I'm coming."

Blizzard did not appreciate the joke.

Shaking his head, Silmanus pulled an apple from his satchel

and held it out to Blizzard, who snapped it up greedily, eyeing Silmanus with a look of indignance.

"Don't you look at me like that, mister," Silmanus scolded with a hard look. "I took you for a good, long ride yesterday. What, you expect me to be paying attention to you with every waking moment?"

Blizzard said nothing in return.

Silmanus let out a sigh and shook his head again. "Look at me, talking to a horse," he mumbled. "And I wonder why I have no friends."

Blizzard shoved his muzzle under Silmanus' arm, a rare gesture of affection from the moody horse. Silmanus smiled. "Well, I've got you, buddy," he said, stroking the horse's neck. "That's enough for me."

Silmanus removed a leather saddle from its hook on a wall, fitting it onto Blizzard's back and buckling the straps. He led Blizzard out of the stable and waved a hand to shut the gate, magically locking it.

Placing a booted foot in the stirrup, Silmanus hoisted himself into the saddle, resting his hands in Blizzard's mane; the horse refused to use a bit and bridle. Silmanus tapped Blizzard's flanks with his feet, urging the horse into a trot and steering his steed along a charming dirt path down the valley.

The path eventually veered into a wider road, lined on either side by graceful trees whose leaves stretched over the dirt path like a canopy. Beams of sunlight danced through the foliage, casting leafy shadows across the ground. Silmanus smiled as a chickadee fluttered over to him, perching for a moment on his shoulder before flying off into the trees, chattering as it went.

Blizzard carried Silmanus along at a brisk pace for the next few hours, pausing every now and then to drink at a glistening stream and graze on some lush grasses while Silmanus refilled his waterskin and munched on some honeyed oatcakes.

It was at such a particular break that something caught Silmanus' attention. At first, he thought it was the warbled cry of some bird or another, but as he pricked his keen elven ears, he realized the sounds were voices.

The familiar feeling of burning curiosity rose in Silmanus' chest as he stood up from the tree he was leaning against. The elf flung himself onto Blizzard's back, rolling his eyes as the horse gave a snort of exasperation, not pleased that his snack was being cut short.

Silmanus ushered Blizzard along the road, noting that the voices were growing louder the farther down they went. There were three, he realized, two clearly elven and one likely human, probably an Eiran, judging by the accent. The elves spoke sternly while the Eiran's voice was desperate and protesting.

"Please, I swear, I had them with me!" Silmanus heard the human say. "They were right here, I swear to Ilbus!"

"Yet they are no longer there, are they?" stated one of the elves in a very imperious tone.

The pleading continued for a few more moments until at last, Silmanus rounded a bend and settled his eyes on the scene.

A human merchant, simply dressed, stood next to a horse-drawn cart loaded with crates and canvas sacks. He carried no weapons, merely a belt holding an assortment of pouches. He spoke with palms open wide, sincerity written into the worried lines in his face.

His interrogators were as Silmanus expected: High Elf soldiers, dressed in light mail beneath their crisp blue jerkins, the crest of Faeryln, a reared unicorn, embroidered on the front with silver thread. They carried long, elegant spears and graceful heater shields in their hands and each wore a short sword on their belts. Flowing helmets sat overtop their long, braided hair, pointed ears poking out of the sides.

"What's going on here?" Silmanus demanded, eyebrow raised.

The merchant snapped his gaze over to Silmanus, eyes wide and round. The guards, however, just calmly turned around to regard the wizard; if either had been surprised, they did not show it.

"What authority do you hold to make such an inquisition?" one guard countered, shifting his spear threateningly.

Silmanus sat up a little straighter in his saddle, peering down his nose at the guards. "I am Silmanus Amarest, Consultant Wizard of the High Council," Silmanus recited in the most condescending voice he could pull off—an easy task for an elf.

He watched with a small amount of amusement as the guards rushed to a flustered stand of attention. "My apologies, Mage Amarest," the first guard replied. Silmanus cringed a little inside; he sometimes hated the formality of High Elf society, particularly his title of "Mage".

"I ask you again, what is the meaning of this confrontation?" Silmanus pressed.

The second guard answered him. "We caught this human travelling without papers," he explained.

Silmanus nodded understandingly. Ever since the war between Eiraland and Faeryln had ended, the High Elves had imposed strict regulations on all human merchants and travellers on Faeryn soil. They needed to have official documentation, approved by the governing High Council of Faeryln, to pass through Faeryln. Silmanus thought it was tedious, and perhaps a little harsh, but it helped keep Faeryln safe.

The merchant, it seemed, simply could not hold his tongue any further. "I had them, I swear! Yesterday, I had them! With me, right here!" The human pointed to one of his pouches.

"But I say again, where are they now?" the first guard snapped. Turning back to Silmanus, he said, "You know the rules, Mage Amarest. Without his papers, this human is trespassing on Faeryn soil."

Silmanus frowned. Faeryn law was very clear regarding

trespassing and was particularly unforgiving concerning humans. Silmanus felt the mistrust could be extreme, but certainly not undeserved. After all, humans had tried to invade Faeryln before, and they were more prone to corruption and greed than any of the other races. Rules were rules.

Yet something bugged Silmanus about the whole scenario. Faeryln was infamous for its extremely tight borders. Some of Faeryln's most elite warriors guarded all roads in and out of Faeryln vigilantly, and Faeryln's forests, Smallwood and Sylvyad, were under constant patrol. Not even the smallest rabbit crossed into Faeryln without being noticed. So how could a bumbling human merchant have passed without his documents?

"He must have had them at some point," Silmanus pointed out, deciding to voice his concerns. "He couldn't have gotten into Faeryln without them."

A look of relief seemed to wash over the merchant's face. "Yes!" he exclaimed excitedly, pointing at Silmanus. "You hear? You see? How could I have gotten in?"

The second guard shrugged. "Does it matter? You have no documents now, and that means you are trespassing. You will be taken to court in Selessa and fined for your crime." Selessa was a small elven town not far from Silmanus' tower.

The merchant's triumphant expression quickly crumbled as his shoulders slouched forward. "Please...you can't...my family...we have very little money. If I cannot trade my goods in Lochadia, I will not even be able to pay my taxes, much less your fine!"

"Then perhaps you should have taken better care of your documents," the first guard said, no trace of emotion in his voice. He set down his spear and shield and moved to bind the human's wrists.

The merchant looked at Silmanus with pleading eyes. "I beg you, sir, convince them otherwise. My wife and children, they will starve."

For a moment, Silmanus wavered. Something about this seemed

wrong. A man was to be condemned simply for losing some pieces of paper and ink. Was that truly any reason for him and his family to suffer? And why should they be punished for a war that had happened over a thousand years ago?

But what could Silmanus do? To interfere would be treason. Silmanus would be revoked of his position, at the very least. He would likely have his land and tower seized as well, and the High Council could even go so far as to exile him. Was that a worthwhile price to pay simply for the sake of some stranger, and a human, no less?

No, Silmanus decided. His hands were as tied as the merchant's. He was not about to risk the life he had built just for a mere human.

Sitting straighter in his saddle, Silmanus looked away from the begging man and said simply, "Carry on."

With that, Silmanus tapped Blizzard's sides and ushered the horse forward, trying to block out the wailing protests that followed him. With each cry and sob, Silmanus' heart grew a little bit heavier. A part of him wanted to turn around and help the man instead, but Silmanus knew he couldn't. There was no point. It wasn't worth it.

A human would have done the same, Silmanus reminded himself, trying to steel his heart against the guilt. They are corrupt and immoral, it's only what they deserve.

As they rode along, Silmanus gradually managed to push the event from his mind. As the sun began to set, the weight in Silmanus' chest lifted, replaced instead by a familiar rumbling in his stomach.

He could tell Blizzard was tiring as well and murmured to his horse, "There should be an inn just ahead."

The night grew blacker as they rode. The silver light of a waning halfmoon cast dim rays between the branches of the valley's trees, spreading faint patches of light across the dark road.

Silmanus, like nearly all elves, loved starlight. He gazed wistfully up at the sky above, the twinkling light reflecting off his pensive green eyes. Silmanus did not need the light of a torch to peer into his surroundings; elves had long ago developed the ability to see as acutely in the dark as an owl.

Faeryln was not known for its hospitality to travellers and had very few inns and taverns along its roads and in its towns. However, roads to Argenrros, frequented by merchants and journeying elves, often had places where travellers could stop and rest for the night. Silmanus was more than capable of constructing himself a magical tent far more comfortable than anything an inn might provide, but he was craving a hot meal, and magically-created food just didn't taste the same. Besides, many of the inns lining Argenrros' roads were family-owned and Silmanus enjoyed supporting his kin.

After roughly another hour of fatigued trudging, Silmanus caught sight of a quaint, wooden inn, with white walls and a thatched roof. A sign reading *The Dryad's Grove* dangled above a wooden doorway. A small, roofed paddock seemed to be the inn's equivalent of a stables.

Blizzard gave Silmanus a disapproving glance as the elf slid from his saddle and led his horse to the communal paddock. "Oh, suck it up, you prissy mule," Silmanus said with a roll of his eyes, earning himself an agitated snort. "You've dealt with worse."

Silmanus unhitched the paddock gate and shoved Blizzard in. The paddock had no lock, as horse thievery was very rare in Faeryln, on account of elven horses forming unusually loyal bonds to their masters. Trying to steal an elf's horse was like trying to drag away a boulder, except the boulder was screaming like an angry child and trying to smash your face in.

Silmanus was about to close the gate when Blizzard let out a whinny, eyeing Silmanus expectantly. The elf sighed and pulled an apple out of his satchel, grudgingly holding it out for the horse. "You're not a horse, you know that? You're a pig," Silmanus jabbed. Blizzard didn't seem to care.

With a sigh, the elf exited the paddock and pushed open the *Grove*'s door, a little bell dinging to announce his arrival.

Human taverns were often loud and rowdy, with the patrons laughing and singing and chugging down mug after mug of ale. The tavern in *The Dryad's Grove* was very different. Mostly empty, the atmosphere was very timid and quiet. About half a dozen elves sat around at small tables, sipping Elfberry wine and dining on various soups and salads. A beautiful elf, probably the innkeeper's wife, played a calming melody on an elegant harp in the corner. Candles burned on ornate wall brackets, casting a warm, flickering light throughout the small interior.

Silmanus noticed two humans sitting uncomfortably at a table in the corner, their meals hardly touched. Merchants, no doubt. Silmanus felt a pang of guilt worm its way back into his heart but pushed it aside.

Aware that his unusual staff was drawing attention, Silmanus hurried to the bar counter, placing an order for a glass of wine and a bowl of rabbit stew and handing the innkeeper a silver Shield in payment. A steaming bowl of warm stew, with a complementary dinner roll, and a glass of blue wine—the colour a result of the blue Elfberries used in its fermentation—were brought to him a minute later.

Thanking the innkeeper with a smile, Silmanus carried away his meal, breathing deeply the delicious scents. He sat down at an empty table, propping his staff up against the side of his wooden chair and taking a sip of his wine before digging into the meal.

As Silmanus gulped down the delectable meal, he noticed the two humans casting him wary, resentful glances, and he sighed internally. He'd had enough of humans for one day. Perhaps even for a lifetime. Their hostility and cynicism were arduous.

Silmanus ignored the stares of the humans, downing the last of his wine and cleaning out the remnants of his stew. Despite his misgivings for mankind, Silmanus genuinely wished the tensions between human and elf would go away. War and hatred were exhausting, and history had produced some very admirable humans. Still, humans were foolhardy and quick to anger and Silmanus found it difficult to respect the race as a whole.

The wizard rose from his chair, pulling out five Shields and trading them for a room key. Silmanus then made his way up a flight of polished wooden stairs that opened into a narrow corridor, varnished doors lining it on both sides. Silmanus found his room, number 17, and slid the skeleton key into the lock, twisting it and pushing the door open.

The room was a combination of elegance and simplicity, featuring a small wooden bed made of lightly coloured wood and an oaken nightstand beside it. An arch-shaped window lined with curving grilles graced the exterior wall, looking out at the forest beyond. Beeswax candles perched on brackets on the side walls, which Silmanus decided to leave unlit; he wasn't planning on staying awake much longer.

Silmanus yawned tiredly, propping his staff up in a corner and setting his satchel and coin purse down beside it. He slid off his boots and robes, walking barefoot over to his bed, dressed only in a simple white tunic and matching pair of pants. Normally, Silmanus had a nightgown that he wore to bed, but he never brought it travelling. He then slid into the soft sheets, sinking his head into the pillow and drifting off into a restful sleep.

CHAPTER 2:
THE SILVER CITY

MORNING SUNLIGHT FILTERED THROUGH THE ROOM'S window, stirring Silmanus from his slumber and illuminating the previously dark room.

Silmanus blinked the sleep out of his deep green eyes, sitting up and stretching before sliding out of the comfort of his bed, quickly changing into fresh clothes and slipping on his green wizard robes once more.

Staff in hand, Silmanus scooped up his satchel and left the room, locking it behind him and descending the smooth stairs, making his way to the tavern for a breakfast. The smell of coffee, bacon, and fried eggs wafted through the tavern, putting a little smile on Silmanus' face as he approached the bar counter.

"Coffee and a breakfast, please," Silmanus requested politely. "Sugar in the coffee." The elvish bartender gave Silmanus an odd look—elves seldom drank coffee and elvish taverns really only brewed it for travelling humans—but went to fetch Silmanus his breakfast anyway. Silmanus paid the bartender seven Helms before carrying off a plate of fried egg and potato and a mug of steaming coffee.

Silmanus took his seat and scarfed down his breakfast, trying his best to savour the bright taste of the egg and the lovely seasonings on the potato but not really succeeding; he was very hungry.

Silmanus gulped down his coffee, noticing with amusement the odd stares he was getting from the elvish patrons. Elves were more inclined toward tea than coffee, but as a wizard, Silmanus found the stimulation provided by the latter drink highly useful in helping him think and work. Coffee was magical in its own right. Besides, he had come to enjoy its combination of bitter and sweet.

With his breakfast finished, Silmanus made his way outside, fetching Blizzard from the stables. The horse did not look very pleased with Silmanus, snorting at the elf as Silmanus unlatched the gate.

"And just what is *your* problem, hm?" Silmanus asked. Blizzard glared, stamping his foot moodily, flicking his head over at an empty metal bucket.

Silmanus chortled. Evidently, the tavern had fed Blizzard oats but neglected to give the horse an apple. Blizzard had something of an apple addiction and got very grouchy when he wasn't given one at breakfast.

"You're a greedy pig, you know that?" Silmanus said with a shake of his head, feeding Blizzard an apple. "At the rate you're eating them, I'm going to have to buy more of these in Argenrros or there won't be any left for the return journey."

Blizzard didn't seem to care. Or, more likely, he just didn't understand. He was a horse, after all. He didn't speak Common. Or Elvish. Or really any language other than snorting and braying.

Silmanus hoisted himself into the saddle, guiding Blizzard once more onto the road. Argenrros wasn't too much farther, Silmanus knew, made apparent by the increasing number of intersecting roads and trails. The signposts labelled "Argenrros →" were also something of a giveaway that he was getting close.

A few hours of riding put the sun high in the sky, blazing down from behind wisps of white cloud, bathing Silmanus in warm, golden light. His silvery skin sparkled in the sunlight, eyes bright and twinkling as he rode along.

Silmanus swelled with pride. There it was: Argenrros, the Silver City, Jewel of Faeryln. It glistened in the distance like a diamond, perched before a shimmering river, the Faewater. As Silmanus drew closer, he could see the city's thin, towering spires, reaching gracefully into the sky like beams of crystallized starlight. A mighty wall, wrought of the same magical alloy of silver and mithril, Silversteel, composing the spires, encompassed the city. A tall, elegant bridge, also forged of that same Silversteel, spanned the wide river, leading up to a pair of soaring Silversteel gates, opened wide beneath a rolling arch in Argenrros' wall. Houses and shops made of polished white marble, same as Silmanus' tower, filled the city's interior, all of them roofed with—to little surprise—Silversteel. Long, flowing banners were draped on either side of the gate, sporting a rearing silver unicorn on a blue background, the coat of arms of Faeryln.

Argenrros was unarguably one of the most magnificent cities in the entirety of Aeternerras. Even the dwarves had to agree that it was a fine piece of architecture, although the dwarves all believed their grandiose mountain halls to be finer while the humans prided themselves in their imposing castles and glorious monuments. Not that it really mattered to Silmanus what the other races thought; he was proud to be able to associate himself with such a splendid city regardless.

There was a lingering sadness that came with that pride, however. Silmanus had been born inside those silver walls, had taken his first steps and said his first words beneath the rooves of its elegant houses. It was where Silmanus had been raised, and for a while, it was his home. Yet ever since his tragedy, 'home' had become a difficult word to associate with the silver glow of the elven city. It had become a difficult word to associate with anything.

Silmanus shook those thoughts from his head, yet again refusing to let decades-old pain haunt his steps, continuing on his way with his head cleared and his mind focused. As Silmanus approached the bridge, he had to slow Blizzard down to a canter. Horse-drawn caravans crowded both sides of the segmented bridge, bustling in and out of Argenrros alongside plentiful other travellers and merchants moving on foot or horseback. Given the tenseness between humans and elves, one might not expect to find many human merchants travelling to and from Argenrros but roughly a third of the people on the bridge were indeed human, with the rest being either elves or gnomes.

This was solely because of Argenrros' importance as the trade capital, and political capital, of Faeryln. Many exotic goods and potions were available in Argenrros, which human merchants would often purchase to sell at higher prices back at home. Furthermore, because of the bitter rivalry between elves and dwarves, many elven smiths were willing to pay higher prices for high-quality dwarven steel and mithril so long as it was sold by humans, which many merchants took advantage of.

Blizzard's canter slowed to a crawl as Silmanus got caught in the thick traffic flowing into Argenrros. It took over half an hour for him to get across the bridge, partly because any humans had to stop to get their paperwork inspected by the guards.

Silmanus did make it into the city eventually though, nodding at the sentries posted at the gate. They were wearing Silversteel half-plate over their chain shirts (called "hauberks", Silmanus recalled), glistening shin guards strapped to their legs and elegant helmets in the shape of unicorns, the national animal of Faeryln, protecting their heads. The guards each carried a leaf-shaped shield and elegant Silversteel glaive. Their Silversteel armament and blue and silver "manes" flowing out of the tops of their helmets marked these warriors as Royal Sentries, the elite of Faeryln's elite. Dozens more Royal Sentries patrolled the ramparts above, although they were armed instead with elegant longbows in their hands and slender scimitars at their sides.

Silmanus passed through the gate and onto the smooth white cobbles of Argenrros' streets, sliding off of Blizzard and guiding the horse to one of several stables lining the beginning of Argenrros' streets. To reduce clutter, only soldiers and merchants with wagons were allowed to have horses past a certain point and merchants were required to stable their horses once their stalls had been set up.

Blizzard put up no fight this time. Because of their similarity to unicorns, horses were regarded with a great deal of respect in Argenrros and every horse was treated like royalty, regardless of the race of their owner. As a matter of fact, every stable in Argenrros had at least one Royal Sentry standing guard before it. Blizzard was immediately offered up a juicy red apple and led to a soft, straw-lined stable where stable hands wasted no time in grooming the spoiled horse.

One of the four sentries guarding Blizzard's stable handed Silmanus a small stone tablet bearing the number of Blizzard's stall. Silmanus tucked it away safely in his coin purse; they took horse thievery very seriously in Argenrros and without that tablet, Silmanus would never be able to reclaim Blizzard.

Silmanus wove his way through the streets, shuffling between and around elves, humans, and gnomes as he made his way toward the centre of Argenrros. His telltale staff marked him easily as a wizard, which brought a wide range of glances Silmanus' way, from suspicion to admiration to downright disgust.

At last, Silmanus arrived in the marketplace of Argenrros, a massive circular clearing in the very centre of Argenrros. White cobble pathways led from eight different directions, conjoining at a spectacular marble fountain in the shape of a unicorn. A carving of Sarissa, the High Elf Goddess of Elves and Magic, sat astride the unicorn, looking regally ahead. Beautiful flowers formed a myriad of cheerful colours in the wedges between the pathways. A different species of tree sprouted from the wide end of each wedge: Rowan for art and creativity, Hawthorn for love and marriage, Willow for magic and the moon, Golden Gorse for hope and the sun, Elven

Oak for strength and nobility, Holly for nature and compassion, Hazel for knowledge and wisdom, and Blackthorn for death and vengeance. Each wedge contributed to a circular pathway, along which countless market stalls were set up, their vendors calling out the names and prices of their goods.

At the western end of the circle sat Argenrros' keep. It was a breathtaking piece of architecture, essentially a massive square tower made of Silversteel with a tall, pointed roof and a narrow spire emerging from each of its corners. A gigantic statue of a reared unicorn was perched precariously at the tip of the keep, staring down regally at the marketplace below. Flags flew from each of the four spires and two banners dangled on either end of each wall. A wide white staircase sat at its enchanted oaken doors, funnelling into one of the pathways leading to the fountain. Two Royal Sentries stood guard on either side of the keep's entrance.

That was not Silmanus' destination, however. His objective was frostpetal, not another lengthy discussion with the High Council, the ruling lords and ladies of Faeryln, about the ethics of permanent magical augmentation (which Silmanus was firmly against).

Silmanus began circling the marketplace, searching around for a vendor selling frostpetal. It took him a few minutes, but eventually he caught sight of an herbalist stall. A young human woman with pale skin and light brown hair stood behind a wooden counter, holding out jars of herbs and plants, calling out prices on medicinal tonics.

Approaching the vendor, he offered her a smile and was about to inquire about frostpetal when the woman sighed and said, "No, I don't have any frostpetal left."

Silmanus was momentarily taken aback. "What…sorry, how exactly did you know I was looking for frostpetal?" he asked slowly, narrowing his eyes.

The woman sighed again and pointed to his staff. "I've had three dozen wizards approach me today, all asking for the same thing," she explained tiredly. "I don't have any frostpetal left. Sold my last bunch three days ago."

Silmanus' shoulders drooped in disappointment. He wasn't surprised, however; he had fully expected that to be the case.

He opened his mouth to speak again, and again, the woman cut him off. "No, nowhere else in Argenrros is selling any," she informed him, speaking in a bored tone as if she were reciting a line from a script for the hundredth time.

Silmanus grinned a bit and shook his head. "And they say wizards are supposed to be unpredictable."

"They say a lot of things," the woman responded. Silmanus couldn't be sure, but he thought he heard a hint of malice in her voice. He wondered what exactly she meant by that.

Probably something to do with us elves, he realized, sighing inwardly. Humans.

"Right, well, I guess that's all then," Silmanus said. "Thank you for your time."

The woman blinked a few times, clearly startled. "Well, there's a first. An elf saying, 'thank you.' I guess wizards really *are* unpredictable."

Silmanus wasn't exactly sure what to make of that so he just went with the old reliable: smile and a nod. The woman gave him a small smile back before going back to calling out her prices.

Silmanus turned and left, feeling rather dejected and not really looking forward to his alternative option. Silmanus wasn't particularly fond of any of the human kingdoms, but of all the goodly ones, Eiraland, where frostpetal was found, was the worst. Constantly warmongering, it had been led by a line of corrupt, power-hungry kings for centuries. Eiraland had obliterated several smaller human kingdoms in the north, gaining complete control of all the land between Faeryln and the Northguard Mountains. Not to mention the fact that there was strong evidence that Eiran nobles held gnomes and other humans as slaves. Silmanus really did not want to go to Eiraland.

He had no other choice, unfortunately. If there was no frost-petal in Argenrros, there wouldn't be any anywhere other than Needlewood in Eiraland. He'd have to go pick some himself.

The sun was starting to set, casting a pale pink light across the western sky, setting the wispy clouds ablaze with shades of fiery orange. The Silversteel of Argenrros glowed with an amber light alongside its normally silver hue.

Silmanus wished he could stay the night in Argenrros. The city looked positively spectacular in the starlight, when Silversteel glowed brightest. Unfortunately, inns were very expensive in Argenrros and the city was even more crowded than usual; finding a room would be both costly and time-consuming.

So, with something of a heavy heart, the wizard fetched Blizzard from the stables. The horse was very reluctant to leave but he seemed to sense that Silmanus wasn't in the greatest of moods and complied with no more than a forlorn sigh.

Silmanus pulled himself into the saddle, guiding Blizzard out of the gates and nodding at the guards as he left. Fortunately, the bridge was much less congested now that nightfall was approaching and Silmanus was able to cross much quicker the second time.

As he and Blizzard passed over the bridge, they plodded by a tetrad of High Elves on horseback. Each was dressed in the same outfit: leather bracers and shin guards, a Silversteel hauberk, and a blue jerkin embroidered with a silver unicorn. Most notably, however, they all wore the same pin above their hearts: a rearing unicorn with sapphire eyes.

Silmanus' heart dropped into his gut. These were members of the Royal Vanguard, a faction of incredibly skilled warriors that acted as a private Ranger division for Argenrros, serving as spies, scouts, shock troops, assassins, and trackers for the Faeryn military. Royal Vanguards were expert marksmen and lethal swordsmen, their skill in combat, throughout Faeryln, at least, matched only by Royal Sentries.

That wasn't why seeing a group of them nearly brought tears to Silmanus' eyes, however. His parents had once been some of Faeryln's finest Royal Vanguards, before settling down to raise Silmanus. And then...

No, Silmanus growled at himself. *No. You are* not *thinking about that.*

Shaking the memories from his mind yet again, Silmanus rode onward, urging Blizzard into a gallop, wanting to reach an inn as soon as possible.

CHAPTER 3:
THE ENCOUNTER

THE JOURNEY HOME WAS AS UNEVENTFUL AS THE JOURNEY there. Silmanus spent another peaceful night in another peaceful inn before setting out on another peaceful ride on another peaceful day. Such was life in Faeryln.

The more he thought about it, the more Silmanus had to admit that he was sort of looking forward to the journey. His life was relatively monotonous: get up, eat, study and practice magic, go to sleep, rinse and repeat. There was typically some more eating involved in there, too. All the same, not much interesting happened in Silmanus' life. Every now and then, he'd make some sort of magical breakthrough or the Council would recruit him to accompany the army on some sort of quest, but really, he led a very calm and peaceful life. Which was certainly nothing to complain about, but it did get rather boring from time to time.

Before long, Silmanus' characteristic white tower came into view. As soon as Blizzard had brought Silmanus up to the tower's curved oak door, the wizard hurriedly dismounted and dashed up the steps, suddenly anxious to get on the road. Whether it was because he wanted to just get the journey over with or because he actually subconsciously *wanted* to go to Eiraland, he wasn't sure, but ultimately, he didn't really care either. He just wanted to get on with the trip; it didn't really matter why.

He flew through his packing, trading his satchel for a large leather backpack and stuffing it with a much wider variety of survival items. A blanket, a bedroll, spare clothing, rations, apples, a mess kit, an extra waterskin, rope, candles, a knife…all of it got thrown hurriedly into the bag. He also grabbed a little wooden box and tucked it into his robes. He'd need that in a moment.

The elf stood up, looking at the pack satisfactorily, running over a quick mental checklist. It felt like he was forgetting something…

Silmanus suddenly snapped his fingers. Books! There was no way he was getting stuck in Eiraland without anything to read. He tossed a couple stories and historical tomes into the bag as well. He briefly contemplated bringing his latest research notes, but he wouldn't be staying long enough to justify bringing them, and he didn't want to run the risk of them getting lost or ruined.

As he collected his books, Silmanus felt his hand brush against something in the extradimensional chest. The excitement in his chest suddenly dissipated, like a flame extinguished by a cold breeze.

Silmanus pulled his swords out of the chest, staring at them in silent lamentation. Memories washed over him once more, drowning him in melancholy, tormenting him with glimpses into a past that dangled just out of his reach.

He didn't understand why, but something prompted Silmanus to buckle those magnificently heartbreaking weapons to his waist, his hands moving separately from his mind, a blank expression on his pained face. Despite their remarkably light weight, the swords felt as heavy as mountains, weighing Silmanus down with the memories attached to them.

The wizard suddenly slammed his fist into a wall, teeth gritted and eyes clenched, tears threatening to spill from his eyes. He checked himself, breathing deeply a few times, burying those painful emotions for what felt like the millionth time.

Wiping his eyes on his sleeves, Silmanus swung his heavy pack onto his back, staggering a few steps until he regained his balance.

Snatching his staff up from the wall he had propped it on, Silmanus carefully made his way down the stairs, not wanting to move too fast in case the weight of his backpack caused him to stumble.

Once outside, Silmanus took note of the sun's position in the sky. Early afternoon. Running some quick calculations in his head, Silmanus figured they should reach Needlewood by evening of the next day.

Magically locking his tower, Silmanus turned to approach a grazing Blizzard but something held him back. A strange nagging feeling had settled in his chest, a little intuition that he would not be coming home for a long time. Silmanus suddenly found himself very reluctant to leave again, those earlier thoughts of a potentially exciting adventure now replaced with fear of what may come of the journey.

Ah, you're just being paranoid, you silly git, Silmanus told himself. *No time for dawdling, you've got places to be.*

Silmanus strode over to Blizzard, patting the horse's shoulder and producing that little wooden box. "You ready, bud?" Silmanus asked.

Blizzard raised his head and breathed heavily out of his nose, a clear exclamation of protest. Silmanus shook his head. Some days he wondered if his horse was actually even a horse at all and not some poor person turned into a horse by a vengeful wizard or something.

Silmanus opened the box to reveal seven large, red berries. Wizards called them Skyberries. They were ordinary enough berries at first, but after a very lengthy and ludicrously expensive series of spells, Skyberries were capable of granting a horse the ability to fly tirelessly for ten hours, and at a pretty respectable speed too. The horse could even fall asleep if it wanted to and it would still stay aloft.

Silmanus knew it would take six of his seven berries to complete the journey there and back. He was loath to use them on account of how difficult they were to procure, but it was better than spending over a week travelling the old-fashioned way. He wanted to get that frostpetal as soon as he could. Besides, it wasn't like Silmanus needed them for anything else.

Blizzard grudgingly swallowed the berry, his entire body shuddering as the magic flowed through him. Silmanus hurriedly mounted his horse, tingling a bit with excitement. He loved flying.

Silmanus urged Blizzard forward and the horse took off at a gallop, charging across the grass and gathering speed. The horse's hooves thundered across the ground, digging up earth with each pounding step, gouging into the soil with each mighty bound.

Blizzard then suddenly leaped up, tucking his forelegs beneath his chest. Instead of falling back to the earth, however, the horse soared into the sky, magically held aloft by the power of the Skyberry. Blizzard let out an excited whinny and flicked his head to the side as they climbed higher and higher into the sea of blue above.

Silmanus laughed and flung his arms into the air, wind whipping through his hair as they glided across the sky, moving about as fast as a human might run. The land below Silmanus grew steadily smaller, blurring into a canvas of greens and browns, punctuated every so often by a splash of colour from a meadow or a city.

The wizard breathed in deeply, smelling the clean, fresh air around him. Flying truly was an otherworldly experience, and the view was simply remarkable. He was flying over top of the hills lining the Elf Valley, their gentle slopes covered in splashes of bright colour from flowery meadows and glades.

Just to the west of those hills was a vibrant forest whose leafy canopy stretched like an ocean beside Silmanus. It was known as Smallwood, so named because of its close proximity to the gnomish kingdom, Gryzland; gnomes were the smallest of the four races.

At that thought, Silmanus reflexively looked to his left, into the west, where he knew the lush, rolling hills and mushroom-filled forests of the gnome lands sat just beyond the elf's sight. Gryzland was riddled with gnome hovels, ramshackle little houses with an irresistible rustic charm, each filled with a sprawl of clever gadgets and gizmos, creating an atmosphere that was a unique combination of random chaos and planned order. Most gnomes built such hovels underground as parts of larger networks of tunnels and caverns that made up gnome cities, but some made their homes in the trees and giant mushrooms of the surface.

To Silmanus' right, in the east, the Faewater cut between the sloping hills on either of its sides, shimmering in the afternoon sun. Argenrros glistened as it always did, a silver pearl hidden in the banks of a crystal river.

Beyond the eastern hills was another forest, this one larger and much less welcoming than Smallwood. It bore the same gorgeous colours, treetops gleaming in the sunlight, but the air about Sylvyad, as the forest was known, was much different. While Smallwood seemed teeming with light and life, Sylvyad seemed much more mysterious, its atmosphere full of illusion and secrecy. This was due to the ancient magics shrouding Sylvyad and the High Elf cities within it, illusory spells that sent shivers down the spines of the unwelcome.

They were well out of Silmanus' sight, but the elf knew that on the other side of Sylvyad sat the Iron Mountains, the longest mountain chain in Aeternerras. Their caverns were, as the name suggested, brimming with iron, the main export of the kingdom situated there, Thelegard. The Iron Dwarves dwelt in those mountains, mining gold, silver, and mithril deposits alongside massive quantities of iron, tunnelling out their majestic mountain halls and building some of the world's mightiest fortresses.

On the other side of those mountains was Marrelnia, kingdom of the Sea Elves, a charming expanse of field and forest curling south behind the Iron Mountains around the Elven Bay, bordering the Elven Sea and the endless Great Ocean beyond. Sea Elves were far more cheerful and friendly than their aloof, mysterious cousins, welcoming members of all four races into their borders, trading with men, elves, dwarves, and gnomes alike.

None of those lands were relevant to Silmanus' quest, however, nor were the kingdoms to the south. Silmanus' journey was taking him north, to Eiraland, a chilly land of grassy plains and coniferous forests. Cold ocean winds and a northern geographical position forced the kingdom to endure frigid winters and cool summers.

Specifically, Silmanus was interested in Needlewood, a sparse forest of pines and spruces that covered the northern half of Eiraland, the only place frostpetal could be found in the wild.

Needlewood gave way to the icy Northguard Mountains, unforgiving peaks notorious for blustery winds and destructive avalanches. Only animals and dragons were able to live in those uncrossable mountains, although the latter had seldom been seen since the Fell War.

The Northguard Mountains were a saving grace, however, protecting Eiraland both from even colder northern temperatures and from the savage peoples living beyond them. Helvark sat at the very tip of Aeternerras, a brutal land of ice and snow that saw grass for only a few months of the summer. It was inhabited by a race of tall, stocky humans who relied on raiding parties to secure the vital resources that were so scarce in their own lands. The Helvans were terrifying combatants and without the Northguard Mountains in the way, they would have long ago overrun Eiraland.

Three hours passed and Silmanus slumped forward in the saddle, resting his cheek on the nape of Blizzard's neck. He had to make sure he was awake in seven hours, when the Skyberry would wear off, so Silmanus figured it was best to get some sleep right away. He closed his eyes and sighed in satisfaction, wind in his ears and sun on his side, sleep creeping into his mind and pulling it into a welcoming darkness.

A little less than six hours had passed when the air suddenly became significantly colder. Silmanus awoke from his nap, cursing himself for not bringing any sort of warm clothing. He grudgingly waved a hand over himself and muttered an incantation, not pleased he had to waste his energy on something that could easily have been prevented. Magical warmth immediately flowed through his body, slowing driving out the numbness of the evening cold.

The sun was gone from the sky, leaving starlit darkness in its wake. The land below was dotted with tiny, twinkling lights, the fires of elven villages. Silmanus was still in Faeryln, but the border to Eiraland was just another three hours away. Silmanus could see human towns lining the sides of the Snowy Lake, which glowed silver in the moonlight.

Waiting another hour first, Silmanus tapped Blizzard on the neck to feed the horse another berry, renewing the spell of flight. Blizzard swallowed it tiredly before drifting asleep, his course magically sustained by the Skyberry. Silmanus slid back into sleep a moment later.

By the time the next ten hours were up, Silmanus and Blizzard were directly over the middle of Valley Lake. The air around them was chilly, the spring sun having only risen a couple of hours ago. A biting wind cut through Silmanus' clothing, forcing the elf to begrudgingly cast another warmth spell. He fed Blizzard the last Skyberry the horse would need before attempting to pull a book out of his bag.

That was a mistake. The fierce winds caught the book and tore it right out of Silmanus' still-numb fingers, sending it plummeting down to the lake below. Silmanus watched with horror as his book fell out of sight, destined to perish in the waters of the Valley Lake.

Silmanus wondered suddenly what the Eirans below were thinking as they watched a white, wingless horse soar across the sky. He wondered what they would make of a book plunging into their lake from the sky.

What an interesting sight that must have been.

At last, after another seven hours, Silmanus was directly over top of Needlewood. It wasn't a dense forest, but it wasn't overly sparse either. The sun was setting in the west, casting long and somewhat eerie shadows through the forest.

Blizzard began his descent, the wind gradually slowing down to gently lower him toward a small clearing. The horse landed on his feet, taking a couple of hurried steps as he slowed down so he didn't topple over and send both him and Silmanus sprawling.

Thin pine trees rose up from the mossy ground, creating a bit of a barrier from the wind, which Silmanus was very grateful for. The forest floor was soft, but also cold and damp from recent rains and melts. A few ferns poked up here and there, as well as some scrawny flowers and saplings. No frostpetal though, which meant Silmanus would have some searching to do.

There wasn't enough daylight left to find the rare flower, so Silmanus decided he would have to set up a camp. The elf tied Blizzard up to a tree with his rope, realizing with a groan that Blizzard couldn't graze on moss. Silmanus gathered a great big pile of fallen pine needles and snapped his fingers, transfiguring the needles into hay for his horse. He then conjured a crackling campfire in the middle of the clearing and unpacked his things, pondering over which spell to use to provide a temporary shelter.

He'd just finished laying his bedroll out when he heard a twig snap behind him. Silmanus spun around, peering into the trees with his keen elf eyes, but spotted nothing. Blizzard looked up from his hay, peering around uneasily and raking at the ground with his foreleg.

Worried it might be a bear or a wolf, Silmanus crept slowly toward the source of the sound. He touched his hands to the hilts of his swords, realizing he had left his staff with the rest of his equipment and suddenly very grateful that he had brought the blades.

A pair of squirrels chattered in the trees as they chased after each other, prompting Silmanus to snap his head up to look at them. The wind whistled in his ears, causing trees to creak and shadows to dance. Silmanus suddenly felt very small and very vulnerable. He was used to the welcoming reach of the valley's trees, with their shining leaves and chirping birds.

There didn't seem to be so much as a chickadee up here.

Silmanus squared his shoulders and pushed his irrational fears aside, deciding that the snap had probably just been from a rabbit. Shaking his head at how jumpy he was, Silmanus turned around to return to his campsite. His eyes went wide with genuine fear and he froze in place.

He was staring down the wrong end of an arrow at a woman with a murderous glint in her cold, blue eyes.

CHAPTER 4:
MONSTER HUNTERS

TWO SHORT FIGURES STOOD AMONGST PILES OF RUBBLE and corpses. Bodies of humans and dwarves were strewn across the rocky ground, bent and twisted in a macabre scene of bloody agony. Faces were distorted in frozen screams, bones were shattered and poking out of skin at odd angles, large chunks of flesh had been rent from the bodies they covered.

There was a disturbing similarity between the bodies and the buildings of the ruined village. Most of the houses were missing their top half, as if they had simply vanished into thin air. Which they had, in a sense; this was made apparent by the black ash slowly floating down from the sky. What few were still recognizable as whole buildings had entire walls smashed in or long gouges raked into their sides. Smoke still billowed from many of the structures, and crackling fires fed off what little wood remained.

The (slightly) taller of the two figures, a dwarf, gave a heavy sigh, slowly shaking her head and looking toward her feet. Short and stocky, she was dressed head-to-toe in thick plate armour, crafted with the sharp angles and overlapping layers customary of dwarven smiths. Long red hair fell down her wide back in one, large braid beneath an iron helmet. She held a mighty warhammer in one hand, styled with golden bands and dwarvish runes. A matching metal shield was strapped to her left arm with an anvil emblazoned on its front. A leather backpack hung from her shoulders overtop of a fearsome battle axe.

"Well," she muttered grimly to her companion in a thick, distinctive dwarven accent, "I suppose there's nothing t'be done here."

The other figure nodded in agreement. He wore a long red coat, complete with lines of golden buttons and large cuffs, overtop of a relatively simple white shirt. His brown pants were dotted with spots of red, presumably blood, that the gnome just hadn't been able to wash out. Light brown hair stuck out at odd angles on top of his round, cherubic face, wisps of grey running through the tangles to betray the gnome's respectable age. Normally, his hazel eyes twinkled with a mischievous light, but that glimmer had disappeared as soon as he took in the grizzly sight before him. A marvellous little rapier was sheathed on the gnome's belt, its jewelled hilt glittering in the sunlight, and a leather backpack hung from his shoulders.

"No, not much indeed," the gnome sighed. "I suppose we could track whatever did this though."

The dwarf looked at him with a dry expression. "'Whatever did this?'" she repeated doubtfully. "Jeddo, ye can't possibly be *that* thick. Isn't it obvious?"

Jeddo sighed again, a note of tired resignation in it. "No, Amber, I know what it was. I just don't want it to be true."

Amber nodded in agreement. A few moments of silence passed, until Amber realized that Jeddo wasn't going to say what they were both thinking. "Dragon," she said for him.

Jeddo gave an acknowledging grunt. "Dragon."

The two companions stood in silence again. Just a few fingers taller than Jeddo's rather humble height, Amber, who was a little on the short side of dwarves, took a moment to appreciate finally being taller than someone before breaking the silence again.

"I guess we should go kill it, huh?" she commented in an uninterested tone, staring straight ahead.

"Yup. We probably should," Jeddo agreed in the same, bored voice. "You think we could?"

Amber gave a slight inclination of her head and lifted her eyebrows briefly, although her expression remained neutral. "Ye've certainly got some skill with that wee stick o' yers," referring to Jeddo's finely jewelled rapier.

"And I guess you do know what you're doing waving that crude block of iron around," Jeddo retorted, though not with any emotion, as he gestured to Amber's sizeable warhammer.

"Well, we best be on our way if we want t' catch the beast," the dwarven warrior decided, hoisting her magnificent weapon onto her broad shoulders and adjusting her grip on her heavy iron shield.

"Right," Jeddo agreed.

"Ye wanna lead the way?" Amber asked.

Jeddo shrugged. "Why not?"

To anyone who might have overheard the conversation, it likely would have seemed like those two were as foolish as they were heartless, running naively into the jaws of death—literally. In truth, however, they were professional fighters, and had slain their fair share of dragons that had crossed the Fire Mountains. Their apparent apathy toward the tragic scene stemmed not from a lack of compassion, but rather from years of experience with the horrible and horrifying that had hardened like a shield around the vulnerability of their hearts.

The two monster hunters ran across the rocky landscape known as the Fields of Flame, so named because large cracks crisscrossed the rock, each glowing with the orange light of magma. Directly south of the Fields of Flame were the Fire Mountains, a long chain of mountains dotted with volcanoes. No plants grew within almost two hundred deciums of the mountains, although that didn't stop people from settling there.

A race of dwarves, the Fire Dwarves, inhabited the Fire

Mountains, using the volcanoes as forges and mining the abundance of diamonds and other jewels found within them. They had crafted a mighty kingdom, known as Pyradia, and where there were kingdoms, there was trade and wealth, so many of the less fortunate set up towns along the Fields in hopes of finding work. Most burned alive during the frequent volcanic activities that occurred in both the mountains and the Fields. It was very unfortunate, but the hope in the possibility for wealth lured those in desperation to its treacherous plains all the same.

It was very fortunate for the rest of the world that the dwarves had mastered the volcanoes and made settlement there, for to the south of those hostile peaks lay a land of pure, untamed evil: The Fell Lands. Inhabited by every kind of vile creature imaginable, it was a desolate realm that frequently tried to break free from the cage of the mountains, and despite the dwarves' best efforts, monsters such as the evil dragon Jeddo and Amber were pursuing still occasionally slipped through and found their way into the rest of Aeternerras.

Jeddo and Amber had found work in slaying such monsters, and the dragon had much to fear if the duo caught up to it.

Which they were quite close to doing, in fact. They had gotten lucky and the dragon had only left a few hours before Jeddo and Amber had arrived. Very full and tired from its raid, the dragon was moving slowly and had even landed to rest a while. A mistake, as it would soon realize. The sun was beginning to go down behind the Sand Mountains in the west when the two fighters finally found the dragon, curled up on the hard, grey rock, eyes closed in a blissful sleep.

Amber was not impressed. It was small for a dragon, no longer than three horses. It was covered in hard red scales that flickered like fire in the dying light, and large, scaled wings were tucked tightly to its sides. Long horns protruded from the back of its head, and a lengthy tail, ending in a spear-like point, was wrapped around its body.

"It looks so young," Jeddo said, almost regretfully. "Pity we have to kill it, wouldn't you say?"

Amber just shrugged. "Ye want t' get paid, ye got t' kill it," she reasoned.

"Fair enough," Jeddo accepted, sliding his pack off his shoulders and laying it on the stony ground. Amber did the same. A burgeoning pack was nothing more than a dangerous encumberment in battle.

Amber raised her shield and banged on it with her hammer, not caring in the least that she might damage the anvil emblazoned on it.

"Foul worm o' the South, surrender now or feel the might o' me hammer!" she yelled in her deep, booming voice.

The dragon, awakened very suddenly by the obnoxious banging and loud shouting, narrowed his yellow eyes at the tiny figures before him. Snorting, it retorted loftily, "I fear you not, dwarf, for just hours ago I devoured several dozen of your folk. It is you who should be afraid. Normally, I squash pesky insects like yourself, but I'm quite full and feeling merciful, so I'll give you a second chance. Flee now or face certain death."

Amber's face broke out into a delighted grin. "I was hopin' ye'd say that!" she laughed. "Come on, ye lizard, let's see what ye're made o'!"

With more speed than the dragon thought she possessed, the dwarf sprinted toward her foe, armour clanging noisily. Jeddo drew his rapier and joined the charge, pumping his little legs as fast as they could go.

The dragon laughed mockingly and arced its neck, taking a breath before spewing a jet of flame at his attackers, engulfing both in the searing fire. The dragon smirked, knowing that no mortal could withstand a blast like that. Dragon fire was among the hottest flames known to the world, capable of melting even mithril and Silversteel, given enough time. These two foolish hotheads would have melted into puddles of steaming metal, their flesh and bones turned to black, smoking ash.

Apparently, someone had forgotten to inform Amber and Jeddo of that fact.

To the dragon's utter surprise, when the flames cleared, both figures were still running toward him, hooting and laughing.

Amber's armour and shield were not crafted of ordinary iron. It was what the dwarves called "Red Iron," harvested and forged from the bellies of volcanoes. Completely resistant to any flame short of magma, it was one of the only substances that could resist dragon fire and had protected Amber from many blasts of dragon breath.

Jeddo, on the other hand, had a far subtler defence; his coat was made of dragon hide, immune to fire and very hard to cut through. He had simply turned around and tucked his head, allowing the flames to just wash over him.

Surprised, the dragon stood no chance. He had gravely underestimated his foes and was now desperately trying to decide how to react.

He lashed out clumsily at Amber, but the dwarf, surprisingly nimble in all her heavy armour, grabbed one of his claws and clung to it tightly, letting the dragon's own swipe carry her to its back.

Jeddo, meanwhile, ran toward the dragon's tail, which the dragon immediately swung at him, just as Jeddo had anticipated.

Dropping onto his back, the agile gnome slid underneath the attack, standing up again once when he felt the tail was far enough above his head.

The dragon had a far more urgent problem at the time, however. Amber was now on his back, running toward his head. Although dragon bones were some of the hardest substances in the world, the dragon feared not even his skull would save him from the dwarf's hammer.

Desperately, he thrashed around, hoping to throw Amber off.

Amber went sailing through the air, unable to keep her footing, but to the dragon's surprise, she seemed to be…smiling.

He realized his mistake a moment before blinding pain erupted from his chest. As the dragon reared up and let out an ear-splitting shriek, Amber saw the golden hilt of Jeddo's rapier imbedded deep in the dragon's chest, the only spot on a dragon where the scales were soft enough and far enough apart for a blade to pierce through.

Amber quickly climbed to her feet, shrugging off the pain of the impact, knowing that the task wasn't over. Jeddo's blade was short, and while he may have dealt the dragon a mortal blow, the rapier could not go deep enough to kill the dragon in that one strike. The creature could still easily kill both Amber and Jeddo, and Jeddo was in a rather bad spot, sprawled out beneath the beast.

As the dragon slammed back to the ground, it stabbed furiously at Jeddo with its claws, and the gnome was only just able to roll out of the way.

Another deadly attack, and another near miss. The dragon kept Jeddo pinned, never giving him the chance to stand, and Jeddo knew it was only a matter of time before he slipped up and the dragon's razor-sharp claws dug into his flesh.

With a profound sense of panic, Jeddo realized that the dragon had stomped on his cloak, preventing the gnome from moving. The dragon's grinning jaws opened wide, moments away from devouring the little gnome.

A sudden movement off to the side caught Jeddo's eye. He smirked. "Look! Another dragon!" Jeddo shouted, doing his best to point in the direction of the movement.

That certainly startled the dragon. Whether it was a rival dragon from the south or one of the benevolent ones from the Northguard Mountains, another dragon spelt trouble. He instinctively flicked his head in the direction of the point.

And received a block of iron in the face.

Hooting with glee, Amber watched as the "other

dragon"—actually her hammer—spun through the air before smacking the dragon right in the snout. Teeth were sent flying and the dragon's nose caved in, shattered from the force of the blow.

Amber bore down on the dragon, which was now sprawled out on its back, yelping and clutching its crushed snout.

The dragon suddenly stopped, noticing movement in his peripheral vision.

"I tried t' tell ye t' flee," Amber sighed, shaking her head in mock disappointment. She had recovered her hammer and now held it above her head with both hands. "Enjoy yer afterlife."

With all her strength, Amber swung the weapon down, aiming for the spot beside the dragon's eye where the skull was thinnest. There was a loud crack as iron split bone, and blood exploded from the skull, splashing all over Amber.

The dragon's tongue lolled in its mouth as the beast tried to cling onto life. But it was no use. His chest sank and the last of his breath heaved out of his mouth. The light faded from his sinister eyes, and the monster went limp.

Amber turned to Jeddo, grinning from ear to ear, despite being thoroughly covered in dragon brains. "Now *that* was somethin'!" she exclaimed.

Jeddo grimaced as he wiped a bit of blood off his cheek. "I don't suppose next time you could be troubled to *not* make a mess of our enemy?" He tried to sound disgusted, but truthfully, he didn't really care. A dead dragon was a dead dragon and a reward was a reward.

"Oh, come on, ye know ye enjoyed yerself," Amber said as she collected her shield.

"It was thrilling, but now we don't have proof of our kill," Jeddo replied, grasping the smooth handle of his rapier and pulling it free from the dragon's flesh. A spurt of blood followed, and Jeddo cursed as it splattered all over his shirt.

Amber looked at him in bewilderment. "What do ye mean? I

got me axe; I'll just lop off the thing's head and we're good!"

Jeddo gestured to the gory mess on the side of the dragon's head. "We can't take that as proof! It looks sloppy. It'll ruin our reputation and disgust anyone who sees!" he said in exasperation.

Amber put a hand on her hip. "Well, we can't just bring the teeth or somethin'. That could've just been gathered from a skeleton. We won't be paid."

"Fine, we can take the head," Jeddo grumbled. "But I'm staying a dragon's-length away from you when we take it in."

Amber didn't care. Grabbing her axe, she set to the grisly task of removing the dragon's head, which was only a little smaller than she was.

All in a day's work, she thought.

Chapter 5:
The Elf and the Human

THE WOMAN, MARA, WASHED HER COLD GAZE OVER THE
elf before her, studying him, trying to work out his intentions. He
was a wizard, that was plain enough, but without his staff, he was
completely useless. She bet those swords he carried were more
for decoration. Still, she kept her hand ready on the bowstring.
She didn't have the bow drawn—maintaining its 65-pound draw
weight for more than a few seconds was no easy task, even for an
experienced archer like Mara—but she knew that she could draw,
aim, and fire in a heartbeat and have another arrow nocked and
flying a heartbeat after.

The elf was quite handsome, she had to admit, but all elves
were, and good looks would not save him here. "What do you
want here, *elf*?" Mara hissed at him, spitting the word "elf" with a
lifetime of resentment.

Slowly, the elf raised his hands. "My name is Silmanus Amarest,"
he said meaningfully, waiting for a reaction. Mara just raised an
eyebrow, not recognizing the name. "I'm a wizard," Silmanus
added, his tone indicating that she should have heard of him.

"What are you doing in this forest?" Mara demanded.

"I'm searching for frostpetal. My stores have run low and I need
it for my healing potions," Silmanus explained. "You know. Magic
that helps people."

"Those flowers are under the protection of Eiraland. You may not touch them," Mara stated calmly, but with a dangerous edge, not caring what Silmanus planned to use the herb for.

Silmanus raised an eyebrow of his own. "You don't have the authority to punish me," he challenged.

"Don't I?" Mara replied.

"Well, I certainly don't see any emblem or document stating otherwise," Silmanus pointed out.

It was true. Mara's simple brown tunic, covered with warm furs, and leggings bore no sign of the Eiraland flag, a silver snowflake on a blue and white quarter background. Her weapons, though very beautiful, were not at all in the fashion of Eiran craftsmanship. Her knives were made of steel and stag antler, and the pommel of her bastard sword was shaped like a stag head. The ends of her recurve bow were carved in the forms of antlers, and the hatchet tucked into her belt had intricate knots worked into its head. Eiran officials had their weapons decorated with snow, frost, and pine trees.

Even her physical appearance didn't line up. Aside from dark hair and pale skin, there was really no generic appearance for Eirans, but with her long red hair and piercing blue eyes, Mara looked exactly like someone from the southern kingdom of Lochadia. Her tall, athletic build didn't help either, nor did the long line of freckles along her upper cheeks and nose.

Unable to think of a retort, Mara simply said, "You will leave now, or I will stick an arrow in your eye."

"Not without my frostpetal," Silmanus said firmly. When Mara replied by pointing the arrow more directly at his eye, Silmanus let out a heavy sigh and muttered, "Oh, for Gods' sakes."

Faster than Mara could take in, Silmanus' swords jumped out of their scabbards and flew into his hands, almost as if they had just materialized out of nothing. An instant before Mara's instincts kicked in, Silmanus drove both of his blades downward in a cross. The first blade severed the arrowhead from the shaft, and he twisted the blade of his following strike outward, so it hooked behind the bow and cut the string. The bow, no longer held in position by the string, snapped back into its natural shape, wrenching the weapon from Mara's hand.

Suddenly realizing her bow had been disabled and was now little more than a pretty stick lying on the ground, Mara shot her hand over her shoulder and drew her bastard sword from her back, just in time to deflect a blow that would have cut into her arm.

Mara's heart began to pound against her chest as adrenaline coursed through her veins, lighting up her senses and sharpening her vision. She allowed fear and anger to simply melt away like ice from a warm roof, melding her sword and her mind into one.

Mara retaliated as best as she could, trying to force the wizard—Silmanus, he had said his name was—on the defensive. Her blade flashed left and right, up and down as she parried blow after blow after endless blow.

A slight frown crept across Mara's brow. Silmanus was good, very good, far better than Mara had expected. Elves were competent swordsmen, Mara knew, but wizards? Wizards seldom knew how to even get a sword out of its scabbard.

This wizard, however, was as proficient with a blade as an elvish warrior, able to maintain his initial momentum and keep Mara pinned down beneath the ceaseless strikes of his twin swords. He moved fast and fluid, calculated and precise, knowing just where to place his blades and just when to move his feet. He was good.

But Mara was better.

She just had to break the stream of attacks that were raining down upon her. Keeping her breathing calm and controlled, Mara allowed Silmanus to push her back, closer and closer to the tree line. Not daring to look at the ground, Mara kept her eyes locked on the battle, praying that she was remembering her surroundings correctly.

A flood of relief passed through her as she felt her foot brush a familiar shape.

Mara's leg suddenly flicked out at the ground, toes hooking beneath a branch she had nearly stepped on earlier. The twisted stick was flung into the air with a spray of pine needles, and Silmanus crossed his arms in front of his face instinctively to protect himself from the earthy shrapnel. The stick crashed into the wizard's leg, not painfully, but enough to be a distraction.

I've got you now, Mara grinned to herself.

Mara came flying through her screen of needles with renewed vigour, sword weaving every which way as she hammered down on the startled wizard. Time seemed to slow as Mara pressed her advantage, battering Silmanus from every possible direction. Each beat of her heart, each rush of her breath, seemed to echo in her skull, all other sounds nullified as her mind focused in solely on controlling her body.

Mara managed to hook her sword around one of Silmanus' blades and twisted it out of the wizard's slender fingers, sending it skittering across the dirt. Smiling, Mara noticed a spike of panic in the elf's eyes, a crease in his brow, the realization that one of his key advantages had been lost.

Mara instantly lunged forward, sword outstretched, vision focused to a single pinpoint as anticipation bubbled in her chest. Silmanus managed to dance out of the way, but Mara was quick to follow up her attack, heart racing faster as she readied her blade for a final blow.

And then cried out as one of Silmanus' sword crashed into the side of her chest.

Fortunately for Mara, her chain shirt had stopped the elf's sword from injuring her, but the blow still hurt, and the surprise of it left her reeling. How had that happened? One of his swords was gone and the other had been in no position to attack.

That was when Mara noticed that Silmanus' lost sword had suddenly reappeared in his hand, faster than Mara had been able to register.

You cheeky little bugger, Mara thought. *I suppose wizards have some tricks up their sleeves.*

Evidently assuming that Mara had lost her edge, Silmanus went hard on the offensive, but Mara was not going to let him take control again. After parrying several of his strikes, she lashed out with her leg and slammed her boot into Silmanus' knee. The wizard let out a sharp cry and fell to the ground as his leg buckled beneath him.

Silmanus hit the ground hard, grunting as he collided with the hard Eiran earth. One of his swords skittered out of reach, but he maintained his grip on the other one.

Mara turned and stepped on his wrist before he could attack with his remaining weapon. She pressed the point of her sword against Silmanus' throat. "Don't even think of trying to summon that sword or I will kill you," she threatened evenly. Just to make sure he really wouldn't try anything, Mara pulled her other knife out of her belt and threw it at Silmanus' sleeve, pinning it to the ground.

Silmanus glared. "This is assault. You are not an authorized guard of Eiraland, and have no right to hold me like this," he said coldly. "Release me now or I will report you."

Mara laughed. "To who?" she challenged.

"Whom," Silmanus corrected instinctively. When Mara shot him a confused glance, he sighed and explained, "It's not to who, it's to *whom.* Who refers to the subject of a verb, whereas whom is for the object. You ruffians are always making grammatical mistakes like that."

Mara rolled her eyes. "So not only are you a wizard and an elf, but you're a know-it-all too," she retorted. "Does it get any more insufferable than that?"

Silmanus grinned slightly. "Well, you could be an uneducated highway robber pretending they own a forest," he countered.

Mara's eyes narrowed. "I'm not a highway robber," she stated.

Seeing Silmanus' doubtful expression, Mara shook her head. "That's it, I'm done." She reached down, grabbed Silmanus by the scruff of his clothes, and hit him over the head with her pommel.

He immediately went limp and Mara dropped him, frowning as she examined the cut Silmanus' sword had left in her tunic. "I might kill him for that," she muttered to herself, then grabbed some rope from her belt and set to the task of tying up Silmanus.

Silmanus' eyes fluttered open. He groaned in pain and tried to reach up to touch his throbbing head. His arms wouldn't move, however, and looking down, Silmanus could see a considerable amount of rope wrapped around him, tying him to a pine tree. The stubs where branches once grew on its trunk dug painfully into his back, and he sighed, knowing that he would have a fair amount of sap to clean out of his robes.

Blinking a couple times, he looked around him, trying to take in his surroundings. It was now well into the night, and a cold wind blew through Silmanus' flimsy, impractical robes. He shivered, wishing very much that his hands were free so he could cast a spell of warmth.

He was still in the clearing he had landed in, and all of his possessions were still where they'd been left. A small campfire was now burning in the middle of the clearing, and Mara's athletic form was hunched over it, running a stone along the edges of her sword.

What a weapon it was! The blade seemed to glow white in the moonlight, a trademark sign of a weapon forged of mithril, and intricate knots ran down the length of it. Silmanus took a moment to observe its beautiful form, from the stag pommel to the antler-shaped cross guard to the perfect shape of the blade. It was magnificent piece of craftsmanship, and Silmanus was impressed that humans could have forged such a perfect weapon.

Its wielder puzzled Silmanus. She couldn't have been any older than twenty-five, if even that, yet fought with the skill of someone who had been training for decades. She wore simple clothes, with the only sophistication being a fur lining along her shoulders, yet her weapons were of a quality reserved for only the most wealthy and important people. Not only that, but she had seemed completely comfortable with them during the duel, suggesting that she had trained with them, not stolen them.

Who was she, then? A renegade noble? No, she seemed far too at home in the wild. A noble wouldn't have been able to pull off what she had. Perhaps a member of some elite guard? Again, no, her weapons were the wrong style for an Eiran. So maybe she'd come from another kingdom? That didn't make sense either. She didn't look at all like a Helvan, and no renegade from the south would have made it through Faeryln without being waylaid. Maybe she came through Gryzland? Why come to Eiraland though, when Gryzland was a much nicer place to live?

Silmanus sat there, studying Mara, trying desperately to figure out who she was, where she'd come from, *anything* to tell him how to get out of his situation. But there were simply not enough facts for him to come to a certain, logical conclusion.

As he thought, he couldn't help but notice that she was a beautiful woman, although brash humans weren't really his type. She was very fit and slim, but Silmanus could also see she was much more muscular than the average woman, particularly along her shoulders and upper back. She wasn't too shapely, but still had prominent curves to her. Her wavy red hair fell about halfway down her back, covering her oval face like a fiery veil. Still, Silmanus could make out her sharp jawline and prominent chin. Her cheekbones were high and strong, combining with her piercing eyes and generally determined features to create a dangerous but also alluring expression. Her thin lips were drawn in a tight line beneath her straight nose, over which ran a thick line of freckles that almost made her look childish and innocent. Almost.

Everything about her, from her rigid posture to her comfort with weapons screamed that she was a strong young woman, able to hold her own in a world dominated by men. Silmanus had no doubt that with a loyal army at her back, she could conquer the world.

The woman seemed to sense Silmanus studying her and snapped her gaze toward him. "Something I can help you with?" she asked far too sweetly, exaggerating the tone so that Silmanus knew she had no interest in assisting him in any way.

"What's your name?" he replied, meeting her steely gaze with one of his own.

"Why? So you can use it in one of your enchantments?" the woman challenged.

Silmanus shook his head in disappointment. "You're far too cynical," he commented. "No. I just want to know your name." When her only response was to intensify her glare, he pressed, "Look, if you're going to hold me captive, the least you can do is tell me your name. You know mine."

The woman stared at him coolly for a few more seconds before finally answering, "Mara."

Silmanus raised an eyebrow expectantly. "Mara what?" he inquired.

"Mara nothing," she answered, the cold tone of her voice telling Silmanus that he would learn no more. He thought he might have seen a flash of pain in her eyes as she said it, Silmanus wasn't sure.

Silmanus nodded. "Well, Mara Nothing, it's a pleasure to meet you," he said cheerfully. "I'm Silmanus Amarest, in case you've forgotten."

Mara stared at him for a few more seconds, and Silmanus could almost see her thinking. "Why are you *really* here, elf?" she asked, still frowning.

Silmanus sighed again, and it suddenly occurred to him how much he did that. "I told you already; I'm here for frostpetal," he explained. "Would you stop being so damn suspicious of me?"

That cold anger returned to her gaze again. "I've learned not to trust elves," she said with no emotion whatsoever.

"Ugh!" Silmanus protested in frustration. "Why won't any of you people *learn*? What is so dreadfully bad about an elf?"

"They are lying cowards," Mara replied. "More likely to flee from a fight than engage in it."

"Have all of you humans forgotten what we've risked?" Silmanus argued furiously. "How many times my people have put their lives on the line to hold back evil? Might I remind you, when Pyradia fell during the Fell War, it was up to the elves of Sylvare and Faeryln to hold back the Dark Army!"

"Using thousands of Lochadians as fodder to save your own skins!" Mara snarled back. "You are cowards, nothing more." She turned her back to Silmanus, signalling that the conversation was over.

Silmanus sighed, slumping back against his tree. Humans could be so insufferable, he found.

A smelly, wet tongue suddenly drenched the side of Silmanus' face, causing the elf to sputter angrily. "Blech!" he spat, wanting to wipe his face but unable to do so on account of being tied up.

Glaring, Silmanus looked to his side and his eyebrows rose in surprise. He was staring at a very familiar white muzzle. "Blizzard!" he exclaimed, happy to see his horse unharmed.

"He's a very fine horse," Mara commented without looking at Silmanus. "Well groomed, very fit. Very loyal to you as well, wouldn't let me tie him up but he sat very patiently beside you. You're lucky to have him."

The compliment caught Silmanus off guard, even though it was more directed at Blizzard. "Yeah, I am," he replied after a moment of shocked silence. Deciding to use that as an opportunity to start another conversation, Silmanus ventured, "Do you have a horse?"

"Don't small talk me, elf," Mara warned flatly.

Silmanus let out another sigh. Being this grouchy woman's prisoner was going to be interesting.

CHAPTER 6:
BAR BRAWL

JEDDO SIGHED AS HE WATCHED AMBER MARCH INTO THE Pyradian trading post. It was a fairly simple structure, just a large rectangle of rock with a door and a couple windows, but it was made by dwarves, which meant lots of intricate designs had been chiselled into the stone that helped set it apart from the mountain it was built into. Most importantly, it was made of stone, and would be much more resistant to any volcanic encounters.

The trading post was a go-between for merchants and bounty hunters, as dwarves were not particularly fond of just letting people into their cities, not to mention the fact that Pyradian cities were constructed in the middle of a mountain range. The post allowed outsiders to barter goods with the dwarves without worrying about journeying through inhospitable mountains.

Jeddo followed Amber into the building, trying to ignore the stares. The room, far bigger than it looked from the outside, was full of simple wooden tables and chairs. Barrels of ale were stacked at the back, allowing the post to double as a sort of tavern; dwarves loved their ale. A long wooden counter, manned by several well-dressed dwarves, was positioned about an eighth of the way from the back. A wide assortment of merchants and artisans were packed into the room, most of them human. Several animals were crowded in as well, mainly dogs and cats, but Jeddo also spotted a curious black dove staring from a corner of the room.

Jeddo smiled quickly before looking down at his feet. Gnomes were a very rare sight outside of their country, and were virtually never seen in a place like Pyradia. As such, Jeddo found himself on the receiving end of far too many questioning and disbelieving looks as people studied his face, trying to figure out if he really was a gnome.

It was fairly obvious, in his opinion. Jeddo had a large, round nose, typical of most gnomes. Large pointed ears poked out beneath messy auburn hair, which was starting to grey slightly. The occasional wrinkle creased his round face, particularly around his thin mouth and hazel eyes. He had big, bushy eyebrows and a large forehead. His skin was somewhere between fair and tawny, permanently tanned from his years in the sun as a pirate captain. All in all, he looked quite like a gnome, which was definitely drawing more attention than it needed to be.

At least they aren't associating me with Amber, Jeddo thought, suddenly grateful he had buttoned up his coat to hide his bloodstained shirt. *Now that would really draw some attention! A gnome and a dwarf, carrying around a mangled dragon head. God, I'd never hear the end of it from anyone who knew me.*

Deciding that he'd need to hear the discussion between Amber and whomever she was selling to, Jeddo walked up to the bar counter, keeping a large distance between him and Amber. "A drink, please," he called, raising his hand so that the bartender knew who was asking.

A short, fat dwarf with a fiery red beard, typical of Pyradians, waddled over with a frothing mug. Jeddo grinned. "Thank you," he said eagerly, tossing the dwarf a coin.

"What brings ye t' Pyradia?" the dwarf asked in the same kind of gruff and heavily accented voice Amber had. "Not many gnomes be comin' 'round here, that's fer sure."

Jeddo's mind raced to come up with a believable story. "Well,

I was doing business in Lochadia when I heard of the infamous Dwarven Ale in Pyradia. It wasn't too far, so I figured I'd grab myself a mug!" Jeddo explained. He really didn't want anyone thinking he was here with Amber and that gory mess of a head. He was not proud of the state of that kill.

"Aye, well, ye be right about that!" the dwarf exclaimed. "Best ale in all Aeternerras, I'd say!"

Jeddo grinned. "Cheers to that," he said, lifting his mug up before taking a good, long sip of the intoxicating liquid.

Closing his eyes in satisfaction, Jeddo licked his lips and patted his belly, remembering the old days when he sailed the oceans, living the good life.

Ah well. You're too old for that now, you prune of gnome you, he told himself. Jeddo couldn't deny it; he *was* getting old. Gnomes had a lifespan of around three hundred years, and Jeddo was well past two hundred.

His pleasant flashbacks of the pirate life were suddenly cut short by some very loud and very agitated shouting.

"*THE BLOODY HELL DO YE MEAN, 'ONLY WORTH FIFTY'?!*" Amber yelled at a bored-looking dwarf standing behind the bar counter. "*YE'VE PAID ME A HUNNERD FER SMALLER!*"

The dwarf, clearly not intimidated, held out his hands in a diplomatic manner. "Now, I understand your frustration, but money's a little tight and—"

"'*MONEY'S TIGHT*'?!" Amber repeated. "'*MONEY'S TIGHT*'?!" Amber turned toward Jeddo, an exaggeratingly bewildered expression on her face. "Ye hear that, Jeddo?" she said to him. "These here *dwarves* are tight on money!" As Jeddo rested his face in his hands, embarrassed, Amber spun on the dwarf she was bartering with. "*YE'RE BLOODY DWARVES! YE MINE GOLD FER A LIVING!*"

"Yes, well, we've had a lot of bounty hunters to pay off," the dwarf explained, starting to lose his patience. Jeddo noticed that he didn't have the typical dwarven accent and wondered if this dwarf had been raised or trained somewhere other than Pyradia. "Lots of folk like you have been coming in with heads asking for money, and we simply don't have enough to go around."

"*I DON'T GIVE A DAMN!*" Amber argued stubbornly. "*I WANT ME PAY! A HUNNERD GOLD OR I'LL GIVE YE THE SAME TREATMENT HE GOT!*" Amber nodded toward the dragon head lying beside her.

The dwarf was clearly done with arguing. Leaning forward, he said through gritted teeth, "Then you'll be charged for assault and thrown in a prison to rot."

Amber laughed. "I'd like t' see ye people try!" she challenged, putting her hands on her hammer. Two armoured dwarves standing at the back also readied their weapons, ready to deal with the situation of it got out of hand.

Jeddo noticed the movement and decided he would have to intervene. Holding up his hands, the little gnome walked over to the two arguers. "Hey, hey, there's no need for violence," he said, trying to signal to Amber to calm down.

Amber shot him a glare that very clearly said, *Back off or it'll be your skull I crush.* Realizing there was no use in trying to create a peaceful solution, Jeddo raised his hands in surrender and backed off to his seat.

Jeddo sat down again and sighed. He knew where this was going. "Three, please," he said to the bartender, holding up three fingers and tossing over a few more coins.

After giving Jeddo a questioning look, the dwarf placed three mugs of mead in front of Jeddo, who immediately picked one up and began chugging. Bar fights were much more entertaining when you were drunk.

As he drank his ale, Jeddo listened intently for the first sounds of the coming fight. It would be any minute now, Jeddo knew, any minute until Amber threw one of her signature haymakers and started a brawl.

Right on cue, Amber balled her fists and threw a powerful punch into the barterer's face.

Jeddo winced at the cry of pain that cut through the tavern's cheerful atmosphere. He knew Amber was still wearing her jagged iron gauntlets, and nearly choked on his ale when he saw the barterer go flying back, clutching a deep gash on his cheek.

The guards were quick to react. Putting up their shields to protect from attack, they ran forward and leaped over the counter, hoping to slam into Amber and knock her over.

Full of adrenaline, Amber laughed and jumped at one of the dwarves. He was completely surprised and tried to reverse his own jump, but only succeeded in clumsily flailing about in the air. Amber crashed into him, elbow leading, and the poor dwarf was hurled right back over the counter.

Amber's landing was sloppy, however, and the other guard knew that. Spinning around, he smashed his shield into Amber's side. Unbalanced, she was sent stumbling and crashed right into some unlucky human, sending both of them sprawling across the floor.

Rather disoriented, Amber punched the human in the face, thinking he was the dwarf. The human's head lolled back, a droplet of blood spilling out of his mouth. The man was lucky Amber's gauntlets had fallen off or that blood would have been in much greater volume.

With an angry growl, one of the human's buddies, a big man with rippling muscles, threw down his mug and stomped over to Amber, slamming a fist into her stomach. He let out a cry of pain as his fist connected with the hard Red Iron of Amber's armour, but the force was still enough to knock Amber off of the man she had punched.

Both dwarf guards ran over to Amber and the humans, grappling Amber and the second human to separate them. Unexpectedly, the guard's actions just made the situation worse.

Neither Amber nor her new enemy had any interest in being held, and both fiercely wrenched the guards off. Amber's was sent tumbling into the floor, bowling several bystanders over, and the other dwarf was flipped right over the human's massive shoulders, colliding with a poor old man as he smashed into the ground.

The old man's son immediately charged the giant human, while the friends of the bystanders attacked the guard and Amber, turning what had started out as a small fistfight into a tavern-wide slugfest.

Realizing the fight was on, Jeddo hopped off his stool, laughing and thoroughly drunk. He ran at one human who was grappling with Amber and kicked the man hard in the knee, then bonked him on the head with an empty mug. The man collapsed to the floor, out cold.

In the nick of time, Jeddo drew his rapier and deflected a powerful blow from a chair leg. Several humans had torn apart their chairs and tables for makeshift clubs, and Jeddo had narrowly avoided what many others had not.

Letting out an excited cry, Amber jumped at a random dwarf, leading with her head. She crashed into his stomach, her helmet doubling the pain of the blow. The dwarf's eyes went wide, and his mouth popped open as the wind was knocked right out of him.

Grabbing him by his scruff, Amber heaved the heavy dwarf into the air and threw him at a human, sending both of them to the ground.

Jeddo grinned as he faced down a new opponent. This was going to be fun.

Even whilst drunk, Jeddo moved nimbly. He ducked another strike from his opponent and smacked the man on the back of the leg with the flat of his blade. As the human whirled around furiously and took another swing, Jeddo ducked into a roll, and the club went soaring over Jeddo's head.

With no object to break the club's momentum, it kept

swinging in a wide arc, then slammed into another human's hip. There was a sickening crack and the victim cried out, clutching his broken pelvis.

Jeddo's opponent, horribly off balance, stumbled forward with his head drooped. Jeddo jumped back to his feet and swung the pommel of his rapier into the back of the man's head. As a dazed look filled the man's eyes, Jeddo swiped a half-empty pint of ale and chugged it back.

"Cheers," Jeddo said before smashing the now-empty flagon into the man's jaw. He fell to the ground, unconscious.

The gnome was just about to kick some human in the back of the knee when something hard slammed into his back. Jeddo fell on his face with a cry, trying to turn the fall into a roll. His intoxicated mind was too slow, however, and he felt a spike of pain in his forehead as it collided with the hard, wooden floor.

As it turned out, getting drunk saved Jeddo's life.

A split second later, a dagger went spinning through the air right where Jeddo's head would have been had he rolled. Instead, the deadly blade embedded itself in the stomach of the man who had clubbed Jeddo. The human dropped his club and clutched his stomach, eyes bulging as blood leaked from his gut.

Before anyone even noticed however, the room exploded into a symphony of agonized cries. Twenty hooded figures darted through the tavern, moving with a grace found only in elves. With each step, they plunged a dagger into someone's chest, never once hesitating. They moved in a fluid dance, each movement flowing into the next as they wove through the carnage.

Jeddo scrambled to his feet, only to dive down again as a dead human toppled over, nearly landing on Jeddo. The human's face was frozen in an expression of true terror and blood gushed out of a cut in his neck.

Once again, Jeddo tried to stand, but his foot was pinned beneath the man's corpse. As Jeddo sat up to try to push the man off, he caught a glimpse of the wound and gulped in fear.

The blow had been placed directly across the jugular, cutting deep into the flesh and stretching across the windpipe. The cut was beautifully made, digging deep into the flesh yet leaving a line so thin it could barely be identified. There was only one group of people capable of dealing such perfect blows while moving so fluidly.

Dark Elves.

Terror raced through Jeddo, clearing away the numbing effects of the alcohol. He'd dealt with Dark Elves numerous times during his time at sea, and they terrified him more than anything else. Frantically, Jeddo tugged at his foot, trying to get it free, glancing around wildly to see if he was noticed.

Finally, his foot came free and Jeddo leaped to his feet, tightening his grip on his rapier despite knowing it would prove useless; as far as the stories went, no one survived single combat with a Dark Elf.

Meanwhile, Amber was having similar thoughts. She had noticed the Dark Elves almost immediately, but unlike Jeddo, Amber wasn't feeling fear. She was feeling pure ecstasy, tempered only by creeping feelings of remorse and grief; the last time she had seen a Dark Elf, he was plunging a sword into her mother's back.

It was time to avenge her.

Amber shouldered her way to the bar counter where she'd rested her hammer and shield. A human, clearly drunk out of his wits, tried to intercept her, but she just kicked him in the groin with her metal boots and he collapsed to the ground.

In the absolute nick of time, Amber picked up her shield. As she did, a Dark Elf stabbed a dagger into the shield, which bounced off with the distinctive shriek of metal.

Acting on instinct, Amber grabbed her hammer and spun around, catching the second dagger as it raced toward her neck. The weight of her hammer sent it spinning out of the elf's hand,

and the blade thwacked into a wall.

Grinning, Amber peered into the cold, grey eyes of her opponent. The Dark Elf's pale face showed no sign of expression, only deadly calm.

The elf ran at Amber, who immediately swung her hammer forward to intercept. The Dark Elf had anticipated the strike, hoped for it actually, and leaped to the side, executing a backflip and landing on the bar counter.

Not once losing his speed, the elf transitioned smoothly into a run, jumping off the counter and lashing out with his boot. Now behind Amber, the elf grinned as his foot, armed with a needle and sleeping drug, drove down toward Amber's neck.

The elf's grin turned to surprise and pain as Amber's hammer swung around and crashed into the elf's foot, shattering it. Amber's body followed, and she spun around to face the Dark Elf, who was now lying on the floor, crippled but trying to stand.

Amber didn't hesitate. She swung her hammer in a deadly uppercut that smacked into the elf's jaw, snapping his head back and cracking his jaw. The Dark Elf collapsed, dead.

"That was fer me mother, ye cowardly worm," she spat, kicking his limp body.

Amber was about to spin around in search of a new elf to kill when a cold, deadly voice commanded, "Drop the hammer, or the gnome dies."

CHAPTER 7:
CAPTURED

AMBER TURNED AROUND SLOWLY, REALIZING THAT ANY sudden movements would likely get her friend killed but desperately wanting to see who was threatening her.

She found herself staring at what was possibly the most terrifying person she had ever seen. He was a Dark Elf, tall and slender, clothed entirely in black. Black cloth covered his mouth and nose, leaving only steely silver eyes and a strip of white skin visible. Knives and swords were strapped all across him, on his legs, his chest, his arms, and his back. Amber figured they were likely more for intimidation than use. The most frightening weapons on him, however, were also the most interesting.

A set of black leather bracers rested on his forearms. Black metal bands wrapped around the leather, all leading to a very curious contraption. It was a thin block of metal with a spool at the end of it, sitting on the back of the bracers. Some form of black wire was wrapped around the spool, disappearing into the metal. A thin blade, extending almost to the end of the elf's middle finger, protruded from the end of the metal. The bracers continued across the elf's palm, where a few little buttons were set. A small, black bird—a dove, by the looks of it—flew from across the room to perch on the elf's shoulder.

The elf noticed Amber staring at the contraptions and grinned beneath the cloth. "Would you like to see how they work?" he asked in an almost playful voice.

Amber had always loved machines and contraptions, even those that could easily kill her. Despite all common sense yelling at her not to, Amber nodded.

The elf's grin reached his eyes. His right arm shot out toward a mug sitting on the bar counter. His middle finger curled in and pressed one of the buttons. There was a little click and the blade suddenly rocketed out of the metal strip, almost faster than Amber's eyes could register. The elf pressed another button and the blade retracted just as soon as it had fired, pulled back to the bracer by the black cord.

Amber had barely seen the motion and was only aware that there was suddenly a mug in the elf's hand, bits of brown ale dripping out of either side.

The Dark Elf pulled down the cloth to reveal a grinning mouth. "Cheers," he said and took a long sip of the mead. Then he tossed it into the air, flung out his left arm, and pressed some buttons.

The mug fell down to the ground in five pieces, and the blade retracted into its bracer.

The elf's smile turned from cocky to sinister just as quickly. "I could do that to your friend here too," he threatened calmly. "Drop the hammer."

Amber decided to try a bluff. "Ye really think I care about this gnome?" she scoffed, trying to spit the word. "Ye're a bigger fool than I was thinkin'!"

The elf's smile was replaced by neutrality. "Very well," he said, then turned to Jeddo. He stretched out his right arm and pointed the blade at Jeddo's forehead.

The bracer made that little click again, and just as it did, Amber cried out a protest and dropped her hammer.

Faster than Amber thought possible, the Dark Elf grabbed the cord in midair and flicked his arm toward Amber. The blade wrapped around the hammer's handle, and the elf flicked his wrist again.

The hammer was in his hands before it had even touched the ground.

The Dark Elf glanced evilly over his shoulder at Amber. "Let's go for a walk, shall we?"

By "walk" the Dark Elf had meant "gruelling seven-hour hike while cuffed and chained without any stopping." Amber and Jeddo were placed in exceptionally thick and strong cuffs and dragged behind a horse across the Fields of Flame, never once being given a rest or a bit of water.

As nightfall approached, the sky began to darken with thick clouds that turned a shade of dark orange in the setting sun. The air became very moist and thick, and the distant rumblings of thunder echoed across the stony landscape. The winds picked up and began roaring, making it difficult to hear.

Amber let out a heavy sigh. She knew they were about to experience one of Pyradia's infamous and surprisingly frequent thunderstorms.

The elves seemed to know that too, and they began barking orders in a silky language that Amber assumed was some form of elvish. Within minutes, several black tents had been set up, although not very well, considering bracing poles in solid rock was no easy task.

An instant later, the sky broke open.

Pyradians often told others that when it rained in Pyradia, it was as if a lake was dropped on your head. Sitting outside one of the waterproof elf tents, Amber realized those tales were grossly understated.

The rain hit like a tsunami wave. Each droplet was the size of a large pebble and were so tightly packed it was hard to distinguish that there were even drops. Within seconds, small pools of water had gathered in Amber's armour and Jeddo's clothes were completely soaked through. Worse still, the wind angled the rain into Amber's face, which smashed into her like a waterfall. She honestly thought she might drown.

Before Jeddo could even let out one of his big sighs, a brilliant bolt of light streaked through the sky, illuminating the landscape for just a moment. A few seconds later, an ear-shattering rumble cut through the air, far louder than any thunder Amber had ever heard before.

"I'm pretty lucky, you know," Jeddo yelled over the howling wind. "Wearing all your metal, you'll keep the lighting away from me!"

Amber rolled her eyes. "The elf tents will be doin' that fer me!" she yelled back. "They're taller than I am!"

Jeddo shrugged, squinting against the rain. "Too bad they aren't doing anything about this bloody rain!"

Amber laughed. "And ye thought the drizzles we'd experienced were bad!"

"Drizzles?!" Jeddo hollered. "I've been in ocean storms with less rain than those!"

"They're drizzles compared t' this!" Amber replied.

"Get up," a sharp voice demanded. Amber looked up to see a Dark Elf staring down at her, his face hidden by the rain and his cloak.

Amber spat at his feet, although with the downpour, the elf didn't really notice. "I won't be takin' orders from elf scum," she retorted.

The elf swatted her across the face with the back of his slender hand. "You will do as I say, dwarf, or I will make your life much more miserable."

Amber grinned, barely even noticing the slap. "Ye'll let me go, elf, or I'll send ye t' kingdom come."

The elf reached down and, with remarkable strength, hoisted Amber into the air so she was level with his face, leaving Amber's small legs kicking and thrashing in the air. "The only reason you are still alive is because the king wants you alive. I could kill you without even thinking about it. So, I suggest you come with me."

"Like hell ye'll be takin' me," Amber challenged. She threw her head back then smashed it forward into the elf's face. He cried out in pain, clutching his throbbing forehead and dropping Amber.

Laughing, Amber rose to her feet kicked the elf in the knee. He went down with another cry and Amber stomped on his back. She wrapped her chains around his neck and pulled.

The elf clutched desperately at the chains, his eyes bulging out as he fought for breath. Amber was much too strong however, and it was a battle the elf was quickly losing.

Amber felt the elf resisting less and less and knew her opponent was almost dead. She pulled harder, hoping to speed the process.

All of a sudden, a small black object streaked through the rain and embedded itself in Amber's neck. She gasped and clutched her neck, grasping for the object.

A little dart fell into her hand, stained at the tip with a drop of crimson. Another dart stuck into Amber's arm, and a third found the other side of her neck.

Dwarves were known for their resistance to poisons and drugs, but three darts of elvish sleeping drugs were just too much, even for Amber. Her eyes rolled back into her head and she swayed, no longer able to concentrate on thought.

The world went black, and Amber's thick dwarven frame toppled over, unconscious.

Amber's eyes fluttered open. Bright light flooded into them and she tried to put a hand up to shield her eyes, but her arms wouldn't budge. She blinked and squinted, trying to get her bearings.

She was inside a tent, that much was clear. Sunlight streamed through the cloth walls, revealing a simple desk, a couple of chairs, and a little table, along with several packs and weapons off to one side. A brazier full of hot embers sat next to the weapons, and several rods of metal jutted out of it. She didn't like the looks of that.

She was currently propped up against a pole with her hands bound in heavy iron manacles; they lacked chains this time though. They catch on quick, Amber thought to herself.

She tried moving her hands and wrists, hoping to relieve a bit of the pressure from the manacles. As she did so, her hands brushed against skin.

"Ah. You're awake," a voice said from behind her. It was a tired and ragged voice, but Amber recognized it all the same.

"Jeddo," she replied. "Are ye all right? Ye don't sound like yerself."

"I'm fine," Jeddo answered, hoping he hadn't hesitated too much. "Just a bit tired."

Amber had caught the slight pause however and knew he was lying. "What'd those bastards do t' ye?"

"Nothing," Jeddo told her, this time too quickly. "They just bound me up."

Amber sighed and shook her head. "Jeddo, I know as well as anyone that ye're a good liar. Just not t' me."

Jeddo's head drooped. "They questioned me," he said quietly.

Amber was about to inquire further, but the door to the tent suddenly flung open and a Dark Elf walked in with that slick, black dove perched on his shoulder. Amber grinned evilly as she noticed the large bump on his forehead and the long bruise around his neck.

"Ye're looking well," Amber taunted.

The elf gave her a baleful smile. "Better than your friend."

That wiped the smile off Amber's face.

"Unfortunately, he didn't tell us anything we didn't already know," the elf recalled. With a sinister grin, he added, "It did give us an excuse to torture him for a while though."

Amber fought furiously against her bonds. "Ye'll pay fer that, ye vile cur! When I'm free o' these bonds, I'll break yer skull apart! See how much yer smilin' then!"

The elf raised an eyebrow skeptically. "I hardly think you capable of that," he mocked casually, inspecting his fingernails to rub salt in the wound. "But your threat is duly noted. All the same, we have much to discuss, so allow me to remove your shackles for just a moment."

As the elf approached, however, Amber thrashed out a leg and caught the elf in the ankle. "We'll be doin' it here," she said stubbornly, glowering at her captor.

The Dark Elf ignored the pain in his foot and gave an indifferent shrug. "It matters not to me," he said. "I'm just a little worried for Jeddo, what with all the screaming you'll be doing. Right in the poor gnome's ear too…"

"The only thing ye'll be gettin' out o' me is a foot up yer ass," Amber shot back. "Now do yer worst elf, and I'll let ye know when it starts t' tickle."

The elf smirked. "You act tough now…" he began, putting on a glove and producing a glowing rod from the brazier. He brought the red-hot tip right beside Amber's neck, stopping just short of the skin. "But how long will that last?"

"Longer than ye will," Amber threatened, trying to mask her fear. She was tough, tougher than most dwarves, but even she had a breaking point, and she was quite worried the elf was about to find it.

The elf sighed. "What is it with you dwarves?" he muttered. "Do you think I'm bluffing? Do you really think angering me is a good idea?"

In what was quite possibly an act of both bravery and stupidity,

Amber shoved aside her fear and moved her neck into the hot metal. As her flesh began bubbling and burning, Amber summoned all her strength and hissed two words. "Hell…yes…"

The elf moved the rod away, and it was all Amber could do not to sigh in relief. She maintained her steady stare, trying desperately not to show any signs of weakness.

Her torturer actually raised his eyebrows in mild surprise. His dove, still perched on the elf's shoulder, tilted its head and stared at Amber with a pair of hollow, black eyes. Amber shivered.

"I'll admit, I'm impressed," the Dark Elf said. "You are indeed resilient. I do have other, more painful methods, but I'm starting to realize there's a much easier way to do this."

Amber's stoic expression faltered as the elf walked around Amber and toward Jeddo. "What're ye doin'?" she demanded, a slight quiver in her voice.

The elf released Jeddo's manacles and dragged the tired gnome to his feet, pulling him into Amber's view. She cringed at the sight of her friend. His face was bruised and puffy and lined with little cuts. His shirt had been removed, revealing deep gashes along the gnome's lean torso.

"Clearly, you are very good at resisting pain," the elf explained. With an evil smirk, the elf looked down at Jeddo, then back up at Amber, eyebrow raised. "Is he?"

Jeddo let out a bloodcurdling scream as the hot poker pressed against his side, searing Jeddo's abdomen with what Amber knew was a blindingly unbearable pain.

"All right, all right, what do ye want t' know?" Amber shrieked, her resolve finally broken.

The elf removed the rod and the screaming stopped. "That's much more like it," he said. "Belligerence accomplishes nothing. Now, roughly a hundred years ago, my people destroyed a dwarf kingdom located in the Hidden Mountains. Do you remember this event?"

Amber's face fell. "One hunnerd an' three," she said quietly.

The elf gave her a confused look. "What?"

"It's been one hunnerd an' three years, four months, two weeks, an' six days since ye and yer kind ransacked me home and killed me family," Amber answered. She looked the elf in his cold, pitiless eyes and said fiercely, "I've forgotten *nothin'*."

The elf smiled. "Excellent. Then you will recall how finding the entrance to that miserable excuse for a kingdom can—"

"—Only be done by a dwarf that was born there," Amber finished. "Yeah. How ye got one o' our own t' turn I'll never be understandin', but ye'll be payin' for it all the same."

The elf raised his eyes to the ceiling. "Again with the threats," he sighed. Looking back at Amber, he asked, "Do you know where the door is?"

Amber glared. "Ye won't be gettin' it out o' me," she said defiantly. "And even if ye could, ye can't get in. The tunnels are all collapsed."

The elf shrugged. "A matter for another time," he replied dismissively. "Now, what were your people mining for down there?"

"Iron, gold, silver," Amber answered lazily. "Same as any dwarf kingdom."

"And what else?"

"We came upon a couple o' veins o' mithril," Amber recalled. "But naught else."

"So, there was no arcanium being mined?" the elf pressed.

"What in the blazes is arcanium?" Amber asked.

This was a bluff on Amber's part. She knew full well what arcanium was. It was a very unique substance, created when magic seeps into rock, forming crystals or gathering as pools of liquid magic in sprawling caverns. It was incredibly powerful and dangerous, especially in the wrong hands, and Amber did not want to let on that she knew anything about it.

The elf waved the poker for Amber to see, although he noticed that it wasn't quite as hot as before and produced a new one from the brazier. "Might I remind you what happens when you lie to me?"

"I'm not tellin' ye any lies," Amber said, although the nearly indiscernible waver in her voice said otherwise. Amber hoped the elf hadn't caught it.

He had. The Dark Elf smiled sadistically and pressed the rod back to Jeddo's flesh. Jeddo began screaming and thrashing violently against the elf's iron grip.

Amber watched helplessly while the elf continued his torture. "How much longer do you think he can resist?" the elf asked. "How long do you think it will take for him to die?"

"Yes!" Amber yelled suddenly. "Yes, we mined arcanium! Now just let me friend go!"

The elf removed his poker and Jeddo slumped forward, breathing shallowly. "And how much did you mine?"

"I've no clue," Amber answered. When the elf raised his poker menacingly, Amber protested, "I really don't! I never kept track o' the stores! I was just a miner!"

"Then guess," the elf hissed.

"Three tonnes?" Amber estimated. "Maybe four? We used a lot o' it though, fer our minin' and defences."

"Did you ever refine arcanium?"

Amber nodded. "Not very often though. It's not easy."

The elf continued interrogating Amber for several hours, drilling her about everything she knew about arcanium. Amber answered to the best of her ability, but that didn't stop the Dark Elf from giving Jeddo another few jabs with the poker whenever Amber didn't provide sufficient information.

Finally, as the sun's light began to dim outside the tent, it was over. The Dark Elf nodded as he considered Amber's latest response, then flashed a quick, hollow smile. He held out a finger and his dove hopped onto the outstretched digit. The Dark Elf whispered some words to it before sending the sinisterly beautiful creature out into the night. Amber frowned as she watched it go, wondering what other uses the black doves served.

He then turned to Amber. "You have been most helpful. Rest well tonight. We're travelling again tomorrow." With that, the elf threw a weak and tired Jeddo at Amber and turned to leave.

"Wait!" Amber called. "Aren't ye goin' t' tend t' him?"

The elf turned back to Amber. "What needs tending? His wounds are all cauterized. He won't bleed out."

"Ye aren't even goin' t' bandage him?" Amber asked.

The elf sighed and walked back to Jeddo, grabbing him by his scruff and dragging him out of the tent. "As you wish."

They were gone before Amber could say anything more. She fought back the urge to cry, instead focusing on the many ways she could snap the elf's scrawny neck.

She fell asleep to those thoughts, smiling contentedly.

CHAPTER 8:
Assassins in the Trees

AFTER A ROUGH SLEEP, SILMANUS' EYES FLUTTERED OPEN and he looked around tiredly. He tried rolling his sore shoulders, but they wouldn't move, and he felt a distinctive pain in his wrists.

Silmanus suddenly remembered where he was and what had happened. He sighed and took in the morning.

The spring air was crisp and chilly, but carried with it the smell of pine needles, which Silmanus had to admit was a wonderful odour indeed. The sun wasn't quite up yet, but what few rays had poked over the horizon cast long shadows across the forest floor. A gentle breeze passed through the tall pines, upon the branches of which a black bird perched, singing to the sunrise. The scent of wood smoke wafted into his nose and his ears picked up the crackles and pops of a fire.

Mara was sitting on a log, warming her hands over a fresh fire. Her expressionless face glanced over at Silmanus for a moment, then turned back to the fire. "You're awake," she said.

"How observant," Silmanus replied dryly. "Perhaps you picked up on my evident discomfort as well?"

Mara didn't look at him but cocked an eyebrow. "Are you asking me to untie you?" She responded in a tone that very clearly stated it wasn't happening.

"I wonder what could have possibly given you that notion,"

Silmanus retorted, his voice dripping in sarcasm.

Mara shook her head, letting out a snicker of amusement. "You are aware that irritating your captor is a very bad way to get what you want, right?"

Silmanus shrugged, or tried to at least. "Well, it's not like you'll let me go either way."

Mara nodded in agreement. "Very true, but you've missed your chance on getting a nice cup of coffee," she taunted, bending down to the little pot and breathing in deeply. "Mm, and it does smell nice. Freshly imported from North Hynar."

Silmanus' mouth began watering slightly. Despite being an elf, he drank a lot of coffee, and the beans manufactured in magical greenhouses just didn't measure up to the produce of Hynar, a human country in the southeastern deserts.

Mara glanced at Silmanus out of the corner of her eye, grinning at his hopeful face. "Oh, so you *do* like coffee," she continued in a teasing tone. "Well, that really is too bad. I even have a spare mug, just for instances like this." Mara made a *tsk* sound in her mouth and shook her head. "But alas, you have offended your host."

Silmanus glowered at Mara and sighed in resignation. "Fine. I'm sorry," he said stiffly. "May I please have a mug of coffee?"

Mara's grin broadened slightly. "What's this? An elf, submitting to a human?" she commented in mock disbelief. "Now that's really something. Well, I suppose that just for that, I could spare a mug."

She leaned over and fished around in a canvas bag sitting beside her, then produced a simple wooden cup. A minute or two later, Mara decided the coffee had boiled long enough and poured the dark brown liquid into two mugs, trying not to let the grinds at the bottom get into the mugs.

Mara rose and set the mug of steaming liquid in front of Silmanus. "Well, there you are," she said. "Enjoy." She stepped back and stared at Silmanus, an expectant look on her face.

Suddenly, she snapped her fingers. "Oh, dear me, of course!

You really can't drink without free hands, can you?" she taunted, exaggerating her forgetful voice and expression. "What a shame, because I really can't untie you, can I?"

Silmanus sighed heavily, more than a little frustrated with Mara's taunting. "I'm sure it wouldn't hurt to untie me for a moment, then bind my wrists again once my hands are in front of me," he reasoned, impatience creeping into his voice.

Mara tapped her chin as if considering it, then shook her head sadly. "I'm afraid I just can't risk it. You might escape." She threw out her hands in a helpless gesture. "Well, I suppose there's nothing to be done. Oh well." Mara turned around and walked back to her own coffee, being sure to make very loud slurping sounds as she drank.

Silmanus shook his head. He really didn't want to do this, but he also really wanted a cup of coffee and to show up this cocky, childish young woman.

Narrowing his eyes in concentration, Silmanus willed the mug over to him. The mug floated into the air and over to his mouth, tilting upward against his lips as if held by actual hands.

Mara heard the sound of slurping coffee and immediately snapped her attention toward Silmanus, eyebrows lifting in surprise. "Wha-but-how—" she sputtered. "I thought wizards needed a focus to use magic! Something to tap into the magical essence of the world."

Silmanus set down the mug and gave a contended smile. "Well, I'd hoped to reveal this later, but I'm afraid you thought wrong. Terribly sorry."

Mara's eyebrows narrowed. "Then why carry a staff at all?"

"Because I can only use simple spells without a focus, and it's much more difficult," Silmanus explained, pleased by Mara's curiosity. "Focuses allow wizards to attune much deeper to magic and help us utilize our power to its maximum potential." Silmanus gave a knowing smile. "While most of my spells require a staff for effective use, I don't need it to do this."

Silmanus spoke a single command word and an invisible force blasted Mara off her feet. She flew backward, knocking over her coffee and narrowly missing the fire.

With another command word, Silmanus' bonds disintegrated, and he shot into a standing position. He stretched out his hand and his staff flew toward him. Silmanus curled his slender fingers around it, suddenly feeling much more at ease.

Mara began to stand up, but Silmanus pointed the staff at her. "No, you can stay down," he instructed. "Unless you want to see what I'm able to do when I actually have my staff."

Mara glared fiercely. "So now what? You're going to kill me?" she challenged.

Silmanus opened his mouth to retort, but he stopped suddenly, his attention drawn to something else. There was something not quite right. Warning bells were going off in his head, but he couldn't place why. Blizzard noticed it too. He was pawing at the ground and whinnying quietly.

Mara didn't seem to notice anything. "What's the matter?" she continued. "Cat got your tongue?"

"Shh!" Silmanus hissed urgently.

Mara laughed. "Or what?" she scoffed. "You'll kill me?"

"I mean it!" Silmanus snapped. "Something isn't right."

Mara was going to make some mocking remark, but something in Silmanus' eyes told her otherwise. "What is it?" she asked, all traces of mockery and sarcasm gone from her tone.

Silmanus pointed his staff into the trees, furrowing his eyebrows as he searched. "String your bow if it isn't already strung," he advised absently.

"You cut the string," Mara reminded him flatly. Still concentrating on the trees, Silmanus snapped his fingers. The string immediately repaired itself. Mara picked up her bow and strung it, nocking an arrow almost immediately after.

Bow outstretched but not drawn, Mara peered into the woods, her eyes straining to see through the shadows.

They saw nothing though. No sign of anything out of the ordinary.

Silmanus' eyebrows moved closer together as Mara shot him a doubtful look. "I could have sworn there was something here…" he said distantly. His eye widened in sudden realization. "Up!" he cried in warning.

Mara glanced up just in time to see a cloaked figure point a bow at her and draw the arrow. Mara was too quick with her own bow and sent an arrow streaking with deadly accuracy at the mysterious figure. He let out a cry of pain as the arrow pierced his heart and his bow went off, sending an arrow harmlessly into the ground.

Several arrows whistled toward Silmanus, but he slammed his staff into the ground and pulled magic from deep within him, shaping it into a protective shield that shot up around him. The arrows ricocheted off and shot into the dirt.

Another archer took aim at Mara, but once again, she took the figure out before he could fire.

"There's a dozen in the trees, and I see another dozen climbing down," Silmanus murmured to Mara. He saw an archer aim his bow at Mara and flicked his arm out toward the assailant. Five icicles, each the size of a long dagger and just as sharp, went flying out of his palm and peppered the figure, who dropped his bow and fell limp.

One of the assassins was on the ground and running, so Mara fired an arrow at him. With lightning-fast reflexes, the attacker snatched the arrow right out of the air, snapping it in half and tossing it aside without ever breaking his stride.

"Who *are* these people?" Mara hissed at Silmanus as she drew another arrow. She already knew the answer. She'd seen this fighting style before but asked anyway in hopes she might have been wrong.

She wasn't. Silmanus read the signs clearly too. The stealthy approach, the attack style, the incredible agility. Only one race could pull off an attack like this, and Silmanus' blood went cold as it occurred to him.

"Dark Elves," he said grimly.

Mara's face paled. She'd clashed with Dark Elves once and barely made it out alive. She doubted she'd get lucky twice.

Silmanus knew Dark Elves very well, and he knew that any slip, any hesitation, could spell death. His eyes were narrowed in concentration and his lips were in constant motion, muttering incantations. His range of spells was limited in a forest; anything too destructive or explosive could cause a forest fire and just make things worse. That meant sticking to ice-based spells, as well as psychic spells and spells that just focused raw magic into physical effects.

Surprisingly to most, Silmanus was at the disadvantage. Dark Elves were no strangers to magic, as with all elves, and were well rehearsed in the spells produced by wizards. They knew how to combat magic better than any other race, and Silmanus continually found his spells being thwarted.

Mara was faring only a little better. She had dropped the bow in favour of her sword, as the archers had all been eliminated and, on the ground, the Dark Elves dodged her arrows easily. Two were on her now, twirling around in a hauntingly beautiful dance of death. Both bore twin daggers and attacked her simultaneously.

Mara struggled to get a fix on where her opponents were. Their black cloaks were constantly aflutter, disorienting her vision and stopping her from accurately placing any attacks. She was forced into a defensive position, blocking the nimble strikes but never being able to land any of her own.

Silmanus gave up on offence and switched to defensive spells, drawing one of his swords. He conjured various shields and illusions to keep his opponents distracted. While he wasn't nearly as good of a swordsman as Mara or the Dark Elves, his combination of magic and natural grace had already overwhelmed one elf, who now lay bleeding on the ground.

With only one enemy to face for the moment, Silmanus risked a glance over at Mara. She was being battered down, and Silmanus could see her struggling to keep up with the elves' incredible speed.

It was the cloaks, Silmanus knew. He had faced both Mara and Dark Elves in single combat, and knew that Mara was, incredibly, superior. But she couldn't seem to get a proper fix on where her assailants were.

Silmanus decided to take a risk. Muttering some magical words, Silmanus dug deep into his magical reserves, flooding his body with the familiar warmth of magic. That comforting warmth quickly grew into a raging inferno, like rivers of liquid fire rushing through Silmanus' veins. Hot pressure built up within the wizard's head, pushing on his skull like molten lead, and at last, when he could stand it no longer, Silmanus released his spell.

A ring of fire erupted from Silmanus, expanding quickly. He threw up a shield around Mara and the flames washed over her harmlessly but seared the cloaks right off of the Dark Elves and set the rest of their clothing aflame. Several of the approaching elves were also caught in the blast and dropped to the ground, covered in magical flames.

Silmanus fought to control the fire and extinguish it before it reached the trees, a bead of perspiration trickling down his temple as he did. He was just barely able to stop destructive flames before they set the forest aflame, and the ring dissolved into smoke.

It had served its purpose, however. Most of the Dark Elves were incapacitated and were now easy pickings. They would likely flee and regroup, Silmanus figured, realizing that they had lost the advantage of surprise and shadows, as well as the fact that they were all burning alive.

Sure enough, the surviving elves began running into the trees, covered in nasty burns. Most of them were still alive, however, protected by their hauberks and innate, albeit weak, magical abilities. Mara was able to drive her sword through the chest of one, but the others escaped, darting away like cowards.

Mara lowered her sword, confident that the battle was won. She turned to Silmanus, who was sheathing his blade. She gave him a nod and an approving smile, deciding she was safe to let her guard down and ask a few questions.

It was a nearly fatal mistake.

Several arrows suddenly came flying out of the trees, streaking straight toward Mara. With her back turned, she had no way of knowing what was coming.

Silmanus cried out in warning, thrusting his hand toward Mara. Magical energy slammed into her, knocking her flat and repelling most of the arrows.

Most of the arrows.

One arrow continued its flight, zipping over Mara and piercing clean through Silmanus' right side. He let out a gasp and his hand instinctively clutched the wooden shaft. Pure horror washed over Silmanus' face. Blizzard let out a screeching whinny and darted over to his master, propping Silmanus up with his muzzle.

Mara sat up immediately. If the Dark Elves were still shooting, any hesitation would spell death. Another few arrows slammed into the ground where Mara had fallen, proving her point.

Heart pounding in her throat, Mara scooped up her bow, nocked an arrow, spun toward the trees, and fired. She wasn't expecting to hit anything, but at the very least, it might force the Dark Elves to find cover, giving Mara the moment she needed to find an actual target.

There, behind a tree, Mara could see black fabric spilling out from around the trunk. In the same instant, she drew and fired, sending an arrow streaking toward her mark. There was a cry of pain as the projectile sank into a Dark Elf's shoulder.

Apparently, that convinced the Dark Elves that continuing the fight was more trouble than it was worth. Shadowy figures flitted between the trees, skittering away into the depths of Needlewood. Mara allowed herself a brief moment to smirk and sheath her sword before she remembered Silmanus and spun around. For as much as she hated elves, Silmanus had saved her life and she didn't want to see him die.

Mara drew in a tight breath as she spotted the arrow jutting out of Silmanus' waist.

"Quick, lie down, I'll get that bandaged. You should be fine though. I don't think it hit anything vital," she observed.

Silmanus shook his head, his silvery skin losing its light. "Poisoned," he managed. "Frostpetal." His eyes began rolling around in their sockets and saliva frothed at Silmanus' lips.

Then he collapsed.

Mara worked in a hurry. She cut the end of the arrow off and tore open the middle of Silmanus' robes to access the wound. Mara slid the remaining arrow through the back of Silmanus' waist, not wanting to risk causing more damage. She slid several layers of cloth bandages underneath the wound to control bleeding, leaving the entry wound exposed so she could apply some herbs.

Quickly, Mara ground some frostpetal (she always carried some with her) into a salve in her mug, adding leftover coffee in place of water in the hopes that the beans would somehow help. She threw in a couple of other plants and a special concoction of her own design, a mixture of several extremely rare herbs that held excellent anti-toxin properties.

Almost afraid of what she might see, Mara inspected the arrow wound. She was right to have been afraid.

Pus was already leaking out of the hole and black lines were creeping through Silmanus' silvery skin. The blood had also turned black, mixing with the pus and forming a nauseating goop that just about made Mara hurl.

Snatching her waterskin, Mara poured water on the wound and rubbed the sludgy gunk away with a bit of cloth. Once she felt the wound was sufficiently cleaned, Mara scooped up the herbal paste and smeared it inside the wound, again feeling the urge to vomit as her fingers rubbed the ointment across the disgusting opening of the wound, lifting Silmanus slightly to do the same to the exit. She felt very glad that Silmanus was unconscious; the pain he would feel otherwise would be simply excruciating.

Happy to finally be done with the sickening arrow wound and hoping she hadn't made the infection worse, Mara wrapped the bandage tightly around Silmanus' waist, trying to ignore the nasty black-green colour it was turning. She then pulled his robes back together and briefly contemplated trying to sew the fabric back together, but ultimately decided it was the least of her concerns. She had no idea if the Dark Elves were coming back, but she didn't want to wait around to find out.

Working as fast as she possibly could, Mara hacked down four spars, two long and two short, with her hatchet and lashed them into a rectangle. She then poked holes in the corners of Silmanus' blanket and tied it across the rectangular frame, creating a make-shift stretcher.

Laying the stretcher on the ground, Mara dragged Silmanus' fevered body onto the stretcher, tying down his legs and chest so he wouldn't slide off. She had a long way to drag him, but elves tended to be much lighter than humans, and Silmanus was no exception.

While she secured Silmanus, Mara took a moment to take in what had happened. She really didn't like elves; they were arrogant and snobbish, believing the other races to be completely inferior. Yet here was an elf who had just saved her life, who had taken a

Dark Elf arrow meant for her.

Guilt began pooling in her stomach like acid, burning its way up her throat and bringing tears to her eyes. Mara tried to push it away, tried not to let emotion take hold.

So, she just focused on Silmanus. She took in his face, noticing the way his jawline bent down into a pointed chin that rested beneath a thin mouth and small nose. His eyes, usually deep green but now pale and unseeing, seemed to be full of wisdom and intelligence, like they held the secrets of the universe within them. His thin eyebrows curved delicately above those knowing eyes, and his long black hair formed a widow's peak above his smooth forehead. He looked very calm, despite being so close to death. She wondered if dying really was as peaceful as Silmanus made it look.

Mara didn't have the time or the will to ponder that, however. What she needed to focus on was making sure her debt was paid and finding out who was responsible for the attacks.

Not that she could do that now. She had a dying elf to look after. Mara sighed, trying to figure out how best to carry the stretcher.

Mara suddenly heard a loud whinny off to her left. She looked over to see Silmanus' horse digging frantically at the ground. A wild look was in its eyes, feral desperation tempered by fear and worry. Mara recalled then that elves formed bonds of friendship as deeply with their horses as with each other. Surely the horse would be willing to help her.

Remembering stories of horse thieves having their ribcages shattered while trying to steal elven horses, Mara took the stretcher as close as she dared before setting it on the ground. She reached very slowly to the horse and, heart racing, gently laid a hand on the horse's flank. She expected the horse to suddenly rear up and pummel her into the ground and just about jumped away.

The horse stood stock still, however, eyes locked with Mara's, a sort of mutual respect passing between them. Mara took a deep breath and stepped back, cautiously approaching the horse from the front with hands outstretched. "Ok, horse," she said nervously. "My name is Mara. I'm not going to steal you. I just want your help getting your master to safety, ok?"

The horse snorted and shook its head. Mara skittered back instinctively but the horse did not attack. Confidence growing slightly, Mara approached again, gingerly laying a hand on the horse's long muzzle, breathing a sigh of relief when the horse didn't lash out.

"Alright," she breathed. "Alright. See? I'm not so bad. Your name is Blizzard, isn't it?"

Blizzard snorted in response. "Ok, I'll take that as a yes," Mara decided. "Blizzard, I'm just going to hitch Silmanus to you, ok?" Mara steadily backed away to the stretcher, keeping her movements slow and deliberate.

Quickly tying her bag to the side of the stretcher, Mara grabbed the ends of the long spars by Silmanus' head and lifted the stretcher up and dragged it over to the horse, sliding the spars into the saddle's stirrups and tying them in place. At one point, Blizzard's side twitched and Mara just about jumped out of her skin, but the horse was just responding to the spars brushing his fur.

Mara let out a long breath. So far, so good. Walking over to Blizzard's head again, she replaced her hand and whispered, "Good boy. Now, I'm just going to hop on your back, ok?" Keeping a hand on Blizzard, Mara moved toward the saddle, reaching toward the pommel.

Blizzard suddenly reared into the air, thrashing his forelegs and whinnying angrily. Silmanus was nearly flung off of his stretcher.

Mara backed away immediately, hands in the air. "Alright, alright, no riding," she said quickly. "May I at least lead you along?" Blizzard looked steadily at Mara. He said nothing.

"Right, you're a horse," Mara mumbled. "You don't talk. Well, here goes." The woman approached Blizzard once more, slowly stooping down to grab hold of the rope that once held Silmanus.

She stood up again, bracing herself for another outburst.

Blizzard seemed to be ok with Mara holding his lead, however, not moving a single muscle as Mara rose. The woman nodded. "Ok. Alright. Um…well, follow me."

Turning to face the sun, Mara set off, guiding along Blizzard behind her. The horse followed willingly, plodding along the stiff ground after Mara. The stretcher scraped across the ground with obnoxious grinding sounds, but Mara pushed the mild irritation from her mind.

She had a much more pressing issue at hand.

Chapter 9:
Mara's Village

After about an hour, Mara decided they had put enough distance between them and the site of the Dark Elf ambush to stop for a bit. She hadn't gotten to finish her coffee and after the fight, she desperately needed the boost.

Mara released Blizzard's lead, figuring that the horse wouldn't try to bolt on her. And even if he did, Blizzard was probably encumbered enough by Silmanus and the stretcher that Mara could catch him. She hoped.

With one eye warily watching the trees, Mara collected the driest branches she could find. Using pine needles as tinder, she stacked the sticks like a log cabin before using her flint and steel to light the fire.

Filling her coffee pot with water, Mara waited patiently for the water to boil, her bow lying ready at her side. She was confident that the Dark Elves weren't pursuing her, but a little extra caution had never killed anybody. Not enough caution definitely had.

Finally, Mara saw steam rise from the pot and added some coffee grinds, waiting a few minutes before pouring the dark brown liquid into a mug. An involuntary smile spread across her face as she raised the mug to her lips.

The heat of the coffee was delightful, helping to wash away the chill of the air. Mara savoured the warmth almost as much as the rich, bitter taste.

Once her drink was finished, Mara packed away the mug and went to check on Silmanus, wincing as soon as she saw him.

It wasn't good.

He was sweating profusely, despite the cool Eiran air surrounding him. His skin had lost its elven glimmer, and every so often one of his legs or arms would give an involuntary twitch.

Frowning, Mara placed one of her hands on Silmanus' forehead, immediately jerking it away with a grimace. He was burning a fever hotter than a Pyradian volcano.

That was her problem. Lying here in the forest, Silmanus would not last long. Mara didn't know much about Dark Elf poisons, but she did know that without proper medicine, Silmanus would die.

Mara sighed. She couldn't let that happen. Mara was a free woman, an outlaw, but she lived by a strict rule: if anyone saved her life, she owed that person a favour of equal weight. Usually, those people were other outlaws and nobodies, and Mara repaid them by welcoming them into her band.

Silmanus was a different matter. This time, Mara would repay her debt by saving Silmanus' life. And that meant she needed to take him to her camp.

On and on, Mara led Blizzard, twisting around towering pines and beneath groping branches, brushing needles from her red tangles every so often. The sun climbed higher and higher into the sky, still with no sign of her home. Blizzard's flanks were wet with sweat, the horse's breathing growing steadily heavier. Comparatively to a human, Silmanus was not very heavy—he couldn't have been more than a hundred pounds—but he was still a significant burden whilst being dragged over the rough ground, and Mara's pack certainly wasn't helping either.

The sound of rushing water reached Mara's ears. The river! A large river known as the Icewater flowed through Needlewood directly from glaciers on the Northguard Mountains, branching off into many other smaller, nameless rivers. Mara's home was built along one such branch river, and unless her impeccable sense of direction had suddenly gone askew, she was very close to it.

A good thing too. Blizzard looked like he needed a rest and a drink. Mara knew she couldn't consume any of the water south of her village—it was used for washing and bathing and was thus contaminated—but Blizzard would be fine. *Besides*, Mara thought, laying a hand on her gurgling stomach, *I could use a moment to rest myself.*

Mara guided Blizzard to the left, grinning as she saw the telltale shimmer of the crystal-clear river. Blizzard's drooping head had perked up at the sound of rushing water and he trotted over to the riverbank as quickly as he could, dipping his muzzle into the cool, clear water, noisily gulping up greedy mouthfuls.

While Blizzard drank, Mara untied her pack from the stretcher and plopped down against a tree, leaning against its rough trunk. She pulled a piece of hardtack from a canvas wrapping, unenthusiastically taking a bite of the dry, flavourless bread and washing it down with a swig of water. Hardtack was definitely not Mara's travel meal of choice, but she'd run out of dried meat a couple days ago and it was better than nothing.

Finishing up her snack, Mara took a good look at Silmanus. He was still pale as a ghost, sweat pooled on his forehead. His breathing was shallow but steady. He didn't seem to be getting any worse, but he wasn't getting any better either. She needed to get him to her village, and fast.

Mara suddenly started sniffing the air, a very familiar scent wafting into her nostrils. Wood smoke! She could smell wood smoke! The village had to be very close. Deciding that they had rested long enough, Mara slung her pack across her shoulders and excitedly grabbed Blizzard's lead. After spending nearly a fortnight on a fruitless expedition, she was finally home, and with a prize that could make up for the lack of answers her quest had borne.

Sure enough, a gruelling half hour later, Mara approached a

very familiar sight. Tall wooden posts, sharpened at their ends, rose from the ground in tight formation, serving as the camp's walls. Three sets of shorter, secondary walls, more akin to fences than actual walls, sprawled off of the rear, right, and left palisades, containing the fields where the village grew its crops. Some scattered crosses filled the ground behind the village, marking it easily as a graveyard. In the middle of the front wall, the posts were cut short so that other posts could be laid horizontally across them, creating a large doorway that was currently filled by a drawbridge made of wooden planks. Smoke rose into the sky from behind the walls, and the sounds of laughing and talking echoed from within.

A tall figure on the front wall saw Mara approaching and shouted down to her in an accented voice. "Halt! You may go no further!"

Mara shook her head. That was Linos, and as much as she loved the carefree Esnian who had become her dearest friend, his antics got on her nerves from time to time. Particularly when she had places to be, like now.

"For Gods' sake, Linos, you know it's me," Mara snapped up at him.

Linos, standing on the battlements of the camp's uneven walls, cracked a grin as he peered down at his friend with keen brown eyes. He was a ruggedly handsome boy, with a roguish, cheerful face and smooth olive skin. It infuriated Mara sometimes how good looking he was. It was hard to stay mad at a man that attractive. Hard, but, as Mara had discovered on many occasions, definitely possible.

"How do I know you're not a doppelganger?" Linos called back in his singsong voice, just to irritate Mara. "I need a password!"

Mara's nostrils flared. "There are no doppelgangers in these woods, Linos," she yelled. "I'm not giving you your password."

Stifling a laugh, Linos decided to take the joke even further. "Then I'm not letting you through!"

Under normal circumstances, Mara would have probably ended up laughing at that point. She had a dying elf with her, however, and did not have the patience for Linos' games. "I'm not joking around here, Linos, and I'm not inflating your ego with that stupid password of yours! Now let me through!"

Still grinning, Linos rolled his eyes clambered down a ladder to open the gate. "You Lochadians are all so damned feisty," he teased as he pushed down the heavy wooden drawbridge.

Mara's face fell for an instant at the mention of Lochadia, but she pushed aside the brief remorse.

No. You are not thinking about that right now, Mara thought to herself. Straightening out her shoulders, Mara strode confidently toward the gate with her usual emotionless expression.

"What's the rush anyway?" Linos asked Mara as she stepped onto the drawbridge. He'd seen Mara dragging something but wasn't sure what it was. "And who's horse is that?"

Mara frowned. "That owner will be dead soon if I don't get him inside."

Linos raised his eyebrows. "'Him'?" he repeated. "Who's 'him'?"

Mara let out a sigh. Linos wasn't going to like it, but he didn't have to. "An elf," she said dryly.

Linos glanced at the stretcher, which really did carry an elf, and shot Mara a bewildered expression. "What the hell are you doing bringing an elf here?" he hissed.

Mara returned his glance with a glare. "I'm in charge, I make the decisions. I have my reasons, and that's all that's important," Mara replied evenly.

Linos glared back. "No, you don't get to pull that shit with me," he retorted. "With the others, fine, but not with me. You're my leader, yes, but not my slaver. Not my queen."

Mara sighed. "You're right, I'm sorry," she relented. "He saved my life, and I'm going to save his in turn."

Linos nodded. "That I can respect. We're not keeping him

though, are we?"

Mara shrugged. "That depends. He's a wizard and he knows about Dark Elves. He could be a real asset."

"Fair enough," Linos agreed. "I don't like it though, and the others won't either."

"I don't like it much myself, but we don't need to like it, we just need to benefit from it," Mara reasoned, untying the stretcher from Blizzard's stirrups. "Now help me get him to Eleanor. He's dying."

Linos nodded and walked behind Blizzard, picking up the other end of the stretcher. Together, they walked Silmanus inside, carrying him through the ragtag huts that made up their camp, Blizzard following anxiously behind. It was a nice little community, around two-hundred strong and filled with welcoming fires and delicious smells. Mara gave a small smile as the smell of smoked meat wafted into her nose.

As Mara and Linos made their way to the back of the camp, where Eleanor and the healer's hut were, a small crowd had begun to gather around. People were pointing and murmuring suspiciously at the sight of an elf.

Eleanor, a thin woman with blonde hair and a kindly expression, had seen the crowd and left her hut to investigate. She smiled warmly at the sight of Mara. "Welcome home, Mara," she said in her soft voice.

Mara gave Eleanor a nod. Mara was unusually fond of the woman. Eleanor was older than Mara was, somewhere in her mid-forties, but still held a great deal of respect for Mara and trusted her judgement, which meant a lot to Mara. Eleanor wasn't afraid to tell Mara when she was wrong either though and Mara appreciated that, too.

"It's good to be home," Mara replied. "But there's no time for pleasantries. I've got a dying elf that I need you to save."

Mara knew Eleanor was one of the few people in the camp who wouldn't mind an elf being around, and as the community's best (and only) healer, that was a very good thing.

The woman's gentle expression suddenly went deadly serious. "Let's waste no time then," Eleanor said, striding over to Silmanus and peeling off his bandages to reveal the ugly wound. "What happened to him?"

"Poison," Mara answered bitterly. "I've applied some herbs, but they didn't seem to do much. I think he's doing a little better than he was this morning, but I can't be sure."

Eleanor nodded and peeled open one of his eyelids, then checked his pulse. "His pupils are dilated, and his pulse has quickened," she commented, leaving Silmanus and moving toward one of the nicer huts. "Get him to my hut. Quickly."

Mara and Linos followed Eleanor, quickening their pace to keep up.

The healer's hut was around a medium size compared to the other huts, built of sticks and mud. It was fairly dark and lined with shelves containing an assortment of herbs and medicines. An elevated bed lay in the centre of the hut, surrounded by incense and candles. A young Hynari boy, only twelve years old, with dark skin and hair stood by one of the shelves, sorting the various herbs and remedies.

"Nazim, get me some hawthorn extract," Eleanor said to the boy, who had become her personal assistant. "Mara, Linos, put the elf on the bed."

Nazim hurried over with a vial of red liquid. Not needing further instruction from Eleanor, Nazim lifted Silmanus' head and poured some of the liquid into Silmanus' mouth, frowning as he did so.

"Eleanor, his mouth is very dry," Nazim said in a heavily accented voice.

"Do you happen to know what poison it is?" Eleanor asked Mara, although she had a guess.

Mara shook her head worriedly. "No, but it's a Dark Elf poison."

Eleanor nodded grimly. She briefly mumbled the symptoms under her breath, then came to a conclusion. "Then it is deadly nightshade." She pointed to some rope on the wall before searching through her vials. "Tie him down. Quickly."

Knowing that there was no time to waste, Mara rushed over to the rope and used it to secure Silmanus by his legs, chest, and arms.

Mere moments after Mara had tied the last knot, Silmanus began convulsing violently, rocking the bed. Mara's face became etched with concern, and even Linos looked a little worried.

"How do you know it's deadly nightshade?" Mara questioned, trying to hide her worry.

"I don't for sure," Eleanor admitted hesitantly. "I have not dealt much with Dark Elves, but I do know one of their choice poisons is a deadly nightshade extract, and these are the symptoms of nightshade poisoning. It's my best guess and all we have to go on."

Mara nodded. "You can treat this, right?" she asked, a hint of desperation in her voice.

Eleanor pulled out a little bottle filled with beans. "Thanks to your little trade establishment, I can," she answered. She placed some of the beans in a mortar and ground them up before placing them in a vial of water.

"What are those?" Mara asked.

"Calabar beans," Eleanor answered absently, and she mixed the ground beans in to milky solution. "The Hynari grow them, but I get mine from traders in Lochadia." Eleanor raised Silmanus' head to pour the bean solution into his mouth. "It contains a deadly toxin, but it counteracts deadly nightshade, and vice versa."

Just before the vial dumped its contents into Silmanus' mouth, Mara grabbed Eleanor's arm. "Wait," she said. "What if you're wrong?"

Eleanor gave Mara a somber look. "Then the Calabar beans will kill him," she answered honestly. "But deadly nightshade is my only guess. Even if the beans weren't toxic, he'd still die from the poison anyway because I don't know what else to try administering. It's a risk, but one we have to take." Laying a reassuring hand on Mara's shoulders, Eleanor added gently, "Don't worry though. I am almost certain that I'm right."

Mara nodded and bit her lip, releasing her grip on Eleanor's arm and stepping away. Eleanor emptied the vial into Silmanus' mouth. Slowly, Silmanus' convulsions slowed, but didn't quite stop. Eleanor's face was grim. "All we can do now is wait," she told Mara. "I'm going to prepare more doses."

Mara nodded. "Will he pull through?" Mara questioned uncertainly. "He saved my life. I owe him his."

Eleanor gave a warm and comforting smile. "I'm sure he'll be fine," she reassured. "Elves tend to have greater resilience to toxins than we do. Something to do with their magical attunement. Dark Elves usually concentrate their poisons too, so if he's lasted this long, I'm sure he'll survive with the antidote being administered."

"Thank you," Mara said gratefully. Then in a much more serious tone, she added, "Strange things are about to happen, I fear. And I think this elf may be the key to solving it all."

Before Eleanor could respond, Linos tugged urgently on Mara's sleeve, motioning to the doorway with his head. Mara flashed Eleanor a quick smile and followed her friend out.

They walked a few paces before Linos stopped and whirled on Mara, a pointed expression on his face. He didn't need to say anything; Mara got the message easily enough. *You're not seriously planning on keeping him around, are you?*

"He's an elf," Mara hissed.

"Exactly!" Linos fired back immediately, not letting Mara finish. "We are *not* keeping an elf!"

"I was attacked by Dark Elves, Linos," Mara said, a little exasperated at needing to have this conversation again. "What do you know about Dark Elves? Hm?" When Linos didn't respond, Mara continued, "Precisely! You know nothing more than I do!" She pointed at the healer's hut. "He does!"

Linos sighed, frustrated. "Do we really have to keep him around though? Why not just torture it out of him then send him on his way?"

"We don't torture people, Linos," Mara replied flatly. Linos opened his mouth to retort, but Mara held up her hand. "And he's a wizard. We could use him." The woman sighed. "Look. I don't like it either. You know as well as anyone that I despise elves, High Elves especially. But he's not just any High Elf. He could be very useful to us, so I'm willing to put aside my misgivings for the sake of practicality. I hope you can too."

Linos was silent for a few seconds, trying to think of a counterargument, but there really was none. Mara was right. Linos had seen the devastating spells wizards could produce and knew that if there was a conflict with Dark Elves, they would be fools to pass up such a powerful asset.

"Fine," Linos relented, a hint of indignance in his voice. "But he's your responsibility. I don't want to be anywhere near him unless we're killing something."

Mara shook her head. "You're stubborn as a mule, you know that, Linos?"

"You'd know a thing or two about that," Linos countered, grinning. His face suddenly lit up. "Oh! I just remembered! The trading party came back last night, and you're going to be pleased with what they got!"

Mara grinned slyly. "Am I going to be pleased with *how* they got it?"

"Oh, come on, have a little faith. We're outlaws, but we can still trade like civilized people without our almighty leader breathing down our necks," Linos answered. After a moment's pause, he added, "Well, Ivar might have knocked a couple skulls together for some extra stuff, but nothing too serious."

Mara rolled her eyes. Ivar was a big, burly warrior from the northmost country Helvark. When he knocked skulls together, it most certainly was serious.

"Let's just go see what your so-called trading party brought home," Mara said.

As they turned to walk away, Mara noticed suddenly that Blizzard was standing behind her, looking at Mara with an expression the human couldn't quite read. "Um," Linos began, "What's up with the horse?"

Mara shrugged. "I haven't a clue," she said. "He's an elf horse. He's not normal."

They took a couple steps forward and Blizzard followed, stopping as soon as Mara did. Linos looked at the horse quizzically. "Is he just going to follow us then?"

"I guess so," Mara replied. "No sense trying to take him to a stable. Elven horses are like their masters: they only do what they want to, damned be the opinions of anyone else." Linos chuckled at her jab at the elves.

Linos led her through the huts and tents toward the camp's centre, Blizzard walking curiously in tow. They had set up something of a town square, with little pavilions and stalls supplying food, clothing, and tools to whomever needed them. Several large huts were used for storage, and a large stone building served as the cookhouse. To the side of the cookhouse was a very long building with sturdy wooden walls and a shingled roof. That was the dining hall and the only really sophisticated structure in the camp. A large firepit was situated in the middle of the square, although it wasn't currently lit.

Every now and then, Mara glanced back at Blizzard, growing more and more worried each time. She barely knew the horse, but she had gotten the impression that he was proud and stubborn, rather like an elf. Yet Blizzard was walking with his head hung low, dark eyes flicking back and forth. He stayed very close to Mara, so close that his nose brushed her shoulder almost every other step.

Mara felt a pang of sympathy for the horse. Of course. Blizzard's master, his *friend*, was dying, and while horses didn't possess the intelligence of people, in Mara's experience, they could still feel emotion. She knew how frightened Blizzard must be. Mara took a moment to stroke Blizzard's nose while they walked, hoping to help reassure the noble creature.

Linos guided Mara toward one of the storehouses, a long, ramshackle building built out of uneven wooden planks. A group of people were moving crates into it.

"Hey! Reynard!" Linos called to one of the people.

Reynard, a tall, blond man with a kind face, turned his head and smiled. "Linos! Good to see you," Reynard called back. Noticing Mara, he smiled wider. "Mara! Been a long time, hasn't it?"

Mara nodded in response. "Indeed. I heard the trading went well." Reynard was in charge of organizing trade sessions. The camp had struck a deal with a group of merchants from the south, and both parties prospered from the agreement.

Reynard grinned. "It did. Ivar had to do a little…persuading here and there, but I think it was a fair transaction."

"Show Mara what we traded those bear hides for," Linos said eagerly.

Reynard nodded. "You're going to love this, Mara," he replied, motioning for Mara to come. Reynard grabbed a crate from inside the storehouse and took off the lid, turning to look at Mara just before he did. Or, more accurately, the large, white figure pressing into Mara's shoulder. "Also, what's with the horse?"

Mara sighed. "Long story."

Reynard shrugged and accepted, reaching into the opened crate. "Coffee, straight from North Hynar," Reynard told Mara as he pulled out a birch bark container. He lifted the lid and sniffed deeply. "Mm, that's the stuff. We got lots of coffee…and something better."

Mara looked at him incredulously. "What could possibly be

better than coffee?" she asked, only half joking.

Reynard pulled out a glass bottle full of amber liquid. "Whisky!" Mara's eyebrows shot up in surprise. "Whisky?!" she repeated. "You got whisky for just a few bear hides?"

"Yup. And maybe a couple concussions, but that's a minor detail," Reynard answered with an amused expression.

Mara grinned as she took the bottle. "I should really be mad at you for risking our trade agreement, but I think I can overlook it this time." Mara pulled off the stopper and breathed deeply, letting the breath back out in a contented sigh. "Can't wait to throw some of this in my coffee tomorrow. Mm!"

"Told you you'd like it," Linos said, walking up behind Mara. "They scored some nice bottles of Esnian wine as well, and the hunting party brought back a few boars."

"It would seem I came back just in time for a feast, didn't I?" Mara observed.

Linos grinned and clapped Mara on the shoulder. "Welcome home."

CHAPTER 10:
THE STRANGER

CLOUDLESS NIGHT HAD FALLEN ON MARA'S CAMP, BRING-
ing with it the kind of darkness that made the air thick and
choking. It was the sort of blackness that preyed on one's fears, the
kind that could make even a fearless veteran tremble in his boots at
the slightest of sounds.

While outside may have been gloomy and mysterious, inside
the Great Hall was a different matter entirely. So many torches and
chandeliers had been lit that Mara honestly feared the wooden
building would burn right to the ground. The tables were packed
with all of the camp's residents, save for the chefs who were busy in
the nearby kitchen preparing mouth-watering dishes for the feast.
Delicious smells wafted from the kitchens to the tables, heighten-
ing the already joyous mood. The musicians of the group were
busy striking up a merry tune to which many danced and sang.

Mara stood off to one corner, smiling absently as she watched.
Her mind kept drifting to Silmanus, hoping that the elf would live.
If he ended up dying for her…

Mara didn't want to think about that. Silmanus was going to be
fine. Eleanor was a very capable healer. Still, Mara worried. Elf or
not, Silmanus had saved her, and she didn't want him to die.

Blizzard was worried too, she knew. Eventually, necessity had
demanded that Blizzard be stabled. It had taken hours of coaxing

and half a dozen apples to get the horse into the stables, and even then, Blizzard refused to settle or lie down.

She was abruptly distracted from her thoughts as an elbow bumped against her arm. Mara jumped, scowling as she noticed Linos standing next to her with a big grin on his face.

"Don't startle me like that," Mara grumbled at him before turning her head back to the festivities.

"Aw, come on," Linos complained. "It reminds us that you're human."

Mara raised an eyebrow but didn't look at Linos. "Oh? And why should you need reminding?"

Linos bumped her arm again. "Because! You're the great and mighty Mara Staghorn, Slayer of Monsters, Queen of Outlaws! It's a bit surreal to some people."

Mara shrugged. "Some people are just idiots," she replied, looking pointedly at Linos with a teasing expression.

Linos just looked over both his shoulders then shrugged, prompting Mara to laugh. "Case in point," she said.

Linos smiled, warmly this time. "It's good to have you back," he told her in a shockingly serious voice. "You were gone a while. Some people were a little worried."

Mara gave him a sly look. "'Some people'?" she repeated.

"Some of the newer people may have been concerned," Linos said, rambling and trying to hide how flustered he was. "After all, they aren't yet aware of your martial prowess and survival skills and may have thought you dead, whereas anyone who knows you would realize you were just fine."

Mara grinned and elbowed him. "Admit it, you big softie, you were worried about me."

Linos gave a mock glower. "Yeah, whatever. Don't let it get to your head."

Before they could say anything else, a dinner bell started ringing and a parade of steaming food was brought into the hall and placed along the tables. To her embarrassment, Mara's mouth began watering profusely at the sight and smell of the delicious platters. Mara and Linos took their seats at an elevated table at the back of the hall, and Linos rubbed his hands together eagerly.

Plates full of pheasants seasoned with sage, onion, cider, and, to Mara's delight, bacon were the first to arrive. They were shortly followed by five roast geese, one for each of the tables, seasoned with saffron, clove, cinnamon, and plenty of other herbs and spices. Venison, prepared in a variety of different dishes to ensure that no cuts went to waste, soon found its place on the table as well. Pots of steaming rabbit stew and loaves of fresh bread came next, and, just when Mara thought it couldn't get any better, in came the bottles of Lochadian whisky.

The whole meal filled Mara with nostalgia. It was composed of game native to Eiraland, but Lochadia and Eiraland shared many animal species and the feast looked very similar to those she had enjoyed back home.

Such a reminiscence of her past may have upset Mara some days, but not this one. She had been two weeks without any good food or company, and she was simply too happy to be sad.

Linos didn't give her time for such foolish melancholy either; immediately after all the food had been set down, he rose from his seat and banged on the table to gather attention.

Mara rolled her eyes. He was about as cultured as a drunken dwarf.

"People of…well…wherever the bloody hell it is we are," Linos began, prompting some chuckles from the crowd. "We gather here to celebrate an extraordinary individual who has brought us all together and defended us from unjust persecution." Linos then took a bow, appeared to remember something, then added with a grin, "Oh, and Mara as well.

"In all seriousness, however, we are here this evening to rejoice at the return of Mara Staghorn, the most fearless woman I've ever known. It is thanks to her that we are all here today, and now that she is back from her travels, our community is complete once more." Linos' sober expression broke into a humorous grin after that, and he continued. "More importantly however, we get to feast!" Much clapping and cheering followed the speech, and Linos gave a few exaggerated bows before finishing his address. "Well, I've done too much talking and not enough drinking, so if you'll excuse me, I'll hand it over to Mara to start this feast!"

The cheering intensified as Mara stood, smiling happily. She waited for the applause to die down, then began. "Good evening, everyone. It's great to be home." She paused for a few seconds, searching for words, but she found none and just shrugged. "I suppose that's all there is to be said. Honestly, all I want to do is eat and I'm sure you do too, so let's all just shut up and dig in!"

There was no applause this time. Instead, Mara's very brief statement was promptly followed by the clatter of dishes and a collective moan of delight as everyone stuffed themselves with delicious meats and breads.

Mara, for her part, was gorging herself on some heavenly venison tenderloin. She had grown up on a lot of deer meat. Her family believed that consuming different parts of a deer gave one physical enhancements, and while Mara thought all that was complete bogus, she'd developed a passionate taste for wild deer. Coupled with the excellent whisky, it brought Mara back to her childhood, but the atmosphere was simply too happy for any sort of wistful lamenting.

Instead, Mara grew increasingly happier with every bite. At some point, she must have been grinning like an idiot because Linos looked over at her and teased, "You know, if you smile any wider, you'll split your entire face."

"If you tease me anymore, I'll split *your* entire face," Mara retorted. The comeback didn't have much weight behind it though; Mara was too contented for anything of that sort. "I'm home, I'm eating good food, I'm amongst my friends...there's just a euphoric feeling in the air tonight."

Linos nodded. "Nice word, 'euphoric'," he commented. Then, with his typical lack of subtlety, asked, "When are you going to tell them about the elf?"

Mara lowered the leg of pheasant she was about to eat with a sigh. "And you just killed it."

"I'm serious! What are we going to do about that?" Linos pressed.

Mara turned to him and waved the leg menacingly. "Right now, you are going to shut up and I am going to eat. That's what we're going to do about it." Then, without breaking eye contact, she took an exaggerated bit of her pheasant.

"But—," Linos protested.

Mara held up a finger and chewed vigorously, giving Linos a meaningful look.

Linos sighed. "I just think we should tell them so that no one wakes up to the sight of a random elf in our camp."

Mara swallowed angrily and glared, barely resisting the urge to punch him. "Seriously! Stop with the pestering and let me enjoy my feast!"

Linos grumbled a consent and went back to his meal. Mara nodded her approval and continued eating.

About twenty minutes later, Mara leaned back in her chair, a hand on her very full stomach. She let out a contended sigh, smiling slowly with half closed eyes.

"Well, now that you're done, what are we telling them?" Linos badgered immediately after.

Mara punched him.

Dim sunlight filtered through the thatched roof of Mara's mud hut, wakening the young woman from her sleep. She rose from her simple bed, which was placed along the side of the circular hut. Mara contemplated relighting the firepit in the hut's centre, but ultimately decided it wasn't of much use right now. Instead, she threw on some warm clothes and went to the kitchens for some coffee, bottle of whisky in hand.

As per usual, Mara was one of the first ones up. Dawn was just breaking over the tops of the trees, and a cool breeze blew through the crisp spring air. It was chilly that morning, but it didn't bother Mara; she was used to the cool Eiran weather.

Unlike every other building in the camp, the kitchen was made primarily of stone, with the wooden roof and rafters making up the exception. Several chimneys protruded from the top of the large building, although only one was blowing smoke, likely from the little woodstove.

"Add some water for me please, Bredon," Mara called as she pushed open the wooden door and reached for a mug. Bredon was an older man and one of the best cooks Mara knew. He was also something of an early bird and often had coffee going in the morning for everyone.

As Mara turned toward the woodstove, she was quite surprised to see that it was not Bredon making coffee but Silmanus. He was wearing his thin green and silver robes as well as some light boots, but he didn't have his staff or his swords.

Silmanus glanced over his shoulder and smiled at Mara. "Good morning, Mara. I already added water for you. Figured someone else would be along soon wanting a cup." Silmanus looked back at the coffee pot, which was beginning to boil, and threw in the grinds. Still paying attention to the coffee, Silmanus asked, "Oh, and do you happen to have a spare coat or something? I'm afraid these robs aren't very warm and I can't seem to find my spellbook. Do you happen to know where that might be?"

Mara was so flustered by Silmanus' sudden healthiness, as well as his unexpected presence in the kitchen, that she actually began to answer. "I've got all your stuff in my hut," she said absently, then suddenly caught up with herself and shook her head wildly. "Wait, hang on a minute. What the hell are you doing here?"

Silmanus turned to face Mara with an incredulous expression, then pointed to the pot. "I'm making coffee."

"You were shot! By a poisoned arrow! Why the hell are you out of bed? Why are you even awake?! You were seizing and unconscious last I saw you!"

Silmanus gingerly rubbed the wound on his waist. "Yeah, that rather hurts. Poison's gone though. Been gone since last night, I think. The stars here are so beautiful. It's quite chilly though, so I didn't stay out long. Pity, that was…" Silmanus trailed off, shrugged, and poured the coffee into a couple mugs he'd already set out. "Coffee?" he asked, offering Mara one of the mugs.

"No, we are not here to drink coffee, we need to talk!" she hissed. Looking at the steaming mug of coffee, deliciously taunting her with its tantalizing smells and rich colour, she reconsidered a moment. Mara loved her coffee. "Well, I suppose we can multitask…"

Silmanus took a long sip of his coffee. "Needs sugar. Or honey. Do you guys have any?"

Mara crinkled her nose. "Yeah, although I can't fathom why you'd want some. Should be up there." She pointed to one of the many cupboards lining the ceiling, adding a splash of whisky to her own.

Mara had a sip of her drink as well, but suddenly scowled. "No! Stop distracting me like this! You can't be here."

Silmanus scooped a spoonful of sugar into his coffee and raised an eyebrow. "Why not?" he challenged. When Mara was hesitant to answer, he answered for her. "Because I'm an elf?"

"Precisely!" Mara agreed vehemently. "Not everyone here likes elves. A lot of them don't."

"A lot of *us* don't, I think is what you meant to say," Silmanus interrupted. "I don't recall you being an elf-lover yourself."

Mara glared. "Fine. A lot of *us* don't like elves. And we have our reasons. Because of that, I'd rather introduce you than have you randomly discovered by someone looking to use the kitchens!"

As if on some mystical cue, a tall human with greying blonde hair, Bredon, walked through the open door. Noticing Silmanus, he cried out, "Mara, what the 'ell is a bloody elf doing in me kitchen?!"

Mara gave a frustrated sigh. "You see what I mean?" she scolded out of the corner of her mouth. Speaking louder and to Bredon, she explained, "He's the injured elf I brought in from my journeys."

"Well, what's 'e doing in me kitchen?!" Bredon repeated. "'E should be in the 'ealer's, not me kitchen!"

Before Mara could answer, a voice called from outside the kitchen. "What's all that ruckus there, Bredon?"

"There's an elf in me bloody kitchen!" Bredon yelled back.

"An elf?" the voice replied.

"Yea, an elf! An elf in me kitchen!"

"Well, what the bloody 'ell is an elf doing in yer kitchen?"

Bredon turned on Mara. "That's just what I'd like to be findin' out!"

"I'm making coffee," Silmanus interjected, holding up his mug. "I could make some more, if you'd—"

"Shuddup, elf!" Bredon bellowed. "I didn't ask you!"

"Bredon, calm down. Go use that booming voice of yours to rouse the camp. We'll have a meeting at the firepit," Mara instructed. When Bredon opened his mouth to protest, Mara yelled, "Now, Bredon!"

The cook threw his hands into the air, spun on his heel, and walked out, hollering, "Meeting at the fire!" as he went.

Mara shot an angry glare at Silmanus. "See what you've done?" she seethed before storming after Bredon.

Silmanus just stood there, shaking his head. "All this over a mug of coffee," he muttered. "Humans are so dramatic."

Soon after, the entire camp, excluding a hunting party and the wall sentries, were gathered before a very large firepit. Mara stood on top of a box across from them, with Linos and Silmanus to her right and left respectively. Silmanus was also now carrying his staff, and a large tome was tucked beneath his arm.

"I told you so," Linos whispered out of the corner of his mouth. Mara glared balefully down at him.

"Friends, I've gathered you here today to discuss something very important," Mara announced. "As some of you may know, there is an elf in our company today, and has been since yesterday." Mara motioned down to Silmanus, who waved awkwardly.

Mara paused, waiting for the grumbling and protesting. There was none, surprisingly, so she continued. "Now, I can understand your reservations about this. The elves didn't welcome us to their forest, so why should we welcome one to ours? The answer is plain and simple: this elf saved my life, and while we may have saved his in turn, he's entitled to our hospitality."

This time, there were protests.

"They never showed us any hospitality!" cried one man.

"Won't even trade with us!" shouted another.

"Me and me child were turned from their border at bow-point!" a mother yelled indignantly. "They pointed a weapon at me baby girl!"

The general dissent continued, snowballing into a discord of complaints. Mara didn't blame them. She was just as reluctant to accept an elf into their community as the rest of them, but she couldn't let them know that. Frustrating as it was, they needed Silmanus and that meant convincing everyone that he could be trusted. Mara raised her hands and hollered at the top of her lungs.

"*SILENCE!*"

Everyone immediately shut up.

"Look, I get it. You all have something against elves. I'm sure they had their reasons for what they did, but that isn't important right now. What *is* important is that I make something *very* clear." Again, Mara pointed at Silmanus before proceeding. "This elf is to be treated as one of us. I don't expect any of you to share a home with him, I'll sort something out, but he gets proper meals, proper seating, and the same general respect as everyone else. If I catch anyone," Mara paused here to look meaningfully at a glowering Linos. "*Anyone* treating this elf otherwise, you will have me to answer to. Clear?"

The crowd gave a grumbled, "Yes," but one man, the one who had spoken up first, yelled out a question.

"Why are we doing this?"

Mara looked the speaker hard in the eyes. She recognized him. He was a young Eiran named Edward. His family had been murdered by a small group of goblins a few years ago while elves sat in the trees and watched. He had every right to be angry, but this time, there was no anger in his eyes, just honest curiosity and perhaps some skepticism. *Good,* Mara thought. *That's a start.*

"On my journey home, I intercepted this elf searching for frostpetal. Shortly after, we were attacked by Dark Elves," Mara explained. Some of the more intuitive people began nodding their heads in understanding, but many others were confused, so Mara elaborated. "Dark Elves, in case you don't know, are among the deadliest enemies the good races have ever faced. If they attacked me, it means they want me dead. They failed once, so they'll likely try again. Having this elf here provides us with a few safeguards and benefits.

"The most hated enemies of Dark Elves are High Elves. Our friend here is one such elf, so he'll know plenty about how to defend against a potential attack.

"Secondly, elves know a lot of things humans don't, and I'm sure there are many areas of our camp that our elf could improve.

"Finally, he's not just an elf, but a wizard. I've seen him fight, and believe me when I say, anyone planning to attack here will have *tenth* thoughts about an assault with him on our battlements.

"That is why we are keeping him around. Are there any further questions?"

Mara was met by silence for a few seconds until Reynard called out, "So what's his name?"

Mara smiled. Whenever somebody new joined the camp, it was custom to approve of them by asking for a name. *This is a good sign,* Mara thought.

"Silmanus," she answered.

CHAPTER II:
Answers or Questions?

SILMANUS HAD HARDLY BEEN AWAKE IN MARA'S VILLAGE
for a day before she had him seated down in a chair, bombarding
him with questions.

Silmanus had been reluctant to go to the "meeting", as Mara
called it. It was a beautiful day, with a shining sun that melted
away the crisp cold of Eiraland's infamous spring air. It was often
a beautiful day down in Faeryln though, that was nothing particularly extraordinary. What was really holding Silmanus back were
the pine trees.

They were remarkable plants, Silmanus found. Faeryln's trees
were all leafy and deciduous, while the conifers bristled with
thousands of long needles, like a tree made of hedgehogs. Silmanus
had seen pines before, of course, but this was the first time he was
really getting to appreciate them.

Sighing, Silmanus leaned back in the chair of the meeting hut, a
circular wooden structure with a large wooden table inside, matching the shape of the building. Mara and what Silmanus assumed
were her most trusted advisors were seated around the table, with
Silmanus between a grumpy-looking Eiran and a burly, bearded
human that Silmanus assumed was from Helvark. Silmanus also
recognized Linos, who was trying (and failing) to subtly glare at
him, and Eleanor, the healer who had taken such good care of

Silmanus. Eleanor, at least, wasn't staring at him as if he had just murdered everyone's families.

"Welcome, Silmanus," Mara greeted formally. "I'm sorry to press you so soon after your recovery, but we have a lot of questions and need a lot of answers. First off, I'd like to know more about how your magic works. I've encountered Druids before, but they're mostly just herbalists desperate for attention. What can you do and how does it work? What are its strengths and its weaknesses?"

Silmanus arced an eyebrow. "If you think Druids are no more than flashy physicians, you are sorely mistaken," he informed Mara. "That's not an important matter, however, because I am not a Druid.

"As you are not an Arcanist—that is, someone who uses magic—you are probably under the impression that living things have souls or spirits. You're not wrong, but that 'soul' is actually magic. It burns within each of us, but only certain people can bring it into the material world. Once they do, magic's only limitations are those of its wielder. Virtually anything can be accomplished with magic, if you know the right spells."

"So, using magic slowly kills you?"

Silmanus shook his head. "Magic can regenerate. It will eventually burn out, that's how people die, but any magic used by casting a spell will return with time and rest."

"Explain spells and staffs to me, then," Mara pressed. "During our fight, you used magic without either. Why use them if they aren't necessary?"

"Simply put, because summoning magic from within you is very difficult," Silmanus explained. "You essentially have to bridge a gap between two different worlds, the real one and the magical one. It's possible to do on your own, but having a staff helps bridge that gap and using a spell helps direct the magic properly. Spells and staffs are often necessary for more powerful magics."

"And what spells do *you* know?" Mara questioned.

"I *know* surprisingly few, but I have a vast number in my spell-book that I can read or memorize when I need them. Spells are extremely complicated though, and I've only completely memorized a few dozen."

"Which would be?"

Silmanus gave a casual shrug. "Some destructive spells, a couple telekinetic and telepathic spells, a healing spell, a good number of defensive spells, some casual spells to help out with every day chores. I have some devastating spells in my book though." Grinning to show he was kidding, Silmanus elaborated, "I could drop a meteorite on this place if you made me angry enough."

Mara nodded slowly, a slightly suspicious glint in her keen blue eyes. "Enough about magic. Tell us about the Dark Elves. What do they want? How will they get it? How desperate are they? How—"

Silmanus cut her off there, laughing slightly. "Slow down and let me answer.

"It's important to understand the distinction between Dark Elves and the other elves. A very, very long time ago, before the Fell War, there was just one race of elves. In time, the elves became divided, with differing views and cultures. They split into three groups that became the races of elves we know today: the High Elves, the Forest Elves, and the Sea Elves.

"However, unbeknownst to the world, a fourth group of elves had been formed, those who had met the Dark God. High Elves call him Uzteus, some humans call him Zakor, some Fitis, whatever, all the same guy. He planted the seeds of evil in their hearts, seeds that blossomed at the dawn of the Fell War. The corrupted elves turned on their kin, and you know what happened next. Uzteus unleashed his Dark Army of orcs and dragons and demons and what have you. But Uzteus lost the war and the corrupted elves were banished to Vanaria, where they became known as the Dark Elves. Hatred and anger festered in their souls long after Uzteus was imprisoned and it is all the Dark Elves know.

"Because of this, above all else, Dark Elves desire death and domination. They want to rule the elves and they want to kill anything that stands in their path. What the Dark Elves want with *you* specifically, I have no idea. They seem to want you dead. I was hoping you would tell me what for." After a few moments of silence, Silmanus raised an eyebrow expectantly.

Mara gave an uncomfortable cough. "I have a vague idea, but I'd rather not speculate," she answered, although something in her tone told Silmanus that she knew exactly what was going on. "To what extent will they go to achieve it?"

Silmanus shrugged. "If it's important, then any. When Dark Elves really want something, they don't stop until they get it. That's one of the reasons we have to be so vigilant all the time, you know. The Dark Elves are constantly finding weaknesses in the mountain border and coastal patrols and ferrying monsters through them."

"How about their tactics?" Mara pressed. Silmanus noticed a suddenly piqued interest in several faces around the table, including the Helvan to his right.

"Stealth and merciless precision," Silmanus answered immediately. "They strike at night, creeping into fortresses and houses and slaughtering anyone they find. They favour long daggers as their weapons, both for their concealability and their freedom of movement, in addition to a simple cultural preference. Some of their elite generals use other weapons, however. They coat their blades and arrows in a variety of lethal poisons to keep physicians guessing." Silmanus looked at Eleanor. "I am very impressed that you were able to correctly identify the poison they used on me. You are a fine physician."

The wizard turned back to Mara and continued. "Most importantly, Dark Elves use fear and magic. There is not a race alive that is not afraid of Dark Elves, not even dwarves or High Elves, although they all deny it. A Dark Elf will take advantage of this. They use the innate magical connection all elves share to manipulate an opponent's emotions, intensifying fear in a way that many struggle to resist. Dark Elf wizards unleash deadly blasts of void magic, which literally suck away the magic of another person, shrivelling and killing the target. Believe me when I say if you do not fear Dark Elves, you are a fool, for there is much to be afraid of."

Silmanus noticed a few faces blanch. He wasn't surprised; the prospect of a poisoned blade pressed to your throat from a figure that seemed to materialize from nowhere was a terrifying one, and Dark Elves were very much like that.

They asked Silmanus a few more little questions about a Dark Elf's skill (Unparalleled), their clothing (Black), and a few other relatively minor details.

After what seemed an awful lot like several years, the bombardment was done. Mara gave Silmanus a polite and grateful nod. "Thank you very much for your input. If the Dark Elves attack again—"

"*When* the Dark Elves attack again," Silmanus corrected her, earning him a brief glare of annoyance.

"*When* the Dark Elves attack again," Mara amended irritably before continuing, "this information should be of great use and knowing your limitations will also be very helpful for strategizing."

Or arranging my murder, Silmanus thought cynically.

"Seeing as you'll be staying with us for a while, I'd like to offer you a tour before showing you to your hut," Mara offered. Silmanus noticed that she spoke forcibly, looking more at her advisors than at Silmanus. The elf held in a sigh. Would these humans ever learn to trust him?

"I'd love that," Silmanus responded warmly, hoping to ease the tension a bit. "I've never had the chance to properly observe a human village."

Mara gave a quick nod and stood up. "Right, well, that's that settled. We all have things to get done, let's waste no time not doing them. Norman, Anne, I want the stores replenished. We used a lot of our meat in that feast last night and we're going to need some more." A couple slender Eirans, looking like they could be siblings, rose and left. "Ivar, run through some training drills with our warriors and double the night watch." The burly Helvan beside Silmanus responded with a grunt and lumbered out, stooping to get out the doorway. "Reynard, Linos, I need those supplies dealt with and our next trade arranged. We're going to need steel and medical supplies, so put those as priority."

"Even above whisky?" Linos asked with a grin.

"Even above coffee," Mara replied, and Linos' eyebrows rose in mock horror.

"Bredon, get the cooking staff preserving as much food as possible. Bryant, I need the forges working nonstop making and repairing weapons. Eleanor, come up with a list of herbs you need and get Norman to look for them. We'll need lots of bandages too, so get Nazim working on that."

"Already done," Eleanor said, pulling a little piece of parchment from her pocket.

"Always nice to know I can count on you, Eleanor," Mara complimented. "Everyone else, get the labourers strengthening our walls." The last of Mara's advisors rose and left with a chorus of murmurs and grunts.

That left just Silmanus and Mara. "Well, what are we waiting for?" Mara asked. "Let's get you acquainted with my fine establishment."

While it was certainly no elven city, Silmanus had to admit Mara wasn't wrong in calling her village fine. Some of the buildings were crude and hastily constructed, and even the Hall had a ruggedness about it, but there was a certain beauty in all the imperfection.

"For the most part, the village is just housing," Mara began as they walked amongst the scattered buildings. "We don't really have shops or banks or anything of that sort. Food and clothing are distributed as necessary, which reminds me, we'll stop in at Cara's to get you something warm." Noting Silmanus' questioning look, Mara explained, "Cara is our tailor. She's very good at what she does."

Silmanus smiled amusedly. "Cara and Mara," he repeated, noting the rhyme.

"No relation," Mara replied.

"So, you have artisans then?" Silmanus asked, bring the conversation back to the village.

Mara nodded. "In a sense. We don't sell anything, of course, but we've got blacksmiths, tailors, carpenters, and the like. It allows us to remain independent and under the radar."

"Are you all criminals?"

"I suppose so, yes. We are all technically outlaws. A lot of us weren't before living here though. Most of the families here were the victims of some injustice or another, leaving them broke and with no one else to turn to."

"You aren't an officially registered village?"

Mara gave a grin that seemed both grim and sly. "Nope. Eiraland is a very corrupt nation. The nobles demand far too much from their people, and no one here has the wealth to pay the king's ludicrous taxes. Not to mention the constant infighting between lords and the fact that slavery is legal, although hushed. Besides, if I tried to register us, they'd probably shoot me on the spot for all the poaching I've done. We don't need their taxes or their protection, and I'd rather not get involved with their nefarious affairs."

Silmanus looked at her quizzically. "Protection from what?"

Mara gave Silmanus an incredulous look. "Seriously?"

Silmanus threw out his hands in surrender. "What?"

"From brigands and monsters, of course. Do you not have any of that in your perfect elf haven?"

Silmanus glowered at Mara. "No. We've spent three thousand

years of blood and tears making sure of that," he answered coolly.

"Well, the rest of the world isn't so lucky," Mara snapped. "We get to deal with bandits and orcs and goblins and all the other nasties that come pillaging. The odd troll or ogre now and then too, and beithirs too."

Silmanus cocked an eyebrow. "Beithirs?" Silmanus was well versed in monster lore. Beithirs, gigantic snakes that spat lighting and could swallow a horse whole, were native to Lochadia, which was south of Faeryln and Eiraland.

"No, not beithirs, sorry," Mara corrected hastily. "I meant basilisks." Silmanus buried a skeptical look, questioning once again Mara's origins. "We have to train people how to fight around here, and there are a good number of people in my village that can swing a sword better than the halfwit Eiran guards."

They approached a large pit in the ground. It was pretty shallow but quite wide and filled with wood ashes. A large ring of stones surrounded it and there was a significant amount of empty space between the stones and the nearest buildings.

"This is our firepit," Mara explained. "We've located it as close to the village centre as possible. It doesn't really have a practical use, but we often hold celebrations here. Keeps morale high. And it's nice to have a 'town square' of sorts."

"And these buildings around it?" Silmanus asked, gesturing to the ring of wooden buildings, all built in varying shapes and sizes.

"We put all of the artisans' workshops here so they're easy to find. There's Cara's tailor house." Mara pointed to a small hut with light wooden walls and a thatched roof.

Moving through the open doorway, Silmanus peered around at the hut's interior. A desk covered with cloths and furs sat off to one side and a small loom was placed across from it. Boxes full of clothing were piled near the entrance.

A young woman leaned over the desk, carefully tracing the outline of a jacket on a thick deer hide. She had long red hair that outlined a soft and delicate face. Her frame was very thin and slight and Silmanus might have thought her fragile were it not for the fierce look in her fiery brown eyes and the long dirk strapped to her side. A small shield with a large iron spike protruding from it hung on the wall, telling Silmanus that this woman was not a girl but a very capable warrior.

"Good afternoon, Cara," Mara greeted, and Cara looked up from her work. "I hope I'm not disrupting anything."

"Yoo're nae disturbin' a thin'," Cara greeted in a very thick and rough Lochadian accent that caught Silmanus fully off guard. "I've only jist started. What dae ye need?"

Mara hid an amused look at Silmanus' apparent surprise. "Just some warm clothes for Silmanus here," Mara requested. "He didn't exactly come prepared."

Cara gave a short bark of laughter. "Aye, Eh'd think nae. Yoo're hardly wearin' anythin' mair than a lady's naicht goon!" Cara remarked. Shaking her head as she rummaged through her bins, she murmured, "Yoo'd think an elf woods hae th' gumpshin tae bring somethin' warm…"

This time, Silmanus couldn't contain a chuckle. "'Gumpshin'?" he repeated.

"Aye, gumpshin. Ye know. General and all-roond knowledge ay whit tae an' nae tae be daein'. Common sense, as ye micht be callin' it," Cara answered, hardly looking up from her bins.

"Do all the Lochadians here speak like this?" Silmanus whispered to Mara, hoping Cara wouldn't hear.

Cara heard. "Nae, jist the northern ones like meself. Th' soothern pansies bag mair or less like an Eiran," she answered, finally pulling out a modest brown jacket. "Haur, this'll dae ye jist braw. It'll keep ye fairly warm an' I've treated the fabric wi' oils, sae it's quite waterproof." Next, she produced a simple white tunic. "Put this under ye jacket."

Struggling to contain his laughter at Cara's odd slang and

accent, Silmanus managed, "Do you have something for my legs?"

Cara snorted. "Yer legs?" she scoffed. "Whaur I'm from, real men wear naethin' but their kilts in weaither colder than thes! Nae e'en any skivvies, jist a plain sark an' a kilt!"

"Shirt," Mara translated, noticing the confused look on Silmanus' face at the mention of a 'sark.'

"Ah, well, I'm an elf, not a man, and I'd be quite grateful if you had a pair of warm trousers," Silmanus said.

"Soot yerself," Cara shrugged, digging through the boxes again until she found a pair of black wool pants. "Weel, they'll be a bit scratchy but they'll keep ye warm."

Silmanus gave a nod and smile. "Thank you very much."

"Nae a problem, laddie, any time."

"See you around, Cara," Mara said as they departed. Turning to Silmanus, she said, "I'll take you to your hut so you can change."

Silmanus followed her to a small dome made of wooden frame wrapped in hides. "Normally, we put five or so people in one of these, but seeing as you won't be staying long, you can have this one to yourself," Mara told him.

"And because I'm an elf," Silmanus pointed out knowingly.

Mara looked like she was going to deny it, but just made an agreeing gesture and said, "Yeah, there's that too."

Silmanus stooped into the shelter, which was empty save for his pack, and wasted no time shedding his robes and putting on the warm clothes. He felt a bit silly—they weren't anything like elven clothes—but he was already feeling much warmer, even if the pants itched something awful. He quickly threw his leggings on underneath, resolving that problem.

Mara gave him an approving nod as Silmanus exited his hut and Silmanus spotted the faintest hint of an amused grin creeping across Mara's mouth.

"What?" he asked, confused.

"You look ridiculous," Mara answered bluntly. "But whatever.

Come on, there's more to show you."

After being shown the crude storehouse where all the food was kept, Mara led Silmanus out of the gates and into the wide clearing between the walls and the tree line. They probably cut down the trees here for their buildings and walls, Silmanus realized, as well as to make way for the crop fields he noticed lining the side and rear palisades.

"I've been here before," Silmanus mentioned as Mara led him into the pines. "I went for a lovely walk before my interrogation."

Mara rolled her eyes. "It wasn't an interrogation, and I'm taking you to the river." Silmanus noticed then a faint trail meandering through the scattered trees making its way to the sound of rushing water.

A few minutes of walking brought them beside a fast-flowing river with shallow, sandy banks. Sunlight glinted off the crystalline water, so clearly that Silmanus could easily see the rocks and sand below the water's surface.

"You see this river?" Mara said firmly, turning sharply toward Silmanus. "Under no circumstances may you pollute this river." It took Silmanus a few moments to realize what Mara meant.

"And where might I find the latrines?" Silmanus inquired.

"Back entrance of the village. Just follow the trail," Mara answered. She pointed to a large wooden post with a prominent "1" carved into it about fifteen paces downriver. A few crude wooden stalls had been erected a little way back from the river and down from the post. "That marks the start of cleaning area. Any water upriver of that post is strictly for drinking and cooking, so don't let me catch you washing your clothes in it. There are a few bathing stalls if you want some privacy while washing yourself." She pointed to another post thirty paces from the first. "There is the start of the dishes area. I know it's a bit of a hike, but it's important to be sanitary when you don't have access to a professional physician. We often do dishes in the kitchen though, so you won't have to worry much about it."

"Anything else I should be aware of?"

Mara eyed Silmanus suspiciously, trying to discern if he was being sarcastic or not. Apparently deciding he wasn't, she answered, "No stealing from each other, take good care of your stuff, help out as you're directed, and don't piss me off. I might kill you." Mara managed to say that with such a straight face that Silmanus actually took a subconscious step backward.

"You wouldn't," Silmanus challenged, although he had to hide the slight quiver in his voice as he did so.

Mara responded by drawing her one of her knives and pressing its razor-sharp blade to Silmanus' throat. "Not for pissing me off, perhaps. But we aren't friends, Silmanus, and the moment I perceive you as more of a threat than an ally…" Mara trailed off, increasing the pressure on Silmanus' throat to drive the point home.

Silmanus' eyes narrowed. "Then let *me* make something perfectly clear," he hissed, deciding he was done playing games. He waggled his fingers behind his back. His swords flew out of their scabbards and hovered magically at the back of Mara's neck, blades crossed and aligned along her spinal cord. "I am not your enemy, nor am I your prisoner. The moment *I* decide you and your quest are no longer worth the time and risk, I will be gone, and if I so choose, I'll leave a village of slaughtered outlaws behind me. Now remove your knife."

Eyes burning furiously, Mara sheathed her knife, glaring balefully all the while. Silmanus' blades returned to their sheaths and he stepped back, smirking.

"Wonderful. Now that that's settled, when do we eat?"

CHAPTER 12:
İNTO THE DARKNESS

AMBER WAS AWOKEN BY THE SOUND OF IRON BEING clapped around her wrists. Startled awake, she gave a growl and lunged ferociously forward, gnashing her teeth in an attempt to injure or kill her captor.

She was instead met by a stinging slap across the face.

"Enough. I have put up with this for far too long," the familiar, icy voice said. The Dark Elf Amber had seen so much of glared down at her. "I know that you have now outlived your usefulness. I'm only keeping you alive because the king asked for it to be that way. However, I have the information we need, so I think he'll understand if you were accidentally killed during one of your futile escape attempts."

Amber stared into the elf's cold, pitiless eyes. There was not a hint of emotion, no sign of any lie. Dark Elves were supposedly expert liars, but for all Amber knew, this Dark Elf really would kill her if she continued to struggle.

She decided he was bluffing and spat on his polished black boots.

"T' hell with ye, Dark Elf," she seethed, every syllable laced with venomous contempt.

That was a mistake, which Amber quickly realized as the elf leaned down and brought a hand to Amber's face, one of his wrist blades sliding out with a dramatic, sinister *click*.

The Dark Elf put the blade to Amber's skin and began cutting easily and slowly down her right cheek. Amber tried not to wince, but it couldn't be helped.

"Don't test me, *dwarf*," the elf threatened balefully. He pulled his face away, tearing the knife sharply down and stopping at the bottom of Amber's jawline. She winced again, hot blood spilling down her cheek like red tears.

"What's yer name, elf?" Amber called after him, expertly hiding the waver in her voice.

The elf smirked but didn't turn around. "And why would I tell you that?"

"So I can damn ye t' hell when me hammer spits yer skull."

The elf's smirk broadened. "Mordasine," he answered. "Learn to fear that name, dwarf." Mordasine strode to the entrance in a few graceful steps and just before leaving the tent, before Amber could ask anything further, he added with a knowing sneer, "Your parents did."

It took Amber a few moments to recover from the shock. This elf, this insidious reptile, had known her parents. He had likely tortured them, broken them, killed them. He had participated in the slaughter of her people, the expulsion of her clan.

Mordasine.

Amber would indeed remember that name.

"Wake up," a harsh voice said.

Jeddo groaned and forced open his one good eye. The other was far too bruised.

All he could really see was a pair of legs standing in front of him. About a dozen knives were sheathed along the figure's slender thighs, and Jeddo gulped.

"We're done with the torture, right?" Jeddo asked weakly, his voice rough and husky from all of yesterday's screaming.

"For now," the Dark Elf answered in a very familiar voice. It was Mordasine. "Get up. We have somewhere to be, and it is not in this miserable excuse for a kingdom."

Working up the nerve to look at his captor, Jeddo quipped, "I didn't realize we were in Vanaria yet."

Mordasine smiled. "The two of you really like being beaten, don't you? Perhaps next time I'll cut out your tongue."

Jeddo pressed his lips together and nodded meekly.

Mordasine's sadistic smile broadened. "Wonderful. Now, get on your feet. There's some bread and meat beside you. Maybe, if you keep your mouth shut, I'll let you have a bit of water too."

Jeddo didn't respond. He just grabbed the food with his shaky hands and forced it down his parched throat.

"Here," Mordasine said, throwing a small water skin beside Jeddo. As the gnome greedily gulped down the refreshing, if a bit leathery, water, Mordasine warned, "Don't be too hasty. You won't get any more than what's in there."

Jeddo snapped his mouth shut and lowered the water, glaring up at Mordasine. His mouth opened again, likely for some quippy remark, but he was interrupted by a Dark Elf flipping open the tent flap.

"We're all ready to head out. Shall we drag the prisoners along again?" the elf asked, grinning evilly.

"No, I want them looking presentable for the king," Mordasine answered, deliberately speaking in Dark Elvish so Jeddo wouldn't understand. Mordasine flashed Jeddo another fiendish smile, prompting a miserable sigh from the exhausted gnome, before dragging the prisoner out.

Jeddo stumbled along the coarse ground behind the Dark Elf, his tired legs struggling to keep up with Mordasine's brisk pace. Jeddo didn't even have the energy to curse as he tripped and fell on his face, nor did he feel like acknowledging Mordasine's derogatory snicker as the little gnome nearly faceplanted again trying to stand up.

Mordasine grabbed Jeddo roughly by the back of his shirt and tossed him carelessly onto the back of a wagon. Another Dark Elf, a woman, to Jeddo's surprise, came forward with a pair of manacles and slapped them across Jeddo's scraped wrists, drawing a grimace from the battered gnome and a grin from the elf. She latched the manacle chain to the bottom of the cart, allowing Jeddo little to no movement of his arms.

"Yer not lookin' so good there, Jeddo," came a gruff voice from beside Jeddo. Although his entire body protested the act, Jeddo turned to see Amber beside him, also chained and looking quite miserable. A nasty gash had been carved down the side of her face. Jeddo had completely forgotten about Amber, so great had his pain been.

"Don't feel so great either," Jeddo replied. "Bit too much ale the other night." It was a poor attempt at a joke and a poor time to be doing it, but both prisoners took a small comfort in knowing that at least Jeddo's sense of humour remained undamaged.

"So, what do ye suppose this Vanaria place looks like?" Amber asked a few moments later, hoping to distract Jeddo from his obvious pain.

Jeddo gave a stiff shrug and opened his mouth to answer but Mordasine walked over suddenly carrying two black canvas sacks.

"It doesn't really matter, because you won't be seeing it," the Dark Elf said, handing the bags to his subordinates. "We can't have you learning anything that might help you escape, not that you ever could break free of our prisons." Mordasine flashed a wicked grin. "Besides, it's far more dramatic this way."

Right on cue, the other two elves gagged Jeddo and Amber shoved the sacks over their heads. "We'll stop every once and a while to consider giving you refreshments," came Mordasine's voice, muffled through the thick canvas.

All was silent and still for a few minutes and Jeddo began to wonder if the elves were just going to abandon them. Suddenly, with a sickening lurch that jolted all of Jeddo's aching bones and muscles, the wagon started forward, bouncing along the uneven ground. Jeddo was sure the driver was deliberately hitting every crack and pothole possible, each violent bump sending a new wave of agony racing through Jeddo's beaten body.

Jeddo had absolutely no idea how long they had been travelling for. His mind was too tired to even contemplate keeping track of time and the canvas sacks were too thick for sunlight to get through. The only time Jeddo caught a glimpse of the outside world was when the elves fed him a few bites of stale bread and gave him a small sip of warm, bitter water that Jeddo honestly suspected was urine. But those quick glances of light told Jeddo nothing. For all he knew, it had been just a single day, although Jeddo doubted that.

Whatever amount of time they spent jouncing along the craggily Pyradian terrain, Jeddo was miserable throughout. He managed a few hours of restless sleep leaning on Amber's burly shoulder, but he was starving, thirsty, exhausted, and still in unimaginable amounts of pain.

At some point, the jostling ceased and the road beneath them grew smoother. Jeddo sent a silent thanks to whatever god had ended the torturous bumping of Pyradia's rocky landscape. It occurred to him, however, that a smoother road likely meant they were now in Vanaria, in the land of the Dark Elves, the most sinister land in all of Aeternerras.

Those thanks quickly turned to curses.

The journey continued on and on, time still tangled in an indecipherable mess. Eventually, to both Jeddo's surprise and fear, he felt cold, slender hands shake him from a deep sleep. He hadn't even realized he'd dozed off but was grateful he had.

"We have arrived. Get up," Mordasine's smooth voice

commanded in its ever-superior tone. Jeddo tried his best to stand up, moving his arms around to his side in order to try to push himself up.

Jeddo suddenly realized that while he was still cuffed, he was no longer secured to the cart. Perhaps if he was quick enough, he could reach up…

"Touch the sack and you're dead," Mordasine warned evenly, seeming to read Jeddo's mind. With a sigh, Jeddo heaved himself off the edge of the cart, but his legs gave out underneath him and he fell on his face yet again. He fell on smooth cobblestone this time, and, while it still hurt, it didn't scrape Jeddo's face and told him that he was definitely out of Pyradia. Whether or not that was a good thing remained to be seen.

Mordasine snickered. "Will that ever not be entertaining?" he mused to himself. "Unfortunately, I don't have time to spare watching you stumble around like a fawn. I have an audience with the king, and you're invited, too! Isn't that wonderful?" Mordasine's over-cheerful tone told Jeddo that this audience would be anything *but* wonderful. Jeddo suddenly found himself wishing for the rocks and heat of Pyradia if only to be free from Vanaria.

Once again, Jeddo was heaved to his feet by Mordasine's strong arm and was hauled across the ground. Jeddo grimaced as his ankle twisted over itself, but again reminded himself that he was at least not stumbling across sharp stones and sudden potholes.

Mordasine stopped suddenly and Jeddo heard him bark a command in Dark Elvish. Jeddo winced. While Elvish was a beautiful language of flowing syllables and gentle consonants that sounded like a melodious song, Dark Elvish was sharp and grating. It was still flowing and graceful, but each word seemed to cut like a knife, or rather, one of the Dark Elves' infamous poisoned daggers.

Jeddo heard a brief clang of metal, like a lock on a gate being opened, then the very faint screech of hinges as the supposed gates swung open. Then Jeddo was being dragged along again, although he had managed to regain his footing. Not that it mattered; Mordasine was still walking far too briskly for Jeddo's injured legs to keep up.

They passed through a couple more gates and doors before hitting some stairs (literally, in Jeddo's case). As they returned to flat ground, Jeddo's battered legs slid along glossy tile, suggesting that they were perhaps within a castle now.

Sure enough, after several more flights of stairs (Mordasine had apologized at the top of one, claiming that he had "accidentally" gone up an extra set of stairs. Going down was even worse than up, Jeddo found) and a few long hallways, Jeddo was thrown to the cold, hard floor and had his gag and sack removed.

Dazed, Jeddo struggled to his knees. He blinked a few times, trying to adjust to the light, although there was very little. A few sinister black chandeliers hung from the arching ceiling, creating the minimal light required for Dark Elves to see. Tall windows lining the room—which Jeddo took to be more of hall—revealed the black and ashy landscape of Vanaria. Banners of the darkest black and embroidered with silver daggers hung from the smooth brick walls, which were, unsurprisingly, also black as night. Two rows of Dark Elves, Jeddo couldn't tell how many in each, were lined up on either side of a—surprise—black and silver carpet that stretched to the bottom of a towering throne which was made of a shimmering black metal that wanted to swallow Jeddo whole. The sides of the throne were lined with meticulously crafted dove wings, which met in a peak at the top. A dove, akin to the one Mordasine had, sat upon that peak, staring thoughtfully down at Jeddo.

Jeddo was not afraid of many things. He had done battle with dragons, orcs, trolls, and sometimes all three at once. But the elf, nay, the demon, the pure manifestation of all that is evil sitting atop that throne struck terror into Jeddo's heart like he had never felt before. A crown made of the same metal and style as the throne wrapped around his head and a jewel sat in the centre of it, blacker than anything else in the room and seeming to suck Jeddo's soul from his body. Long, ebony hair fell down he elf's slender shoulders, on which rested a cloak made of black fur and lined with glistening drops of silver. Tight-fitting robes were worn beneath that, outlining the elf's muscular arms and torso. Lines of silver along the collar reflected the pale light onto the elf's face. It was long and narrow with a pointed chin and sharp, distinguished features. Silver eyes in that pale, pale face shimmered and glistened in the most sinister way imaginable. The elf was beyond handsome, but it was a deadly, superior sort of handsome that brought fear rather than admiration from Jeddo.

This was, without a doubt, the Dark Elf king, and while his powerful body and murderous visage were a whole new level of terrifying, he was nothing compared to the Dark Elf at his side.

Sitting in a throne identical to her husband's, the Queen of the Dark Elves stared at the prisoners with a set of silver orbs that seemed to less shimmer and more burn with a fire that seemed both excruciatingly hot and icily cold at the exact same time. Her beautiful face seemed to have been sculpted from porcelain and her raven-black hair framed it perfectly, like the night sky around a shining moon, yet in a far more sinister way. Her long, narrow dress clung to every alluring curve of her shapely body, but not in a seductive way. Rather, it appeared to Jeddo that every accentuation of her body just brought out the aura of death and malice that seemed to surround her. If the king was the image of dread, the queen was dread itself, casting her shadow of hatred and darkness in an almost mystical manner. She, too, had a dove, although hers was sitting on one of her narrow fingers.

A few agonizing moments of silence passed. Maybe they were hours or days or years. At that moment, every beat of Jeddo's trembling heart was a millennium apart.

"So. These are the pitiful souls that will assist in our victory?"

the king asked in an offhanded manner. Jeddo winced at the sound of his voice, which seemed to be laced with an icy poison.

"Good luck with that, ye heartless reptile!" Amber spat, a look of pure rage written on her face. "I'll be killin' meself before I help the likes o' ye, and there ain't nothin' ye can do t' make me!"

The king's mouth curled slowly, so slowly, into the most sinister sneer Jeddo had ever witnessed. "Isn't there?" he said simply, calmly, but in a voice that sent a shudder down Jeddo's spine.

Suddenly, a door near the back of the throne room was thrown open with a dramatic bang. Two Dark Elves with barbed whips hanging from the sides of their belts emerged, each dragging a stocky, limp figure. The prisoners were wearing torn and blood-stained rags that revealed a mess of scars and cuts, most oozing pus, along the backs and arms of the poor prisoners. There were sacks over their heads, so Jeddo couldn't see their faces, but he suspected his face looked clean and pristine by comparison.

The prisoners were dragged to the foot of the king's throne where they were thrown to their knees. Too weak to hold themselves up, the prisoners began slumping forward, but their captors grabbed the backs of their shirts—if the tattered rags could even be described as garments—and yanked them upright again, removing the sacks as they did so to reveal what were, despite the countless scars and bruises, undoubtedly dwarven faces.

It took Jeddo a few moments to catch on, but Amber recognized the prisoners immediately.

"Ma? Pa?"

CHAPTER 13:
An Unhappy Reunion

AMBER'S MIND WAS A BLUR OF EMOTION.

Joy, for her parents were alive.

Sadness, for they were the prisoners of Dark Elves.

Disgust, for they were in a state worse than death.

And, most prominently, outrage, for someone had hurt her parents.

"Ye give them back, ye wretched elf scum!" Amber shrieked, fighting desperately against her bonds. "Ye cannot have them! I'll tear yer throat out, ye murderous son o' an orc!"

Mordasine kicked the back of Amber's head and she flew into the tile, wincing as her nose banged against the hard floor. Amber was lucky it didn't break. "Silence," the Dark Elf hissed, allowing Amber to rise to her knees once more.

Fury burning in her eyes, Amber studied her parents. They looked so lost, so defeated. Her mother, a gentle dwarf, but possessed of fiery spirit, seemed broken, the twinkle gone from her dulled brown eyes, the weight of a mountain seeming to sit on her slumped shoulders. Her father, normally a loud and indomitable man with a merry attitude, had a look of pure submission on his face, resigned to his brutal reality.

"What have ye done t' them?" Amber breathed, hardly able to comprehend the utterly defeated state her parents were in.

A stinging slap from Mordasine snapped her head to the side. And snapped something inside of Amber's father.

"If ye lay another hand on me daughter, I'll tear off that hand and beat ye t' death with it," he growled, an angry light rising in his tired brown eyes.

The Dark Elf king raised his eyebrows in surprise. "So, you *do* still have some fight left in you," he laughed. "Here I thought we beat it out of you years ago."

Amber's father barked a laugh. "Ye hear that, darlin'? The pixie king thinks he broke me!"

Amber's mother gave an empty smile. "Ye cannot know how happy we are t' see ye, lass," she said softly to Amber. "Ye've been the only thing keepin' us goin'. Ain't nothin' can break yer folks when we got ye t' live for."

"Aw, how sweet," the king mocked. "Family reunions are such a joy, aren't they? Although it pains me dearly, we'll have to put these happy tidings on hold. You are, after all, here on a business call, not a personal one."

"I ain't doin' nothin' fer ye while ye've got me parents like this," Amber hissed.

"No, actually, you will," the king said menacingly. "They're only alive for as long as you cooperate."

"So what is it ye want from me?" Amber asked, voice taught with frustration.

"I'm so glad you asked! I need something from somewhere. Unfortunately, I don't know how to get into that somewhere and these two incompetents refuse to help me," the king answered gesturing with his foot to Amber's parents. "You, however, *do* know how to get into this place and your legs still work well enough to help me." An evil grin spread across the king's face as he finished, making Amber's stomach churn.

"Ye want arcanium from me home," Amber concluded dryly.

"You're a bit brighter than I'd thought. Yes, arcanium is indeed my desire and I finally have the means to get it."

"What do ye want with it?"

The king laughed. "You think I'd tell you? I take it back, you're as idiotic as every other dwarf."

"I'll not help ye," Amber growled defiantly.

The king shook his head, resting his head against his fingertips. "Why is this so complicated for you? It's really quite simple. We make for The Forgotten Mountains in two weeks. Either you help me enter the mines or I subject your parents to an eternity of pain and suffering until finally ending their misery before your weeping eyes." He said it so matter-of-factly that Amber was actually put back on her heels for a moment, so to speak.

Amber glared balefully back at the Dark Elf, fury broiling up inside her like one of Pyradia's volcanoes.

The king let out a heavy sigh. "Fine, be that way. Listen, I'll cut you a deal. Stay in my prisons and mull over my offer and I'll stop torturing your parents. How's that sound?"

"Like a filthy lie," Amber spat.

The king gave an evil grin. "You've got me there. Well, I tried giving you a choice. Mordasine, please take these disgusting cretins to a cell," he ordered dismissively, waving a hand at Amber and Jeddo. "Her parents too, although I'll be needing them later."

Mordasine bowed and snapped his fingers. Four Dark Elves each grabbed and blindfolded a prisoner, shoving them along the tiles with echoing footsteps. Amber fought and struggled against the cold hands of her escort, but he jabbed a dart into her neck after a few seconds of thrashing.

As the sleeping poison worked its way through her veins, Amber's vision, impaired by the sack though it was, swam and her head spun. The last thing she heard before her legs collapsed beneath her was the king sniffing the air and complaining, "I'll be ridding the stench of dwarf from this hall for a week. Disgusting vermin."

Then her mind went blank.

Groaning, Amber blinked her eyes, trying to adjust them to the darkness around her. A musty smell hung in the air, combining with the stench of sweat and rotting food to create an overwhelming odour that had the hardy dwarf gagging in moments. The smoke coming from a single dim torch didn't help either.

Fortunately, because they spent so much time in dark tunnels and mines, dwarves had developed excellent night vision, so Amber was able to take in her surroundings anyway. She was in a rather cramped cell, with uneven stone walls and a black iron door on the wall to her right. Amber noticed there was no doorknob or lock on the door and assumed the elves locked it with magic. A cubby sat next to the door, probably for giving the prisoners food.

The prisoners. Amber looked around at them, seven in total, excluding herself. Each was wearing thin rags that were tattered and covered in stains. They were shackled to the walls by long black chains cuffed to their thin, bony wrists. Amber noticed she also had a set of heavy iron manacles restraining her to the wall as well as a scratchy beige tunic draped over her shoulders.

The two prisoners to her left were elves. Their pale, gaunt cheeks sunk beneath their high cheekbones, bringing out the sharp, narrow features elves were so well known for. Both had long dark hair, although it was tangled and knotted and looked nothing like the fine hair elves typically had. Both were skeletal and their bony frames looked like they would fall apart in a gentle breeze. The light had faded from their blue eyes, and they clung to each other tiredly. Amber realized then that one was male and the other female and guessed they were a couple. They looked so tired and resigned, so accepting of their fate, like they had been stuck here a hundred years and knew there was no getting out.

Chained to the back wall across from the door were a couple of humans, also one man and one woman. They didn't look much better than the elves. Both were slumped down, almost lifeless, eyes closed as they rested against the stony wall. Their clothes seemed to be in slightly better condition, so Amber wondered if they were more recent prisoners.

Across from her were a couple of dwarves. Amber's parents, leaning into one another as their gentle snores rumbled through the cell. She winced the moment she saw them, unable to keep her gaze on the fresh display of cuts and bruises lining their ragged faces. Still, she had noticed a hint of resolve in her parents' eyes in the throne room, a sign that they did indeed have some fight left in them. A desperate, burning urge to talk to them overwhelmed Amber, but they seemed to be asleep and she didn't want to wake them.

So, heart aching, Amber instead turned to her right to see Jeddo, hunched over with his swollen head in his hands. He was staring intently at the ground, gears turning behind his hazel eyes. His face bore no expression, brow furrowed in concentration. He was thinking about something…

"What're ye thinkin'?" Amber mumbled, noticing that her mouth was dry and numb.

Jeddo raised his eyebrows and snapped his gaze to Amber's. "Oh, you're awake," he replied. He began looking around at the cell. "I've been in a lot of prisons, you know. Escaped all of them too."

"Ye sayin' ye can get us out?" Amber asked, hoping for a bit of good news.

"Nope. I'm saying I think this is the prison that's going to beat me."

"Oh," Amber said, deflated.

Jeddo let out a sigh. "Never thought I'd end up in a cell again, much less a Dark Elf one."

"Aye, I know what ye mean," Amber replied. "Didn't expect t' be runnin' into these bastards again."

"Again?" Jeddo asked, turning to her and raising an eyebrow.

Amber had never told Jeddo about her past. She might as well now.

"Aye, back when I was a wee girl, I lived out in the kingdom t' the east, right along the edge o' Longwood. Arcantia, it was called, the Halls o' Magic. Finest dwarf kingdom ye could lay eyes upon, and finer than those damned elf halls too. We were the pinnacle o' trade and minin', pullin' up mountains of gold, mithril, and other valuable ores and metals.

"But for all our gems and metals, what we really prided ourselves on was arcanium. Ne'er before had any civilization found or mined the stuff, but we did it. Mined it, refined it, shipped it off t' yer gnome pals fer their inventions or t' them crazed wizards t' experiment on. It was a risky business, arcanium explosions are things o' nightmare, but a profitable one indeed.

"The Dark Elves caught whiff o' what we were doin'. Ne'er will I understand how, but they stormed our kingdom. Found a way in, likely thanks t' some rat. They slaughtered me people tryin' to get t' the arcanium.

"They never got the arcanium though. Some dwarf with more common sense than most o' us had the idea t' blow the stores. Took down more than half the mountains with that explosion, he did. But it was worth it. Not a single drop o' arcanium was left fer those elven buggers t' steal and the blast took more than a few o' them t' hell.

"It was the end o' our kingdom though, both figuratively and literally. Our mountains were gone. All that's left is a little section o' them now called The Forgotten Mountains." Amber spoke the name bitterly, hating the disgraceful title the proud kingdom had been given. Sadness replaced the anger quickly, however, as Amber finished her tale. "Hardly a dwarf survived that massacre. I watched me parents die that day." Amber glanced across the cell at the two weary dwarves. "Or I thought I did."

Amber's voice must have stirred her mother from her sleep

because she spoke then, her voice raspy and quiet but carrying hints of a former jolly ring. "Ye did, me girl. I was dead, or as close as ye can get. I'll not ever understand why they saved me and yer father, why they kept us alive, but they did. And every day, it's broken me heart t' know that ye thought we were dead when we weren't. Probably fer the best though. Knowin' ye, ye'd have charged right in t' save us." Amber's mother gave a little laugh. "I wished every day I could come back t' ye."

Tears threatened to spill from Amber's eyes as her mother's words sunk in. "I found ye though," Amber whispered.

"Wish ye hadn't like this," her mother lamented.

The two dwarves stared into each other's eyes, remembering the days passed when they had laughed together, a mother and her daughter playing in the stone halls of their home. How long ago those memories were, how far away that life had been. Now here they sat, prisoners to the people who had stolen away those memories, reunited by those who had torn them apart. It was almost poetic, Amber realized.

A slight cough shook Amber from her memories. "Care to introduce us?" Jeddo urged.

"Jeddo, these're me parents, Guralyn and Harik Ironheart," Amber introduced, motioning first to her mother and then to her father. Guralyn had to shake Harik out of his own slumber before Amber continued. "And this is Jeddo Hilltop, an old pirate and a friend o' mine."

"I'd say it's a pleasure, but we're stuck in a Dark Elf cell at the moment," Harik said gruffly with a tired smack of his lips, trying a hand at some humour, although to little effect.

"Can ye get us out?" Guralyn asked, a note of hope rising in her tired voice. "Surely a criminal such as yerself has some experience with this sort o' thing."

Jeddo looked as though he might contradict Guralyn's statement about him being a criminal, but the gnome instead replied in a sad voice, "Not this prison. Magically sealed door, Dark Elf guards hiding in the hallways, no way to pick these blasted cuffs… I'm afraid there's nothing I can do at the moment."

Guralyn's shoulders slumped. "So that's it then? We just wait here until that maniac Zarat lets us go?"

Jeddo gave Guralyn a confused look. "Zarat?"

"Aye, that's the king o' these devils," Harik explained. "Sindra is the queen, and if ye ask me, she's an even more bloodthirsty weasel than he is."

"King Zarat and Queen Sindra," Amber mused. "Elf names are so bloody stupid."

"I'll give ye that," Harik laughed. "But ye mind what ye say about elves." He nodded his chin toward the two elven prisoners. "These two here aren't half bad. Been through hell an' back, they have, just like meself."

Amber turned to regard those two elves once again. "What're yer names?" she asked.

"Thalassar," the male elf said in a husky—yet still melodic—voice. "This is my wife, Ayra."

"Yep, still stupid names," Amber commented. "But if ye managed t' earn me father's respect, ye're deservin' o' mine. How long ye been down here?"

"A hunnerd years, just like me and yer mother," Harik answered for the elves. "They don't talk much anymore."

"An' the humans? Who're they?" Amber asked.

"Evalyn an' Percival," Harik answered. "They only been here fer a month, but the Dark Elves have been harder on 'em then on any o' the rest o' us." Lowering his voice, Harik added, "I'm not fer thinkin' they'll last much longer."

"What'd they do?"

"Dunno." Harik shrugged. "Ne'er got a word out o' them, though I'm suspectin' they were trespassin' or somethin'. Can't imagine why the Dark Elves would be treatin' them the way they do if they were wantin' them alive."

"And the elves?"

"Arcanium experts. The Dark Elves are plannin' somethin' big, mark me words, and they're needin' those two t' help."

Amber nodded. "So. What happens t' me and Jeddo?" she asked.

Harik shrugged. "Ye're likely t' be beaten, tortured, and starved until ye give in, just like the rest o' us."

Jeddo shuddered a bit, subconsciously touching the wound on his torso and wincing immediately after.

"Damned Dark Elves think they can break us?" Amber scoffed. "We're bloody dwarves, fer the love of Hutos!"

Guralyn gave Amber a sad smile. "Ye sound just like yer father did a hunnerd years ago," she said quietly. "Yer father was wrong."

Hearing those words, the tones of defeat in her mother's voice, the implication that her parents had indeed been broken, hurt Amber more than any torture the Dark Elves could throw at her. She slumped back against the wall, the hopelessness of her situation finally sinking in.

She was stuck here forever. There would be no getting out.

CHAPTER 14:
A HUMAN LIFE

THE EIRAN AIR WAS COOL ON SILMANUS' FACE, THE CRISP breeze tousling his bangs as he stood next to the village's river, marvelling at the shimmering water as it rushed by. Droplets of water were tossed into the air as the river crashed against its banks, catching rays of sunlight before they fell back into the river.

Silmanus gave a small smile. He had always loved nature, as nearly all elves did. There was a beauty to it that could not be found anywhere else in the world.

"Are you just going to stand there, or do you plan on actually doing something useful around this place?"

The gruff female voice startled Silmanus from his gazing. At first, he thought it was Mara, but upon turning around, he instead saw a woman he'd never met before. She was short and plump and had a round face that reminded Silmanus of a bullfrog.

"I-I-I," Silmanus stammered, rather startled by her sudden and hostile appearance. "I wasn't really sure what to be doing."

The woman gestured to the washing bat, wooden board, and big basket of clothes she was carrying. "Well, for starters, you could give me a hand with these," she stated. "If you know how?"

Silmanus straightened indignantly. "Of course I know how!"

The woman cast a doubtful look at Silmanus' smooth, callous-free hands, but nodded anyway. "Then get a move on. These clothes won't clean themselves."

Silmanus grinned. "Actually, I rather think they will."

Waggling his fingers, Silmanus enacted a spell similar to the one he had used to repair his tower. In moments, the clothes were floating into the river and onto the board to be beaten by the levitating washing bat, all while Silmanus waved his hands, grinning.

A sharp pain suddenly ran up the back of Silmanus' left hand, causing him to drop everything he was controlling. The woman had smacked him!

Silmanus whirled on her angrily, magic bubbling up within him. Fury rose into his eyes. How dare this human strike him?

The woman was completely unfazed, however. She met Silmanus' fiery gaze with cool stubbornness. "Around here, we wash things the proper way," the woman said.

With that, the woman kneeled down on the river bank and retrieved her board and stick from the water. She laid a shirt across the board, dunking it into the river and whacking it with her stick, repeating the process until she felt the shirt was thoroughly cleaned. She then handed it to Silmanus, who dumbly held the dripping garment in outstretched arms.

"Well?" the woman snapped. "Don't just stand there, wring it out and hang it up!" She pointed to a length of rope stretched along several trees.

It took Silmanus a few moments to swallow his indignation, but he eventually took the shirt to the edge of the river and furiously twisted it in his hands, pouring his frustration into it. Dirtied water spilled back into the river and Silmanus wrung it out a few more times before stretching it out across the line, muttering all the while.

After a time, Silmanus' anger at being slapped and ordered around faded and he settled into the relaxing monotony of his task. He had to admit, despite its lack of efficiency compared to using magic, washing laundry by hand did have a certain calmness to it. And it really was quite cathartic.

The woman didn't make any attempt at conversation with Silmanus, which the wizard was just fine with. He wasn't very good at making small talk anyway, probably because of how much time he spent squirrelled away in his tower. She did tell him her name though, which turned out to be Agnus.

Silmanus got lost in the rhythm of washing the clothes, time just floating by without any meaning. Eventually though, Agnus startled him from his thoughts.

"Well, that's all of them," she said, pointing to the empty basket.

Silmanus gave an internal sigh of relief. Relaxing though it might have been, it was also horribly boring, and the cold water was turning his fingers numb. "Great," Silmanus replied. "Well, thank you for showing me how to do things the old-fashioned way. I'll see you around, Agnus."

Silmanus turned to leave, anxious to find something else to do, but a sharp cough froze him in his tracks. "Just where do you think you're going?" Agnus demanded. "We still have four more baskets to do."

Silmanus' jaw dropped. Four more baskets?!

Agnus smirked at his expression. "Come on, bring one back with me. This time, you can do the actual washing."

Silmanus had to hold back a groan. This was *not* how he had meant to spend his day.

Silmanus continued to work around the village, loaning assistance to the villagers. The following day, he spent some time amongst the horses, helping to groom and feed them. The "official horse-master" of the village was hardly a horse-master; he was a seventeen-year-old boy with shaggy hair and a youthful face who had grown up on a farm and happened to know a bit about horses.

Silmanus showed him how to earn a horse's trust and some special grooming techniques, which made Blizzard very jealous.

The day after that, Silmanus went on a hunting excursion with Norman and Anne. He didn't have much to offer by way of advice, the Eiran siblings knew what they were doing, but he helped them bring back a small deer and a plump pheasant.

Nothing of particular significance happened until, a few days after laundry with Agnus, Silmanus was in the healer's hut, helping Eleanor with some medications. Nazim was busy making general rounds across the village and Eleanor needed to restock a number of her tonics and ointments after a recent outbreak of the flu.

"Teach me," Eleanor said suddenly.

Silmanus looked at her in confusion. "I'm sorry?"

"Teach me. Magic. Show me how you do it," the woman pressed.

Silmanus shook his head sadly. "It doesn't work like that. I can't just teach you magic."

"Then how does it work?" Eleanor's curiosity seemed genuine.

"Were you not at the conference, when Mara asked me that?"

"Yes, but you didn't explain it in full."

"Do you actually want to know?" Silmanus asked, surprised at Eleanor's interest.

"Yes," Eleanor said. "If it could help me heal people, then yes."

Silmanus let out a deep breath. "Well. Okay. As you know, people who can use magic are called Arcanists, and there are four kinds: priests, druids, warlocks, and wizards.

"Magic is…well, it's your soul, I suppose. Or at least, that's how many non-Arcanists refer to it. It's that spark of life that burns within all of us, a little well of power that keeps us alive. It is found within every person, plant, and animal, anything that lives and breathes. Arcanists learn how to summon this power to influence the world around us. Priests are given the ability by the Gods, druids by the ancient knowledge of the natural world, and warlocks are simply born with the connection.

"Wizards, on the other hand, draw on the power of mental discipline to utilize our magic. We train our minds to overcome the barrier between physical and magical, to bridge the gap between body and spirit. By doing so, we can tap into the magic that resides within us and bring it into the physical world."

Eleanor frowned. "But…does that not mean every time you cast a spell, you sacrifice a part of your soul? Your life?"

"Well…yes and no," Silmanus answered. "Magical strength is very similar to physical strength in that regard. You can be sapped of it, but as long as you take some time to rest, it will come back to you."

Eleanor looked at Silmanus with concern. "Then…you can kill yourself by using too much magic."

Silmanus nodded solemnly. "Yes. You can. But it's a very difficult thing to do. It's hard to convince yourself to go past the breaking point, just like how it's hard to deliberately hold your breath until you die. Your mind knows better and it will try to stop you."

Eleanor considered this and nodded. "So…hang on a moment. If everyone has magic in them, then why can't you teach me?"

"Because it is a very difficult thing to do. It's why wizards are almost always apprenticed from a young age. As the mind ages, the barrier between the physical world and your magic becomes harder, and it's even harder for humans to overcome that barrier as adults."

Eleanor crossed her arms. "Just what is that supposed to mean?"

"Sorry, I don't mean to say that humans are incapable," Silmanus stammered. "It's just…well, everyone has different amounts of magic. On average, the longer a person lives, the more magic they were born with. Elves are the longest-lived race because we have the most magic. Humans live the shortest, so the average human has less magic, which makes it harder for them to become Arcanists."

Eleanor frowned again. "But…wait, so, if a human is born with as much magic as an elf, does that mean the human will live as long as the elf?"

Silmanus nodded sadly. "Yes. That's why the greatest Arcanists of human history are so old. The more magic you have, the longer you will live. Such is the curse of an Arcanist."

"Curse?" Eleanor asked. "What do you mean 'curse'? How could longevity be a curse?"

Silmanus looked at Eleanor with sad eyes. "Eleanor, an elf lives for a thousand years. Even if I were not a wizard, I would outlive you more than tenfold. Any humans I befriend today will be dead before I am even a fifth of the way through my life. And that is just as an elf!" Silmanus shook his head. "Because of how much magic *I* have, I could very well live to be two thousand years old. Can you imagine that? The amount of loss I will experience in two thousand years of life?"

Eleanor fell very quiet. "I...didn't think of it like that," she whispered.

"And it only gets worse the more powerful you become. Through practice and study, an Arcanist can increase their magic, and therefore how long they live. The most powerful Arcanists of history are also the loneliest." Silmanus looked grim. "And those who crave longevity, who do not see its terrible burden? They are driven to madness and to terrible acts as their craving for power and immortality consumes them."

"That's terrible..." Eleanor whispered. "Why would anyone want to use magic, then? Why do you?"

Silmanus shrugged. "I was born with more magic than most. It is something that has always fascinated me, and my parents thought it fit that I should learn wizardry. It may come with a terrible price, but I love studying it, and using magic...it is an indescribable feeling that I am not sure I could live without."

Eleanor nodded. "Thank you."

"No need to thank me," Silmanus said with a smile. "People don't often take interest in my work."

"There is nothing about this knowledge that will help my

healing though, is there?" Eleanor realized.

Silmanus grinned. "Actually, there is," he corrected. "Like I said, magic and your soul and your life force, they're all the same thing. Ergo, if you can restore someone's magic, you can restore their life force and heal them. That's how priests and druids are able to cure poisons and purge disease."

"But what can I do to heal people without magic?"

Silmanus' grin broadened. "Because," he said, picking up a bundle of fresh herbs and shaking them, "there is magic in everything that lives. If you're willing, I can show you how to make a few tonics that will transfer the life force in herbs to a sick person."

Eleanor's face lit up as if she were a young child. "I would like that very much indeed."

The pair immediately set to work. Eleanor brought out her supply of her herbs and Silmanus began sorting through it, pointing out which herbs were beneficial for what. "Swordleaf is important for drawing magic out of plants," Silmanus explained. "Feverflew helps direct it to a person's life force." Silmanus talked about a few more herb before producing one that he was quite familiar with.

"Frostpetal is the key to this tonic," Silmanus said. "It is used in almost every healing potion because of its unique magical properties."

The pair set to work squeezing out the herbs, mixing together the various juices under Silmanus' careful direction. It was painfully tedious work, precision was an absolute must, but Eleanor was a medical veteran and was very familiar with the practice of exactness.

At long last, Silmanus and Eleanor had created a vial of pale green liquid, with a single bud of frostpetal floating inside of it.

"Is it ready?" Eleanor asked.

"Not quite," Silmanus said. "There is one more thing you must do. Hold it in both your hands."

Eleanor did as she was told and Silmanus continued. "Just

because you are not an Arcanist does not mean it is entirely impossible to use your magic under the right circumstances. With enough concentration, you can allow the tonic to act like a sponge and soak up a little bit of your magic, just enough to activate it."

"How do I do that?" Eleanor inquired, her green eyes twinkling.

"Close your eyes and think about only your breathing, nothing else. You have to completely clear your head of any distractions and just think about breathing in, breathing out, breathing in, breathing out…"

Eleanor shut her eyes and her head bowed a little, her features softening completely. Silmanus saw her breathing begin to steady, gradually growing slower and deeper as Eleanor meditated. A silent hum filled the air, a noise that Silmanus heard not with his ears, but with his soul. The tonic glowed briefly and then settled to its original colour.

Silmanus was about to tell Eleanor she could open her eyes but the physician didn't need him to, already widening her green orbs and staring at the potion in her hands.

"Did it…" she began, her voice tensely quiet.

Silmanus smiled warmly. "It worked."

Eleanor beamed. "I used magic."

Silmanus was about to correct her (technically, she didn't *use* the magic, she just allowed it to flow out of her) but instead, he placed a hand on her shoulder. "Indeed you did."

The wizard suddenly grew very serious and looked Eleanor in the eyes with a grave expression. "You must be very careful with this, however. Do not ever attempt to open yourself like that under any other circumstances. You are not in control of how much magic leaves you and opening up your life force to anything else could kill you. Promise me you will never experiment with this."

Eleanor nodded. "I promise."

Her face was earnest, and her eyes were honest, but Silmanus was still a little worried; humans were foolhardily curious, and

Silmanus did not want to see Eleanor dead. She was goodhearted
and kind, and she had saved Silmanus' life.

"It'll take about a week for the potion to finish…fermenting,
for lack of a better word, but once it does, it should be able to
greatly aid in curing a person from disease or poison," Silmanus
said. "It will do nothing for physical wounds however; that requires
the precision of a practised Arcanist."

Eleanor nodded gratefully. "Thank you for teaching me this. I
am sure it will help me save a great many lives."

"My pleasure," Silmanus said. "It's the least I can do after you
saved mine."

At that moment, the flap of the healer's hut was pushed aside
and a young Hynari boy stepped through. He didn't look any older
than eleven or twelve, with soft features and chocolatey eyes the
same colour as his skin. He seemed vaguely familiar to Silmanus.

"Ah, Silmanus, this is Nazim," Eleanor introduced, and Nazim
gave a shy smile. "I don't believe you two have formally met yet,
but he is my apprentice. He helped me heal you."

Silmanus gave the boy a grateful smile in return. "Then I have
much to thank you for, Nazim." Nazim's expression went from shy
to slightly embarrassed.

"He's quite the prodigy," Eleanor commented. "We are very
lucky to have him." Addressing Nazim more directly, she asked,
"Was there something you needed?"

"Yes. Margaret has a cough. I came to get her some medicine,"
Nazim answered.

Eleanor frowned. "I hope that's not her pneumonia returning,"
she muttered. "Well, you know what to do. Ask her parents to keep
a close eye on her and let me know if it gets worse."

Nazim nodded and began rummaging through Eleanor's collection of vials, selecting a pair of them and slipping them into his
pocket. As he did, the sleeve of his jacket rolled up slightly and for a
moment, Silmanus could see an ugly scar wrapped around his wrist.

Eleanor caught his gaze and shook her head at him slightly, telling him not to ask. Nazim waved goodbye to Silmanus and Eleanor and left the hut.

"He used to be a slave," Eleanor said quietly once Nazim had left. "Mara, Linos, and a few others stumbled across a small slave escort a couple years ago. Needless to say, they ambushed the soldiers and freed Nazim and five others. They were offered a place in our village, which only one, a gnome, declined. There are a few others here with the same scars."

Silmanus felt like he was going to throw up. He had heard rumours that some Eiran nobles still used slaves, but he had hoped it wasn't true. He opened his mouth to say something but couldn't find any words.

Eleanor placed a hand on Silmanus' arm. "Best not to talk to any of them about it though. This place is all about forging a new path and leaving old hardships behind. It won't do any good to stir buried memories."

Silmanus nodded. He understood that very well.

"Well, I had better get to work," Eleanor announced. "If Margaret does have pneumonia again, I want to be ready for it." She gave Silmanus a smile that warmed the elf's heart. "Thank you again for teaching me and for helping me with my medications."

"Any time," Silmanus replied, returning the smile. He rose to his feet and stooped out of the healer's hut, a mixture of emotions swirling in his heart.

As he walked to his own hut, Silmanus thought about something Eleanor had said. "This place is all about forging a new path and leaving old hardships behind."

Everyone here had been cheated by life, had lost something to the chaos of the world. They had built themselves new lives out of the ashes, an island of calm amidst the swirling storm of reality.

Silmanus knew he could never stay here, could never live amongst the fleeting lives of humans, but for a moment, for one, longing moment, a flicker of hope rose up within him. Hope that he could build himself the future he needed, tormented no longer by the losses he had experienced.

Or the ones he knew were yet to come.

Chapter 15:
A Walk in the Woods

THWACK!

The arrow thudded into the target, roughly 50 paces away. The wooden shaft quivered from the impact, about a pinkie's width from the bullseye. The noise startled a pair of black birds, who flapped quietly away into the trees.

Silmanus frowned, swinging the simple recurve he had borrowed over his shoulder as he inspected the shooting. Most of the arrows were barely within a hand's breadth of each other and not a single bullseye. Silmanus was slipping.

He pried the arrows out of the straw target, sliding them into a fine leather quiver hanging from his belt. Silmanus didn't know who worked all the leather around Mara's village but they had some talent.

Silmanus had been with the village for about a week now. One long, uneventful week of trying to help the villagers. Other than doing laundry, tending to horses, hunting, and preparing medicines, Silmanus had also spent time working with the village's farmers to improve their agricultural techniques and helping the smiths heat and work their steel. He had even shown a few elvish recipes to the cook, Bredon, although the grumpy Lochadian had been quite reluctant to learn.

Come to think of it, the whole village had been rather

begrudging about working with Silmanus. He didn't quite understand why. He was just trying to show them a better, more efficient
way to perform their tasks, to save them time and energy. He
figured it probably had to do with him being an elf.

Typical humans.

Mara was no exception either. Despite having told the entire
village to treat Silmanus with respect, Mara had been avoiding him
since their fight at the river bank and over the last couple days,
Silmanus had often found himself with nothing to do but practice
his spells.

At least Blizzard was enjoying himself. He was fed apples and
oats until his heart's content, and, knowing Blizzard, that took a
great many apples and oats indeed. The horse was living a life relatively close to luxury, surrounded by good food and other horses,
as well as a number of curious children who would come stroke
his muzzle. And feed him apples.

Silmanus wasn't entirely without recreation, however. Yesterday,
he had discovered a supply of bows and arrows in the storehouse
and, after a bit of negotiation with Reynard, had been gifted a
recurve, quiver, and two dozen arrows, which he frequently practised with. Not the quality of equipment Silmanus was used to—
elves held very high standards for their weapons—but the bow
worked well enough, offering what Silmanus judged to be about
fifty pounds of draw weight.

He knocked another arrow, sighting down its shaft as he drew
back with three fingers, being careful not to grip the bow and
instead letting the tension from the draw hold it against his open
hand. As soon as he felt his thumb touch the back of his jaw,
Silmanus slid his fingers off the string, clasping his hand around the
bow immediately after—but not before—the arrow was in flight.

Silmanus smiled as it smacked into the target. A bullseye at last.

"Took you long enough," a cool voice quipped from
behind him.

Silmanus whirled around in alarm, nocking an arrow as he did so and lifting the bow in the direction of the voice.

He relaxed his aim with a glare as Mara stepped out of the trees, an amused look on her face.

"How long have you been standing there?" Silmanus asked, a bit annoyed that Mara had been spying on him.

"How long have you been shooting?" Mara replied, her smirk widening. "I thought you elves were supposed to be supernaturally perceptive or something."

"And I thought you humans weren't supposed to be insufferable narcissists. Guess we're both wrong," Silmanus shot back.

"Ouch," Mara responded dryly. "I'm so hurt."

Silmanus just shook his head and turned back to the target, briefly imagining it to be Mara's smug face. Bullseye again, just a hair from his first arrow.

"Damn," Mara whistled. "Not only do you have some skill with a blade but you're actually a pretty good shot too. What kind of wizard *are* you?"

"An elven one," Silmanus answered, firing another arrow, though not quite striking the bullseye that time.

"Do they just teach everyone that stuff in elven society? Even the peasants?"

Silmanus arced an eyebrow but didn't look at Mara. "There's no such thing as a 'peasant' in elven society, but yes, we are all trained in swordplay and archery. I've been shooting since I could walk, and I first learned to swing a sword when I was just six."

"And how long ago was that?"

Silmanus gave a little chuckle. "Longer than any human could remember." *Thwack!*

"Exactly how old are you?" Mara inquired, seeming genuinely curious.

"One hundred and twenty-six," Silmanus answered, loosing another arrow with commendable accuracy.

Mara whistled. "You wear it well; I'll give you that."

"Of course I do. I'm an elf. I've looked like this for a hundred years and I'll look like this for hundreds more. We live for a millennium, you know." *And me for even longer,* Silmanus added mentally.

"That must suck."

"How do you figure?" Silmanus knew exactly why it "sucked," but it seemed like the appropriate response.

"Well, all of the other races live for a much shorter time. Dwarves get five hundred years, gnomes two hundred and fifty and us humans just seventy-five. Any non-elven friends you have are going to shrivel up and die long before you."

Silmanus was surprised at Mara's insightfulness, but he didn't let on to it. "Hence why I don't have any."

Mara gave a little snort. "Do you even have any elf friends?"

Silmanus considered the question for a moment, then fired another arrow and answered, "No."

"Figures," Mara agreed. "Wizards don't get out much, do they?"

"I had a girlfriend once," Silmanus told her, still focused on the target.

Mara's eyebrows shot up in surprise. "Really? What happened?"

Thwack! "She wasn't into wizards."

"Can't say I blame her," Mara muttered. Silmanus winced visibly, a movement Mara did not miss. "Sorry. I haven't known many wizards, but the ones I have known were…eccentric, to say the least."

"Or insufferable elves that you look to save one moment and kill the next," Silmanus spat bitterly, the apology doing nothing to take away the sting of her words.

Mara rolled her eyes and gave her head a shake. "Look, I'm sorry about the river. You must understand though, I have dedicated years to building this place. When someone wielding as much destructive power as you walks in, I'm naturally going to be defensive."

"Then why bother saving me? Why bother keeping me around?" Silmanus asked, not letting it go.

"Because *you* saved *me* and because we may end up needing you."

"But you don't trust me."

"Can you blame me for that?"

"You don't like me either."

Mara threw her hands up into the air. "I give up. I was going to invite you on a walk to see if I could make up for our earlier disagreement, but clearly, you don't want that."

"No, wait," Silmanus protested tiredly. "A walk would be lovely."

Mara stopped and turned back to him. "Then what are you waiting for?"

Silmanus jogged a few steps to bring himself beside Mara. They walked in silence for a while, Mara guiding them through the clustered trunks of Needlewood. A few clouds hung in the sky, but the sun's rays found their way to the forest floor, shining through the reaching branches to cast dancing shadows across the needle-ridden ground.

"Sort of," Mara said after a short silence.

Silmanus frowned, not understanding. "Sorry?"

"You asked me if I had a horse," Mara answered, recalling her first encounter with Silmanus. "The answer is sort of. I don't have a horse, but I befriended a Pegasus several years ago. She lets me call on her when I need her."

Silmanus' jaw dropped. "You have a *Pegasus*?!" he exclaimed in equal parts awe and disbelief.

Pegasi, essentially winged horses, were cousins of the unicorn and highly revered in High Elf culture. They were also incredibly rare and mysterious. Silmanus had never even encountered one, much less befriended one.

"Well. Not *have*," Mara amended. "You can't own a Pegasus. They are free and noble creatures, bound to nobody but themselves. I saved Blackthorn from some Eiran hunters though, so when I need her help, she returns the favour."

Silmanus was still trying to wrap his head around how incredible that was. "Will I ever get to meet her?"

Mara shrugged. "She's not very social. Pegasi are very aloof, you know. But there's potential."

Silmanus felt a little giddy at the prospect. He very much wanted to meet a Pegasus.

The conversation soon faded into another awkward pause, neither party quite knowing what to bring up or what to talk about.

"Who were you before you became this Queen of Outlaws?" Silmanus asked suddenly.

He caught the briefest flicker of pain in Mara's icy blue eyes, which seemed so strangely vulnerable in that moment. But it was a moment and no more, and her eyes were once again as hard as her voice.

"Nobody of importance," she answered cryptically, her cold, bitter tone making it clear that she was not elaborating any further.

"I'm not stupid, Mara," Silmanus pressed anyway, ignoring the obvious warnings in her voice and expression.

"Then figure it out yourself," Mara snapped.

Silmanus stopped. "You lived in Lochadia for most of your life. You belonged to a noble family, explaining how you came across your magnificent weapons. But in the aftermath of some tragedy, perhaps involving those Dark Elves that want you dead, you fled and started a new life here, hidden amongst the pines and surrounded by souls as lost as your own."

Mara froze in her tracks, her entire body rigid, and Silmanus knew he had hit the mark.

"Don't be absurd," Mara replied, although Silmanus was sure she was lying.

"I'm not."

"Then you're just wrong," Mara retorted, continuing to march along with heavy, angry footfalls that signalled beyond a doubt that the conversation was over.

Silmanus chose yet again to ignore those signals. "Are you always this guarded?"

"Yes," was Mara's flat reply.

"Even around Linos?"

"Yes."

"What's the deal with you and him anyway? Are the two of you friends or a couple?" Silmanus inquired, figuring he might as well investigate another part of Mara's private life.

"Yes."

Silmanus' eyes narrowed in suspicion. "Are you just answering with the word 'yes' to everything I say now?"

"Yes."

Silmanus threw his hands up in the air. "I give up," he exclaimed, exasperated. Voice thick with sarcasm, he jabbed, "Thank you for the lovely walk. You were such pleasant company."

"My pleasure," Mara responded indifferently.

Silmanus whirled around, shaking his head. He didn't pay any mind to where he was walking; he just walked, furious thoughts racing through his head.

Of all the stubborn humans in this world, why do I have to be stuck with this one? he thought. *To think I'd find myself preferring the company of a headstrong dwarf over that impossible woman!*

It was quite a while before Silmanus looked up from his thoughts and noticed he was hopelessly lost. The trees suddenly seemed completely identical, the ground perfectly undisturbed. Silmanus wasn't even sure if he'd been moving in the same direction the entire time, so utterly lost in thought had he been.

Worse still, he didn't have his staff, his bow, or his swords with him. He might as well have been naked and blind, dumped in a strange forest full of…well, Silmanus had no idea what dwelt in a forest such as this, but he suddenly recalled Mara having mentioned something about a basilisk.

The sun was still high in the sky, it couldn't have been much past noon, but Silmanus felt as though it were the dead of night. Everything seemed so dark and evil and, without his staff, Silmanus felt weak and helpless against the hateful forces that were closing in on him.

A twig snapped behind him. Silmanus jumped and spun around, eyes wild. He didn't have his staff, but he did still have magic, and he began muttering the beginnings of a shielding spell as he peered into the trees. The warm, tingling feeling of magic began spreading to his fingertips, which were starting to glow silver.

Although he had no idea what it was, some instinct told Silmanus to turn around in that instant. He did, and there was Mara, bow pointed right at his face, cold blue eyes glaring balefully at Silmanus.

Déjà vu, Silmanus realized with an internal grin, remembering his first encounter with Mara.

Only this time, Mara drew the bow back and released, sending an arrow streaking right toward Silmanus.

CHAPTER 16:
THE TABLES TURN

BETRAYAL FLASHED IN SILMANUS' EYES AS HE WATCHED the arrow fly toward him.

He had put trust in Mara. He had given up his time and patience to help her and had been willing to fight alongside her if the need arose. Despite that, after some petty argument, there she stood, a murderous glint in her eyes as she sent an arrow to do what the Dark Elves could not.

There really wasn't anything Silmanus could do. Seeing Mara had startled him, and he'd lost concentration on his spell. He couldn't react in time to stop the arrow and he knew it. It was going to hit him and kill him and there was nothing he could do.

As the arrow whipped past his head, Silmanus readied himself, prepared himself for the pain, braced himself for the end. His eyes closed, his features softened, his mind slowed to a numbing acceptance of his inevitable fate. Perhaps he would see his parents again. Perhaps life would be better on the other side, in whatever afterlife awaited him.

Wait.

Past his head?

Silmanus' eyes snapped open and he whirled his head around, following the arrow as it zipped through the air, sinking deep into the throat of its actual target.

A Dark Elf.

Silmanus realized immediately what was happening. He ran toward Mara, ducking his head as another arrow flew over it, the shot just barely missing another Dark Elf. Planting his foot, Silmanus spun around behind Mara, facing the approaching Dark Elves with a determined expression on his face.

There were six of them, five now that one lay dead on the ground. Three were carrying sinister recurve bows, the other two wicked daggers. As the first archer reloaded with blinding speed, the other two fired, sending arrows streaking toward Mara.

Silmanus reached out with his mind, pushing himself to call upon his magic without the use of his staff. His mind burned with the fury of a dragon's breath and his heart pounded in his ears. It took a significant amount of concentration, but the wizard succeeded, his hands flying out to create a shimmering, one-way barrier between Mara and the arrows.

Meanwhile, Mara already had another arrow of her own in the air and was drawing yet another from her quiver. Her target was a bit too quick, rolling to the side and loosing an arrow at Mara as he came out of the somersault. Silmanus' barrier deflected it, however, and Mara's third arrow found its mark.

Four Dark Elves still remained, however, and three of them were closing in on Mara, daggers ready for a kill. Mara dropped her bow and drew her sword, giving it a quick twirl as she awaited her opponents.

Struggling to maintain concentration on the barrier, Silmanus tried to reach even deeper, tapping into his power to conjure a barrage of giant icicles. The icy spears shot out of his hand, zipping toward the charging elves. Two managed to dodge the spell but the third was not so lucky, taking two shards of ice to the chest and dropping to the ground, dead.

The other two elves kept coming, stabbing furiously at Silmanus' barrier until at last, the wizard's concentration snapped, and the spell shattered into oblivion, leaving nothing between Mara and her deadly opponents.

Mara was ready however, sword already moving into a parry as the Dark Elves closed in. She moved quickly, keeping her sword away from her body to force the elves back. Mara was outnumbered two to one, but her weapon was much longer, and its reach would be the only way to come out of the battle alive.

The Dark Elves danced around Mara, trying to rush forward any time that spinning sword provided an opening. But Mara was too quick, sword flying into place just before the elves could find themselves an opening.

They were at a stalemate, Mara recognized. She couldn't launch a proper counterstrike without leaving herself vulnerable to one of the two elves. So, she kept up her defensive dance, hoping she could keep the elves at bay long enough for Silmanus to assist her.

The wizard was having his own problem, however. The remaining archer was firing a continual stream of arrows at Silmanus, not giving Silmanus the time he needed to cast a spell. The High Elf was forced to dodge this way and that, ducking behind trees as he tried to evade the deadly barrage.

Silmanus did have one advantage, however. His opponent only had so many arrows and Silmanus could see the Dark Elf's quiver starting to run dry. Five arrows left.

Silmanus threw himself into a roll, barely dodging an arrow that whizzed over his head. Four arrows.

Planting his feet, Silmanus skittered backward to avoid an arrow that would have caught him coming out of the roll. Three arrows.

The Dark Elf's next two shots thudded into a tree as Silmanus jumped for cover. Just one more arrow.

Silmanus' eyes popped wide as the Dark Elf's final shot soared right through the loose fabric of his jacket, missing the wizard's side by a hair.

At last, Silmanus had a reprieve from the arrows. As the Dark Elf drew a pair of daggers, Silmanus waggled his fingers and muttered some strange words before sending a ray of shimmering magic flying at the elf. It slammed into the Dark Elf and exploded into a net of barbed vines that wound around the elf's torso and legs, sending the evil creature tumbling onto the ground, incapacitated.

Silmanus threw another ray at one of the elves attacking Mara, hoping his aim would hold true. It did and the Dark Elf writhed in pain and frustration as the thorny plants twisted around him, tearing into the elf's flesh as they brought him to the ground.

Mara sent Silmanus a silent thanks before turning her full attention to the remaining Dark Elf, sword flashing as she fought with renewed vigour. The Dark Elf quickly found himself put on his heels, unable to outmanoeuvre his deadly foe. Daggers flying this way and that, the Dark Elf tried to position himself where Mara's sword was not.

But Mara's sword was everywhere, dancing around faster than Silmanus' eyes could track. Mara had her sword in place to parry before her opponent had even moved his blades for the attack, anticipating every single strike with almost supernatural ability. Parries flowed into counterattacks, deflecting each dagger strike before lashing out to send the Dark Elf skittering away.

Silmanus hadn't even noticed the Dark Elf's mistake. Neither had the Dark Elf, it seemed, for he continued his intricate dance even after Mara's sword had cut two long gashes in his chest, the mithril blade cutting smoothly through the Dark Elf's chain armour. The elf eventually just sort of stopped fighting, never actually realizing he had been wounded until he was falling to the ground, dead before his head hit the dirt.

Mara pulled a rag from within her tunic, wiping off the crimson blood staining her blade before sliding it into its sheath. "How long will your spell last?" Mara asked, looking at the two incapacitated Dark Elves.

It took Silmanus a few moments to realize he was being spoken to. He was still entranced by the movements of Mara's sword. Shaking his head clear, Silmanus answered, "Uh, an hour or so."

Mara nodded. "Good. We should be able to get them back to the village before it wears off." She reached down and grabbed the foot of one elf, dragging him across the ground as she made her way home.

Silmanus waved his hands and uttered a spell, levitating both elves high above the ground. "We can move faster this way," Silmanus explained, pushing back the beginnings of fatigue.

Mara shrugged and continued onward, leading Silmanus through the pines. They walked in silence, Mara making it clear that she had no interest in conversing with Silmanus. The wizard was fine with that. He was still a bit irritated with Mara.

After about forty-five minutes, the edges of Mara's village became visible through the branches. Shouts of excitement came from the battlements at the sight of Mara's approach and the drawbridge was hastily lowered.

As soon as Mara was inside her village, she began barking orders. "Linos, lead Silmanus somewhere we can put the prisoners. Ivar, find your sister and follow them. I want you two guarding the prisoners twenty-four seven. If they escape, it's your ass. Eleanor, if you have anything in the ways of a truth serum, I will need all of it."

"I have spells for that," Silmanus put in, trying to be helpful.

"I don't need your spells," Mara snapped at him. Noticing that nobody was moving, Mara yelled, "Let's go, people!"

Linos shook his head in confusion. "Mara, what's going on?"

Smiling grimly, Mara pointed to the two Dark Elves, still bound and suspended and enjoyed the look of surprise on Linos' gaping face. "We finally have an edge."

Silmanus stared blankly at the crackling bonfire, its roaring flames soaring as high as three men into the night sky and sending showers of glistening sparks raining down like fireflies. He absently fingered the fresh stitches along the side of his jacket; Cara had graciously repaired it for him—after cursing him for ever having let it happen in the first place.

The elf rubbed his temples. What was he even doing here? He was surrounded by humans that hardly acknowledged his existence except to throw him a suspicious glance now and then. He could be home at his tower, studying magic in the company of the only person he needed: himself. Instead, Silmanus was fighting Dark Elves with a woman who hardly seemed to care about him.

Why? Why put up with hateful glares, uncomfortable weather, and murderous Dark Elves? Why help somebody who refused to tell Silmanus anything about herself and treated the wizard like nothing more than a tool?

It occurred then to Silmanus that there was a very simple answer: it was exciting. Although he wanted to, Silmanus could not deny how much he enjoyed the rush of adrenaline that seized him when the Dark Elves were about. Life in his tower was comfortable and enjoyable, each day full of fascinating discoveries and stimulating analyses. But it lacked excitement and Silmanus was realizing how much he truly enjoyed this action-filled life he was now living.

There was, perhaps, something more to it than just that, but if there was, Silmanus had no interest in soul-searching for it.

Silmanus frowned, mind wandering back to before the attack. He had been practising archery, nothing more. There had been two birds though, two black birds. He'd thought nothing of them at the time, but now…

They had been doves. Silmanus was sure of it. But since when were doves black?

He'd seen them before, he realized. The morning when the

Dark Elves had attacked him and Mara, when he'd been shot by a poisoned arrow. There had been one perched in the trees. Silmanus wanted to dismiss it as coincidence, didn't want to believe that the Dark Elves had such birds at their disposal, but the knot in his stomach told him otherwise.

Approaching footsteps shook Silmanus from his thoughts. It was Linos, walking over with two leather-wrapped flasks in his hands.

"Here," the human said flatly, sitting down on the log beside Silmanus and handing him one of the flasks. "Whisky."

Silmanus shook his head. "I don't drink liquor."

"And I don't talk to elves. First time for everything," Linos replied. "Drink it, don't breathe it."

Wrinkling his nose at the acrid smell wafting from the flask as he opened it, Silmanus raised the flask to his lips and took a tentative sip.

Silmanus gave a wild cough as the liquid slid down his throat. It prickled and burned, especially in his throat, and had a bitter taste that disguised a bit of a sweetness, but not like coffee did. No, this was far different, and Silmanus found it positively disgusting. He liked wine, but the alcohol concentration in the whisky was far too high for Silmanus and he found the taste repulsive.

Silmanus raised his flask again for another long sip.

Linos grinned a bit as he took a swig from his own flask. "Good stuff, huh?"

"It's dreadful," Silmanus replied, his voice a bit husky, before taking another sip.

"Love this stuff," Linos said, taking another drink himself.

After a brief silence, Silmanus asked, "So, I take it you're from Esnia?"

"Born and raised."

"Why'd you leave?"

Linos sighed, his next sip of whisky lasting longer than all the others. "I stole some money to buy medicine for my sick mother."

Silmanus hesitated a moment before speaking. "Where is she now?"

"Dead," Linos said without a hint of emotion. "Didn't survive the road here."

"Medicine wasn't enough?"

"Nope. And your damned elf kin didn't do a thing for her," Linos spat bitterly, drinking more of his whisky.

Silmanus felt a twang of guilt. "I'm sorry."

"Yeah, well, wasn't your fault, I guess."

Another brief silence. "Why are you talking to me?" Silmanus asked. "You hate me, or at least, you don't like me very much. Why talk to me? Did Mara make you?"

Linos snorted. "Not even Mara could make me talk to an elf if I didn't want to. No, I figured that if we're going to go fight a bunch of Dark Elves together, I might as well ensure you'll watch my back instead of sink a knife into it."

"Wouldn't be a knife," Silmanus replied honestly. "And wouldn't be your back."

"How comforting," Linos said dryly. "What's *your* deal, then? Where are you from?"

"Faeryln. I've got a home and a life there." Silmanus pushed away the doubt that suddenly crept into his mind as he said that.

"Then why are you here?"

Silmanus thought carefully before answering. "Turns out I like killing shit." Something panged in Silmanus' heart, that little feeling one gets when they tell a lie, but Silmanus ignored it.

Linos gave a bark of laughter and clacked his flask against Silmanus'. "I'll drink to that."

The two continued their dry conversation, trading vague stories of their pasts, snorting over dark and sarcastic comments, and engaging in several rather heated debates about magic. Despite the disagreements, Silmanus found himself liking Linos more than he'd expected. The human was brash and stubborn, not to mention his obvious distaste for elves, but Silmanus respected the man's considerable intelligence and enjoyed his sardonic sense of humour.

Linos, for his part, was rethinking his opinion of the wizard. He'd expected Silmanus to be like typical elves, arrogant, haughty, and overly sophisticated, but this one was different. Silmanus was far more…human than Linos had expected, and he certainly didn't seem to give a damn about refinement. Silmanus was brilliant and logical and definitely not afraid to hold his ground on an opinion, and Linos both respected and liked that. Silmanus did have a bit of an ego on him, but Linos could get past that. And it wasn't like Linos was Mr. Humble either.

A little while later, Silmanus wasn't sure exactly how long, Silmanus gave a long yawn. "Well, I, for one, am getting quite tired. It's been an interesting discussion, Linos. I look forward to fighting alongside you." The elf rose then, handing Linos back his flask, now empty of even the tiniest drop.

"Yeah, you too, elf," Linos replied, staring at the dancing flames of the fire.

Silmanus walked off, noticing a very slight dullness to his mind, which surprised him. Elves had a supernatural resistance to both toxins and intoxicants and very seldom suffered any effect from drinking alcohol. *That whisky must really be something*, Silmanus thought as he ducked into his hut.

With a sigh, Silmanus lay down on his bedroll and pulled his warm blanket close around him. The calming blackness of sleep soon fell over his mind, carrying him off to the land of dreams.

CHAPTER 17:
HOPELESS

AMBER HARDLY SLEPT THAT NIGHT. THE ROUGH STONE OF the walls dug into her back and if she tried to lie down, her arms were forced into an equally uncomfortable position.

Recognizing that sleep was nothing more than a hopeful fantasy, Amber mulled over what had happened, trying to figure out exactly what Zarat's goal was.

He wanted arcanium, that much she knew. But what he wanted it for, that was unclear. There were a great many things one could use arcanium for. Amber's people had used it to create tools and weapons far more powerful and complex than anything anyone else had ever created, even the gnomes. Perhaps that was what the Dark Elves were after? Some sort of super weapon?

It was feasible and there were an almost unlimited number of possibilities. A super-powered catapult, ballistae with explosive bolts, bombs…Amber had even heard rumours that crystalized arcanium could act as a powerful magnifying lens, turning the sun's rays into destructive beams of unimaginable power.

Super-soldiers were another possibility. The dwarves had been experimenting with the possibility of using arcanium to augment the physical and mental capabilities of the black bears that served as their mounts, hoping to create an unstoppable cavalry. Maybe the Dark Elves were trying to do something similar.

One thing really confused Amber, however: where would they get the arcanium? All of Arcantia's arcanium reserves had been destroyed and no one else had the tools to mine more. How did the Dark Elves expect to acquire the necessary arcanium?

Maybe that's where Ayra and Thalassar came in. Perhaps they had discovered a way to excavate arcanium. It was unlikely but the only sensible conclusion.

Amber continued thinking her situation over for hours and hours until, after an eternity of discomfort, a loud banging rang from the cell door.

"Up and awake, you miserable worms," a smooth voice said from outside. "It's time for breakfast."

The cubby creaked open and a metal casket was shoved through, landing on the stone floor with a crash.

Guralyn sighed and reached for the casket, just barely able to drag it toward her. Opening the box, she looked in and saw eight small biscuits, each crawling with maggots, as well as a small waterskin. With another sigh, Guralyn pulled out one of the biscuits and passed the casket to Harik.

Amber's mouth dropped a little at the sight of the food. "This is what they been feeding ye?" she asked incredulously.

"Yep," Harik confirmed with a sigh, half-heartedly taking a biscuit from the box and handing it to Percival and Evalyn. "Ye get used t' it eventually though. And the maggots aren't all bad. Add a little flavour an' protein."

"I just wish I could get me a nice leg o' lamb," Guralyn grumbled, taking a tentative bite of her biscuit.

"Ye wish that e'eryday and it ne'er happens, so why don't ye just shut yer trap about it and stop torturin' me with talk o' food!" Harik snapped.

"There's no need t' be speakin' t' her like that!" Amber scolded angrily. "Ye apologize this instant or so help me, I'll find a way to shove that biscuit o' yers right up yer—"

Harik cut her off with a laugh. "Ye're yer father's daughter," he chuckled. Regret and tiredness creeping into his voice, Harik turned to Guralyn and added, "But ye're right. I shouldn't have spoken t' ye in that way, me dear. Please be acceptin' me apologies. All this has just been gettin' t' me."

Guralyn smiled sadly and patted her husband's arm. "I know ye didn't mean anythin' by it, ye stubborn ol' git. Ye ne'er do. Next time though, I'll be takin' yer daughter's advice and place that biscuit where the sun don't shine, see how ye like the maggots then."

Amber smiled, happy to see her parents being humorous with each other. She figured that was probably a good sign, a sign that they hadn't lost all hope, or if they had, they'd managed to find some again.

Thalassar passed the casket and Amber took out a biscuit for herself and handed the last one to Jeddo. The old gnome accepted his gingerly, grimacing at the sight of the maggots.

"Never thought I'd have to eat something like this again," Jeddo sighed, taking a tired bite.

"When have ye before?" Amber asked, wondering if closing her eyes would help her get past the disgusting sight of bugs in her food.

"Well, you can't have a roast boar and fresh bread every day on a pirate ship," Jeddo answered. Considering that for a moment, he added, "Or any day, for that matter."

"Remind me ne'er t' take t' the seas," Amber commented, finally working up the nerve to bite into her food.

The biscuit was dry and flavourless, tasting sort of like what Amber assumed stale parchment tasted like. The maggots had a disgusting flavour, like rotten meat. Which actually made a lot of sense, considering that's what maggots ate. They tasted horrible and wriggled around in Amber's mouth, which was one of the most nauseating sensations she had ever had the misfortune of experiencing. And considering Amber had once been sneezed on by a troll, that was saying something.

Amber choked down the biscuit anyway; she wouldn't be getting anything else. The waterskin was passed around, everyone taking only a small sip which did very little to quench their thirst, especially after eating such a dry biscuit.

Amber wasn't sure how much time had passed before the Dark Elves came and got her. Time didn't really have much meaning in the cell. Every minute Amber spent in that rancid, damp, uncomfortable cell felt like a year.

The cell door gave an odd click, more like a pop, actually, before swinging open. Mordasine stood there, looking down at Amber with a smug expression on his narrow face. Oh, how Amber wanted to punch him in his perfect teeth, see how much he smiled then.

"The king wants to see you now," Mordasine said casually, inspecting his perfectly manicured fingernails. "And please, struggle. I was told I can punish you however I choose if you resist, except by death. Which is most unfortunate, your filthy ilk is a sickness to this world."

"Sickness?!" Harik growled. "Come over here and I'll show ye sickness! Ye'll be puking up yer own heart by the time I'm through with ye!"

Mordasine smirked, raising an incredulous eyebrow. "As much as I truly would enjoy teaching you your place, I have other, more important matters to attend to. I'll be seeing you later though. King Zarat has some extra special torture planned for you, doesn't that sound fun?" Leaning against the cell entrance, Mordasine gave a little wave and two Dark Elves glided into the room, unlocking Amber's cuffs and dragging her to her feet.

Briefly, Amber considered fighting against them, but she decided against it. She didn't want to give Mordasine the satisfaction. Instead, she just threw an icy glare at the haughty elf and let the guards lead her along, head held high.

Amber was led up several long flights of staircases, each made of smooth black stone just like the castle's walls. Torches sat in metal brackets along the walls, each decorated with blooming roses and thorny vines. Apparently Dark Elves had a thing for roses.

Makes sense, Amber figured. They're pricks, after all.

As she was led along, Amber noticed something that seemed rather peculiar to her. Every now and then, a small group of Dark Elves would walk down the staircase. That wasn't the strange part. What caught Amber so off guard was the state of these Dark Elves. Every Dark Elf she had seen so far was impeccably dressed in either fine clothes or glistening armour, their jet-black hair perfectly styled and straightened, their narrow faces strong and healthy.

These Dark Elves were very, very different. They wore ragged black clothing, like the Dark Elf equivalent of peasant clothes. Their faces were tired and gaunt, sunken cheeks bringing out their sharp cheekbones, tired eyes staring at the floor. At first, Amber thought they were prisoners, traitors of some sort, but then she noticed most groups had a male adult, a female adult, and at least one child. They also were not escorted by any guards.

These were families, ordinary subjects of the Dark Elf kingdom. As soon as the realization sunk in, Amber lingered her gaze on one of the passing families, wondering why they were so thin.

She got a sharp slap to the back of the head for that. "Keep your unworthy eyes off of those who are above you," Mordasine scolded coolly.

Amber snuck a glance at him out of the corner of her eye. She noticed then that there was a certain thinness even to Mordasine, although elves were slender and lithe as a rule, Dark Elves perhaps even more so. Still, there was something about the Dark Elf that just looked…Amber wasn't quite sure. Off, she supposed.

Amber didn't have long to contemplate it. She was soon pushed through the doors to the throne room, strong arms shoving her forward and into the tile.

Growling, Amber pushed herself to her feet, but Mordasine's boot shoved her back down. "On your *knees*, filth," he hissed.

With a glare hot enough to melt a glacier, Amber rose to only her knees, glowering at King Zarat.

The king had assumed a very casual position, legs draped over one armrest of his throne, leaning his back over the other while the queen played lazily with his hair, not even noticing Amber's presence.

Amber had to fight hard to resist the urge to start yelling, knowing that it would just make her situation worse. The Dark Elves' constant superior attitude infuriated Amber and the nonchalant way they acted around her, as if she was no more than an obedient dog, just further raised her ire.

The throne room was silent for about a minute before Zarat finally pretended to take notice of Amber, turning his head slightly and raising his eyebrows in mock surprise before crinkling up his nose. "What is she doing here?"

"You requested I bring her to you, my liege," Mordasine answered, playing along with Zarat's frustrating act.

A look of feigned realization swept over Zarat's face. "Oh, yes. I did say that," he said. Turning his head back to the room's curving ceiling, Zarat carried on in an uninterested voice. "I was wondering if you'd changed your mind about helping me at all."

"Ye really think it's that easy t' break a dwarf?" Amber snarled. "Just stick me in a prison fer a day and feed me maggots and I'll come running t' yer e'ery request?"

Zarat pretended to consider that for a moment before shrugging. "I thought I might give it a shot. You're right, I should have known better though. It didn't work on your parents either, after all." Zarat turned his gaze to meet Amber's, smiling in a way that made Amber's insides squirm. "That took some more…extreme forms of persuasion. Would you like an example?"

"Touch me, and I'll tear yer throat out with me bare hands,"

Amber growled.

Zarat gave an exaggerated sigh, turning his head back to the ceiling. "They never learn, do they, my love?" he lamented to Sindra. "You can't speak to your superiors that way."

"No, you cannot," Sindra agreed with a silky voice that somehow managed to be sharp and icy at the exact same time. A wicked smile stretched across her face as she looked at Amber. "Perhaps she needs to be taught a lesson."

"No, I doubt that will work," Zarat sighed. "A good suggestion, but dwarves are such trivial creatures. Even a concept as simple as learning her inferior place is beyond her pathetic mind's ability to comprehend and no amount of torture will drive that through her thick skull." Zarat grinned sadistically. "Doesn't mean we can't try though. Mordasine, I am so sorry to have made you spend so much time around a dwarf mongrel like her. As a gesture of apology, you're welcome to do with her as you will. Make it painful."

"You are too kind, my lord," Mordasine said, bowing low with an evil smirk. "Come along, little dwarf, it's playtime." The Dark Elf guards grabbed Amber by her shoulders and pulled her out of the hall.

Amber never stood up though, never turned around. She made the Dark Elves pull her to her feet and drag her across the glossy tile, glaring hatefully at Zarat all the way.

After hours of the worst agony she had ever been subjected to, Amber was tossed back onto the cold floor of her cell. Her head felt like it had been filled with molten lead, too heavy to lift off the ground and throbbing with a burning migraine. Her veins were on fire, various drugs and poisons flowing through them like lava. Giant purple bruises covered her torso and one of her eyes was swollen shut and bleeding. She had lost three teeth as well.

"Oh, me girl, what did they do t' ye?" Guralyn gasped as soon as he saw Amber's grisly state. The guards dragged Amber to her cuffs, deliberately smashing hands against the stone wall as they locked her cuffs.

Amber's arms dropped to her sides the moment the guards let go, all the strength gone from them. She winced as her left hand smacked into the floor, sending another jolt of pain up her arm. Amber would have cried out were her throat not already completely raw from screaming.

"Nothin'...I can't handle," Amber managed, her voice husky and weak, head slumped forward.

"The bastards!" Harik cursed angrily, tugging violently on his cuffs. "I swear, I'll kill e'ery single one o' them fer what they've done t' ye." Turning to the cell door, he yelled, "Ye hear that? I'm comin' for ye, ye sick piles o' troll snot! I'll split yer pretty skulls with nothin' but me head!" He fell back against the cell wall, tired and defeated.

"Are you all right, Amber?" Jeddo asked, concerned.

Amber hesitated before replying. "No! No, Jeddo, I am not! I'm stuck here in a cell, bein' fed maggots and not gettin' near enough water! Me head aches, me hands ache, me throat aches, me whole damn body aches! I been cut and punched and loaded up with poisons and drugs and all I want t' be doin' right now is fallin' over and dyin', if only t' get me out o' this place!" she shrieked, painful sobs wracking her body. She began coughing soon after that, lungs feeling like they were going to explode with each violent heave of her chest, throat burning like someone had dumped a bucket of acid down it.

Jeddo laid a comforting hand on Amber's shoulder, but she flinched away, that gentlest of touches sending waves of agony rolling across her body.

"Have hope, good dwarf," Ayra said, her voice hoarse but still with a songlike tone to it. "We will get out of this, that I truly believe. As the old generals used to say, 'a single man with a sharpened stick and nothing left to lose can win the battle.'"

"Aye, but we've not even a twig," Harik pointed out grimly. A gloomy silence claimed the room.

Dinner arrived shortly after, tumbling through the cubby in another metal box to land beside Guralyn. Salted meat, which would have been a great treat were the meat not stale and overly salted.

Just before the cubby closed, Amber called out in the loudest voice she could muster, "Wait! I'm needin' t' relieve meself. Can ye come and take me t' a privy?" She winced as the words scraped against her burning throat.

She heard nothing but silence from the other side until a small wooden bucket tumbled through the cubby.

CHAPTER 18:
THE MOST DANGEROUS HUNT

"GET UP," A COLD VOICE DEMANDED.

Silmanus groaned a bit and blinked open his eyes, adjusting them quickly to his surroundings. They focused in on Mara's deadpan face staring down at him, arms folded over her chest.

Silmanus sighed. "What do you want?" He pushed his blanket aside, stretching as he rose from the ground.

He caught a flash of annoyance cross Mara's face as she hesitated to answer. "Your spells," she mumbled.

Silmanus had to fight back the urge to gloat, instead politely replying, "I'll need a few minutes to review the necessary ones."

Mara gave a stiff nod, her face still expressionless. "Be quick about it and meet me in the prisoners' hut."

As Mara turned to leave, Silmanus asked, "And which one is that?"

"The one with a pair of living mountains standing in front of it."

Silmanus dug through his bag a bit, pulling out a worn leather book with numerous slips of parchment tucked between the yellowed pages. Taking a moment to appreciate the smell of an old book, Silmanus scanned through the pages, upon which were scrawled notes and incantations, the former written in Elvish and the latter in a strange, archaic language known as Arcanian, the language of spells.

After roughly ten minutes, Silmanus was confident he had properly memorized the necessary incantations. Arcanian was a very difficult language to memorize and spells often required very specific gestures to accompany the verbal components, making memorizing spells, especially those Silmanus less frequently used, rather difficult.

Staff in hand, Silmanus strolled out of his hut and scanned the village, looking for these "human mountains" Mara had referred to.

Silmanus spotted them right away. Ivar and Helga, twins from the northern land of Helvark, Silmanus recognized. He'd seen them around here and there but had never spoken to or paid much attention to either.

Human mountain was an accurate description, Silmanus noticed. They were both very tall, about two heads taller than Silmanus, with Ivar standing no more than an inch taller than his sister. Each wore a tunic and trousers made of hide and fur, likely wolf. The tunics had no sleeves and the trousers didn't extend beyond their knees, revealing the twins' massive, trunk-like arms and legs. Silmanus had no doubt that either of them could snap him in half with so much as a flick. They both had long blonde hair, although Ivar's stopped at his shoulders while Helga's ran halfway down her back in a thick braid. Piercing blue eyes stared stoically ahead, massive battleaxes propped up on the hut wall beside them.

Silmanus gave a slightly nervous nod as he passed between the twins, feeling very, very small next to them. He composed himself quickly before stepping into the hut.

Inside, the two Dark Elves were bound by thick ropes and tied back-to-back to a pole in the centre of the hut, glaring out of their pitiless silver eyes. Mara stood over them, arms crossed and a threatening expression on her face.

Silmanus noticed a series of bruises and cuts lining each of the elves' faces. "Torture?" he asked Mara skeptically.

"I guess," she answered. "Simply asking them wasn't working so I got Ivar to throw some punches, but to no avail."

Silmanus winced a bit, knowing that a punch from that monstrosity of a man probably felt like being hit by a sledgehammer. "And you didn't torture them further?"

"I don't torture people beyond what Ivar did. And even then, it's a last resort."

Silmanus nodded. "Well, let's see how I fare." Silmanus studied the two Dark Elves carefully, trying to discern which would be easiest to break. The elf on Silmanus' right had a significantly more inflamed eye as well several cuts on his puffy lips. He'd taken a worse beating.

Narrowing his eyes in concentration, Silmanus began murmuring and waggling his fingers, compelling the Dark Elf to be truthful. The elf put up a commendable resistance, pushing back against Silmanus' power with far more strength than the wizard had expected. But Silmanus proved the stronger and the Dark Elf's resolve broke, his mind charmed by Silmanus' magic.

"Ok," Silmanus said, brow furrowed and strain evident in his voice. "Ask him anything."

"What is your name?" Mara demanded, figuring she'd start small.

"Berrelzia," the Dark Elf hissed, twitching as he (futilely) continued to try to resist Silmanus' spell.

"And your friend?"

"Liathodon." Liathodon tried to elbow his companion, hissing what Silmanus assumed were curses and insults in Dark Elvish.

"Wonderful. How many of you are in this forest right now?" Mara asked.

Berrelzia gritted his teeth and hesitated, but Silmanus forced the truth out of him. "There are thirty-six of us left, counting Liathodon and I."

Silmanus whistled. A force of thirty-six Dark Elves was powerful indeed.

"Where?"

Again, Berrelzia tried to resist and almost succeeded, but Silmanus managed to hold his spell of truth. "Twenty deciums downstream of your pathetic village." Berrelzia couldn't lie, but he could still insult.

"What is your mission?"

Veins were popping out of Berrelzia's neck at this point as he fought desperately against the spell. "To...kill...you," he hissed.

With a cry of fury, Berrelzia pushed back against Silmanus with all his might, somehow managing to throw the wizard out of his mind. Silmanus gasped as the spell broke and Berrelzia's head lolled forward, asleep.

Silmanus began the casting again, but Mara held up a hand and stopped him, a pained and knowing look in her eyes. "No, they've told me enough." She walked out of the hut, motioning for Silmanus to follow.

Speaking in a hushed voice, Mara said, "I don't understand something. Over forty of them came north, probably close to sixty in total. A force that large could have easily killed me by now. So why haven't they?"

Silmanus frowned. That was a very good point. There was absolutely no reason why the Dark Elves hadn't struck yet. They knew where the village was, as Berrelzia had implied. Getting to Mara couldn't be that hard.

Silmanus shook his head. "I don't know," he answered.

"Then guess."

Silmanus thought hard for a few moments. "The first attempt contained about a third of their forces. Likely they assumed that would have been enough, so they split into groups in order to patrol a larger area. It would have been enough had they caught you alone, but I was there, and we managed to fight them off."

Mara seemed a little insulted that Silmanus thought she couldn't have won on her own, but there was no way one person could have battled that many Dark Elves alone. Not even Mara.

"The second attack yesterday was probably just a scouting patrol that I ran into by chance. So, I think they're casing the village out for now and likely waiting to establish a critical weakness before striking."

Mara nodded slowly. "Yes, that makes sense. So, by your logic, they are trying to find the most effective way to eliminate me?"

"That would be my best guess, yes."

"Meaning all of their attention is focused on planning an attack?"

"Yes…"

"Meaning they do not expect, nor are they prepared for, a counterattack?"

Silmanus considered that for a moment. "That's actually not a half bad idea."

"Let's do it then," Mara decided.

Something clicked in the back of Silmanus' mind. "I almost forgot!" he exclaimed. "Doves. Have you ever heard of a dove being black before?"

Mara frowned. "No…"

"When we first met, there was a dove, a black dove, in the trees. And again, when we got attacked yesterday," Silmanus explained. "I've never heard of Dark Elves employing birds before, but I can't dismiss it as coincidence and it's not a radical idea. Let people know to report any sightings right away."

"I'll get the word out," Mara said with a nod. "Thank you. Now, pack your bags, we're going hunting." With that, Mara turned to leave but Silmanus grabbed her arm.

Mara whirled back around, blue eyes shooting daggers at Silmanus. The elf promptly released Mara's arm, holding his hands up in surrender. "Sorry, I know, you've got a strict 'don't touch me' policy. But we need to talk about something else, right now."

Mara sighed. "What about?"

Silmanus made an exasperated expression. "About the way you've been treating me! Look, I get it, you don't trust me, and I've been asking some personal questions. But you have to understand the position I'm in! I know absolutely nothing about you and you're expecting me to go risk my life for you! Not to mention the fact that you're treating me like an object, a means to an end. Show me some damned respect, for Gods' sake, instead of expecting me to come to your beck and call and tossing me away when you're done!"

Something snapped in Mara's blazing eyes. "The way *I'm* treating you?" she snarled. "You've been prancing around this place with your head held high, thinking you're so much better than us humans with your fancy staff and pointy ears. You think we're all so beneath you and it's sickening. You want to get respected around here? Try looking at the rest of us like equals."

Silmanus opened his mouth to retort but something hitched in the back of his mind. He thought about all the times he had dismissed humans as corrupt and uncivilized, all the times he had thought of how greatly humanity could progress if only they were more elflike. He thought about how he had spent the last weak essentially telling the village to be more like elves in order to improve.

He thought about the merchant he had passed on his way to Argenrros.

Silmanus opened his mouth again, although this time, his features had softened, and guilt hung in his eyes. But no words came out. Silmanus knew he should apologize, knew he *needed* to apologize, but he couldn't make a sound.

Mara didn't seem impressed. Putting a hand on her hip, she snapped, "What, cat got your tongue?"

"You're right," Silmanus managed finally, pushing past the shameful lump in his throat.

"Sorry?" Mara asked, furrowing her brow. Silmanus wasn't sure if she hadn't heard him or if she just didn't believe it. Maybe both.

"You're right," he said again, a little louder. "For as much as I think I am fair to humans, you're right. I have been arrogant. And I am sorry."

Mara blinked a few times, processing Silmanus' words with something of a surprised expression. "Right. Well then. Glad to have that sorted out."

"Yeah," Silmanus replied shortly, a little frustrated by Mara's reaction. He turned to leave, wanting to just be done with the conversation.

"Wait," Mara called after him.

Silmanus stopped. "Yes?"

Mara sighed. "I also owe you an apology. You're right, I haven't been very fair to you either. I've asked you to dedicate your time to helping me, to risk your life for my sake, and yet all I have shown you is distrust and anger. For that, I am sorry. I just…I'm not particularly trustful of elves, or anyone, for that matter, and there are parts of my past I just don't discuss with people. You deserve to know though. Pretentious though you've been, you've been loyal and trustworthy, too, and if we're to fight beside each other, you should know who I really am.

"My past isn't a story for right now, however. Go gather your things. We set out at midday. If you're with me?" Mara stuck out her hand, which Silmanus grabbed and shook.

"I am," Silmanus told her. "Let's go hunt some Dark Elves."

Mara nodded and turned, striding off to assemble her team.

Silmanus stood there for a few moments, guilt mixing with relief in the pit of his stomach, before marching off to his own hut.

"Linos," Mara called. Her tall, grinning companion turned from the conversation he was engaged in immediately.

"Yeah?" Linos answered.

"I'm leaving for a while. We know the general location of the remaining Dark Elves and I want to take the fight to them. Catch them off guard and reduce civilian casualties," Mara explained. "I'm leaving you in charge."

"Hell no!" Linos protested. "You aren't going alone!"

Mara shook her head. "I won't be alone. I'm bringing Silmanus, Cara, Norman, Anne, Ivar, and Helga."

"And me," Linos said firmly. "There is no way I'm letting you go off fighting Dark Elves without me."

Mara sighed. She'd figured Linos would react like this. "Linos, I need someone I trust running things while I'm gone."

"Then get Reynard to do it! I don't want to be stuck here twiddling my thumbs while you're out fighting Dark Elves and risking your life!"

"Linos, you are staying here and that is an order."

Linos straightened, his whole body rigid. A defiant light blazed in his brown eyes. "You do *not* get to order me around like that. Mara, I am your friend. Your *best friend*. You don't tell me what to do and you certainly do not leave me behind when you go out fighting Dark Elves."

Mara sighed again. "Fine. I'll get Reynard to look after things here then. Go pack your things and meet by the firepit."

With an excited grin, Linos sped away to his hut, anxious to finally get some action.

Mara shook her head. Linos was just as stubborn as she was, although secretly, she was glad for that. She felt much more comfortable knowing Linos would have her back, even if it meant leaving the village in the hands of someone else. But Reynard was a capable leader, she knew that. He would manage things just fine without Mara or Linos.

Quickly locating Reynard by the storage building, Mara broke the news to him. Reynard gave her a nod and assured her that the village would be well looked after.

"Good luck out there, Mara," he said. "Come back to us."

Mara clasped the man on the shoulder. "I plan to."

Mara rushed to her hut, quickly stuffing items in her leather backpack. She didn't think she would need much. Some provisions, a water skin, a bedroll and blanket, that was it.

She looped her quiver around her belt and slung her sword across her chest and onto her back. She strung her bow and attached it to the side of her pack, figuring it would be better left ready for use. Mara grabbed her hatchet and knives and slid those into their respective places on her belt.

Deciding she was all set, Mara swung her backpack onto her back, the fur on the shoulders of her shirt helping to keep the straps from digging in. Not that the pack was very heavy anyway. She took a few moments to adjust the pack comfortably overtop of her sword before making her way to the firepit.

The others were all already at the firepit. Silmanus, dressed in the same clothes as always, staff in hand and pack on his back. Ivar and Helga, both with their massive battleaxes and leather packs. Norman and Anne, the two Eiran siblings that had become Mara's chiefs of hunting, carried their longbows and longswords, sporting simple clothing beneath their leather packs. Cara had her spiked targe on one arm, long dirk sheathed on her belt and a wild expression on her face. And of course, there was Linos, trident in hand and grinning from ear to ear.

Mara felt very confident knowing she would be travelling with these folks at her side. They were all very capable warriors, even Cara, who, despite looking so frail and fragile, had easily held her own against a variety of powerful foes. She trusted each and every one of them with her life, even Silmanus.

Mara stopped in front of them and they all turned to face her. "Well, this is it," she announced. "We're leaving this place and there's a chance we may not come back. Are you all still up to this?

There's no shame in backing out now."

"Ah, quit yer jabberin'! We've got Dark Elves tae kill!" Cara yelled at her.

Mara grinned at her. "I'll take that as a yes," Mara replied. She led the group out, pausing every now and then to take one last look at her home.

Mara knew that day could be her last, that she may never see her village again. These were no goblins. They were Dark Elves, and while Mara had already held up relatively well against them so far, they were not to be underestimated. Death by a Dark Elf's hand was a very real possibility, so Mara found herself trying to savour what could be the very last sights of a place she had called home.

As they marched out of the gates and across the village's draw-bridge, Mara shook such thoughts away. She was surrounded by the strongest warriors she knew. The Dark Elves didn't stand a chance. So, as Mara strode out of her walls and into the towering pines of the forest around her, she did so with her head held high, her eyes bright and twinkling, confident that she would make it home again.

This was the most dangerous hunt she had ever been on, yes, but her hunters were the deadliest around.

CHAPTER 19:
THE DEAL

JEDDO AWOKE TO THE HARSH CRASH OF METAL AGAINST metal as the guards banged their weapons against his cell door.

Groaning and clutching his head, which was aching from dehydration, Jeddo blinked open his eyes. Because gnomes had poor night vision, Jeddo could only make out the dimly illuminated figures of his fellow inmates, their features dark and blurred in the lacking torchlight. He coughed a bit. The smoke from the torch wasn't vented very well, if at all.

Curiosity suddenly spiked in Jeddo's mind. The torch…how did it stay lit? The guards never changed it during the day, or what Jeddo assumed was the day, there really was no knowing in their cell, which meant they must come in at night. That, or the torch was enchanted to perpetually burn. With a sigh, Jeddo realized it was probably the latter possibility; Amber hadn't noticed any guards come in during their first night.

Jeddo looked over at Amber. She was slumped forward, fast asleep, chest heaving with husky, ragged breaths. Deep snores rumbled out of her half-opened lips, both of which had doubled in size from swelling. At least she was asleep. Some rest would do the dwarf good and she hadn't got any the night before.

Jeddo smacked his lips, noticing how dry his mouth and throat were. Last night's meal had been particularly devious, the extra salt on the meat just worsening Jeddo's already unbearable thirst. The gnome had no idea how Amber's parents had managed to live like this for a whole century. After just two days (or, at least, what Jeddo had guessed to be two days), Jeddo was honestly considering finding a way to put himself out of his misery.

He couldn't do that though. He refused to let the Dark Elves win again, not after what they'd done to his ship and crew.

Jeddo hung his head forward in lamentation as he brought to memory that fateful day.

His ship, the *Ocean's Hearth* had been running up and down the east coast, smuggling goods and plundering merchant ships. Jeddo had been a pirate, after all, although he and his crew of gnomes took every precaution to spare lives, instead simply incapacitating the sailors of a ship and stealing its loot. Jeddo's crew had been infamous for it, in fact, using gnome technology to raid ships without any casualties. It had been a good life, a fun life, one of adventure and excitement.

And then disaster struck. Nine years ago, the *Ocean's Hearth* had been heading south on a smuggling run, carrying various contrabands to a black market in southeastern Pyradia. A storm had caught their ship, however, carrying it farther south than they had intended, past the Black Strait and into Dark Elf waters.

Jeddo had been confident that there would be no trouble. The ship had come out of the storm relatively unscathed and he doubted the Dark Elves would have a ship anywhere near the Black Strait.

Jeddo had been wrong. Not two hours after the storm had let up, a sleek black ship closed in on the *Ocean's Hearth*, racing through the waters like shadow as it cut toward Jeddo's ship. They were boarded and slaughtered, Jeddo just barely managing to escape in a lifeboat. He was, to his knowledge, the only survivor.

A determined expression came over Jeddo's face. He had taken a coward's way out with the Dark Elves once before. Never again.

The cubby creaked a metal casket fell onto the stone with a crash, just like always. Breakfast. To Jeddo's surprise, a large waterskin followed the casket. Not only did the size of the waterskin catch him off guard, but their water usually came in the casket, which meant there was likely more food than usual.

And indeed, when Guralyn picked up the casket, she commented on how warm and heavy it was. Opening it, she found is was full of porridge, along with eight spoons. "The Dark Elves takin' pity on us or somethin'?" she asked rhetorically.

Picking up a spoon, she shovelled a lump of porridge into her mouth, smacking thoughtfully on the sludgy food. "Well, it doesn't taste great," Guralyn mused. "But it actually doesn't taste bad. And there's a good amount o' it too." The casket was passed around, everyone taking a spoonful of porridge before passing it on to make sure everyone got an even serving.

Jeddo noticed Amber struggled to eat. Opening her mouth brought a wince to the wounded dwarf and any time the spoon touched her split and swollen lips, Amber grimaced. Swallowing didn't seem to be a pleasant experience for her either.

The water was passed around next and Jeddo took a couple greedy, grateful gulps to empty the last of it. Feeling much more refreshed than after the previous day, Jeddo began mulling over a possible escape.

Deciding to work at it methodically, Jeddo laid out the facts.

Three times a day, the cubby would open up and a metal casket of food would be pushed through.

The cell door was magically locked and could not be picked by any means.

The guards only opened the cell door to take someone out.

The cubby only opened from the outside.

They had no tools or weapons.

Conclusion: they were screwed.

Jeddo sighed. There were only two ways he was getting out of his cell: either with Amber on a quest to The Forgotten Mountains or in a coffin. And considering going to The Forgotten Mountains meant giving the Dark Elves the tools they needed to complete whatever devious plan they had, the first option would probably put him in a coffin too. Not to mention the nightmarish reality of a Dark Elf plan coming to fruition.

The cell door creaked open suddenly and two Dark Elves stood in the entrance, dressed in tight-fitting black uniforms overtop of their chain shirts with crossed daggers embroidered in silver thread. Without a single word, they uncuffed Jeddo and hauled him to his feet. The gnome's legs were still a little weak from his earlier torture sessions, but he found enough strength to stumble along beside the guards as they led him out of the cell and down the winding, black halls of the palace.

Jeddo was led back to the throne room and tossed roughly to its glossy black floor. Jeddo slid on his face a bit before stopping himself and rising up to his knees.

"You have more manners than your dwarf friend," King Zarat observed, dismissing the guards and looking into Jeddo's eyes with his malevolent silver orbs, burning a hole through Jeddo's very soul. The king's legs were crossed casually as he leaned back in his throne, one arm propped up on its elbow with the hand draped nonchalantly back.

Sindra sat beside him, smiling in a sinister, chilling sort of way as she stared unblinking at Jeddo. The gnome shuddered and looked away from her.

"Do you know why you're still alive, gnome?" Zarat asked, eyes wandering to the walls of his throne room. When Jeddo didn't answer, Zarat pressed, "I asked you a question."

"Uh…good looks?" Jeddo ventured nervously, unable to think of a legitimate answer.

Zarat smirked. "I've seen orcs more attractive than you," he insulted disinterestedly. "No, you are alive because you are a friend of the dwarf. She won't see reason, not through any amount of pain or suffering. That much has quickly become clear. Her parents were the same and I do not doubt she will be too.

"You, however, can convince her otherwise. She seems to trust and respect you. You need to convince her to help me."

"And why would I do that?" Jeddo challenged nervously, swallowing the lump in his throat.

"Well, if you don't, I'll kill you," Zarat said in an unnervingly casual voice, like killing people was just an ordinary part of an ordinary day. Which didn't seem like an unrealistic comparison, considering he was a Dark Elf. "And if Amber refuses to help me, I'll kill her too."

Jeddo tried to hide the fact that he was shaking. "What happens if I *do* help you?" he asked, fighting hard to keep the stammer out of his voice.

"I won't kill you," Zarat stated as if it were the most obvious thing in the world. "I might even consider continuing to give you improved rations." Ah. The improved breakfast was a bribe.

"But you won't let me go?"

Zarat snorted. "Of course not. Don't be ridiculous."

Jeddo bit his lip. His options were not great. On the one hand, he could refuse to help. Zarat would kill him and Amber but the Dark Elves probably wouldn't get what they wanted, and the world would be saved. Jeddo really didn't want to die though.

On the other hand, Jeddo could help Zarat, giving the Dark Elves what they wanted and likely condemning the world to a horrendous fate. Plus, Jeddo would remain a prisoner for the rest of his life. But he would at least be alive, if the Dark Elf's word was to be trusted. Which, in honesty, it really wasn't.

"H-how long do I have to think about it?" Jeddo stuttered.

Zarat shrugged and looked over at Sindra with a raised eyebrow. "Four days," Sindra decided.

Jeddo gave a shaky nod. "What happens if I can't convince Amber?"

Sindra gave a delighted smile. "We get to kill you!" she told him cheerfully.

Wonderful.

"Well, I'll let you think about it then," Zarat declared, about to clap his hands to summon back the guards.

"Wait!" Jeddo blurted, his mind racing. Zarat raised an expectant eyebrow, hands still poised to clap. "I'll do it, but I have some more conditions."

Zarat smirked. "You are in no position to bargain."

"Actually, I am," Jeddo shot back with a confidence he didn't even know he had. "You're right, you will never convince Amber to help you. She would rather die than aid the people that slaughtered her kingdom."

"That can easily be arranged," Zarat threatened.

It was Jeddo's turn to smirk. "But then you'll never get what you want."

Zarat kept his expression cocky and uninterested but Jeddo could see the slightest hint of worry creepy into his voice. "I still have her parents."

"Who are just as unlikely to help you, even less so if you kill their daughter," Jeddo countered. "Face it, I am your only chance at getting Amber to help you."

"There is always another way," Zarat hissed.

"But I'm the best one," Jeddo reasoned, his confidence growing has he realized he had won this round.

Zarat's eyes narrowed into slits, his glare almost enough to steal Jeddo's confidence away. "What are your demands?"

Jeddo grinned. Finally, he was getting somewhere. "Get me and the others out of that cell. Start treating us like your guests, not your prisoners. And when we're done helping you, let us go."

Zarat considered that for a moment. "Absolutely not."

"Then I won't help you."

Zarat growled, clearly very frustrated that Jeddo now held the cards. "Fine. You stay in the cell, but I will uncuff you. Except for the humans, who may be treated how I please. Your rations will be improved to the level they were this morning, and when you are done, you and Amber will be moved to guest suites. The others will be killed."

Jeddo shook his head. "Not good enough."

Zarat rose from his throne, eyes blazing with a hateful fire. His shadow seemed to swallow what little light could be found in the room, sucking Jeddo into its malevolent vortex of darkness and fury. The gnome fought very hard to retain his confident composure, although he wasn't sure to what end.

"You do not make the demands here!" Zarat roared. "I am a Dark Elf! No lowly gnome has the right to speak to me in such a way! You will pay for your insolence! Guards, take him back to his cell. Tell the others that they will receive no food and no water until the gnome agrees to help." Zarat sneered. "Let's see how long you stay stubborn while your friends' survival depends on your cooperation."

As the guards returned and grabbed Jeddo's arms, the gnome thrashed and called out. "No! Wait! I agree to your terms, please, don't do this!" he protested desperately.

Zarat shook his head, grinning wickedly. "That deal has been terminated. You lost your chance. Here's the new deal: help me or you and your friends die of thirst and hunger. Think it over. Now guards, please, get him out of my sight." Zarat finished with a dismissive wave, turning to look at Sindra.

The guards hauled Jeddo off with strong arms while the gnome kicked and squirmed violently. "No! Don't do this!" he cried. "You're a monster! A *monster*! You'll never win! No, get off of me!"

But Jeddo's words meant nothing. He was pulled out of the throne room and its heavy black doors shut in the gnome's face, the embossed twin daggers gleaming down at him with an evil silver light, the guards stationed beside smirking at Jeddo. One even gave Jeddo a cheerful smile and a little wave, snickering as the gnome was hauled away.

Back down the stairs he went, body jolted and bumped against every step until they reached the dank, musty dungeons below. Jeddo's cell popped open and he was tossed inside, slamming into the stony floor with a groan. The guards heaved him violently up and spun him around, cuffing him in place once more.

Sneering down at the prisoners, one of the guards announced, "Your friend here has refused to help the king, and until he does, you will receive no food and no water. You now have him to thank for your misery." With that, the cell door was slammed shut and the guards strode away, cackling as they went.

Amber looked at Jeddo in alarm. "What're they talkin' about, gnome?" she asked anxiously.

Jeddo hung his head shamefully. "The king wants me to convince you to help him. I tried to bargain with him, tried to get us out of this damned cell, but it didn't work. It's like the guards said, until I agree to help, we get nothing, and I suspect that if I stop helping at a later date, the rations do too." Jeddo pressed his hands to his eyes. "I'm so sorry."

Amber nudged him with her elbow. "Ye're talkin' crazy," she decided. "It ain't no one's fault but that damned King Zarat. Don't ye go beatin' yerself up about it."

"We have to get out of here…" Jeddo whispered.

"Aye, that we do, but we've no way."

"What are we going to do then?" Jeddo asked, looking up at Amber, his voice empty and defeated.

Amber thought for a moment. "Accept his deal," she suggested. "I'll pretend t' be convinced and that'll buy us some time. He's not movin' out fer another, what, two weeks?"

Jeddo nodded. "Minus a couple days, but yeah."

"Right. So, we pretend t' be willin' t' help, we all get food, and we have two weeks to figure out an escape."

Jeddo shook his head. "Amber, there *is* no escape. We are *never* getting out of here!"

"Not with that attitude, we aren't," the dwarf said stubbornly. "Just ye wait, somethin' will turn up. We'll get that sharpened stick and bust out o' this place."

Jeddo shook his head again, wishing he had Amber's optimism. He didn't though. He didn't believe there was any escape. There was no way out. He was going to die here. That, or the Dark Elves would get their arcanium and the world would burn before them. No matter what, Jeddo was doomed. There was no hope, no chance.

He had never felt so small, so powerless, so completely unable to do anything except make an already-horrible situation even worse. With those thoughts in mind, Jeddo slumped his head against the wall of the cell, closing his eyes and trying to will away the discomfort.

CHAPTER 20:
HUNTERS OR HUNTED?

NIGHT HAD FALLEN. TWINKLING STARS SHINED DOWN from between the branches, sparkling across the cloudless night sky. Darkness surrounded them, darkness that could conceal Dark Elves behind every bush, every tree, but the group could not have felt safer. They even had a small campfire crackling in the centre of the clearing where they'd stopped, upon which several squirrels and two rabbits had just been roasted.

Sucking the last remains of grease from his fingers, Silmanus stared into the dancing flames, lost in their every leap and flicker. Mara sat beside him, gnawing absently on the last scraps of flesh clinging to the bones of the squirrel she'd eaten. Norman, Anne, and Linos were on watch, hidden in the branches of the trees while Cara, Ivar, and Helga slept comfortably below.

"I used to do this a lot with my father," Mara said suddenly.

Silmanus raised an eyebrow. "Oh?"

"He would take me out on hunting trips all the time. We would spend weeks wandering the wilderness, foraging for our own food, spending the evening around a campfire eating the day's yield."

"Was your father a hunter then?" Silmanus asked.

Silmanus flinched instinctively, noticing the flash of irritation that crossed Mara's guarded eyes. He expected her to tell him to piss off and mind his own business, but something softened in her expression and she answered. "Sort of. He was a Ranger."

Silmanus' eyes went wide and his mouth fell agape. "A Ranger?"

Silmanus was quite impressed. Rangers were elite members of an ancient and mysterious organization, The Guardians, founded millennia ago by the Lochadians to protect the lands from the threats of South Hynar, Helvark, Vanaria, and The Fell Lands. They were recognized throughout the goodly nations as protectors and defenders, roaming Aeternerras to eliminate threats, secure borders, and perform espionage. The leaders of Faeryln, Marrelnia, Sylvare, Eiraland, Lochadia, Esnia, North Hynar, Pyradia, Thelegard, and Gryzland all respected Rangers, who had saved each nation from annihilation countless times throughout history. Armed with weapons of pure mithril and possessed of skills contested only by Faeryln's Royal Vanguards, Rangers commanded admiration from friend and foe alike.

"Yes. Not only that, he was the king of Lochadia, although his Ranger duties often called him away, leaving rule to a chieftain.

"I was his only child. My mother died in childbirth and my father never found the heart to remarry. From the moment I could walk, he was training me to become a Ranger, teaching me to shoot and track, to duel and forage. Many of his advisors and rivals criticized his decision, believing that he should be raising me to be a ruler, not a Ranger.

"Eight years ago, when I was sixteen, he was assigned to a scouting mission in Vanaria. There had been reports of increased Dark Elf activity in the south, so he was sent to infiltrate a stronghold and find out what was going on. He took me with him, believing the experience would be very beneficial to me. I was already quite skilled at the time and he believed I could both assist him and gain a significant level of field experience.

"The mission was almost a success. We were able to steal a set of plans and documents and escape Vanaria, but not undetected. The Dark Elves pursued us, chasing us all the way to Longwood before finally catching us." Mara stopped suddenly, her voice hitching at the painful memory.

"My father sacrificed himself for me. He gave me the plans, but I lost them. I failed him. The Dark Elves recovered them and I barely escaped with my life."

Mara's eyes began to water, but she wiped them dry with her sleeve.

"How did you end up here, in Eiraland?" Silmanus asked quietly after a few silent moments.

"One of the chieftain's of Lochadia had secretly been gaining support behind my father's back. By the time I had returned, he had managed to persuade almost all the other clan leaders of the land that my father was not fit to rule. The chieftain had planned to confront him and seize control of the nation but he never got that opportunity. A better one presented itself instead." Mara's eyes burned with indignation. "Women are not allowed to sit in positions of leadership in Lochadia. Worse yet, I was still not even a proper woman yet. I was forced out of power, made to flee my own home. The chieftain, now king, banished me on pain of death.

"So, I fled north, taking along anyone that would join me."

"Cara and Bredon?" Silmanus asked, giving Mara an apologetic look as he realized he'd interrupted.

"Well, some others too, but yes, they came with me. My plan was to live in Faeryln. My father was greatly respected amongst the elves. I figured they would take us in." Mara's voice grew very bitter.

"They did not. They told me I was not my father, that I was not even a Ranger yet. I was no more than a civilian to them and they turned me away.

"But I could not go back. I had no way to cross Ilbus' Lake either, so I led my companions through the Iron Mountains. It was a long, hard journey, and we foolishly strayed into Faeryln's borders at one point. We almost got caught, but we made it through. I'm wanted for trespassing in Faeryln now though, and I was expelled from The Guardians.

"Eiraland was a chance to start fresh. I built a new life in a nation that did not know my name. I earned a new one, of course, and I'm wanted here too, but it's a better life than I had in Lochadia. I am respected here, with friends and allies."

Guilt wormed its way through Silmanus' heart. "Don't feel bad for your people's mistakes," Mara told him, apparently noticing how he felt. "I once believed that no elves could be trusted, but you have proved me wrong."

Silmanus nodded. "I am glad," he said. "But I am still sorry for the way my people treated you. In truth, our leaders are no less corrupt than those of Eiraland or Lochadia. They believe in putting High Elves above all others, showing little concern for the other nations north of the Fire Mountains and acting only in their best interests. Although, we have at least recognized the importance of equality. An equal number of males and females lead Faeryln, as it has always been. I am sad to hear that not every country has caught on yet."

"The world is a terrible place," Mara sighed. After a brief silence, Mara asked, "How about you? What's your story?"

Silmanus took a deep breath and steeled his pounding heart. It was time to stop running from the pains of his past.

"I was born and raised in a small village. My parents had served as members of Faeryln's elite guard, Royal Vanguards, until they had me, at which point they began practising magic and studying arcanium." Silmanus gave a nostalgic grin as he continued. "I wanted to be just like them. 'Daddy, daddy, teach me to shoot like you! Teach me to use spells like you and mommy!'"

Silmanus shook his head, still grinning. "So, they apprenticed me to a kind old wizard, Toronil, when I was ten, and my parents taught me how to shoot a bow and swing a sword. I didn't see them much, however. Much of my time was spent with Toronil.

There is no room for family in wizardry. It consumes every part of your life, demanding the utmost focus and sacrifice." Silmanus' grin was replaced by an expression of deep sorrow. "I love what I do, but it is one of my greatest regrets that I did not spend more time with my parents."

Silmanus could feel tears climbing up his throat, but he swallowed them back down before continuing. "Exactly one hundred years before the day I met you, my parents disappeared. Nobody knew where they went. Nobody knows where they are. I spent decades searching for them but didn't even find a trace of where they went. No one did. It has haunted me ever since.

"After their disappearance, I continued my studies, believing that one day, I would become powerful enough to find them. I didn't though, so I've made a life for myself as a researcher, studying magic for Faeryln's government, the High Council, as well as an emergency War Mage when the Royal Vanguards need the help."

For a moment, Mara was very quiet. She stared blankly at the ground, and in that moment, Silmanus saw in her eyes the same pain that lived in his own heart, the same loss that had plagued him for a hundred years.

"Is that why you're still here?" Mara asked suddenly, still looking at the ground. "Why you're *actually* still here?"

Silmanus gave a little smile. She must have heard about his conversation with Linos, where Silmanus had claimed he stuck around for the excitement.

And that was it, was it not? The danger, the adrenaline, the adventure, that feeling of being so alive that came with being so close to death. Silmanus had lived a life sorely deprived of risk and had found it to be dangerously seductive.

Yet in his heart, he knew that Mara's guess was correct. He was not just here for the danger; he was here for his parents.

"I suppose it is," Silmanus said quietly. "Now that I think about it…well, my parents vanished without any warning, and then suddenly, precisely a century later, I stumble across a mysterious woman with Dark Elves nipping at her heels. I don't believe much in fate, but I have a hard time believing that my life getting turned upside down on the centennial of my parents' disappearance is just coincidence.

"So, I guess it's hope that's keeping me here. Hope that you and your band of ragtag outlaws will help me find the answers I've been looking for."

As Mara nodded slowly, Silmanus saw the empathy in her eyes intensify, a stubborn light flickering behind it.

"I can't make you any promises, Silmanus," Mara said, "but I'll help you to the best of my ability. I owe you that much, at least."

Silmanus smiled sadly. "Thank you." He didn't know what more to say than that.

"You'd be welcome to stay, you know," Mara offered. "When this is all over. We could use a wizard around here."

Silmanus looked hesitant. "I'm not sure," he said slowly. "I'm here for now, but once all this is done…well, I'll cross that bridge when I come to it."

Mara nodded. "Fair enough."

Silmanus thought he saw a sliver of hurt in her eyes and placed one his hands on top of hers. He expected her to recoil, but she just stayed still, looking at Silmanus with a mixture of sadness and curiosity.

"Mara, you need to understand, it's not that I don't want to be here," Silmanus explained. "Well…in truth, I'm not really sure what I want anymore, but this village you built…it's incredible, and there is a part of me that wants to stay. It's just…well, you're a human. You're all humans. I'm an elf, and not only that, I'm a wizard. I will outlive you and everyone else in this village twenty times over, perhaps even longer."

Mara frowned. "Wait, what do you mean 'twenty times'?" she interrupted. "Elves only live to be a thousand years."

"Yes, but wizards…alright, well, let me explain how magic *really* works," Silmanus said. He half expected Mara to roll her eyes, but the woman just looked Silmanus in the eyes, earnest curiosity written on her face.

As Mara listened patiently, Silmanus explained to her what he had told to Eleanor, about how magic is tied to life force and how his life was doomed to be long and lonely by the very thing he had devoted himself to.

"So…I just don't know," Silmanus finished. "When this mess is sorted out, I don't know where I'll go, but I promise you this: I will fight by your side against the Dark Elves for as long as you need my help."

Mara nodded with an expression that Silmanus didn't know how to read, trying to process everything Silmanus was saying. For a tense moment, Silmanus feared he had just undone everything he had tried to mend.

But Mara finally broke the anxiety with a warm smile. "Thank you, Silmanus," she said kindly. "I appreciate that. And as I had said before, I promise to do whatever I can to help you find out what happened to your parents."

A solemn quiet fell over them. Silmanus hadn't opened up to anyone about his parents in a very long time, not even to himself, and he could tell Mara had done the same concerning her own past. Despite the grief it had stirred, it had felt good to share his pains with another person, especially a person who understood how he felt. Silmanus realized suddenly how much he had grown to value Mara, in spite of their past differences.

After a minute or two of silence, Linos approached the two. He gave them a questioning look and seemed about to ask what had happened, but shrugged it away. "Your shift," he said simply. "Can the two of you take it or should I wake someone else up to help?"

"I think we'll be fine," Mara replied, rising to her feet and grabbing her bow as she made her way to the tree Linos had occupied.

Any trace of emotion had fled from her voice, but Silmanus could see the echoes of their conversation deep in her eyes.

Silmanus did the same, collecting his staff before taking up a watch position. Blasting a quick burst of telekinetic energy at the ground, Silmanus vaulted himself into the branches of a gnarly pine, suddenly grateful for his light, wiry build.

Waggling his fingers, Silmanus began reading a series of spells from his tome, warding the campsite against prying eyes and magical scrying; he didn't want any nasty Dark Elf surprises.

As Silmanus continued with his casting, pulling magic out of his soul and enveloping the camp with it, his thought drifted back to his conversation with Mara. He could scarcely believe what she had been forced to endure, the losses she had felt and the struggles she had pushed through. He respected her now more than ever before.

And to think Silmanus had once believed humans to be weak.

Shaking his head to relieve the knot of guilt that was growing in his stomach, Silmanus turned his focus back to his spells. Once he felt the camp had been sufficiently warded, he settled back against the rough trunk of his tree, being careful not to get too comfortable lest he fall asleep prematurely.

A couple quiet hours passed before Mara collected Silmanus to wake the next shift. As Cara, Helga, and Ivar went to take up their positions, Silmanus laid back along his bedroll, nestling his head into his pack and pulling his blanket over him. Sleep came quickly that night for Silmanus.

Mara did not enjoy the same luxury.

Mara awoke to the sound of chirping birds, who sat in the branches of the trees above, welcoming the first rays of warm sunlight. Reluctantly, she pushed her blanket aside, rubbing her arms as she sat up in the cold morning air. Her breath wafted out of her mouth in a visible cloud, like a little plume of smoke.

Everyone else was still asleep. Mara decided to give them a little longer, quickly gathering some branches and tinder and creating a fire. After a few practised strokes with her flint and steel, Mara had a small fire going.

She roused her companions, who each groaned at her before sitting up and stretching off their sleepiness. Ivar and Helga seemed to be the only two that weren't bothered by the chilly morning, understandable considering they came from a land that was almost perpetually freezing cold.

They all gathered around the campfire, which was slowly growing to a respectable cooking size. Mara pulled out a coffee pot and noticed Linos do the same; they had only brought a couple to travel lighter. She poured some water into the pot, adding some from Silmanus' waterskin as well.

"I'll brew you a coffee, but I'm not using my water for it," she explained as she set the pot in the flames to boil.

Ivar shook his head. "Why do you make coffee when we are on the hunt?" he criticized in a thick Helvan accent. "We do not have time." Helvans, Ivar and Helga included, did not drink coffee, especially not when they had more important things to be doing.

"Ah, and that is where you are wrong, my muscly friends. There is *always* time for coffee," Linos corrected, drumming the leather pouch containing his portion of grinds.

While they waited for their water to boil, the group broke into their rations, largely containing deer jerky, dried berries, and hard bread. Not the most delicious of meals, but Mara wasn't complaining. She enjoyed the salty, smoky flavour of deer jerky.

At last, the water came to boil, and Mara threw her grinds in, begrudgingly adding extra for Silmanus, who shot her a grateful look. She waited a few minutes, fishing out a pair of wooden mugs and pouring herself and Silmanus each a cup of dark, steaming coffee.

Mara took an appreciative whiff of her coffee before taking a tentative sip, not wanting to burn her tongue.

"Is there any sugar?" Silmanus asked. Linos handed him a pouch and Silmanus added a small amount to his mug, earning him a confused look from Anne, Norman, and Mara, who all drank their coffee as it was. Ivar and Helga just sent a confused look to everyone.

Now warmed by their coffees and with relatively full bellies, the group quickly packed their things, following Mara south with their weapons ready.

The sun climbed higher and higher into the sky with each passing hour. The air around the group was tense, each person well aware that Dark Elves could lurk around every tree, behind any bush, waiting to spring like a pack of wolves. Worse yet, they were all now aware that the Dark Elves had eyes in the sky as well, which just made everyone even more nervous.

Mara scanned the ground with a furrowed brow, looking for any signs that might point to the exact location of the Dark Elf camp. They had only a rough idea of where the camp would be, so they would have to rely on tracks to lead them to the Dark Elves.

They made slow, methodical progress, travelling with their backs covered and their eyes peeled, stopping only to refill water-skins at brooks and replenish themselves with strips of jerky and handfuls of berries. No one wanted to be caught surprised by the Dark Elves.

As the sun began its descent across the horizon, tension just continued to rise. Twenty deciums was not an outrageous distance and they had likely travelled that far by now, meaning they could be a mere minute away from the Dark Elf camp.

The suspense was clearly starting to get to people. Although Ivar and Helga remained as stoic as ever, Mara noticed a nervous light had crept into Linos' eyes, which darted back and forth like a wary animal. Anne and Norman kept fingering the drawstrings of their massive longbows, peering anxiously through the trees. Silmanus had been repeatedly casting the same spell on himself for the past hour, although Mara had no idea what it did.

On one occasion, Silmanus had seen a flicker of movement in a tree and, thinking it to be a black dove, yelped and flung an icy dart at it. It had turned out to be a simple crow, who tumbled to the earth with a dagger of ice in its heart.

But anxiety hit Cara the worse. She was not a patient person and all this waiting and sneaking had worn her self-control thin. "'Main 'en it and barnie us, ye pale-skinned freaks! Lit me shaw ye whit a targe can dae!" she had screamed at the trees, startling a pair of squirrels.

That had earned her a steely glare from Mara. "Shut up!" she hissed. "Do you want them to know we're coming? And for Gods' sakes, if you're going to tell our enemies to come out and fight, at least do it in a way they'll understand!"

Silence had taken hold again shortly after that, broken only by the shuffle of footsteps and scurrying of animals.

At last, Mara's keen blue eyes spotted something, but not what she was looking for. It was a large pawprint, bigger than Ivar's hand and shaped like that of a dog or a wolf, except for that the claws were far too long. This evidently did not belong to any natural dog or wolf. Whatever had made these tracks was huge, monstrous, and, knowing the nature of monstrous canines, likely evil.

Worse yet, the track was fresh. Whatever had made it was still nearby.

By now, the sun was hanging low in the sky, casting long and disorienting shadows across the ground. It would be easier for something to sneak up on Mara's party now.

"Form up," Mara instructed, nocking her bow and backing toward the others. "Make a circle, be ready for trouble."

"Why? What's going on?" Linos asked anxiously.

"I think we're being hunted," Mara answered.

"Dark Elves?"

Mara shook her head. "Some kind of monster. Long claws, big paws, probably a canine."

"Barguest," Norman breathed, his voice shaking slightly.

"Don't be ridiculous, Norman," Anne said, although she too spoke with fear in her tone. "They aren't real."

"Aren't they?" Norman hissed. "Do you know that for sure?"

"What, exactly, is a barguest?" Mara interjected.

Suddenly, a deep growl echoed through the trees. It was low and fierce, like the rumble of a bear but worse. A pair of glowing ice-blue eyes appeared, thin wisps of smoke wafting from them as they bored through Mara's soul. A massive, wolf-like creature emerged from the trees, bigger than a horse and approaching with slow, deliberate footsteps. A trail of black smoke followed its steps. It had a coat blacker than anything Mara had ever seen, which seemed to glow and ripple with a spectral blue light. Its lips were drawn up in a snarl, revealing a jaw full of razor-sharp teeth that dripped saliva.

"That," Norman gulped. "Is a barguest."

Chapter 21:
The Barguest

Releasing another terrifying growl, the barguest pushed off the ground with its muscular legs and leapt straight at Mara, who seemed frozen in fear. Its deadly maw opened wide, preparing to snap closed over Mara's throat.

Silmanus was the quicker, flinging up a shimmering shield of magical energy in front of Mara as he shrugged off his encumbering pack. To the wizard's surprise, however, the barguest just shrank into a puff of black smoke, passing through both the shield and Mara before reforming inside the group.

Everyone was pushed to the ground as the beast's massive form filled the space between them. Silmanus hit the ground hard as the barguest's muscled flanked appeared beside him and smashed him aside. Rising to his feet, Silmanus quickly rose and fired off a rapid series of magical icicles, which stuck fast in the beast's hind leg. It let out a ghostly howl of pain, spinning around and swatting at Silmanus with a massive paw.

Silmanus gasped in pain as he was flung through the air before landing on his shoulder and rolling into the base of a tree. Face twisted into a grimace, he struggled to rise but his body gave an agonized protest.

With a fierce cry, Ivar, also free of his backpack like the others, swung his mighty axe at the barguest. The monster just transformed

again, zipping through Ivar to reappear behind him, already preparing a deadly swipe at the man's exposed back.

Helga was there, however, axe racing to intercept the barguest's
sickle-like claws. A loud shriek pierced the air as the barguest's
claw scraped across the flat of Helga's axe. The mighty woman
tried to sweep her axe toward the barguest, but the beast dove
its head toward her, forcing Helga to drop into a roll, narrowly
avoiding decapitation as the barguest's jaws snapped shut above her
like a bear trap.

Yelling in some sort of crazed gibberish, Cara threw herself at
the barguest, spiked targe held out in front of her. The spike drove
into the monster's side, bringing forth a roar of agony and a slow
trickle of thick black blood. A mad light creeping into her eyes,
Cara stabbed furiously with her dirk while the barguest shook and
thrashed, trying to fling Cara off its flank.

Realizing there was no getting rid of the warrior stuck to its
side, the barguest transformed again, and Cara fell to the ground,
landing with a thud on her face. The barguest appeared suddenly
beside Norman, who instinctively dove to the ground just as a set
of lethal claws swept over him. Anne fired off an arrow, a perfect
shot that lodged itself in the monster's neck, although it hardly
seemed to notice.

Mara shook herself free of whatever fear had consumed her, firing
off a volley of arrows as she backed away from the beast. Apparently
tired of the annoying pinpricks raining down from Mara's bow, the
barguest turned and leapt, crashing into Mara and smashing her
into the ground. Hot breath that smelled of rotting flesh wafted
over Mara's face as the barguest's maw closed in.

Linos raced to Mara's rescue, flashing her a grim look as he
drove the barguest away. Mara rose shakily to her feet, trying

to control the racing of her heart. Mara had seen monsters in Needlewood many times before. They were a constant threat lurking like a shadow at the edge of the life she had built for herself, an ever-present danger that she had to be totally prepared for. Normally, it was just hulking ogres, serpentine basilisks, or tribes of orcs or goblins.

Mara had never seen any beast like the barguest before. It danced around the battlefield like a black cloud, darting around her friends as it switched from a hulking canine to an incorporeal shadow. It was a figment of pure nightmare that Mara hadn't even known existed.

She wondered what the appearance of such a terrifying creature could mean.

There was no time for wondering, however. Mara pushed aside her fear and steadied her breathing, taking a quick moment to survey the battlefield. Norman was on the ground, bleeding heavily from a series of slashes in his arm. Anne stood beside him, longsword drawn, glancing anxiously in every direction and swinging at the barguest anytime it got close enough. Linos, Cara, Ivar, and Helga were all running around, chasing after the spectral beast with their weapons at the ready. Silmanus stood off to the side, flinging spells at the barguest whenever it showed itself and trying to shield the others from its teeth and claws.

Mara fired off an arrow as her friends continued trying to pin down the barguest. Mara could see that it was beginning to tire, bleeding from many wounds and struggling to manoeuvre as quickly. That was good. They needed to keep up the pressure.

A sudden cry of pain rippled across the battlefield and Mara whipped her head around to see Cara pinned beneath the barguest. The barguest's teeth clamped down on Cara's arm and the woman shrieked as excruciating pain ripped through her. She was flung to the side, rolling across the ground as the barguest zipped after her.

Mara felt her chest tighten with fear for her friend, but she let it out in a relieved breath as Silmanus lobbed a ball of telekinetic energy at the beast, knocking it away from Cara's vulnerable figure.

With the barguest temporarily incapacitated, the group pounced, trying to defeat the beast right there. The barguest battled back, sluggishly trying to repel the thrusts and slashes that battered its fur-lined flanks. At last, Mara drove her sword into the mouth of the barguest, stabbing up into its brain and finally killing the beast.

A ghostly shriek filled the air, seeming to come from every direction. Mara clutched her ears in pain, gritting her teeth against the piercing scream. The barguest's body glowed a spectral blue before vanishing in a cloud of black smoke that rose into the sky and disappeared.

Panting, Mara lowered her sword to the ground, her entire body aching. She was exhausted, and the others were too. She didn't blame them; it had been a difficult fight.

Anne rushed over to Norman, worriedly inspecting her brother's wounds. Mara joined her, pouring water along the cuts in an attempt to clean away the blood. But the gashes were deep and kept bleeding.

Mara raised Norman's arm, sliding his pack underneath it. Tearing off the bottom of his sleeve, she pressed the rag firmly against the wounds, bringing a tortured grunt from Norman. Anne grabbed his other hand, murmuring assurances to her bother and trying to distract him from the pain.

Mara swore. "This isn't working," she muttered, rummaging through her bag for a spare belt, which she tied around Norman's arm in a tight tourniquet. Immediately, the bleeding slowed significantly. Mara produced a needle and thread and began stitching Norman's wounds closed. The injured Eiran grimaced and groaned with each pass of the needle.

After what seemed like an eternity to poor Norman, Mara tied off the sutures and bandaged the arm, releasing the tourniquet.

Norman slowly sat up, wincing as he gingerly touched the bandages.

"Know any spells for healing?" Norman managed, looking at Silmanus.

The wizard bit his lip. "I do have one," he said slowly. "But it's slow and excruciatingly painful."

"Do it," Mara ordered. "We need him able to fight. Those wounds are really bad too, perhaps more serious than a simple set of sutures can fix."

Silmanus nodded. "Hold him down, please," he instructed, fishing through his pack for his spellbook. Silmanus flipped through the pages until he found the spell he was looking for. Ivar and Helga pressed their strong hands down on Norman's shoulders while Linos and Mara pinned his legs.

Placing a slender hand on the bloodied bandage, Silmanus began chanting arcane words. His hand glowed white and magical energy rushed into Norman's arm.

Norman's screams were almost as loud as the barguest's, his tortured cries echoing through the forest. The pain was nearly unbearable, hurting even worse than the initial wound had. It was working, however, the cuts steadily knitting themselves back together. After about a minute of the worst pain Norman had ever experienced, the spell finished, and Norman's arm was as good as new.

There was no time to celebrate, however. Cara was injured as well, just as badly. A line of deep red punctures curved along either side of her arm in the shape of the barguest's jaws, bleeding heavily. The fierce woman was paling and weak, as crimson blood pooled beside her.

There was no time for a medical procedure. Cara was pinned down just as Norman had been and Silmanus set to work, beginning his chant once again. Cara shrieked as well, a bloodcurdling wail that seized Mara's heart. Another minute passed, and just like with Norman, Cara's wounds finished healing, leaving not even a scar across her wiry arm.

Cara sat up and gave Silmanus a weak nod.

"Hurt loch a bugger but I owe ye one, laddie," she said. "Ah owe ye a bevvy ur something."

"I assume a bevvy is a favour?" Silmanus guessed, confused by Cara's slang.

"Nae, better," Cara answered, stretching out her thumb and pinkie and tipping her thumb into her mouth as if it were a bottle.

"Ah," Silmanus said, cluing in. "A drink."

Cara threw a wink at Mara. "He's smarter than he looks, isnae he?"

Mara shook her head, helping Cara to her feet. "Come on, let's get your bed set up. You need some rest."

"Ah, shove it up yer erse! Ah dornt need rest, Ah need tae kill a Dark Elf!" Cara protested. "Let's fin' those shady buggers an' stick 'em!"

"It's almost dark and the light is weird right now," Silmanus put in. "Hunting Dark Elves when we can't see properly will be nearly impossible, fighting them even more so."

"Braw, yoo're right. We'll gie them tha' moorns nicht," Cara relented with a sigh. Silmanus figured she was saying they'd get them in the morning, but he wasn't quite sure. He never was with Cara.

Silmanus looked up at Mara. "You didn't mention there were barguests in these woods," he commented.

Mara held up her hands. "I didn't even know they were a figure of folk stories, much less actual creatures!" she replied. "You're telling me *you* knew they existed?"

Silmanus nodded. "I read a lot," he explained. "Barguests are a very notable part of Eiran legends. They weren't supposed to exist anymore though."

Mara frowned. "What do you mean, 'anymore'?" she asked slowly.

"Well, they were a part of the Dark Army in the Fell War," Silmanus explained. "Ravaged the northern kingdoms for centuries afterward. Supposedly, the last one was hunted down nearly two thousand years ago." There was a look in Silmanus' eyes as he spoke, and Mara didn't need him to explain it.

The appearance of Dark Elves followed by an attack from a supposedly extinct demon dog? That simply could not be coincidence. Something dark and evil was at work.

Mara just didn't know what.

She tried to push it out of her mind, however. One thing at a time, and the Dark Elves were the more immediate issue. The group laid down their sleeping gear but didn't build a fire. Not this close to the reported location of the Dark Elves. They ate their rations in silence, not even Linos up for conversation. Everyone was tired and sore after the battle.

Unfortunately for him, Silmanus had first watch, which dragged on for what seemed like days before Mara finally came to relieve him. Silmanus laid down on his mat and pulled his blanket around him, asleep an instant later.

Chapter 22:
Shatter

When Jeddo awoke, the first thing he realized was his throbbing headache.

It felt like his skull was contracting, closing in on his brain and squeezing the life out of it. With a grimace, Jeddo put a sluggish hand to his forehead, eyes squeezed shut and teeth gritted, as if touching his head would make it all better. It didn't.

Dehydration. That would be the death of Jeddo. The pain in his head would get worse and worse. He would grow more and more sluggish, his skin would shrivel, he would start fainting. All of this would grow worse and worse until finally, his kidneys stopped working and the toxins in his body killed him.

What a wonderful way to go.

Amber's plan was their best, and only, hope. But could it work? Would Zarat even believe Jeddo? What if he realized the whole thing was a scam? If he didn't beforehand, he certainly would when they marched off to The Forgotten Mountains. How would he and Amber even manage an escape? What about the others, would they be killed?

Jeddo sighed. It didn't matter. Unless they got water soon, they would all be dead. Glancing over at Evalyn and Percival, Jeddo realized that some of them might not even survive the next hour.

"Guards," Jeddo croaked, his voice husky and his throat dry.

"Guards, I need to speak with Zarat."

"That's *King* Zarat to you, filth," a guard's muffled voice replied.

"*King* Zarat then, please, I need to speak to *King* Zarat," Jeddo amended desperately.

Jeddo heard silence and wondered if the guards were just going to ignore him. But then the cell door creaked open and the two guards stepped inside to unlock Jeddo's cuffs.

The poor gnome was so weak, he could barely stand. He hadn't had any water since yesterday morning and for at least a week, although Jeddo really wasn't sure how long it had been since his capture, Jeddo hadn't been getting enough food or water. His legs didn't work properly, and the guards did more carrying than leading as they took Jeddo to the throne room.

The guards didn't need to shove Jeddo this time. They simply let go and the old, dehydrated gnome crumpled to the ground like a sack of potatoes. Struggling, Jeddo managed to bring himself to his knees and stare into the amused eyes of King Zarat.

"My, don't you look pitiful," the Dark Elf king smirked. "Have you reconsidered?"

Jeddo nodded weakly. "Yes," he whispered hoarsely. "I'll talk to her. But I don't know if I can convince her."

"Oh, you will," Zarat said confidently. Leaning forward in his throne, he hissed, "Because if you don't, I will kill you. If the dwarf still refuses to lead us into The Forgotten Mountains, I will kill you. And I will kill her parents, slowly, painfully, right in front of her. Then, when she breaks, I will kill her too."

Zarat sat back and crossed his legs. "But, I am a merciful lord, so I will give you this chance. Convince the dwarf to help within a week or I go back to starving you all."

"A week?" Jeddo blurted, hoping that such a reaction would make it easier to convince the king of his facade. "You don't leave for almost two!"

Zarat shrugged. "You have a week."

Jeddo pretended to seethe with frustration, but truthfully, the time was irrelevant. Just so long as Amber was "convinced" by the end of the time period, the prisoners would be given food and water.

After an "angry" hesitation, Jeddo nodded his agreement. "May I have some water?" Jeddo asked quietly.

"What am I?"

Jeddo was confused by the question. "A king?" he ventured uncertainly. *A monster, a heartless, wretched beast that even the deepest pits of hell would spit out in disgust,* Jeddo answered to himself.

"That I am, but I am not your king. What am I to you?"

My enemy, Jeddo thought, although he knew saying it out loud would sabotage everything. "My captor?"

Zarat smirked. "I suppose I am that. But I am also your superior. Your master. So, ask again, but address me properly this time."

With an irritated hesitation that he actually didn't have to fake, Jeddo repeated, "May I have some water…Master?" He spoke the last word with a great deal of reluctance, eyes flicking to the floor as he did.

A sadistic grin spread across Zarat's face. "Come here," he commanded. "Crawl."

Broiling with indignation, Jeddo complied, crawling sluggishly on hands and knees right up to the base of Zarat's throne. "Kiss my boot," Zarat ordered in an amused voice. He held out one of his polished leather boots, the black material glistening in the torchlight.

Jeddo glared up at Zarat, quivering angrily. "Do you want the water?" Zarat asked when Jeddo hesitated. The gnome nodded stiffly and Zarat leaned forward, hissing through gritted teeth. "Then kiss. My. Boot."

Hazel eyes never leaving Zarat's, Jeddo bent forward and pressed his lips to Zarat's boot, feeling like he might explode with fury at being so humiliated. Zarat suddenly flicked his leg forward, shoving Jeddo onto the floor. The gnome groaned as he landed on the hard stone, aching body screaming at him.

"Bring him some water," Zarat called absently to his guards. One left and returned a moment later with a glass full of water, which Jeddo snatched and drank greedily.

"Remember that, little gnome," Zarat said. "Remember the kindness your master showed you today. Am I not a kind and merciful lord?"

Jeddo glared, unable to hold back his outrage any longer. "You are the vilest and—"

"Am I not a kind and merciful lord?" Zarat interrupted loudly and pointedly.

Hesitating furiously, Jeddo replied with a simple, "Yes."

"Yes what?" the Dark Elf king demanded menacingly. Sindra gave a delighted giggle at seeing Jeddo so humiliated and indignant.

Lacing every word with enough fire to melt the smirk from Zarat's face, Jeddo corrected himself. "Yes, Master, you are a kind and merciful lord."

Zarat smiled in amusement. "That's more like it. Guards, take him back to his cell and bring his fellow inmates some food and drink."

With a little sigh of relief that Zarat had bought his act, Jeddo allowed the guards to heave him to his feet. As they led the gnome out of the throne room, Zarat called after him, "Oh, and gnome? If you are lying about helping me, I will know. If you and your friends attempt to cross me, I will know, and I assure you, you will be punished quite extensively."

Jeddo gave a grim nod and the guards led him back to his cell, tossing him inside and cuffing him up. They slammed the door shut and left, returning a few minutes later with a casket and a large waterskin.

Guralyn picked up the casket, as per usual, and opened it up with a gasp. "There's proper bread in here!" she exclaimed. "And meat!" Picking up a piece of dried meat, she took a tentative bite. "Properly dried meat too, not that overly salted crud they often give us!" Shaking her head in disbelief, Guralyn asked Jeddo, "What did ye do, kiss the darned king?"

Jeddo felt himself blush in embarrassment. "Yes, actually, he made me kiss his boot," Jeddo muttered, utterly humiliated. "It was the most demeaning thing I have ever done."

"Aye, he's a patronizin' lump o' pond scum, but ye got us some proper food, so it's all worth it in the end, eh?" Amber pointed out with an optimistic clap on Jeddo's back.

"I guess," Jeddo mumbled, not feeling very comforted at all. He wanted nothing more than to sink his rapier into that smug Dark Elf's heart.

"Well, cheer up," Amber said, passing Jeddo the casket. "Ye can have some o' my rations as a thanks."

Jeddo shook his head. "No," he protested, although he did desperately want the extra food. "You're hurt. Take your fill."

Amber flashed Jeddo a grateful smile, passing Jeddo the casket once she had taken her share.

Guralyn had been right; the meat *was* good. It was salty, of course, any dried meat was, but as salty as it should be, not over-seasoned to dehydrate the prisoners. Although Jeddo couldn't quite tell what animal it had come from, the meat had a wonder-fully smoky taste.

The bread was decent too. Far from the greatest bread Jeddo had tasted, although that came as little surprise considering the agricultural state of Vanaria, but it was infinitely better than the maggoty biscuits they'd been served before. It was soft and fluffy and Jeddo savoured every bite.

Finally, the water came to him and he once again finished the waterskin with deep and greedy gulps. The water wasn't cold and it tasted leathery, as always, but it was still water.

"So, I take it he bought the plan?" Amber murmured quietly,

hoping the guards wouldn't hear.

Jeddo nodded. "He said I have a week, so pretend to be stubborn about it for a few days before giving in. Also, he told me he'd know if I wasn't convincing you at all, so we need to stage a bit of an argument."

Speaking louder now, Jeddo said, "Look, Amber, we need to help Zarat. I know you don't like it, I don't either, but it's our only hope of survival."

Amber gave a furious snort. "Ye think I'm fer helpin' a *Dark Elf*?"

"It doesn't matter what he is, he'll kill us if we don't!"

"He'll kill us anyway! Ye don't really think the treacherous bastard will be lettin' us go after this, do ye?" Amber roared, throwing a wink at Jeddo.

"Well, not let us *go*, but he said he'll at least improve our conditions," Jeddo said. "Who knows, maybe he *will* let us go eventually."

"Yer trustin' the word o' a Dark Elf?" Amber said skeptically. "Ye're a bigger fool than I'd thought, and an even bigger one than that if ye think I'll be helpin' someone who tortured me parents!"

Jeddo raised his eyebrows, impressed with how well Amber was acting all this out. Although, thinking of it, she really only had to feign the anger; everything else she said was true. "Amber…" Jeddo ventured.

"Don't ye 'Amber' me!" the dwarf snapped. "I'm not helpin' Zarat and there ain't nothin' ye can do t' change that, so ye can take yer pleadin' t' someone who actually cares!"

Jeddo heard some mumbling in Dark Elvish from outside the cell, followed by the oh-so-quiet footfalls of Dark Elves. Their guards were probably bored and off to do something else.

"Well, how was that?" Amber asked.

"Wonderful," Jeddo told her. "You played your part perfectly."

Amber shrugged. "Didn't take much pretendin'," she said, confirming Jeddo's suspicions.

"So, what now?" Harik questioned. "We just sit here for a

couple o' weeks an' wait for them t' let us go? Ye know they won't be takin' all o' us."

"That is true," Jeddo said slowly with a nervous glance and Evalyn and Percival. "They're planned to be executed." He hoped the humans hadn't heard and was already opening his mouth to mention something else, but Evalyn had heard him and her distressed sobs interrupted the gnome.

"I knew we never should have come down here!" the woman wailed. Percival hugged her tight a grim expression on his face.

Jeddo opened his mouth again, but Amber spoke first. "What exactly did ye do t' wind up here?"

"I'm a craftsman," Percival explained. "Or I was. I get jewels and metals from the Fire Dwarves and turn them into works of art that even the elves have admitted are impressive. I shape the metal and set the jewels and Evalyn adds her magic touch to style the pieces.

"I've had a hard time finding a market back in Lochadia though, so I decided to try selling in some of the trading posts around the Fire Mountains." A shadow crossed over the man's face. "On our way between two of them though, we stumbled across a Dark Elf convoy. Evalyn and I tried to run away, but we were too slow. We were caught. Taken prisoner for trespassing and spying, even though we didn't see a thing." Panic came over his face. "Are they really planning to execute us?"

"Yes, but—" Jeddo began, but he was cut off again by another sob from Evalyn.

"We'll never get out of here!" she cried.

"Maybe we can convince the elves ye're o' importance," Harik suggested, interrupting Jeddo, who was now getting quite annoyed.

"What would you say though?" Percival asked. "We're just ordinary humans!"

"There's no need—" Jeddo began but Amber interrupted him.

"We could make it a condition," she suggested. "Maybe I agree only to help if the humans are spared."

"What about the elves?" Percival asked selflessly. "We need to save them too."

Thalassar shook his head. "Don't worry, the Dark Elves need us."

"Why?" Amber asked.

Thalassar tapped his head with a grin. "They need this thing," he answered. With an apologetic glance at his wife, he added, "And Ayra's, too."

"This is all quite irrelevant, if you'd just listen—" Jeddo started again.

"What're they needin' yer minds fer?" Amber inquired over top of the gnome.

"We're arcanium experts," Thalassar said proudly. "I think they need our help building their weapons. Maybe even mining, if you've all forgotten how." Thalassar looked at the dwarves with that last statement.

"What're ye sayin'?" Harik demanded indignantly. "That I'm fer forgettin' me people's proudest achievement?"

Thalassar held up his hand in surrender. "I meant nothing by it, good dwarf. I just didn't know if you still knew how to perform such a difficult operation. It's been a hundred years, after all."

"I remember how," Harik said defensively. "I'll need me tools, but I remember. And I remember what those tools look like too!"

"It really doesn't matter—" Jeddo said tensely, quite annoyed at being interrupted so many times.

Guralyn cut him off. "Not that ye'd ever help the Dark Elves, would ye, Harik?"

Harik shook his head fiercely. "Not in a hunnerd years."

"It's *been* a hunnerd years," Amber pointed out.

"Well, not in a thousand, then!" Harik amended. Narrowing his eyes suspiciously, Harik accused, "How about ye? Are ye helpin' em then?"

Thalassar's eyes flashed dangerously. "How dare you suggest that I would do such a thing!" he snapped.

Harik sat up straight. "Oh, ye think ye can tell me what I can and can't be doin' now, eh?" he roared. "Typical elf!"

"I'm not saying that at all! You're just blowing it out of proportion like a typical dwarf!"

"Ye lookin' down yer nose at us, elf?" Guralyn growled.

"You know what, yes, I am!" Thalassar seethed. "You dwarves are all so stubborn and irrational, blowing up at the slightest suggestion that perhaps you're at fault for something! I am quite sick of it!"

"Don't ye speak t' me parents that way!" Amber yelled. "I'll break yer skull open if ye do!"

"Touch him and I'll break your neck," Ayra hissed balefully.

Jeddo was quite finished with all the yelling and interrupting. "Will you all just shut up?!" he screamed. The entire cell fell silent and all eyes snapped to him. "Thank you! Just for the record, your petty rivalries are childish and irrational and need to stop if we are going to get out of here."

Amber gave an exasperated sigh. "Jeddo, we've got a week t' wait before that! There's no gettin' out sooner, ye said so yeself!"

"If you would all just listen to me, you'd know that isn't true!" Jeddo snapped angrily. "I can get us out!"

"With what?" Amber snorted doubtfully.

Grinning Jeddo reached into his sleeve and pulled out the glass from earlier. In their arrogance, the Dark Elves had forgotten all about it and Jeddo, his knack for pickpocketing still as strong as ever, had managed to slip it unnoticed into his sleeve.

Amber wasn't quite catching on. "What're ye goin' t' do with a bloody glass?"

Grin broadening, Jeddo held the glass up to the light. "It isn't a glass though," he said ominously before smashing it against the floor. The glass shattered into dozens and dozens of shards, a few of which were rather long and pointed. A knowing look came over Amber's face as Jeddo scooped up one of the shards.

"It's a sharpened stick."

CHAPTER 23:
JAILBREAK

HIDING ALL OF THE SHARDS HADN'T BEEN EASY, ESPE-
cially since the prisoners were all chained up, but the group had
managed, tucking the useless pieces away against the wall and
saving the three good ones. Jeddo and Amber each held a long,
pointed piece of glass concealed in their palms while Ayra, who
was reportedly very skilled in the use of knives and daggers, hid
the other.

"Guards, we're needin' an audience with the king," Amber
called out.

"You don't have the right to request an audience," the guards
replied haughtily.

"It's about the quest," Jeddo said. "Amber said she'll help but
she has some conditions."

"King Zarat as already given you the conditions."

"Well, I've got some new ones," Amber snapped impatiently.
"And I'd like t' be takin' them up with him."

Jeddo played his ace. "Do you really want to be responsible for denying the king his chance to get what he desires?"
Jeddo challenged.

There was a long hesitation from the guards before the door
finally opened. The Dark Elves glided over to Amber, drawing out
their keys to uncuff her.

"He comes too," Amber demanded. With an irritated sigh, one of the guards moved to uncuff Jeddo.

The Dark Elves hoisted Amber and Jeddo onto their feet. Amber used the movement to conceal her attack, swinging her arm up as if to steady herself. As she did, she slid the shard of glass forward into her fingers and stabbed it into the guard's vulnerable throat, noticing Jeddo do the same.

Blood bubbled out of the wound, the Dark Elf sputtering angrily as he tried to sound an alarm. Amber wouldn't let that happen. Leaving the glass embedded in the elf's throat, she grabbed both sides of his head and twisted violently, snapping the Dark Elf's neck with a satisfying crack. Jeddo used his piece to cut the trachea of his Dark Elf, silencing the guard before he had the chance to cry out.

Jeddo and Amber took the guards' keys and began uncuffing the rest of the prisoners, who all thanked Amber and Jeddo gratefully. Thalassar rolled his sore wrists. "Been far too long since I had those things off."

Harik gave him a grim look. "Knowin' what happens when the bastards *do* uncuff ye, ye should be grateful they haven't," he said, looking pointedly at Amber's injuries.

There was no time for celebrating the removal of their shackles, however. "You two, put their uniforms on," Jeddo ordered, motioning to Thalassar and Ayra.

The High Elves crinkled their noses. "I will not wear the garb of any *Dark Elf*," Thalassar spat. "Besides, they'll know we aren't Dark Elves, our skin is too silvery."

"Ye want t' get out o' here?" Amber roared. Thalassar gave a meek nod. "Then put on the damned clothes!"

Thalassar sighed. "All of you, turn around. I'll not change in front of you."

Amber shook her head, turning around as instructed. "Elves," she muttered.

After a few minutes, Thalassar announced that they were done. The two High Elves were now dressed in the black clothes of the Dark Elves, twin daggers sheathed along their belts, the bottom of their hauberks poking out from beneath their black jackets.

Ayra handed off her piece of glass to Harik, who took it with a wicked grin. "It's goin' t' feel good t' drive this into some Dark Elf's pretty throat," he said.

"Does anyone know where they keep our stuff?" Jeddo inquired. Amber was glad he'd thought of that. She missed her warhammer.

Everyone shook their heads in answer. "Not a clue," Harik said.

"Perhaps down the right corridor?" Ayra suggested. "I've never seen any sort of storeroom going down the left."

Amber shrugged. "Worth a shot," she decided. Turning to Ayra and Thalassar, she instructed, "Ye two are guards. Ye're movin' us t' a new cell on order o' the king. It was one o' me demands, we'll say." Shooting a pointed glance at her father, Amber added, "As much as I'd like t' be bashin' some skulls in, we don't want t' be raisin' any alarms, so don't ye go stabbin' any Dark Elves until I get me hammer."

Thalassar sighed. "That, my dear dwarf, will be the hardest part of the whole operation."

Amber grinned. "I know what ye mean."

"Well, let's not waste any more time. Come on, let's go!" Jeddo urged. He put his hands behind his back and stepped out of the cell, side by side with Amber as he turned right. Harik and Guralyn followed, with Evalyn and Percival behind them and Thalassar and Ayra taking the rear, putting on the haughtiest faces they could manage. Which, considering they were elves, was not a very difficult thing for them to do.

The group walked quietly down the dark stone passage, glancing around nervously as they searched for something that might serve as a locker for confiscated equipment.

Amber began considering the very real possibility that their gear had just been dumped. The Dark Elves likely had no need of it, after all. Why bother keeping it?

She didn't have the time to consider that possibility any further because right at that moment, a pair of Dark Elf guards walked around the corner. They stopped suddenly, looking suspiciously at the prisoners.

"Where are you taking these prisoners?" one of the guards asked.

"They're being transferred to a new cell," Thalassar answered smoothly. "King Zarat agreed to it in exchange for their coopera- tion. Waste of my time, if you ask me though."

The guard smirked. "Well, carry on then. I don't want to make you spend more time around these disgusting creatures than you have to." The two Dark Elves continued on, walking right past Thalassar and Ayra without a second glance.

Amber allowed herself a slight sigh of relief. They hadn't been caught. She was just about to take another step when she heard a very unnerving sound: a boot turning against the floor.

"Hang on," one of the guards began. "Aren't there supposed to be two elves with them?"

Thalassar and Ayra exchanged a glance just as realization swept over the guard. The two Dark Elves drew their daggers but the High Elves were quicker, already slashing at the guards' throats. Both Dark Elves went down, blood seeping forth from their necks like a fountain.

Thalassar wiped off his daggers on one of the guard's uniforms before returning them to their sheaths. "I have been waiting to do that for a hundred years," he lamented wistfully.

"Durned elf, stealin' all the fun," Harik grumbled. In response, Thalassar took off the guard's belt and tossed it to Harik. Ayra did the same for Guralyn.

"Here," he said. "You can kill the next one."

Harik grinned as he put on the belt, handing his glass shard to Percival. "I always knew ye were a good one, elf."

"Come on, let's go!" Jeddo hissed.

"Shouldn't we do something about the bodies?" Evalyn suggested.

"Doesn't matter. By the time anyone finds them, we'll be armed enough t' crush their pretty skulls!" Amber exclaimed.

After just a few more bends and corners, a door made of some black metal loomed on their left. Not a cell door, an actual door, with a rose-shaped doorknob and a label written in the harsh—yet also surprisingly beautiful—Dark Elvish script.

"This has got to be it," Jeddo breathed as Thalassar moved toward the door, keys in hand. He jiggled several around in the lock until finally, he felt a click. Turning the handle, Thalassar opened the door.

Inside, rows upon rows of weapons and equipment lined several tall shelves. None were of Dark Elf make.

With a delighted laugh, Amber spotted her beautiful warhammer and fine plate armour, grouped up together along with her backpack, shield, axe, and underclothes on one of the higher shelves. Next to it, a one-of-a-kind red jacket, jewelled rapier, and a backpack and clothing. Amber looked down at Jeddo with a grin.

She reached up on tiptoe, waggling her fingers which fell just a hair short of the handle of her warhammer. Face reddening in embarrassment, Amber tried again, but to no avail.

"I'm too short," she mumbled, looking at the floor.

Jeddo tried to hide an amused grin, as did the elves. "What was that?" Thalassar asked teasingly, even though he had heard properly.

"I said I'm too short," Amber snapped. "Could ye get them down fer me?" Amber's whole face was as red as Jeddo's jacket, eyes boring shamefully into the ground at the prospect of asking someone else, and an elf, of all people, for help.

Thalassar strode over, barely able to contain his grin as he reached up and retrieved Amber's equipment, doing the same for Jeddo. Thalassar paused as he grabbed the rapier, taking a moment to admire its hilt.

Thalassar drew the blade from its sheath, his hand almost too big for the gnome-sized handle. He bounced his arm, feeling the balance of the rapier before giving it a few practised swings.

"Shorter than what I'm used to, but that's a fine blade you have," Thalassar complimented, returning it to its sheath and handing it to Jeddo, who took it with a grateful nod. "Beautifully balanced. The gnomes made that?"

Jeddo nodded. "Forged by my own cousin, actually."

"Well, the gnomes have as much skill with the anvil as they do with clockwork," Thalassar said with a warm smile.

"Don't ye be forgettin' about me hammer!" Amber said a bit defensively. "Finest piece o' smithy work ye'll ever lay eyes on!"

Thalassar grinned a little. "Well, I beg to differ on that, but yes, it is indeed a marvellous weapon," he agreed, noting the intricate golden designs woven into the hammer's bulky head. "I have always respected the dwarves' talent for metalcraft, even if the weapons they make are unwieldly and graceless."

"Let's see how graceful ye are when ye've taken a swing o' me hammer t' yer little twig leg!" Amber shot back, although not with any malice, instead wearing a jesting grin.

Thalassar grinned back. "You'll have to catch me first," he said with a wink before striding off to look for his own weapons.

Amber noticed Percival and Evalyn standing still. "Ye don't have anything?"

Percival shook his head. "Not other than our clothes, no."

"Here, I've found my equipment," Ayra called, holding up a shimmering chain shirt made of silver metal. "You can have the Dark Elves' stuff. I have no further need of it."

Amber hid herself away in a corner, not particularly wanting to change in front of anyone else. It took her a little while—plate armour was very tedious to put on, especially with injured fingers—but she eventually emerged, fully dressed in her glinting red armour and giving her warhammer a practised swing, testing the weight of her shield.

"Oh, how I missed ye," Amber sighed.

"Now aren't ye a sight fer sore eyes," Harik whistled. He was dressed in a bearskin tunic and simple brown pants; neither he nor Guralyn had been armed when they were kidnapped.

"Ye look like a true dwarvish warrior, me girl," Guralyn said with a smile, also dressed in simple dwarfish clothing.

"Ye're needin' some weapons," Amber pointed out, completely ignoring the compliments. She handed her axe to her father, thank goodness she always packed a spare, and scanned the shelves for something for Guralyn. She eventually found a hefty broadsword that appeared to be of human craft. It was relatively simple, with a spherical pommel and a leather-wrapped handle.

"This'll suit ye fine," Amber said, handing the blade to her mother. Guralyn took it out, testing its balance before swinging it in a couple wide sweeps.

"This takes me back," she said. "Ye know I used to be a member o' the cavalry."

Amber raised her eyebrows. "Ye did?"

Guralyn nodded. "I retired after I had ye, but I did. Rode around on me black bear, swingin' a great big hammer at all the filthy orcs and goblins that slipped through Pyradia. Those were some good days. How I met yer father, actually."

Amber was about to ask for the story, but she was interrupted by a little cough. Ayra was standing there, wearing a blue jerkin embroidered with a silver unicorn overtop of her hauberk and green tunic. A pair of slim leather bracers, decorated with leaves in typical elvish fashion, were clasped around her wrists, one of which extended down the three middle fingers of Ayra's right hand to form a finger guard for archery. She wore a pair of tall leather boots atop her brown leggings and a long, narrow sword was sheathed across her back. A quiver of arrows hung from her belt and a gorgeous yew recurve was clutched in her left hand.

A silver unicorn with sapphire eyes was pinned above her heart, marking her as one of Faeryln's Royal Vanguards.

Thalassar stood beside her, dressed almost identically and also sporting a Royal Vanguard sigil. They both cut stunning figures, even if they did appear gaunt and ragged, with plenty of dirt and grime coating their silvery faces and a healthy amount of dust caking their uniforms. Looking closely, Amber could even see that the uniforms were just a little too large for their thinned, starved figures. Still, Amber found their appearance quite inspiring, even if they were elves.

She was surprised to see they had found their equipment. They'd been prisoners for about a hundred years. The fact that the Dark Elves had kept the weapons, armour, and clothing for so long was rather shocking. Honestly, Amber hadn't even expected to find her own stuff. But then, Amber figured they must make nice trophies. And where was the sense in disposing of fine armour and weaponry when it could potentially be reused?

Frankly though, she didn't really care about the why or the how. All that mattered was that they were now armed to the teeth.

Percival and Evalyn came out from behind a shelf, clad in Dark Elf armour. Now that Amber looked at it, the Dark Elf armour was very similar to what Thalassar and Ayra wore, just black and much more menacing. The two humans looked very uncertain, nervously fingering their daggers.

"Have ye ever fought before?" Amber asked them.

Percival shook his head. "Never even held a sword."

That was bad. Percival and Evalyn wouldn't stand even the slightest chance against a Dark Elf warrior. "Well, don't ye worry, we'll take care o' the fightin'," Amber said. "More fun fer the rest o' us!"

"Ye watch yerself, girl," Harik said sternly. "Ye're still hurtin' from yer torture, o' that I'm certain."

Amber realized he was right. She hadn't really noticed it

through all the adrenaline, but her body screamed and ached and she was still quite hungry and thirsty. The others probably were too. Amber figured adrenaline was the only thing keeping the prisoners on their feet.

Still, Thalassar and Ayra looked confident indeed, despite how thin and weak they were. They stood strong with determined expressions, as did Harik and Guralyn, as did Jeddo. All five of them were weak and tired, but they were ready for a fight.

So was Amber.

"Ah, quit yer worryin'," she said, shrugging away the pain. "Ye'll be fightin' me as much as the Dark Elves t' get yerself a kill!"

Harik clapped a rough hand on Amber's shoulder, sending a little jolt of pain up Amber's arm, which she completely ignored. "That's me girl!" he roared. "Now let's get out o' this miserable prison!"

Harik whirled on Thalassar suddenly. "Ye keep good on yer word, elf," he said. "Next kill is mine, ye hear me?"

Thalassar held up his hands. "My dear Harik, I wouldn't have it any other way."

Harik shook his head and turned back around, striding eagerly out of the storeroom. "Come here, ye shifty elf buggers!" he murmured to himself. "Me axe is waitin'!"

The other prisoners—or rather, ex-prisoners—were quick to follow. Harik and Amber took the point, with Guralyn and Jeddo diagonally behind each respectively, Percival and Evalyn tucked nervously in between, and Thalassar and Ayra taking the rear, arrows nocked and ready, forming a sort of ragtag hexagon.

The sound of footfalls crept around the corner, followed by a cry of distress in Dark Elvish. They'd found the bodies.

Amber grinned and tightened her grip on her warhammer. This was going to be fun.

Time to crack some heads.

CHAPTER 24:
THE PALACE

WITH A LOW, RUMBLING CRY, HARIK RAISED HIS AXE AND leapt around the corner. Five Dark Elves stood there, one of whom was running away to raise the alarm. Not on Harik's watch.

Raising his arms above his head, the mighty dwarf threw his axe. It spun through the air with deadly force, cutting through the fleeing Dark Elf's armour and digging deep into his back. With a cry, the Dark Elf was thrown forward, landing dead on his face.

The other four Dark Elves smirked. "Now you're outnumbered and unarmed," one observed, slowly pulling out his daggers with a sinister grin.

"Ye think I'm alone?" Harik scoffed.

Amber jumped out from around the corner, hollering a fierce battle cry as she raced toward the Dark Elves. Jeddo and Guralyn followed quickly, as did Thalassar and Ayra.

Grinning as she did, Amber threw herself at a Dark Elf, crashing into the lithe warrior and bringing him to the ground beneath her weight. He cried out in pain, cries Amber soon silenced with a fierce shield bash that likely fractured the elf's skull.

Jeddo danced toward a Dark Elf, rapier twirling as he batted aside a couple hasty dagger strikes. His small, nimble form was able to manoeuvre around the tall Dark Elf quite easily and Jeddo had soon landed three crippling strikes along the elf's legs. The

Dark Elf toppled to his knees and Jeddo stabbed his rapier into the elf's heart.

"This is for the torture," Jeddo hissed into the elf's pointed ear, happy to have finally gotten a bit of revenge.

Guralyn ran at her chosen foe, sword drawn as she bore down on her startled enemy. Suddenly, an arrow whizzed over her shoulder, skewering the Dark Elf right through the throat. Another arrow dropped the final Dark Elf simultaneously, both Dark Elves dead before their heads hit the ground.

Guralyn spun around angrily, glaring at the two High Elves who each already had another arrow nocked. "That was *my* kill!" Guralyn shouted.

Ayra shrugged sheepishly. "Couldn't help myself," she said with a grin.

"Ye owe me fer that!" Guralyn declared, pointing her sword at the elf before turning back around and falling into formation.

The prisoners made it out of the dungeon with no further trouble, ascending the stone stairs and arriving in the black tiled palace. A flight of stairs rose up in front of them and two corridors, one to the left and one to the right, stretched out beside them. Black banners bearing crossed silver daggers lined the walls, along with torches set in black metal braces. They all stopped suddenly, realizing no one knew where to go.

"Um…which way?" Amber asked, glancing around.

"Right is right?" Percival suggested uncertainly.

Amber shrugged. She didn't have any better ideas. "Right is right," she agreed, turning in that direction with Harik by her side.

The group slunk down the corridor, Thalassar and Ayra walking backward to ensure no one could sneak up on them from behind. The two elves moved with absolute silence, hundreds of years of practice not forgotten, their padded boots making not a sound upon the glistening floor.

The others, however, were much nosier, a symphony of squeaks and thumps as they walked along, trying to be quiet but really not succeeding very well. Amber was particularly noisy, her metal plate armour clacking and scraping with every step she took. Each clatter of her armour seemed to echo endlessly off the smooth stone walls of the corridor.

The prisoners quickly noticed how eerily quiet the palace was. Normally, castles were bustling with the sounds of servants rushing from this place to that, cooks preparing kingly feasts in their kitchens, guards patrolling the halls, and nobles laughing and talking amongst themselves. The only sounds in this palace were made by the prisoners.

Amber bit her lip. Another fork. There weren't even any windows to help them get their bearings, just endless black walls, banners, and candles.

"Go right," Thalassar suggested, turning his head to observe the situation.

"Why right?" Amber asked.

"Well, we went straight out of the dungeon, then right. If we go right again, we'll be looping back to the edge of the palace," he explained. Amber tried to visualize the C-shaped movement he was describing.

"Unless the dungeon isn't at the edge of the palace, in which case the direction becomes irrelevant," Ayra pointed out.

"And if it's at the other edge, going right actually just takes us deeper into the castle," Percival realized.

"So which way am I turnin' then?" Amber pressed, frustrated. She could not picture at all what her comrades were discussing.

"Right," Thalassar said while Percival simultaneously suggested, "Left."

"Eeny meeny miny moe," Jeddo proposed.

Amber looked at him with a confused expression. "'Eeny meeny miny moe'?" she asked, not familiar with the expression.

"Yeah, eeny meeny miny moe," Jeddo repeated. He turned

to everyone in the group, all of them wearing confused expressions. "Has no one heard of eeny meeny miny moe?" Head shakes answered him.

"It's a way of randomly choosing something," Jeddo explained, still a bit skeptical that no one knew of the operation. "Really? No one else knows what this is?"

"No, will ye just get on with it already?" Amber snapped impatiently.

"Alright, alright," Jeddo said. "Eeny meeny miny moe, catch a goblin by the toe…" With each word he said, Jeddo pointed his finger between the two corridors. "…if he hollers, let him go, eeny meeny miny moe." Jeddo finished with his finger pointing to the right. "Right it is."

"I'm confused, why would you catch a goblin by its toe?" Thalassar asked. "Knocking it out or using a net is much more effective."

"Forget yer net, ye grab goblins by the throat!" Harik argued. "And don't let the durned thing go, or it'll bring more o' its kind along t' stab ye!"

Jeddo gave them both an exasperated look. "It's a kids' song!" he exclaimed.

"Ye're teachin' kids t' let goblins go?" Harik criticized skeptically.

"Oh, for Gods' sakes," Jeddo muttered, resting his forehead in his hand. "Let's just go already."

They carried on to the right, Harik still confused by the lesson of the rhyme. As they passed by a flight of stairs, a young voice cried out in alarm.

Amber snapped her head to the side to see a Dark Elf woman hugging a little Dark Elf girl protectively, staring nervously down at the prisoners as she shouted what Amber assumed were threats in Dark Elvish.

Instinctively, Thalassar and Ayra both took aim, but upon realizing they were just aiming at a mother and her child, they lowered their bows uncertainly.

"What're we t' do about them?" Amber asked.

"Kill them!" Harik blurted as if it were the most obvious thing in the world. "They're bloody Dark Elves, fer Gods' sakes!"

"She's just a child!" Ayra exclaimed, looking sympathetically at the little girl, who seemed genuinely terrified.

"She's a *Dark Elf*," Harik argued, gripping his axe tighter. "They're not fer carin' about how old or young *our* people are!"

The mother was still shouting, slowly backing up the stairs.

"She's goin' t' summon the guards," Harik warned. "We need t' do somethin' now, and I vote fer somethin' involvin' me axe!"

Jeddo was already moving, however. Looking the mother right in her silver eyes, Jeddo slowly bent down, one hand raised above his head. He placed his rapier on the ground with a soft clatter, raising his other hand as he slowly stood back up. The mother stopped yelling and narrowed her eyes suspiciously.

Jeddo pointed to himself. "Jeddo," he said, figuring that putting a name on himself might make him seem like less of a threat. He motioned to the group and raised his hands above his head as if in surrender, trying to communicate that, "We are not going to hurt you."

The Dark Elf woman nodded slowly and relaxed a bit, seeming to understand.

Jeddo gestured again to the group, then mimed walking and opening a door before spreading his arms wide. "We are trying to get out." Jeddo was really hoping he had made sense with that one.

The Dark Elf seemed to understand though. She nodded again, eyes narrowed once more suspiciously.

Jeddo pointed to her, tapped his head, made a searching gesture, and mimed a door again. "Do you know where the exit is?"

The Dark Elf seemed stuck in contemplation. Jeddo understood why. After all, all four races the Dark Elves called enemy were standing before her. Jeddo knew that if *he* saw Dark Elves in *his* home, he would summon help immediately.

Perhaps it was the weary state of the group or the many visible injuries on Amber. Perhaps the Dark Elf simply didn't care for her nation, or perhaps she didn't believe they were the enemy. Whatever the reason was, the Dark Elf woman nodded and pointed straight, then right, then left.

Jeddo gave her a grateful smile and threw a wink at the Dark Elf girl, who giggled in response. "Keep going, right, left," Jeddo said to himself with a nod. "Then freedom."

The prisoners rushed off, wondering why the woman had helped them.

Not that it mattered. There was another fork up ahead, but there was no indecision this time. Amber led the group right, hoping that the Dark Elf hadn't been lying.

They rushed along, moving quicker now that they knew where to go. The next fork loomed up ahead, with one corridor going left, one going right, and one straight ahead. Freedom was just around the corner.

Shouts of alarm suddenly echoed down the corridor as a patrol of guards, six in total, emerged from the right-hand passage. They each drew their weapons and dashed toward the prisoners.

"Ha *ha*, time fer some fun!" Harik cried excitedly, rushing to meet the charging elves.

Thalassar and Ayra immediately opened fire but their first arrows were dodged, screeching off the tile and skittering down the corridor. An instant later, the two elves each had another arrow in the air, and this time, their aim was truer. One Dark Elf took a hit to the shoulder while the other cried out and clutched his thigh. Two more arrows were all it took to finish them off.

Ayra already had another arrow nocked and was taking aim at another Dark Elf but Thalassar pushed her arm down. "No, we promised to let the dwarves have their fun."

Guralyn gave a happy roar, broadsword swinging as she rushed to meet her foe. Sparks flew as Guralyn's sword screeched along the crossed daggers of the Dark Elf. The elf kept moving his legs, running forward and dropping his block as soon as his torso was out of the way, swinging the daggers at Guralyn's side.

The dwarf warrior was a hardened combatant, however, and she had been waiting for decades for her revenge. Feeling more alive than she had in a century, Guralyn easily kept pace with her Dark Elf foe, exulting in the familiar feeling of a sword in her hand.

The Dark Elf stood no chance.

Harik swung his axe down in a mighty chop but his Dark Elf just dashed out of the path of the axe, smirking as he stabbed at Harik's unarmoured side.

Harik knew that, in a fight, anger was a dangerous emotion to have, as it often clouded one's judgement and left one susceptible to mistakes and oversights.

Instead of flushing away the anger, however, Harik simply harnessed it, fuelling his movements with the red-hot flame of rage as he blocked the Dark Elf's attack and came on hard with his axe, fury springing into his eyes as he battled.

Amber, for her part, was swinging her warhammer low at her Dark Elf's ankles, although the nimble elf just leapt aside and spun, thrusting her daggers down as she came out of the twirl. Amber anticipated the strike easily, blocking it effortlessly.

Amber was not afraid of Dark Elves. She had been tortured, starved, and imprisoned, but none of that mattered now that freedom was close. All of the pain and the suffering was swallowed by the hope and anger that welled up within her, driving every swing of her hammer.

Jeddo flashed and spun his little rapier, twisting aside a series of deft thrusts and slashes from the Dark Elf's daggers. Using his small size to his advantage, Jeddo tucked into a roll and passed right through the elf's outstretched legs, springing back up behind her. Jeddo thrusted at the Dark Elf's back, although she instinctively leapt to the side, spinning on her toes as she landed.

Jeddo could not help the flood of memories that came rushing back. The sturdy tile beneath his feet became a rocking deck, the sweat on his skin turned to the salty spray of the sea. He was back on the *Ocean's Hearth*, defending his crew from a Dark Elf raid.

He wouldn't lose a second time.

Thalassar and Ayra watched the battle unfold with eyebrows raised and bows lowered. Both had been ready to jump into the fray if the need arose, but there clearly was not going to be a need. The other prisoners fought skillfully and furiously, and before long, the Dark Elves all lay dead on the floor.

The elven pair wore very impressed expressions as the others turned around, their battles won. "You each have commendable skill with a weapon," Thalassar complimented as he went to retrieve his arrows. "I am impressed."

Jeddo took a bow, sheathing his rapier as he did. "Your prowess with archery is remarkable as well," Jeddo replied, mimicking Thalassar's refined manner of speech and glancing over at the fallen Dark Elves, two of whom sported an arrow perfectly placed in their heart. "Lady Ayra's as well, of course."

"Such polite manners from a gnome," Ayra commented with a little grin. "Were you but a little taller, there are some who might mistake you for an elf."

"Can we spare the fancy talk and just get out o' here?" Harik interjected impatiently, pointing to the left passage. "If that Dark Elf was tellin' the truth, our escape is just around the corner."

"Lead the way, good dwarf!" Thalassar called, earning himself a head shake from Harik.

With Amber and Harik on point again, they moved to the left passage, Thalassar and Ayra each aiming their bows down the other passages in case there were more Dark Elves coming.

"Aha, she was tellin' the truth!" Amber exclaimed excitedly. At the end of the corridor were two tall, black doors, covered in barbs and sporting two massive daggers crossed over them.

Two more Dark Elves were in the passage, weapons drawn as they moved to investigate the sounds from the corridor the prisoners had just come from.

"Surprise," Harik said with a grin before Thalassar and Ayra each sent an arrow streaking toward the charging Dark Elves. Their accuracy was impeccable and both Dark Elves went down instantly, arrows in their chests.

Harik turned to the High Elves, eyebrows raised. "Well, I always knew ye two were good fer somethin'."

Thalassar just grinned as he pulled his arrow free, wiped it clean, and returned it to his quiver with a flourish. Harik rolled his eyes.

Ayra breathed deeply as she eyed the doors. "There's a gate with guard towers outside these doors," she recalled, straining her memory back to one of the reconnaissance missions she had performed many years ago. "They'll have a clear shot at us for the length of the walkway. We walk out of those doors, we're likely to be riddled with arrows."

"What about battlements?" Jeddo asked. "Surely there's a wall around the palace."

Ayra frowned, diving deep into her memory. "There is, but the one around the palace isn't meant to house guard patrols. It's just there to keep unauthorized civilians out. Still though, those towers are going to be an issue."

"What do ye propose we do then?" Harik asked anxiously, frustrated that escape was so close yet impaired by another obstacle.

Amber turned to the High Elves. "Do ye think ye can take 'em out?"

Thalassar looked at Ayra with a raised eyebrow and she nodded back at him. "Yes."

Amber nodded, a plan forming in her head. "Right, here's what we're goin' t' do. Ma, pa, yer goin' t' open those doors. There're probably a couple o' guards right outside. Me and Jeddo will take them and draw the fire from the guard towers. Ye two need t' take out the archers fast."

"And what about us?" Evalyn asked, feeling rather useless.

"Get back and don't get killed," Amber instructed.

"But I want to help!" she complained and Percival nodded his agreement.

Amber shook her head. "Ye'll not stand a chance."

"You all seemed to do fine!"

"We're all trained fighters. Ye've ne'er even fought a goblin before, so much as a bloody Dark Elf!"

"It's for your own good," Ayra put in softly.

Clearly still upset, Evalyn gave a reluctant nod and Percival led her around the passage they had come from, figuring they'd be out of the way there.

Amber adjusted her grip on her warhammer. "Ye all ready?"

"Let's get out of this place," Jeddo replied.

Amber nodded, taking a deep breath. "Open those doors."

Grunting in effort, Guralyn and Harik pulled on the heavy metal doors, which swung open with a noisy creak. Amber raised her shield and charged forward, Jeddo hiding behind his coat as he ran.

Sure enough, a Dark Elf sentry stood to either side of the doors, each brandishing a long glaive instead of the usual daggers. Amber's Dark Elf whirled around in surprise to see an angry dwarf running at him, hammer raised as she charged.

The elf swung his glaive across, aiming for Amber's right side where the shield wasn't. Amber accepted the blow with a grunt, knowing her armour would stop the attack. Frowning, Amber noticed that the glaive had made a small dent in the metal.

"Ye bastard, ye dented me armour!" Amber cried in outrage. She smashed her shield down on the outstretched shaft of the glaive, knocking the weapon down and spinning to her left, warhammer outstretched.

Her hammer gained momentum as she spun, slamming into the Dark Elf's lower back with enough force to shatter his pelvis and snap his spine. Roaring in agony, the elf dropped to the ground, legs no longer able to support himself. Amber swung her hammer into his chin, shattering his jaw and snapping his head back, breaking the elf's neck.

"That'll teach ye t' dent me armour!" Amber snapped, spitting on the Dark Elf's corpse.

Amber suddenly heard a whistle and looked up just in time to see two arrows racing toward her. Amber raised her shield and the arrows bounced harmlessly off, clattering onto the tile walkway.

Four Dark Elf archers were situated in a pair of watchtowers at the edge of the palace grounds, overlooking a twisting metal gate and low stone wall, topped with tendril-shaped fencing covered in little barbs. Thick clouds hung in the sky above, only letting a few eerie rays of sunlight through to illuminate the castle grounds.

"Durned elves!" Amber called to Thalassar and Ayra, raising her shield again to block two more arrows. "Think ye can take out those archers sometime this year?"

Jeddo pressed himself against the wall of the castle, feeling the smoothness of its cold stone against his back. His guard hadn't noticed him yet, but the Dark Elf *had* noticed Amber.

Spinning around in alarm, the Dark Elf gripped his glaive and ran to attack Amber, not even noticing Jeddo as he dashed forward. The gnome sprang suddenly, rapier thrusting at the Dark Elf's thigh. He was rewarded with a cry of pain as his blade poked into the Dark Elf's leg.

Spinning around, the guard swept his glaive in a powerful diagonal swipe that Jeddo ducked into, springing up behind it and thrusting furiously with his rapier. The glaive's momentum was already reversing, however, and Jeddo was forced to turn his thrust into a parry as the weapon raced toward his side.

Jeddo spun forward, whipping his rapier around and swinging it toward the Dark Elf's back. The Dark Elf spun too, placing his glaive to parry the strike and wincing as he set his wounded leg back on the ground. Jeddo spun again to the left, forcing the Dark Elf to pivot on his wounded leg which brought a cry of pain. Jeddo took advantage of the Dark Elf's distraction to feint left before stabbing low at the elf's midsection. Distracted by his throbbing leg, the Dark Elf fell for the fake, exposing himself to the real blow, which slipped through the elf's armour and into the soft flesh beneath.

Instinctively, Jeddo ducked to the side and two arrows slammed into the ground where he had just been standing. Another two arrows flew into the air, although these arrows were flying *away* from Jeddo. Thalassar's and Ayra's aim held true and their arrows found their marks, dropping two of the archers instantly. The other two were quick to follow.

"Nice work," Jeddo called to the High Elves, genuinely impressed by their extraordinary level of marksmanship. Thalassar and Ayra acknowledged the compliment with only a nod, already busy collecting the scattered Dark Elf arrows.

That's when they heard the screams.

CHAPTER 25:
THE BONFIRE

SILMANUS ROSE WITH A YAWN, SHIVERING IN THE COOL morning air. The rising sun cast an orange light on the clouds as it peeked over the treetops.

Like the morning before, Mara was already awake and stoking a small fire, which Silmanus knew was something of a risk. "Not worried about the Dark Elves seeing?" he asked Mara, rubbing his arms as he approached.

Mara shook her head. "Not this early in the morning. Besides," she said, holding up a cluster of squirrels. "I figured we could use a little moral boost."

The fresh meat proved a welcome supplement to the hard rations the group ate for breakfast and Silmanus noticed that spirits did seem to rise slightly as the group munched on smoky squirrel meat and sipped their coffees.

Soon after, they were off again, travelling cautiously through the trees, Mara searching even more intently for signs of Dark Elves while the others scanned the trees for doves. She led the group around in something of a circle, turning toward the east as they continued south and looping back north before repeating the process west.

As the sun began to sink yet again, Mara kicked a tree in frustration. "This is hopeless!" she proclaimed. "How do we even know the Dark Elf was telling the truth?"

"He was telling the truth," Silmanus assured her. "Lying under the influence of that spell is impossible."

"Then where is the camp?" Mara demanded, whirling on Silmanus with angry eyes. "We have searched this area for a whole day and found nothing! Not even a single footprint!"

"Mara, calm down," Linos intervened. "Maybe they moved the camp."

"Then where are the signs of one having been here?" Mara countered. "This is pointless! We're never going to find them!" She slumped down against a tree, tossing her bow to the side.

"Maybe we should turn back," Silmanus suggested. "Refresh our supplies, question the prisoners again, maybe try to organize multiple search parties."

"No!" Mara snapped. "We are not giving up! We just need to keep searching."

Linos shook his head. "Did you not just say this was hopeless?"

"Turning back won't do us any favours! There must just be something I missed…"

"Mara, you're grasping at straws here," Silmanus put in. "Face it. We aren't going to find the Dark Elves today and we might not tomorrow either. Let's just go back. Our rations are starting to run low. Plus, we can get the prisoners to lead us to the camp."

"Aye, an' Ah, fur a body, woods loch tae hae a proper rest efter havin' mah arm chewed up by a big ghost doggie!" Cara added, rolling the shoulder of the arm that had been injured.

Silmanus saw a measure of defiance in Mara's eyes, but she sighed and relented. "Alright. We'll rest here for the night and head home in the morning," she agreed. "I don't like wasting all this time though."

With that, the group set up camp, arranging bedrolls and blankets. Norman and Anne disappeared into the trees to go hunting while Cara helped Silmanus get a fire together. Linos and Mara stood to the side, murmuring quietly to each other about something Silmanus couldn't make out while the Helvan twins sharpened their axes.

As dusk began to fall, the two Eiran hunters returned with a brace of rabbits and a bag full of elderberries and blackberries. Mara helped skin the rabbits, placing each on a sharpened stick to roast over the fire. Soon, a hearty dinner of rabbit, jerky, and both fresh and dried berries filled the stomachs of the group who spent the rest of the evening swapping stories. Cara led the group in a few Lochadian chanties which proved more comedic than melodious with her thick accent.

Silmanus, never one for extended conversation, left to take his watch early, enjoying a bit of time to his own thoughts as he scanned the trees for signs of movement. Nothing approached, however, and a few hours later, Cara came to relieve him and Silmanus crawled happily under his blanket, ready for a rest.

A thick blanket of clouds hung in the sky when Silmanus awoke, hiding the sun behind their greyish-white wisps. A cold wind blew through the trees, biting through Silmanus' jacket and forcing the wizard to enact a spell of warmth on himself.

"It's not going to rain today, is it?" Silmanus asked Mara, who, once again, was up early prepping a fire.

Mara shook her head. "It shouldn't, no."

"That's good. I don't want to get wet in this blasted cold."

Mara nodded her agreement, placing one last stick on the crackling fire before sitting down and hugging her legs, eyebrows creased in a frown.

"You alright?" Silmanus asked, concerned.

"I'm fine, just frustrated that we didn't find the Dark Elves," Mara answered.

"Well, they are the masters of hiding," Silmanus reasoned. "We'll find them eventually though. Or they'll find us and we'll kill them then."

"And how many innocents will die in that fight? I've told you before, a lot of the people in my village are simple commoners that needed a safe place to live outside of the law. Many of them have barely even held a sword before. If the Dark Elves come to us, how many of them will be killed?" Mara challenged, although not maliciously. She seemed genuinely concerned about the future of her people.

Silmanus didn't blame her either. That village was her pride and joy, a safe haven she had crafted with nothing but willpower and some loyal friends and followers. It was her kingdom, a place she could rule without being undermined by selfish advisors and power-hungry chieftains. The people in that village were Mara's subjects, her people, and she had a duty to protect them.

"I don't know," Silmanus answered quietly. "Maybe many, maybe none." He wanted to say more, but he had no words of comfort for Mara. Only false hopes and unkeepable promises.

"Could you save them?" Mara asked, a hint of hope creeping into her voice. "If they died could you bring them back? Or heal them? Surely there are more healing spells than the one you had used on Cara and Norman."

Silmanus shook his head. "There are more healing spells out there, and many are much less painful and much more effective, but I'm afraid I simply don't have the capacity to learn those spells. Such knowledge of magic is beyond the grasp of a wizard. It must be granted by the power of the Gods or the primal energy of the world itself. And bringing someone back from the dead..." Silmanus shook his head again, sadly this time. "That is a power beyond any mortal."

"There are no other healing spells for you?" Mara pressed desperately.

"I'm afraid not. But do not fear, Mara. I may not be able to help those who are wounded but I can stop them from being wounded in the first place."

Mara nodded. "I can live with that."

Silmanus winced internally, taking Mara's comment as an insult to his apparently insufficient abilities but he shrugged it off. The others were getting up now as well with a symphony of yawns and groans that quickly became sighs of contentment as coffee was brewed and sipped.

Under the knowledge that they would soon be home, the group was rather liberal with their rations, saving only enough for lunch. Mara had been unsuccessful with her hunting that morning, which was understandable. No matter how good you were at hunting, and Mara was very good, sometimes there was just nothing around to catch.

All the same, spirits were high as the group began the trek home, except for Mara, who remained glum after their unsuccessful mission. Silmanus figured the cloudy sky wasn't helping her mood much either.

After a relatively uneventful journey, the wooden palisades of Mara's village came into view between the trees. The drawbridge was lowered and the group was welcomed home by the guards.

Reynard soon found Mara, clapping her on the back with a wide grin. "Welcome home!" he said. "How did it go?"

"We found nothing," Mara answered bitterly. "All we got for our troubles was a close encounter with the biggest damned hound you've ever seen."

Reynard's eyes went wide. "Barguest?" he guessed nervously.

"Aye, a barguest!" Cara confirmed. "Mingin' bugger bit mah arm somethin' awfy tay!" Only through years of friendship was Reynard able to understand Cara had said, "Nasty bugger bit my arm something awful too!" Silmanus was left slightly confused.

"Are you all right?" Reynard asked. "Is it gone?"

"Yeah, we killed the beast. Norman and Cara were hit pretty hard, but Silmanus fixed them up," Mara said.

Reynard looked at Silmanus. "You're a healer?"

The wizard shook his head. "Not really. Trust me, you don't want me tending to your wounds."

"Hurt waur than a thistle up th' erse, it did!" Cara described, drawing a slight chuckle with her crude, but accurate, comparison.

"Anything interesting happen while I was gone?" Mara asked.

Reynard shook his head. "Nothing. Managed a good deal on some more wheat and potatoes though, and a good thing too. The crops won't be ready for a while yet."

"How are the prisoners?"

"Grumpy. They refuse to eat and I've barely been able to get them to drink. I think they're trying to starve themselves."

Mara grinned wickedly. "Ivar can get them to eat," she said. "We're going to need them soon."

Reynard nodded. "And what are we doing for the evening?"

Mara gave him a questioning look. "Sorry?"

"Do you not know what day it is?" Reynard asked.

"No. It's a bit hard to keep track of time when you're trying to find a group of people that want your head on a spike," Mara replied dryly.

Reynard, far too used to Mara's sardonic comments to be put off, just grinned. "It's the first day of Somaig."

Silmanus looked confused. "Sorry, what's Somaig?"

"It's the fifth month of the Lochadian calendar," Mara answered, her eyes still on Reynard. "And we're not doing anything. It's too dangerous."

"Doing anything? What do you mean?" Silmanus inquired, still very confused as to what was so special about Somaig. Human traditions were one of the few areas the wizard had never bothered investigating.

Mara gave a small sigh and turned to the elf. "In the Common tongue, Somaig roughly translates to 'Near Summer.' It's the Lochadian equivalent to the Elvish month of Floritha. The first day of Somaig marks the beginning of fairer weather. The flowers bloom, the air is warmer, the snow is gone, you get the idea. Because of this, the Druids regard the First of Somaig as a sacred day, the Day of Renewal, or 'Resgal,' in our tongue.

"Each year, on Resgal, the people of Lochadia celebrate the return of warmth by throwing massive parties. There's lots of drinking and feasting and music and dancing. And, of course, fires, because Lochadians kind of have a thing for bonfires. Normally, we keep the tradition alive in our village here." Mara gave Reynard a hard look before continuing. "But *not* this time. It's too dangerous to be lighting giant fires and playing loud music while there are Dark Elves out there, actively trying to kill me and anyone who stands in their way."

"Oh, come on, Mara," Reynard pleaded. "The people need this. Most of them already suspect something bad is going on. If we suddenly don't celebrate Resgal, they'll know for sure, and it will scare them. Isn't that what Silmanus said the Dark Elves do? Strike fear into their targets to make them easier to kill?"

"He has a point," Silmanus put in. "The Dark Elves prey on fear. If your people show that they are nervous, the Dark Elves will capitalize on that and plunge your entire village into a state of utter terror, making us all the easier to defeat."

"Ok, but a bonfire isn't exactly inconspicuous. Neither is loud music. I might as well give the Dark Elves a map to where we are and scream 'Come and get me!'"

"I can ward the village," Silmanus suggested. "Make it harder for the Dark Elves to find us, if they don't already know where we are."

"'Don't already know where we are?'" Mara repeated nervously.

"Well, they've been here for a while. They haven't just been sitting around and waiting for you to stumble into their clutches.

They'll have done plenty of scouting and surveillance. I would not be shocked if they've found you village by now, especially if they've got doves working for them."

That was more unnerving that Mara could describe. The fact that such a lethal force could already have found her home, could have the entire place surrounded at that very moment, terrified Mara more than she would admit.

Reynard gestured to Silmanus. "See? The wizard thinks it's a good idea."

Silmanus smiled uncomfortably. "I don't know if I'd go so far as to call it a good idea. Mara does still have a point, and a party would leave the village rather distracted."

Reynard frowned, then snapped his fingers. "Ok, so what if we doubled the guard? Silmanus said he can ward the camp. Between that and extra guards, who would be regularly rotated so that everyone can have fun, I'm sure we'd be fine."

Mara and Reynard both looked at Silmanus expectantly. The wizard shuffled uncomfortably, not enjoying having so much responsibility resting on him. "Well…it's something you do every year?" Silmanus asked slowly. Reynard nodded. "And it's important to the people?" Another nod.

Silmanus sighed. "Well, then I think it's worth the risk. Keeping people's spirits high is very important, and it might send a message that you aren't afraid. As long as we're vigilant, I think you should do it."

Mara nodded and took a deep breath. "Alright. Get Helga and Ivar on that immediately. I want them on the walls at all times. They aren't fans of parties anyways. Silmanus, you go do your thing. Give it everything you can." Silmanus nodded and ran off to find the twins and "do his thing."

Mara turned to Reynard. "I guess we have a party to plan."

Despite the short notice, Mara and Reynard managed to pull off a magnificent celebration. That evening, the chefs prepared a massive pot of delicious rabbit stew, with tender cubes of fresh rabbit meat, soft cuts of potato, slices of carrot, and plenty of onion and seasoning. It was a delicious stew made all the better by loaves of golden-brown bread and a glass of delicate red wine straight from Esnia. Just what Mara needed to lift her spirits after such a disappointing day.

The dining hall that evening was alive with chatter and conversation, everyone appreciating the fine meal after a long, hard day of planting and tilling. It was early spring still, so the seeds needed to be planted and without many horses or any oxen, that was a difficult, tiring job.

Silmanus remained relatively taciturn throughout the meal, leaving Mara and Linos to a very heated but seemingly friendly debate about the superiority of a trident versus a sword.

"I'm telling you, the extra reach and its potency against an enemy charge makes up for the lack of cutting area!" Linos argued emphatically.

Mara shook her head. "A sword is a far more manoeuvrable and versatile weapon. Any time you block with a trident, you risk having your hands cut open!"

They carried on like that for most of the evening while Cara entertained the others with a variety of folk tales and ghost stories that most people seemed to have heard dozens of times already. Silmanus hadn't, however, and found himself quite enjoying listening to Cara spin tales about shapeshifting sea people and fierce lake monsters, even if he couldn't understand half of what the spirited Lochadian said.

The evening finished with a large bonfire, as requested. Silmanus marvelled at how high the crackling flames reached once the blaze had reached its peak, easily triple Silmanus' height. Great showers of sparks flew through the cool night air like swarms of fireflies, dancing around in the smoke with each pop and snap of the flames.

All was very merry that evening. Cara, always one for a good time, led the village in a few highland jigs, which were very energetic dances to some very loud music that had Silmanus laughing and clapping despite himself. The elf had never been one for dancing and had very specific musical tastes, but despite their loud droning, Silmanus found himself enjoying the merry tunes of those funny Lochadian instruments. Bagpipes, he believed they were called.

Mara, too, got onto the dance floor, jumping around to the time of the music, laughing as she did so. Her flowing red hair bounced atop her shoulders as she danced this way and that. Silmanus was surprised to see the serious young woman being so happy and carefree. Perhaps it was the wine?

Or maybe it was the music, the energy in the air. These were tunes from Mara's past, after all, traditional songs and dances that must have reminded her of home, of a time when things were better. Silmanus wondered how many times a younger Mara had danced like this with old friends and forgotten family, around fires blazing in the Lochadian highlands.

Cara noticed Silmanus sitting passively to the side after a little while. "Oi! Elf! 'Main 'en up haur an' hae a wee fin fur ance in yer life!"

Silmanus held a hand to one of his long, pointed ears, unable to hear Cara properly over the bagpipes and drums and not exactly understanding her accent anyway.

Mara overheard and helped him out. "She's telling you to get up here and dance, you old stick in the mud!"

Silmanus shook his head. "I don't dance!" he yelled over the music.

"Ay coorse ye dorn't! Yoo're a bludy elf, efter aw, walkin' around wi' a stick up yer erse! Gie up haur an' learn!" Cara called back to him, lifting her knees high up in the air as she clapped her hands in the air.

"I'm fine here, thanks," Silmanus said.

Linos walked past him, grabbing Silmanus by the ear with his thumb and forefinger. "Come on. Anyone'd think you're a dwarf with how stubborn you're being about this."

Silmanus winced and slapped Linos' hand away, holding his sore ear. Linos spun back around with raised eyebrows. "Let's go, elf. About time you learned what fun is!"

Silmanus gave a heavy sigh. "Fine." he relented. "But don't touch my ears."

"Fair enough," Linos agreed. Silmanus followed the human up to the bonfire, making his way to Cara, who Silmanus figured was the best person to be taught by.

Cara gave a delighted laugh. "Aye, that's maur loch it!" she exclaimed as Silmanus shuffled beside her. "Noo watch me, yer leg goes up loch thes…" Cara began instructing Silmanus on how to do a proper jig.

The elf learned quickly and soon, he was dancing and laughing just as well as the others. "That's th' way!" Cara laughed.

Mara snickered at the sight of Silmanus hopping around and clapping his hands like a highland hooligan. "Never thought the day would come where I'd see an elf dance a highland tune!"

"Never thought the day would come where I'd be dancing with a bunch of humans!" Silmanus shot back, grinning.

Cara clapped him on the back. "We'll make a highlander it ay ye yit!" she proclaimed.

As the night progressed, the dancing stopped and changed to a series of friendly contests and showcases of skill. Some of the villagers juggled, some performed clumsy acts of acrobatics, a couple attempted lousy miming shows. There were caber tosses, archery contests, and wrestling matches. People showed off the various skills and talents they had or attempted to do things they were quite bad at for comedic value. Ivar was even allowed to take a break from guard duty to absolutely dominate the wrestling events. The Helvan never could resist a good fight.

"You'd think this was winter solstice or something," Mara commented to Linos as they watched Cara futilely try to tackle Ivar to the ground, succeeding only in dangling from his neck with her scrawny arms before the hulking Helvan plucked her off his back and placed her gently on the ground.

"We certainly are a merry bunch this evening," Linos agreed. "And all because you couldn't find some Dark Elves. Guess it's a good thing we came back, huh?"

"Oh, shut up," Mara grumbled. "You do not get to say I told you so."

"Ok, but I still told you so."

"Bugger off," Mara muttered.

Linos grinned. "No way. I was right and I am enjoying my victory."

Mara slugged him hard in the stomach and Linos doubled over, the wind knocked right out of him. "Still enjoying it?"

"You know, someday I'm going to hit you back," Linos said weakly, still trying to find his breath again.

"For your sake, I pray you don't."

The bonfire "celebration" carried on late into the evening, the night filled with laughter and singing as everyone partied and enjoyed themselves. Even the little kids were still up and awake, clumsily dancing and giggling, much to the amusement of the adults.

So cheerful was everyone that no one noticed the tiny, black bird that had suddenly perched itself on a tree branch overlooking the village, head cocked curiously as a pair of pale eyes stared down from out of the shadows.

CHAPTER 26:
VOLHAD

JEDDO'S HEART FROZE AS THE SCREAM PIERCED THE AIR. It was a shriek of pure terror, one of horror and pain, a last pleading cry for help.

It was Evalyn's cry.

Jeddo sprinted back into the palace, little legs carrying him as fast as he could. Thalassar and Ayra were already there, backing away as they fired arrow after arrow down the corridor where Evalyn and Percival had gone to hide.

Sliding across the glossy floor, Jeddo rounded the corner and froze. Before him was a squad of Dark Elves, roughly fifty of them, weapons drawn as they bore down on Evalyn and Percival, who were running as fast as they could toward Ayra and Thalassar.

The *thrum* of bows filled the air, the sound wrenching Jeddo's heart as he realized what was happening. Twenty black arrows arced through the air, racing toward Evalyn, Percival, Jeddo, and the High Elves.

Jeddo hit the floor, swinging his cloak up around his head. He felt the sting of three arrows smash into his jacket and the clatter of a fourth landing just beside his head, but the cloak's enchanted dragonskin proved stronger and the arrows merely bounced off.

The instant he felt the impacts, Jeddo sprang up to his feet. Thalassar and Ayra were both coming out of rolls having narrowly dodged the arrows fired at them. With looks of despair and deep regret, the two elves bolted down the exit corridor, heading for the doors.

Jeddo spun around to see Percival lying dead on the floor, his back riddled with arrows. Evalyn was trying to drag herself forward, three arrows jutting out of her left leg, crimson blood spilling across the black tile and leaving a bold red line as the woman tried desperately to get away from the Dark Elves, who were now close enough for Jeddo to see the whites of their eyes.

"Help me!" Evalyn shrieked, looking at Jeddo with wild, tear-filled eyes. "Please, Jeddo! Don't let them catch me!"

At the same time, Jeddo heard Amber calling from the castle doors. "Hurry, Jeddo! There's nothin' ye can do, save yerself! Let's go!"

Jeddo looked back and forth between Evalyn and Amber, knowing that Amber was right and that Evalyn was doomed, no matter what Jeddo or anyone else did, but unable to tear himself away from Evalyn's desperate, pleading cries. Evalyn's face seemed to ripple and shift as it changed to the screaming face of his first mate, of his boatswain, of his crew.

"Jeddo! Let's go!" Amber hollered. "Ye can't save her, run!"

Feeling like the lowest person to have ever lived, Jeddo began walking hesitantly toward Amber, breaking eye contact with Evalyn with a guilty grimace.

Evalyn's eyes went wide. "No! *No!* Jeddo, don't leave!" she wailed, fighting harder to escape. "No! You monster! I hate you! I hate all of you! No! *Nooo!*"

Tears welling up in his eyes, Jeddo sped from a walk to a run, pushing away Evalyn's tortured screams as he made his way to freedom. As soon as Jeddo was out of the palace, Harik and Guralyn slammed the doors shut with a mighty *crash* that rattled Jeddo's chest. Harik slid the guards' glaives into the circular handles on the doors, hoping they would be enough to keep the Dark Elves contained.

Then the group turned and ran, sprinting as fast as they could down the walkway, heading toward the twisting metal gates. Jeddo threw one last guilty look over his shoulder at the palace.

Jeddo noticed then how magnificent the castle was. A high, cylindrical keep made of black stone rose from the ground like a jagged black mountain, pointed towers lining its sides. Black trees sprang from the ground, perfectly still in the breezeless air, standing like statues carved of jet. Great banners displaying Vanaria's silver dagger emblem hung from the walls. Against the eerie light peeking through the thick cloud cover, the castle seemed nightmarish, yet also beautiful in a strange and terrifying way.

There was no time for observing the Dark Elf palace, however. The prisoners were almost at the gates and freedom lay beyond.

Amber rattled the gates furiously. "Locked!" she cursed. Raising her warhammer above her head, Amber smashed the weapon into the centre of the gates but her hammer just bounced off.

Jeddo spun around in alarm at the sound of a deep crash coming from inside the palace. The doors heaved forward, but the glaives held strong, keeping the palace entrance shut. "Hurry!" Jeddo hissed, knowing it was only a matter of time before the Dark Elves found a way out.

Amber swung again, bringing her hammer down right on the lock, but to no avail. The weapon just bounced off again with a noisy *clang*. Growling, Amber struck with all her might, and this time, the gates gave in. The lock snapped and the gates opened a little. Amber kicked out at one, swinging it wide with a loud creak.

Jeddo gave a delighted laugh, clapping Amber on the back and wincing as his hand smacked against the hard metal. The prisoners ran forward, out of the gates and into the city beyond.

They all froze suddenly. All around them, Dark Elf citizens stood gaping from outside their simple stone homes. They were all dressed in modest, often torn clothing, staring at the prisoners with ragged, hungry features. The houses stretched on and on, lining the black cobble streets of Volhad, along with what Jeddo assumed were shops, market vendors, and soup houses.

Jeddo was very confused. Vanaria was supposed to be a nation full of bloodthirsty Dark Elves, all trained as deadly warriors, strutting around in fine black clothing, wielding daggers and tormenting lesser creatures and slaves. But these…these just looked like ordinary people, most of them poor and starving.

What was going on here?

There was no time to stop and contemplate though. Amber was already shouting, pointing down one of the streets. Jeddo followed her finger and, with a start of hope and elation, noticed a faint, rippling glimmer on the horizon beyond. Jeddo knew that glimmer anywhere.

The sea!

Specifically, the Black Sea, but the name was completely irrelevant. All that mattered was that before them, mere deciums of streets away, there was a sea. Even better, Jeddo picked out the familiar sight of masts rising above the cityscape, towering black poles sporting wide black sails and flags decorated with the Vanaria coat of arms. They could steal a ship, sail north across the Black Strait, and take refuge in Fort Vanguard, the dwarven fortress-city along the Black Strait.

They were going to escape.

But first, they actually had to get to the ships.

Feeling very self-conscious amongst all the suspicious stares, the prisoners made their way down the street, speed walking on account of their weak bodies being unable to run any further.

Jeddo winced as a Dark Elf man pointed and shouted something angrily in Dark Elvish. Jeddo wondered then if any of the citizens actually spoke Common.

Jeddo considered stopping to ask but another echoing rumble from the palace urged him on like a whip does a horse, reminding him that slowing down will result in plenty of pain and suffering.

Jeddo hurried on, panting as his little legs swished back and forth, carrying him across the smooth cobbles.

"Traitors!" a Dark Elf spat, glowering and pointing at Thalassar and Ayra.

"Murderers!" another hissed, pushing back her child as she glared daggers at the High Elves. Thalassar and Ayra held their heads high in response, refusing to acknowledge the insults.

"What're they goin' on about?" Amber murmured, confused. "They're the traitors and murderers!"

"The Dark Elves try to justify their radical acts of violence by painting the Light Elves, as in the High, Forest, and Sea Elves, as evil hypocrites," Thalassar explained. "They perceive the banishment of the Dark Elves as an act founded on jealously, revenge, and a genocidal mindset, when of course, it was done as a means of containing the Dark Elf threat."

Before anything more could be said, a cry of alarm rang across the streets and four Dark Elf guards marched forward, daggers drawn.

Thalassar and Ayra were quick to act, raising their bows and taking aim. Jeddo shot them a warning glance. "We don't want to risk civilian casualties," he hissed.

Thalassar looked at him, frowning a bit. Ultimately, the High Elf decided Jeddo was right, returning the arrow to its quiver and dropping his bow. Ayra did the same, drawing her graceful longsword instead.

Combat broke out in the streets of Volhad, Dark Elves dancing around the prisoners with daggers flashing. The civilian onlookers shouted and screamed, many shielding the eyes of their children.

Amber faced off against one Dark Elf, as did Harik and Guralyn. Jeddo, Ayra, and Thalassar joined together to take on the presumable leader.

The fighting was brief but fierce. After an exchange of blows, Amber managed to trip her Dark Elf opponent, sending the lithe warrior sprawling across the cobbles. The Dark Elf tried to stand but Amber quickly threw a powerful hook at the side of his head, spinning the Dark Elf back to the ground, out cold.

Guralyn fared similarly, powering through her opponent's offensive with ease. She disarmed one of the Dark Elf's hands, sending the dagger clattering to the stone road. The pommel of Guralyn's sword connected with the Dark Elf's cheek and the elf went down hard, already unconscious as she slumped to the ground.

Like all Dark Elves, the patrol leader was a formidable warrior, but Thalassar, Ayra, and Jeddo were all superior fighters individually. Banded together, they proved a simply indomitable force for the lone Dark Elf. She put up a valiant defence, but the three prisoners quickly overwhelmed her. Jeddo cut the Dark Elf's right hamstrings, taking her out of the fight but leaving her alive; the prisoners could not afford to anger the Dark Elf civilians any further.

Harik growled as he met his foe, quickly overpowering the Dark Elf warrior. The burly dwarf was too close to freedom to allow a measly Dark Elf to stand in his way. Harik kicked one of the Dark Elf's legs, sending the elven guard to the ground, left prone and vulnerable.

Harik raised his axe above his head, about to split open the Dark Elf's skull and finish the nasty creature, but something caught his eye instead.

A little Dark Elf girl, no older than four, staring at Harik with big, frightened eyes and holding her mother's hand, mouth slightly agape. There was innocence in those wide, silver eyes, innocence as well as genuine fear.

Something inside Harik's gruff old heart twanged, some peculiar emotion that took control of the dwarf's arms. With a sigh, Harik lowered his axe, instead bending down and lifting the Dark Elf up by his scruff. Harik held the elf's dazed face to his own.

"Ye listen here, elf," Harik growled lowly. "I'm done bein' a prisoner in this filthy place. I'm leavin' and if ye try t' stop me again, I'm not showin' ye any more mercy. Ye get me?"

The Dark Elf nodded weakly, his head spinning too much to properly register anything Harik had said.

"Great. Now get ye gone. I've places t' be and none o' them are in Vanaria," Harik said, pushing the Dark Elf over.

The crowd was still gathered, watching the spectacle with mixtures of fear, outrage, confusion, and curiosity. Finally, one Dark Elf pointed and shouted a commanding word in Dark Elvish, charging toward the prisoners with raised fists. The rest of the crowd followed suit, rushing forward to attack.

Ayra held forth her sword, a dangerous glint in her eyes. "Stand down," she ordered sternly. The crowd hesitated, eyeing Ayra's deadly blade warily.

"We are not your enemy," Ayra continued, hoping someone in the crowd spoke Common.

"Yes, you are!" a Dark Elf man shot back. "You have always been our enemies and now here you are, infiltrating our home!"

"We are not infiltrating!" Jeddo explained. "We were prisoners! We're just trying to escape. We don't want to hurt anyone."

"We can't let you escape," the Dark Elf said threateningly. "You were prisoners for a reason."

"We were kidnapped," Jeddo said. "Taken against our will by your people. Please, we just want to leave. Let us through."

"If ye don't, I'll be cuttin' me way though!" Harik announced menacingly, waving his axe.

"If not for our sake, then for yours, step out of the way," Ayra pleaded.

After a few mumbles, the crowd reluctantly dispersed from the streets. "Thank you!" Jeddo proclaimed. "Your kindness will not be forgotten!" Turning to the others, he nodded and said, "Let's get out of here."

Moving with renewed vigour, the prisoners ran down the streets, their eyes set and focused on the ships ahead. Jeddo's heart dropped a little as his eyes caught the shape of a towering, black wall overlooking the harbour, but he tried to keep his spirits high.

"We're going to do it!" Jeddo panted happily, a smile breaking on his face. "We're going to make it! We're going to get out of here!"

Jeddo learned that day never to say such words pre-emptively. For just as he finished his hopeful exclamation, a slick voice froze him in his tracks.

"You're not going anywhere."

The group froze and spun around, weapons at the ready as they turned to face whatever new threat was trying to stop them from leaving. A hateful glare passed over Jeddo's face as he recognized the speaker instantly.

Mordasine.

CHAPTER 27:
SHADOWS FALL

THE GUARD GAVE A DEEP YAWN, HOLDING A HAND TO HIS mouth as he did so. It was late and he had taken a double shift, the result of losing a bet and owing another guard a favour.

Not for the first time, the guard questioned what he was doing. It wasn't like anything had attacked the village before. There were wild animals that dropped by every now and then, sure, but they went away on their own quickly enough. The hunting and trade parties had run into trouble, but never on village grounds. And besides, hadn't that wizard cast spells around the village or something? Nothing ever happened, so why bother guard when he could be enjoying a party instead?

In that very moment, the guard found out why.

A bolt of black energy raced toward him from the trees, trailing wisps of black smoke as it flew unseen toward its target. The spell smashed into the guard with deadly force, exploding into a cloud of black smoke that leeched into the guard's skin, causing him to writhe and scream in pure agony. A few seconds later, he fell dead from the battlements, veins black and full of dark magic, eyes rolled back in his head and face distorted into an expression of fear and torment.

The other guards weren't even given a chance to react. Black arrows dripping with Dark Elf poison sailed toward them, each arrow finding its mark and bringing down a guard.

Despite the loud shrieks of anguish that erupted from the walls, none by the bonfire were alerted to the attack. The bagpipes were still playing at full blast, their droning mixing with the laughs and cheers of the village folk to completely block out the screams of the dying.

It wasn't until the first dozen villagers lay dead that anyone realized something was afoot.

Silmanus had just been dancing, finally getting the hang of the jig and laughing as he jumped around. One moment, everything was fine, and the next, a ball of black energy the size of a man's head slammed into the ground beside a group of villagers.

The ball exploded, sending dirt and debris flying into the air. Tendrils of black magic raced towards the innocents, piercing them through the torso and flooding their bodies with necrotic energy. After a few seconds of pure agony, the villagers fell dead, stained black by the dark magic.

Silmanus froze for a moment, caught completely off guard by what was happening. Dark Elves! Dark Elves were attacking! Worse yet, they had wizards! Silmanus knew Dark Elf wizards wielded an arsenal of spells designed specifically for killing their targets in the most painful way imaginable, sucking out their life force—their magic—and replacing it with dark, necromantic energies. Silmanus felt a flicker of rage surge in his heart; such effects were despicable to him, the magical equivalent of sadistic torture.

Silmanus didn't snap out of his surprise until Mara began shouting orders. "Get to cover!" Mara was shrieking, her voice full of fear and desperation but still wielding the same authority as ever. "We are under attack! Run! Hide! Flee this place! Anyone who knows how to fight, to me! Give the others a chance to escape!"

Silmanus kicked into action immediately. He dashed to his staff, scooping it up and turning to face the direction from which the spell attack had come. A storm of arrows was racing out of the darkness, raining down on the panicked citizens below.

Silmanus planted his staff and braced his legs, taking a deep breath as he bowed his head and began to mutter. A warm feeling began pooling in his gut as he poured more and more of his magic into the spell. Raw power filled his veins and crackled in his ears, his eyes glowing white like tiny stars and silver light radiating from his skin.

All of the magic suddenly rushed out of Silmanus like a bursting dam and the wizard threw up a shimmering wall of protective energy, an impenetrable barrier that deflected the Dark Elf arrows easily. His crystalline wall spread like liquid glass, flowing to engulf the village beneath its protective frame.

"Move, move, move!" Silmanus shouted at the villagers. "Get back, run away from the wall!"

Frightened though they were, the villagers found the common sense to listen, grabbing their children and running as fast as they could toward the village's rear exit. Another hail of arrows smashed down against Silmanus' barrier, bringing a few terrified shrieks from the villagers as they ducked down and covered their necks with their arms.

Silmanus' spell held strong, however, deflecting the barrage yet again. By then, Cara, Norman, Anne, Linos, Mara, Ivar, Helga, and about four dozen other men and women were gathered behind Silmanus, weapons in hand, while arrow after arrow continued to smash into the wall, which had grown and grown and now touched the village palisades.

"How many arrows can it take?" Mara asked worriedly.

"As many as they shoot," Silmanus answered confidently, knowing it to be the truth. He could feel the spell slowly beginning to slip, however, like a wet rope inching through someone's hands. "I can only hold the wall for a few minutes though. You should leave, protect the villagers as they flee."

Mara shook her head fiercely. "We stay and fight."

"Aye, ye think we're gonnae lit ye hae aw th' fin?" Cara said.

Before Silmanus could say anything else, a massive explosion of black magic rocked the barrier, sending rolling clouds of smoke cascading across the wall's curved face. Silmanus gritted his teeth, fighting to hold the wall against the Dark Elf's spell attack. If Silmanus' hold on his spell was indeed like holding onto a rope, each Dark Elf spell was like twenty men heaving on it with all their might.

"And how many of *those* can it take?" Mara asked, nervousness finding a place in her voice again.

"Not many," Silmanus answered honestly, grimacing in concentration. "I think they only have one wizard though, so it'll take them a little longer."

Right then, three more black spheres smashed into the wall, causing to Silmanus to wince. "Ok, I guess they have a few," he observed. His head felt like it was starting to split and his eyes burned, but Silmanus held strong, trickling more and more magic into the wall to strengthen it.

The Dark Elves kept up the barrage, sending spell after spell at Silmanus' barrier, which gradually grew weaker and weaker until finally, a giant crack spiderwebbed across the wall with a sound like ice cracking beneath one's feet, only a hundred times louder. All those gathered behind the wall held their hands to their ears to block out the deafening sound.

"I'm dropping the wall!" Silmanus announced, breaking his spell to prevent another thunderous crack from disorienting the warriors. The air rushed out of Silmanus' lungs as he severed that mental cord and the wall disappeared into a cloud of silver dust.

The Dark Elves struck immediately, raining arrows down on the gathered defenders. Most had shields that they hid beneath, but some did not, Silmanus included. He threw up a smaller, silvery shield around himself while those without a shield or magic leapt to the sides, trying to get behind someone with cover. Two warriors were struck down in the barrage, pierced several times by those insidious poisoned arrows.

The barrage ended soon, the Dark Elves either out of arrows or deciding that the attack was not effective enough. The only sounds to be heard were the crackling of the bonfire and the nervous breathing of the defenders. Otherwise, all was silent and still, the Dark Elves making not a sound as they jumped across rooftops and skittered through shadows, making their way to the defenders.

The silence was broken by a shriek of anguish as a poor woman, Silmanus believed her name had been Ula, was laid low by a Dark Elf blade, which had cut a curving smile across her throat. The Dark Elf responsible quickly dashed forward, leading the charge as nearly three dozen Dark Elves ran out from all directions, daggers drawn and staffs in hand.

Silmanus picked out three wizards, identifiable by the black skull-topped staffs they carried. They would be the most danger-ous targets. Throwing caution to the wind, Silmanus pointed his staff and shot a fist-sized ball of fire from it, savouring the feeling of magic roiling through his arm. The spell arced toward one of the Dark Elf wizards, smashing into the ground at his feet and exploding into a massive ball of flame that engulfed several Dark Elves and two nearby huts.

The huts were set ablaze, crackling flames rising high into the night sky. Four Dark Elves lay dead and charred in the wake of the spell, but the wizard still stood, surrounded by a swirling black cloud that sank into the ground shortly after the flames had cleared.

A ray of black magic raced toward Silmanus, but he held forth his staff and poured his magic into it. A shimmering white shield met the dark spell and Silmanus juggled with the Dark Elf's magic, spinning it around and flinging it back at his opponent.

The Dark Elf wizard dove to the side moments before his own spell smashed into the ground where he had previously been stand-ing, sending dirt flying as it exploded into a cloud of black smoke.

The other two wizards tried to pin down Silmanus with spells of their own, various rays and bolts flying at the High Elf in an effort to take him down. Silmanus vanished in a puff of smoke, reappearing a little way away and flinging an orb of telekinetic energy at one of the wizards. His spell hit home, blasting the Dark Elf off his feet and shattering his ribs.

One down, two to go.

Mara gave an angry snarl and charged at a Dark Elf, sword drawn as she rushed to intercept. The Dark Elf ducked and stepped to the side, thrusting forward with his daggers as he did so. Mara was too quick, spinning her sword up along the side of her body to bat the daggers away and spinning on her toes to face the Dark Elf.

Pitiless silver eyes locked with Mara's steely blue orbs as the Dark Elf rushed forward. Mara rushed to meet him, determined to finish off this foe as quickly as she could. The Dark Elves had made attempts on her life before, but never had they attacked her home, harmed her people, killed her friends.

The Dark Elves were about to be given a taste of Mara's fury unlike any they had before.

Mara hit fast and hard, battering the Dark Elf into submission. Mara watched the elf's eyes widened in fear as he realized the situation he was in. This was no meagre human warrior. This was an unstoppable force of unmatchable prowess, a virtual angel of death.

And soon, the Dark Elf found his death delivered.

Given a temporary reprieve from the fighting, Mara quickly surveyed the battlefield. She was a swordswoman of nearly unmatched skill but most of the others were not and Mara noticed that many of them were struggling against their opponents. Several already lay dead or dying on the ground, bleeding out of wounds in their necks and torsos. Mara felt bile rise into her throat at the sight of her friends scattering the ground as corpses.

Ivar and Helga, however, were having no such trouble. They were bleeding from multiple small scratches and gashes across their muscled torsos, but the massive Helvans shrugged aside both the pain and the poison, accepting minor blows to deal devasting axe strikes and punches to their fragile attackers. The pair had already plowed through four Dark Elves and were quickly overpowering a fifth, a very impressive number indeed.

Norman and Anne were also holding up quite well. Although not quite as skilled as Mara, both were formidable duelists, wielding their longswords with commendable skill. They were pressed back-to-back, covering each other's vulnerabilities and preventing the Dark Elves from properly exploiting any blind spots. Three Dark Elves lay dead in the dirt as a testament to their considerable martial prowess.

Cara wasn't proving to be anything of a pushover either. Through either dumb luck or her totally unpredictable fighting style, the erratic Lochadian was holding her own against not one but two Dark Elves, laughing wildly as she thrusted with her spiked targe and slashed with her long dirk. The Dark Elves were forced to give her a wide birth, completely unable to predict where she would strike next and already each sporting a small gash as a consequence for underestimating the scrawny woman.

Linos fought with as much strength and skill as ever, wielding his trident like an extension of his own arm. He thrusted and stabbed, catching daggers between the prongs of his weapons and twisting them aside before lashing out with a powerful kick to knock back whatever Dark Elf he was fighting. His trident spun and twirled to bat away oncoming blows as he pressed through every Dark Elf that came his way. Two already lay dead behind him, a trademark line of three puncture wounds stretched across their bleeding chests.

And in the middle of it all, Silmanus raged like a fiery thunderstorm, flinging spell after spell at the wizards.

Silmanus just barely moved his foot out of the way before a bolt of wispy black energy crashed into the ground where it had previously been. Silmanus flung a spear-like icicle at the spell's caster, although the attack was easily dodged and Silmanus' spell just smashed through the wall of a hut.

The High Elf spotted one of Mara's warriors, Silmanus thought her name was Brenna, being quickly battered down by a Dark Elf. She was twisting her axe desperately, trying to force the Dark Elf back while moving away from his daggers. She was not going to last very long.

Silmanus stepped in, shooting a ray of dancing fire right at the Dark Elf. The elf didn't see the blow coming and it caught right in the back, burning through cloak and armour to sear away his flesh. The spell gave Brenna all the time she needed to drive her axe through the Dark Elf's skull, which she did with a grateful nod to Silmanus.

The assist nearly cost Silmanus his life. An orb of crackling black electricity flew toward Silmanus, who just barely threw up a shield in time. The orb struck his glowing white barrier, sending arching tendrils of electricity in all directions. A spinning blade of dark magic, trailing wisps of black smoke, spun toward Silmanus from the other wizard, but Silmanus pushed magical energy into his staff and batted the blade aside, sending him harmlessly into the ground.

The High Elf wizard struck back with a barrage of magical icicles, managing to injure a couple nearby Dark Elves but failing to strike his intended target.

The air suddenly hissed and popped as Silmanus began building electrical energy around himself. Sparks leapt from his skin and his staff began to glow bright blue. Eyes flashing, Silmanus sent a brilliant beam of lightning streaking toward the Dark Elf wizard. The

Dark Elf had tried to raise a shield, but Silmanus' spell fried right through it, blasting into the Dark Elf's chest with deadly electricity. The dark wizard collapsed, his skin charred and smoking.

Silmanus was beginning to feel the familiar cold, empty feeling that came with extended use of magic, like a part of himself was starting to shrivel away. Beads of sweat were rolling down his cheeks, his heart pounding in his labouring chest. He had to be careful. The giant shield he'd cast had used a lot of magic, and so had the wards he'd put in place. But he couldn't let up. His friends still needed him, and he was almost finished with the wizards.

Just one more left.

Mara deftly spun her sword around in a wide parry to deflect two lightning-fast dagger strikes, stepping around her opponent as she did so. Three powerful sword strikes rained down on the Dark Elf, who just barely crossed his daggers in time to block. The Dark Elf hacked and stabbed, trying to break Mara's impeccable defences, but to no avail.

Desperate, the Dark Elf flung one of his daggers at Mara, hoping to catch her off guard.

He did. Mara let out a cry of pain as the Dark Elf's dagger scraped against her shoulder, delivering a poison into her body that burned like acid.

Despite the pain, Mara still managed to deflect a sharp stab at her side, kicking out at the Dark Elf's chest as she did so. The elf was sent sprawling onto his back and Mara's sword was quick to finish him off.

But the damage was done. Mara pressed three fingers to her shoulder, wincing as she did. They were stained crimson when she removed them. Already she could feel poison burning through her veins. It wasn't much, she knew, and perhaps not enough to kill her, but certainly enough to encumber her.

Trying her best to shrug away the pain, Mara whirled to face her next opponent, swinging her sword in a quick feint before diving underneath the Dark Elf's defences with a powerful thrust. The Dark Elf spotted the feint however, sidestepping the thrust and counterattacking with a couple quick strikes of his own.

Teeth gritted, Mara moved her sword to parry, relieved to find that her injury was more of a nuisance than an actual hinderance. But how long would it be before the poison changed that?

Allowing himself a cocky grin, Silmanus turned to face the final wizard, who was in the midst of casting a rather long spell. That was bad. Almost always, the longer a spell took to cast, the more powerful it became. Hastily, Silmanus prepared the strongest defence he could muster, praying that his spell would finish in time.

When the Dark Elf finished his casting, a jagged line of black energy raced toward Silmanus, just as the High Elf set a glistening shield in place. Much to the High Elf's surprise, however, the dark spell smashed his shield apart, spraying Silmanus with glass-like shards of magic that scraped up the wizard's face.

That was hardly the worst of it. Although its effects had been cushioned, the spell still retained its potency and slammed into Silmanus' chest with startling force. Silmanus gasped as deadly necrotic energy coursed through him, eating away at his magic and bringing forth pain worse than Silmanus had thought possible. He toppled to the ground, writhing and screaming as the Dark Elf's spell did its work.

It was one of the worst feelings Silmanus had ever endured. All his life, he had been in tune with the magic within him. It had been an ever-present comfort to him, a familiar warmth that never left his side. And now, Silmanus could feel it dying, could feel *him* dying, his magic beginning to blacken and shrivel, the warmth turning to icy cold. Silmanus felt alone, so alone, cut off from the very thing that made him who he was.

The spell was no longer lethal, Silmanus' shield had done that much, but the pain was excruciating and Silmanus was now a sitting duck for whatever else the wizard decided to throw at him. Silmanus was crippled, with no way to defend himself against the orb of black magic that was now soaring through the air toward him, trailing black smoke as it raced to deal a killing blow.

Executing a flawless corkscrew manoeuvre, Mara managed to smash aside the Dark Elf's defences and drive her sword in for the killing blow, flicking it toward the Dark Elf's chest like a serpent tongue. The elf gasped as his body went limp and he slumped to the ground.

It was then that Mara heard the screams, the shrieks of agony coming from Silmanus as Dark Elf magic tore apart his soul. Mara spun around and saw Silmanus collapsed and thrashing on the ground, veins black and bulging out of his silvery skin. Mara also noticed a black orb sailing through the air, heading straight for Silmanus.

She could do nothing for him. It broke her, because over the many days they had spent together, Mara truly had grown fond of the brilliant wizard, even if she tried to hide it. He had proved himself and his worth to her time and time again, standing by Mara in every time of need, fighting alongside her even though he owed her nothing.

Now here she was, completely unable to save him. He was going to die and there was simply nothing Mara could do about it. She was too far away and did not possess the tools or powers necessary to protect Silmanus from the oncoming spell.

So, swallowing her hurt, Mara drew one of her knives, gripping it by the tip as she took aim. Blue eyes wet with tears of grief and regret but blazing with an icy fury all the same, Mara snapped her arm forward, sending the dirk flying toward the final wizard. The knife spun once, twice, three times before sinking into the throat of the unsuspecting Dark Elf. He gurgled as blood welled up in his throat, bubbling out of his mouth as his weak hands clamped against the wound.

The final Dark Elf wizard sank to his knees, the life gone from his eyes as he fell dead onto his face. The battle was almost won, the last few Dark Elves struggling against the combined might of the remaining defenders. And so, with nothing else to be done, Mara dropped her sword and fell to her knees, watching helplessly as Silmanus' doom fell upon him from the sky.

Chapter 28:
Mordasine

MORDASINE STOOD THERE, HIS USUAL COCKY SNEER stretched across his imperious, narrow features, a sadistic twinkle gleaming in his cold, silver eyes. He was dressed in the typical Dark Elf uniform—tight-fitting black with a chain shirt underneath the shirt and jerkin—but with his signature bracers glinting menacingly along his forearms. Two more Dark Elves stood to either side of Mordasine, daggers drawn and wearing the typical arrogant smirk of a Dark Elf.

"Where are all of you off to in such a hurry?" Mordasine asked. "King Zarat still has need of your generous services."

"Don't ye try t' stop me," Amber snarled. "I've no qualms about splatterin' yer brains across the cobbles."

"You think I'm intimidated by you, dwarf?" Mordasine scoffed.

"I think I'm tired o' hearin' yer voice!" Guralyn snapped, brandishing her broadsword. "Either ye get runnin' back now or me and mine will teach ye a whole new meanin' o' pain!"

Mordasine laughed. "This shall be entertaining."

Thalassar and Ayra raised their bows and fired, sending two arrows streaking toward Mordasine's chest. The Dark Elf just pressed a button on each of his bracers, rocketing the daggers forward and flicking his wrists to tangle the wires around the oncoming arrows. Another flick of Mordasine's wrists sent each arrow spinning to the side, just as two more raced forth.

Mordasine spun and whipped his arm up, slapping the cord of his bracer into the arrows and deflecting them off course. Thalassar and Ayra reached down to their quivers only to find them empty.

"Out of arrows?" Mordasine mocked. "Good. Now the *real* fun begins. Because, you see, the king has given me permission to kill you at last."

Amber scoffed. "Ye really expect me t' believe that?" she chortled. "Ye need the lot o' us alive and we're knowin' it."

Mordasine smirked. "Oh, Amber, dear, you truly are as thick as they come. We only *need* you, your mother, or your father; the rest of you have been kept alive out of hope that you'd see reason and join us. Evidently, however, that's not happening. So, we get to kill all of you but one!"

Tightening her grip on her hammer, Amber spat on the ground. "Take yer best shot, ye ugly son o' an ogre."

"Spilling your filthy dwarf blood shall be my greatest pleasure," Mordasine shot back.

With a cackle, Mordasine spun low and forward, springing back up with a violent flick of his wrists and sending his daggers straight at Guralyn and Harik. The dwarves swiped down at the flying daggers as they leapt to the side, batting the flying blades into the cobbles.

Gripping the cords with his hands, Mordasine yanked the daggers back up, tangling them around Guralyn and Harik's weapons. The two dwarves held on tight as Mordasine clicked another button and the cords started retracting into the bracers.

Guralyn and Harik proved stronger, however, maintaining a tight grip on their weapons as Jeddo and Amber charged at Mordasine, weapons drawn.

Thalassar savoured the smooth feeling of his sword's grip in his hands as he drew it from its sheath. The sword, just like Ayra's, had a long, curving blade, made of Silversteel and forged by the finest elven smiths. It was decorated with silver runes that shimmered with a faint blue light and an ornate pommel sat at the end of its curved wooden hilt.

Thalassar charged toward one of the Dark Elf guards, pushing away the fatigue and exhaustion that threatened to impair his movements. Thalassar came on with all the grace of a seasoned High Elf warrior, corkscrewing down at the Dark Elf with devastating force. The Dark Elf angled his daggers, stepping forward around the blow and allowing Thalassar's blade to simply slide along the daggers.

The two elves quickly settled into the familiar dance of sword combat, twirling around each other with their weapons spinning and flashing. Even tired and wounded, Thalassar was an impeccable warrior, one of the finest Faeryln had ever bred. In spite of that, however, the Dark Elf was keeping pace with Thalassar's rapid attacks.

Thalassar narrowed his deep blue eyes. This was no ordinary Dark Elf. All Dark Elves were quite skilled with their blades, but Thalassar had studied their movements and determined that they were not much of a match for his own prowess. This Dark Elf, however, was even more skilled than usual. Thalassar would have to be careful.

Ayra followed Thalassar's lead, drawing her own sword and rushing toward the other guard. The sword's long, curving blade flashed, its silvery designs glinting as Ayra feinted high and struck low.

Like Thalassar across from her, Ayra had to push away the tiredness that lingered in her body, clinging to her like a leaden blanket.

The High Elf shoved it aside, focusing solely on the fight at hand. She weaved in and around her opponent, slashing and parrying wherever necessary.

In her day, Ayra had been among the finest warriors in the Royal Vanguards, possessed of skill beyond many of the captains that led her. She had never before met a Dark Elf that could keep pace with her.

This particular Dark Elf was good, however, very good, yet Ayra managed to deflect every single blow despite the nauseous feeling rising from her stomach. The only hit Ayra managed was a grazing blow across the Dark Elf's side, which was turned aside by the chain armour beneath.

Hatred broiled in Amber's chest, pure and unbridled, hatred toward this Dark Elf that had kidnapped her and her parents. Amber resented every single part of the arrogant elf before her and it showed in the fierce light burning in her eyes.

With a roar, Amber charged forward, Jeddo at her side. Mordasine noticed the charge and quickly realized he had bigger concerns than disarming Harik and Guralyn. Pressing a third button on each of his bracers, Mordasine detached the daggers, whose cords fell limply to the ground. Snapping his arms down, Mordasine replaced the old daggers with two new ones and pointed his wrists at Amber.

Amber heard a *click* and raised her shield as two daggers raced toward her. Much to Amber's surprise and horror, the first dagger punched into and through her shield, an inch of its deadly tip poking out of the back of the dwarf's shield. The other dagger wrapped around Amber before Mordasine yanked it back, smashing it into Amber's back. The dwarf's armour held strong, however, deflecting the blow with a crash.

The four former prisoners surrounded Mordasine, trying to pin down the slippery Dark Elf. Each of them fought with strength they had never known they had, fuelled by emotions ranging from rage to hope to desperation to a burning drive to exact vengeance on the looming shadow that had stood over their lives.

Mordasine was not so easy a foe to vanquish, however. There was a reason he led Vanaria's armies. Armed with his mesmerizing bracers and astonishing agility, the Dark Elf captain outmanoeuvred and outmatched everything that his foes threw at him, an endless supply of ballistic daggers at his disposal.

Thalassar came on fast and hard, powering forward with unrelenting strikes at every single angle of the Dark Elf's body. Abandoning all caution, Thalassar focused his movements solely on offensive attacks, his body spinning around in a graceful dance of flashing steel as he rained down blows on the Dark Elf.

The Dark Elf was put back on his heels by Thalassar's sudden ferocity, struggling to keep with the High Elf's lightning-fast attacks. The Dark Elf sent his daggers flying this way and that, batting aside every sword strike in the absolute nick of time, desperately searching for an opening for counterattack.

Thalassar did not allow for one. He kept up his intense attack routine, forcing the Dark Elf back and using offence as defence, never giving the Dark Elf the time he needed to counterattack.

But Thalassar's routine had a distinctive weakness: it was very tiring, and no matter how strong Thalassar's willpower was, his weakened body could not sustain the highly energetic offensive for much longer.

Thalassar ignored that fact, pressing his attacks even faster, hoping he could wear down the Dark Elf before his own body succumbed to exhaustion. Thalassar hammered again and again with his sword, slashing at every conceivable angle as he battered away his opponent's resolve.

Yet something in those lightning strikes betrayed the High Elf. Each blow that rained down on the Dark Elf came just a bit slower, hit just a bit weaker. It was a difference too subtle for a novice to notice, but the Dark Elf was a seasoned veteran. He knew that Thalassar was tiring.

And when the High Elf could fight no more, then he would fall to the daggers of Vanaria.

Where Thalassar chose to use aggression to batter down his opponent, Ayra focused her energy on defence, keeping her movements tight and close to her body, waiting for the opportunity for a counterattack to present itself.

Despite having put herself in a defensive position, Ayra was actually not at a disadvantage. She held her ground, expending as little energy as possible to keep up her very patient defence, waiting for that perfect moment to arrive, the moment when she would strike back and lay low the Dark Elf.

That moment did not seem to be arriving, however. As more and more dagger strikes rained down, Ayra began questioning whether or not her strategy had been a smart one. But she kept up her defensive posture, flicking her sword out to either side to quickly bat away two slashes.

As the Dark Elf ducked and spun, twisted and turned, stabbed and slashed, Ayra simply held her ground, keeping her footwork small and tight, her sword weaving around her body but never straying far from it. It was working, Ayra noticed. Her opponent was gradually beginning to tire.

But Ayra was in trouble too. Despite her highly conservative fighting style, her body wasn't in a very good state to be fighting.

She was hungry and weak, each blow she blocked sapping more and more of her limited strength.

Decisively, Ayra suddenly switched to the attack, trying to startle her opponent into a mistake. The Dark Elf was indeed surprised, pushed suddenly into a defensive posture that left her struggling to keep up.

But she was keeping up all the same, blocking every single one of Ayra's strikes. And Ayra's arms were beginning to burn with fatigue.

Suddenly appearing behind Harik and Guralyn, Mordasine retracted his blades and shot them out again immediately, sending the lethal projectiles flying toward the backs of the dwarves. Amber was just barely able to get her shield in place in front of Harik's back, angling it so Mordasine's daggers just glanced off instead of penetrating the shield.

Guralyn was not so lucky. Jeddo flung himself at the dwarf, protective cloak outstretched, but he wasn't quick enough.

The dwarf let out a roar of pain as Mordasine's dagger sunk into her shoulder, piercing flesh and bone as it came out on the other side. Mordasine grinned and yanked his arm back, snagging the dagger on Guralyn's wound and bringing forth another agonized cry from the dwarf. Guralyn was pulled backward, stumpy legs stumbling as they tried to keep the stout dwarf on her feet.

Hollering as she did, Guralyn grabbed hold of the cord behind her back and threw all of her considerable weight forward. Mordasine, a lithe and lightweight Dark Elf, was thrown off his feet, pulled forward by his own weapon and skidding across the cobbles with a wince.

In the absolute nick of time, Mordasine detached the dagger he had shot at Guralyn and rolled to the side before Amber's warhammer came smashing down, shattering the stone that had been covered by Mordasine's head just a moment before.

The battle continued, although Guralyn was no longer a part of it. The others did not let Guralyn's injury get to them, however, trying their best to maintain the aggression they needed to lay Mordasine low.

But the Dark Elf had taken control of the battle and he had no intention of giving it away. While Jeddo, Amber, and Harik stabbed, swung, and slashed, Mordasine ducked and rolled between every blow, firing his deadly daggers at every opportunity.

"How many daggers does this bloody elf have?" Jeddo muttered as he ran toward Mordasine, breathing hard.

The charge was cut short, however, as Mordasine swung a pair of daggers toward the gnome, forcing him to take cover beneath his cloak.

Amber cursed. Every single attack the trio unleashed at the dancing Dark Elf was thwarted. They could not break his seemingly impenetrable defences. Mordasine didn't even seem to be tiring at all, fatigue apparently a foreign concept to this indomitable warrior.

Off to the side, Guralyn grimaced as she slowly pulled the cord and dagger out of her shoulder. Tossing the weapon to the side, Guralyn hunched over, panting, waiting for whatever lethal poison coating Mordasine's blades to take hold.

Thalassar felt his arms slowly growing heavy, his sword becoming harder and harder to move with every swing he took. Each jolt of steel against steel became gradually more painful, each step of his graceful feet sapping more and more strength from Thalassar's tired legs.

The Dark Elf was tiring too, but much less noticeably than

Thalassar. Gradually, the Dark Elf pressed the offensive, Thalassar's fatigued arms unable to maintain that unending barrage of strikes that had kept the High Elf alive for so long.

Now their positions had been reversed. The Dark Elf's blows were raining down from every angle and Thalassar had to duck and spin desperately to avoid the deadly strikes, his sword flashing here and there as the High Elf tried fiercely to keep himself alive.

The Dark Elf sneered as his dagger dove over Thalassar's parry, stabbing into the High Elf's shoulder. Thalassar roared in anguish, his shoulder burning in pain as the Dark Elf's blade twisted in the wound. Laughing sadistically, the Dark Elf pressed the dagger farther and farther into Thalassar's shoulder, twisting the slender blade as he did. Thalassar was driven to his knees, sinking into the cobbles as the strength seeped out of his legs.

Each movement of the Dark Elf's insidious dagger brought fresh waves of agony rolling across Thalassar's body. Tears sprang into the High Elf's eyes, tears brought forth not only by the physical pain of the Dark Elf's dagger but also by the knowledge that Thalassar had lost. Here, so close to freedom, he would meet his end. The High Elf could already feel the vile Dark Elf poison creeping through his veins, eating away at Thalassar's strength and vitality. The edges of Thalassar's vision started darkening, his mind began dulling.

Indignation flooded through Thalassar like a wave of fire, broiling inside him and sharpening his dulling mind. This was *not* how it ended. It couldn't be.

With a guttural roar, Thalassar heaved his sword up, using the last of his fading strength to drive the blade into the Dark Elf's chest. The Dark Elf gasped, blood pumping out of his chest.

Thalassar's head lolled back, his limp hand falling from the hilt of his sword. Darkness clouded over the High Elf's vision. It could be over now. He would die, but he would do so with the knowledge that he had taken yet another of the Dark Elf scum with him.

As his body hit the cobbles, Thalassar's last thought was of Ayra, a silent apology to his beloved wife. Perhaps someday, he would see her again, in another life.

Thalassar closed his eyes and the darkness swallowed him whole.

Ayra fought against the exhaustion that was slowly creeping into her muscles. She steeled her mind against the fatigue, trying to simply will away the soreness she felt across her entire body.

It wasn't enough, however. There are some things that not even willpower can defeat. No matter how much Ayra told herself she wasn't, the High Elf was still tired, still fatigued, and her body was beginning to succumb to it.

Ayra couldn't press the attack much longer. Her blade fell slower and lighter now, each strike harder and harder to bring about. Ayra simply could not keep fighting.

Just as the High Elf thought her arms might fall off, so badly did they burn, a small miracle happened. The Dark Elf took a step backward, placing her foot right in the crater Amber's hammer had made earlier. With a cry, the Dark Elf crumpled to one knee, her ankle twisting and sending a shock of pain up the Dark Elf's leg.

A rush of hope surged through Ayra's body, suddenly giving her the strength she needed to continue. Ayra's sword hammered down again and again, battering continuously against the Dark Elf's crossed daggers. The Dark Elf could not stand, could not move out of the way. She held her daggers in that crossed parry, arms slowly giving out against Ayra's renewed ferocity.

Ayra swung down but suddenly darted her blade to the side, cutting it into one of the Dark Elf's arms. The Dark Elf cried out, her tortured shriek piercing the air. One of the Dark Elf's daggers clattered to the ground.

Ayra struck again, severing the Dark Elf's other hand at the wrist, sending hand and dagger falling to the cobbles. The Dark Elf screamed again, clutching the bleeding stump to her chest. A fountain of scarlet spouted from the wound, drenching the Dark Elf's uniform in blood.

Ayra's blade came across one last time, cutting a deep, crimson line across the Dark Elf's pale throat. With a breathless gasp, the Dark Elf's eyes widened, lines of blood dribbling out of her mouth. Her limp body crumpled to the cobbles, which were now stained deep red, and the light faded from her sinister silver eyes.

Panting heavily, Ayra rested the tip of her sword on the ground, scarcely able to believe she had won the fight. Exhaustion hit her suddenly like a sledgehammer, nearly knocking the tired High Elf off her shaky feet.

Ayra managed to look up, taking in the fierce battle being fought against Mordasine. The Dark Elf was proving to be a very formidable foe, but Ayra believed, or perhaps hoped, her companions would beat him. She would not be needed, not that she had any help to spare.

A hollow grin crept across Ayra's face. They were going to win. She had won her fight, Mordasine would surely be defeated, and Thalassar…

Ayra's face blanched as her eyes settled on her beloved splayed out on the cobbles, eyes closed and bleeding from a grisly wound on his shoulder.

Guralyn waited, hunched over against her knees, blood oozing out of her shoulder. She waited for the dizziness, the pain, the darkness to consume her mind, for the poison to take control and drain her of life.

Guralyn frowned. She should be experiencing something by now, some form of pain or wooziness. Dark Elf poison was always fast-acting. There was no reason Guralyn was not suffering from the symptoms of some poison or another.

Unless Mordasine's blades weren't poisoned.

Wincing, Guralyn reached down and scooped up the dagger that had pierced her shoulder. She gave it a tentative lick with the tip of her tongue but tasted only the metallic taste of blood and steel.

There was no poison.

Guralyn grinned. For whatever reason, Mordasine did not, or perhaps *could* not, poison his blades. Which meant Guralyn was not yet out of the fight.

With a fierce yell, Guralyn raised her broadsword and charged at Mordasine's back, all pain forgotten. The Dark Elf immediately turned to face her, whipping one of his daggers at the dwarf's face. Guralyn smacked the dagger aside with the flat of her sword before swinging her blade at Mordasine's chest.

Jeddo, Amber, and Harik each shared a grin as they noticed Guralyn's charge, their spirits rekindled by the sight of their comrade fighting once more. They pressed the offensive, hoping that Guralyn's return would be enough to finally over-whelm Mordasine.

The Dark Elf was not making it easy. Mordasine's daggers whipped around at Harik, and this time, the dwarf was not so lucky. One dagger missed, but the other wrapped around Harik's axe arm, the sharp blade slicing into Harik's flesh as it struck skin. Mordasine whipped the other dagger back around and it sliced into the back of Harik's shoulder, bringing a roar from the mighty dwarf.

In what seemed to be the same second, Mordasine yanked his daggers free of Harik, worsening the existing wounds and causing the dwarf to crumple to the ground, shaking in anguish and bleed-ing across the cobblestones.

The others tried to pounce on Mordasine, but Jeddo's luck ran out right then too. As the gnome jumped over a flying dagger,

Mordasine snapped his wrist back, tangling the dagger's cord around Jeddo's ankle. With a mighty yank, Mordasine pulled Jeddo's leg out from underneath him. The gnome went into the air and slammed back down on his back, cracking his head against the cobbles and splitting his scalp. Jeddo lay there, stunned and bleeding superficially from his head.

Quickly dodging a furious swipe of Amber's hammer, Mordasine reloaded his bracers and fired at Guralyn, piercing the dwarf through her left thigh. Guralyn cried out and Mordasine heaved on the cord, slamming Guralyn to the ground. The dwarf clutched her bleeding leg, moaning and unable to stand.

Mordasine turned to Amber with an evil sneer. "That just leaves you."

With a roar, Amber rushed at Mordasine, hammer raised. Mordasine just laughed, sidestepped the blow, and shot two daggers out at Amber. She raised her shield desperately, but the daggers punched through, smashing through Amber's gauntlet as well to root themselves in the dwarf's arm.

Amber screamed, agony racing up her injured arm. Mordasine yanked his arms back, pulling Amber close to him. Amber tried to raise her hammer but Mordasine caught the weapon in a strong hand and twisted it out of Amber's grasp, tossing the weapon to the side with a crash. As Amber attempted to bash Mordasine with her shield, the Dark Elf grabbed the shield and yanked it off of Amber's arm, sending fresh waves of anguish rolling up the dwarf's arm as the daggers were torn out with it.

Mordasine reloaded his bracers, grabbing Amber by the throat with one hand and sticking the bracer of the other under Amber's chin.

"Did you really think you could get away, dwarf?" Mordasine sneered. "You never stood a chance. I'm going to kill you now. It will be a quick death, far quicker than vermin like you deserve. Your parents, however, will be saved. They will be tortured and broken and made to help us where you would not, do you understand? I am going to end you, destroy your parents, and burn the world. And there is nothing, *nothing*, you or anyone else can do to stop me."

Amber gave a weak grin. "Actually, I can think o' something," she gasped against Mordasine's choking grip.

Mordasine snorted. "You're thinking of something?" he asked incredulously. "What's this, a dwarf trying to use her head?"

Amber's grin broadened. "Yep."

She suddenly smashed her head forward, driving her forehead into the bridge of Mordasine's nose. Mordasine gave a cry as his nose snapped, blood spurting from his nostrils. Amber drove her head against Mordasine's again, cracking her skull against his. Dwarves had notoriously thick and hard skulls and Mordasine was getting a full dose of one.

The Dark Elf dropped Amber, hunching over and clutching his throbbing head. A large lump swelled where the skin of his forehead had been split open, blood now trickling into his eyes.

Amber staggered tiredly over to her hammer, scooping it up off the ground. "Listen here, ye pale-skinned bastard," she said, walking back over to the agonized Mordasine. "Ye and yer kind killed me people once. Ye'll not be doin' it again. Ye end here, and with ye, whatever futile plan yer deranged king has brewin' in that twisted mind o' his."

Amber swung her hammer in a wide, powerful arc. It cracked into Mordasine's jaw, shattering bone as it spun the Dark Elf off his feet. Mordasine's limp body slammed into the ground, his neck broken.

Amber spat on his face. "That'll teach ye t' mess with a dwarf."

With that, Amber turned to congratulate her friends, to enjoy a small moment of victory before they had to start running again. Instead, her heart fell into her stomach as she saw Ayra huddled over Thalassar's limp body, tears flooding from her eyes.

CHAPTER 29:
THE KINDNESS
OF STRANGERS

"NO! NO! NO!" AYRA PROTESTED WILDLY, CRADLING Thalassar's head in her arms as she rocked back and forth on the ground. Tears flowed freely from her eyes like waterfalls, spilling across the ground as she mourned for her husband.

Amber staggered over, looking down regretfully at the High Elves. "I'm so sorry," she muttered. "There's nothin' ye can do."

"I can't lose him," Ayra whispered hollowly, big watery eyes staring down at Thalassar. She pushed a strand of his long, dark hair out of his handsome face, stroking her slender finger along the side of Thalassar's neck.

Ayra's eyes suddenly widened in surprise. "Oh my Gods," she muttered, pressing her hand against the side of Thalassar's neck. A joyful smile split her face. "A pulse! He's still alive!" Ayra looked up at Amber, eyes twinkling. "He's alive!"

Amber gave her the saddest smile Ayra had ever seen. "Aye, but not fer long," the dwarf said solemnly, pointing at the fallen Dark Elf's dagger. "Poison."

Ayra looked at Amber with one last glimmer of hope in her eyes. "But-but you're fine," she stammered, pointing at Amber's wounded arm. "And Harik and Guralyn, none of you are poisoned!"

It killed Amber to have to crush that light in Ayra's eyes. "Ayra, I'm sorry. Mordasine's blades weren't poisoned. I'm fer guessin' they were magical or somethin'. But that's just a regular Dark Elf dagger. It'd be poisoned. And look, ye can already see the signs." Amber pointed to the yellow-green tint of Thalassar's wound.

Desperation crept back into Ayra's features. "No," she breathed, turning her head back to Thalassar. "No no no no no, he's alive, he's alive, he can't die." She was screaming now. "No! This isn't *fair*! Somebody, help him! Someone, please!"

Amber noticed then that a large crowd of Dark Elves had gathered to watch. They were standing in a large ring, staring at the wounded prisoners with the same mixture of expressions as earlier. None of them moved.

Ayra turned to the crowd. "Why won't any of you save him?" she shrieked angrily. "*You* did this to him! It is *your* people's fault that he's here! You kidnapped him, dragged him into a cell for a *hundred years* and now here he is, dying for trying to escape the nightmare *you* forced him into! Why won't any of you *do something*?!"

There was an uncomfortable shift in the crowd as those who spoke Common digested Ayra's words. But still, no one moved. Amber looked at Ayra with sad eyes. "There's nothin' ye can do," she said again softly.

"Out of my way," a smooth voice suddenly said in slightly accented Common. Amber spun around to see a Dark Elf pushing his way through the crowd. He was dressed in simple black clothes and carrying a large leather bag.

Quickly, the Dark Elf strode over to Thalassar. Ayra eyed him suspiciously. "What are you doing?" she asked in a wavering voice.

"Saving his life," the Dark Elf murmured, opening his bag and rummaging through it. He pulled out a small glass vile full of a dark purple liquid, removed the stopper, and tipped it into Thalassar's mouth.

Several Dark Elves in the crowd began shouting angrily. Cries of "Traitor!" and "Heretic!" rang through the air but they were quickly shushed by the other Dark Elves.

The Dark Elf then produced a needle and thread and quickly stitched Thalassar's wound shut, wrapping it in a bandage after he was done, all the while Amber and Ayra watched in disbelief.

The Dark Elf rose, nodding with a serious expression on his face. "He is weak, but he is also a High Elf. With the antidote, I am confident he will recover, although he will need rest." Nodding at Amber's shield arm, the Dark Elf said, "Please, remove your gauntlets and bracers, I'd like to inspect your wounds."

Dumbfounded, Amber did as she was told, absently raising her arm and removing the armour on it. The Dark Elf clicked his tongue and quickly wrapped the arm in a bandage. "You should be fine. I see no signs of poison and they are small wounds."

The Dark Elf scooped up his bag and moved on to Jeddo, but Amber caught his arm. The Dark Elf whirled around.

"Why are ye doin' this?" Amber asked, honestly confused about why the Dark Elf was helping them.

The Dark Elf took a deep breath. "Because it's the right thing to do," he said at length. "And some of us are tired of doing the wrong thing." Then the Dark Elf pulled his arm free and inspected Jeddo's wounds, patching him up as necessary before doing the same for Guralyn and Harik.

"Zysta," the Dark Elf called suddenly. "Bring it here."

A little Dark Elf girl, perhaps twelve years of age, waddled through the crowd, which parted curiously for her. She was dragging a heavy sack across the cobbles.

The Dark Elf tossed some bandages into it and handed it to Amber. "It is full of food and water. Take a ship and get out of here."

Amber accepted the sack gratefully. "What's yer name, elf?" she asked.

"I am Sylatus," the Dark Elf answered. Sylatus pointed to the young elf he had called for, Zysta. "This is my daughter. My wife is named Namara, but she is ill and at home."

Amber nodded. "I'll be rememberin' those names, Sylatus," she promised. "Mine's Amber. Amber Ironheart. Ye saved Thalassar today and spared Ayra, his wife, a great deal o' grief. And ye patched up me friend, Jeddo, and me parents, Harik and Guralyn. Ye remember those names too, Dark Elf. Each o' them owe ye a tremendous debt."

Thalassar suddenly let out a heavy gasp, his lungs snatching greedily at whatever air they could find. The colour had returned to his keen blue eyes and he propped himself up on a shaking elbow, his body suddenly wracked by barking coughs.

Ayra ran over to him, dropping to her knees with an expression of pure joy on her face, flinging her arms around her husband and burying her face in his good shoulder. "You're ok!" she exclaimed.

Thalassar's voice was husky and weak when he spoke. "I'm ok," he whispered back, falteringly draping an arm across Ayra's back in the closest thing to a hug he could manage.

Her heart swelling with happiness, Ayra helped Thalassar to his feet, wrapping her arm around his back to support him.

"No, I'm alright," Thalassar protested. "I can manage myself."

Ayra gave him a concerned look. "Thalassar," she scolded. "Now is not the time to be prideful."

Thalassar smiled meekly. "You are right," he answered. "Alright. Help me along then, as you have always done."

Amber let out an exasperated sigh. "Can't the two o' ye save the sappiness fer when we're actually on the damned ship?" she snapped. "We gotta run before the Dark Elf reinforcements get here!"

"Wait!" Sylatus called after them. Amber stopped and turned to regard him. "You can't go that way. The gates to the harbour are magically shut and dozens of guards swarm the battlements."

"Then how do we get out?" Amber asked anxiously, struggling to stop herself from yelling.

"Follow me," Sylatus said, darting through the crowd toward a side street.

Jeddo and the dwarves followed, with Ayra and Thalassar hobbling after them, moving painfully slow across the cobbles. Anxiety broiled in Amber. If they took too long, the Dark Elves would catch them. Amber very nearly picked Thalassar right up to carry him and would have if not for the state of her arm.

The prisoners stumbled slowly along, Sylatus hissing at them to hurry and glancing nervously around. He led the group down an alleyway, pointing to a grate at the end of it.

"There," he said. "It's a storm drain. Empties out at the base of the harbour. You'll need to be quick, however. If the guards on the battlements notice you, they'll open fire."

As Jeddo began fiddling with the rusty lock on the drain, Amber nodded to Sylatus and held out her uninjured arm, which Sylatus firmly shook. "I thank ye again, Dark Elf," Amber said. For the first time in her life, the dwarf said the words "Dark Elf" without any malice. "Ne'er will I forget what ye did."

Jeddo finished with the lock and threw it to the side, opening the grate and clambering down, followed by Harik, Guralyn, and the elves.

"Just get out of here," Sylatus ushered. "Get out of here and win the war against my king."

Amber nodded again, lingering her gaze on Sylatus' silver gaze for just a moment. Perhaps not all Dark Elves had evil in their eyes.

With that, Amber slipped down the drain, wincing as she landed on the stone floor of the drain tunnel.

The drain tunnel was dank and musty, lacking in any lighting whatsoever. The gurgling of water echoed off the tunnel's curved walls, coming from a small stream that ran down the centre. The tunnel was tall enough for Amber, her parents, and Jeddo to stand, but Thalassar and Ayra had to stoop.

They couldn't see where they were going, but they didn't need to. There were no forks in the tunnel, no way to go but forward or backward. A pinpoint of light at the end of the tunnel marked the direction they needed to go.

Amber wasn't sure how long they trudged through that musty passage, but it felt like eternity. Eventually, however, they reached the tunnel's end, noticing with frustration that it was covered at the end by a thick grate.

Amber wasn't going to let that stop them. Praying that the waves would be enough to mask the sound, she hammered furiously at the metal bars, grimacing as a rush of pain flamed up her arm with each strike. Finally, after several loud, ringing blows, the side of the gate popped loose from the stone it was embedded in and Amber managed to pry it open.

The prisoners stumbled out, each of them fighting back a cry as they fell from the drain to a stone ledge below, presumably placed there for access to the drains for maintenance.

Amber gasped as she looked up. Her parents swooned and the elves nearly fell over with delight. Jeddo just smiled.

Before them was water. Not a wall, not a gate, not a patrol of armed Dark Elves. Just water and waves, rolling out for as far as the eye could see. A gentle sea breeze filled their nostrils with the smell of salt, waves lapping up at the ledge, spraying drops of water up at the group. The sky was still dark, and the water was a murky black, but none of them cared.

It was freedom all the same.

To their left, Amber noticed a set of stairs that led up to a series of long docks. Roughly a dozen ships sat moored against those docks, their black masts towering into the cloudy sky, flags flapping in the breeze.

Hugging the wall behind them so as not to fall into the black water below, the prisoners inched their way toward the stairs, all of them with pounding hearts. Escape was close, but so much could still go so wrong.

Jeddo went first, creeping up the stairs to peer around at his surroundings. After a moment, the gnome slipped back down the stairs to report to his friends.

"There are no guards on the docks," Jeddo told them, seeming almost giddy. "They must be on the inside of the wall, waiting for us. The guards on the battlements have their backs turned, too. They're not paying attention to harbour."

Amber felt like she was a child. This was it. Their chance to escape was finally upon them. "Ye find us a ship?" she asked. Jeddo nodded. "Then lead the way."

The group made their way hurriedly up the stairs. Jeddo pointed to a small, nimble ship, with two towering masts and bundled black sails. Like all the other ships, and apparently everything else in Vanaria, it was painted midnight black, silver lettering scrawled along the bow. Ropes and lines hung from the masts and the railings, seeming like a great big mess to Amber. "That one," he said. "Fastest one they've got, I reckon."

Dwarves weren't exactly fond of boats or sailing so Amber had absolutely no idea which ship was the fastest. Personally, she thought they should take the great big one, with three giant masts and armed with four ballistae and two small catapults. But Jeddo was the (ex) pirate, not Amber, so she took his word for it.

A narrow plank was the only way to access the sloop from the stone docks of Volhad. Guralyn was the first up it, wincing as the board bent and creaked beneath her weight. It held, however, and the dwarf made it safely aboard the ship.

"Watch yerselves across that," Guralyn called down to the group. "It's not very stable."

Thalassar followed, Ayra right behind him to catch him if he fell. The board didn't even shift as they limped across it.

Thalassar grinned at Guralyn as he joined her on the deck. "Time for a diet, maybe?"

"Stupid elves," Guralyn grumbled.

Harik was about to cross the plank but Jeddo held him back. "Help me and Amber undo the mooring lines."

"How in Gods' names do I do that?" Harik explained, glancing nervously over his shoulder at the wall. They still hadn't been noticed.

"Ye just untie the knot, knucklehead," Amber sighed.

Harik waggled a finger at her. "Ye watch how ye speak t' yer father," Harik scolded humorously before moving to undo the heavy ropes securing the sleek ship in place.

Jeddo darted across the wobbling plank, Amber traversing it nervously behind him, arms outstretched for balance.

Harik was the last to cross. As he reached the centre of the bowing plank, a loud *snap* suddenly rang out as the board splintered apart and broke in two beneath Harik's weight. With a cry of alarm, the dwarf plummeted into the murky water below, landing with a great splash and a cascade of water.

"Harik!" Guralyn cried, racing to the edge of the sloop and leaning over the railing, scanning the water for her husband. Jeddo's eyes flicked up to the battlements, trying to see if the Dark Elves had heard the splash or the shout. Miraculously, it seemed that they hadn't.

Gasping, Harik suddenly broke the surface of the water, his tangled red hair matted to his face as he floundered about, struggling to stay afloat.

Jeddo acted fast, tying a quick bowline and throwing it down to Harik. The dwarf slapped at it, grabbing it and slipping it over his shoulders. Amber and Guralyn grabbed hold of the rope, grunting as they hoisted Harik aboard, Amber only able to use one of her arms to pull.

Harik flopped down on his back across the deck, a pool of water growing around him, his hair and beard a complete mess. He lolled his head to look at the elves. "If either o' ye say a thing, I'm sending the both of ye for a swim," he growled. Ayra and Thalassar both cupped a hand to their mouths to hide their grins.

Amber, however, was not grinning. She cast an anxious look at the harbour wall, then breathed a tremendous sigh of relief. The Dark Elves were still scanning the inside of the wall, not realizing the group had evaded them. But then, even if they did notice, it was too late. The group was already on the ship. Freedom was moments away.

Jeddo, meanwhile, got to work scrambling up the ratlines, letting down the sails and tying them in place, doing all sorts of fancy sailor things that went way over Amber's head. The gnome called down to Amber every now and then, telling her to tie this rope to that and pull on that line and whatever else Jeddo needed a hand with.

It took a short while, but Jeddo soon had the ship ready for sailing, taking a spot at the wheel and guiding it north. Amber had absolutely no idea how Jeddo knew which way was north. They didn't have a map and even if the stars were out, the cloud cover was too thick to see the sky. That worried Amber a bit, but she had learned to trust her companion's sense of direction.

Harik and Guralyn made their way below decks, both clearly very tired and anxious to get to bed. Ayra and Thalassar moved to the bow of the sloop, leaning over the railing and gazing at the horizon. At freedom.

"Do you think he's waiting for us? Our son?" Ayra asked.

"I do," Thalassar replied.

Ayra smiled. "I can't wait to see him again," she said. Thalassar had no reply, so she dangled one of her arms at her side and drifted it toward Thalassar, fumbling for his hand. She couldn't seem to find it blindly, so she looked down—and screamed.

Thalassar's hand was gone. And so was the rest of him.

Ayra whipped her gaze to the ship's port side, panic seizing her body as she saw a dozen Dark Elves lined up along the docks. One of them had her hand outstretched, a tendril of black magic reaching from it, coiled around Thalassar's helpless body.

Ayra rushed to the ship's railing, crying Thalassar's name in protest, reaching her arm desperately across the rail, fingers stretching for Thalassar's. He reached back, terror and desperation in his watering eyes, straining weakly against the Dark Elf's magical grasp.

As Thalassar was pulled farther and farther from her grasp by the Dark Elf's spell, Ayra collapsed against the railing, tears springing from her eyes as she watched the Dark Elves steal away her beloved for the second time that day.

Amber rushed on deck to see what was going on, eyes widening in horror as she watched what was happening. Fighting back tears of her own, the dwarf ran over to Ayra, grabbing the elf's arms and pulling her back just before Ayra dove over the side of the ship.

Arrows flew across the water, thudding into the ship's hull and deck, several of the shots just narrowly missing Amber and Ayra. Jeddo spun the ship's wheel, veering east in an attempt to increase the distance between them and the Dark Elves.

Another tendril of black magic shot toward the ship suddenly, groping fiercely at Amber, trying to grab hold of the dwarf the Dark Elves so desperately needed. Amber was just out of reach, however, and the tendril dissipated.

An explosion suddenly rocked the ship. The Dark Elf who had stolen Thalassar was bombarding the ship with magic, sending wispy orbs of dark energy flying at the ship's hulls. Each one blasted a hole in the wood, sending splinters flying in all directions. Water sloshed into some of the lower holes, bringing surprised cries from Guralyn and Harik below.

The dwarves were surprisingly quick thinkers, however, shoving barrels up against the holes wherever they could, managing to reduce the water intake.

Eventually, the sloop had sailed out of the Dark Elf's reach and her spells fell short, splashing into the water with sinister hisses, staining the water an inky black and sending clouds of black smoke rising into the air.

Amber grunted as Ayra elbowed her injured arm, forcing Amber to release the desperate elf, who immediately ran to the stern of the ship, her body shaking with both fury and sadness, watching helplessly as Thalassar was kicked and beaten. Two soldiers scooped Thalassar up by his arms, dragging the senseless elf back toward the palace.

Amber felt the familiar sensation of her heart falling like a stone in her chest. She had never been fond of elves; they were arrogant and ignorant, not caring about anyone beyond their borders except for the purposes of trade. But Amber had grown quickly attached to those two. She respected them both as warriors and as people, and something about escaping from sadistic tormenters together just caused instant bonding between people. Losing Thalassar was a blow to Amber in its own right and seeing Ayra so heartbroken just made it even worse.

The dwarf blinked away a couple drops of moisture that had gathered in her eyes, trying to stop her voice from breaking as she spoke.

"What do ye want me t' do about those holes?" she asked Jeddo.

At first, Jeddo did not reply, and it was only then that Amber saw the ache in his eyes. He, too, had grown to like Thalassar. Watching one of his friends be captured and seeing another in so much pain was not easy on Jeddo either.

"Take the wheel," Jeddo answered at length, heartache filling his voice. "Spin it right to turn right, spin it left to turn left. Keep us within sight of the coastline. I'm going to go help your parents."

Amber did as she was told, grateful to have the wheel there to help support her. Her arm was screaming and her legs felt weak. She knew it was much worse for Ayra, however. Amber had never loved someone in the way Ayra loved Thalassar but watching her parents "die" in front of her all those years ago had broken Amber and left a hole in the dwarf's heart that had not been filled until she had been reunited with her family.

After a few hours passed, the sky grew even darker as night set in, clouds still hanging thick above the sea, blotting out whatever stars might have been shining in the abyss above.

Jeddo emerged from belowdecks, giving Amber a tired smile as he walked over. "Ship should be all good to go," the gnome informed. He was trying to look strong, but Amber could still hear a note of sadness in his voice. "I've got to hand it to those Dark Elves, they do actually know what they're doing. There's plenty of tar and planks down there. I wouldn't go sailing this thing through a hurricane just yet, but it should get us safely to Fort Vanguard."

Fort Vanguard, Amber knew, was a stronghold in southeastern Pyradia, guarding the Black Strait and maintaining watch over any ships that passed across or around it. The stronghold was more of a massive wall running completely alongside the strait but Fort Vanguard itself was a highly secure citadel perched in the southernmost of The Forgotten Mountains. It contained the only port in Pyradia, where a formidable fleet of dwarven ships—a very rare concept indeed—was constantly ready to intercept any Dark Elf vessels.

Amber nodded. "I'll be sleepin' if ye need me," she said, clapping Jeddo on the back and casting a long look over at Ayra before descending to the bunks below.

The light of dawn crept slowly through the choking clouds above, eerily illuminating the murky waters through which the prisoners sailed.

Jeddo fought to keep his leaden eyes open, wanting to do nothing more than fall asleep but knowing that he needed to keep steering the ship. Jeddo hadn't slept much since they escaped

Volhad. He'd gotten Amber to take over a few times, but he wanted Amber to get her rest. She had been through a lot. They all had.

For the billionth time since Thalassar's capture, Jeddo felt his heart break apart, full of pain for both his captured friend and his heartbroken one. Jeddo couldn't fathom the kind of loss Ayra was suffering from.

They had been at sea for a day. One long, agonizing day, through which they had all struggled to cope with the barrage of emotions that constantly weathered their hearts. Rest brought remembrance, and remembrance brought pain. Ayra, in particular, had been struggling to deal with the inability to do anything except sit on the ship and wait.

As if his thoughts had somehow summoned her, Ayra suddenly appeared on deck. Dark circles hung beneath her bloodshot eyes, dried tears staining her cheeks. She was fully dressed for battle and a fierce light burned in her eyes.

"Turn this ship around," Ayra ordered coldly. "We're going back for him."

Jeddo felt his heart break a little bit more. This wasn't the first time Ayra had told Jeddo to turn around. "Ayra, we can't," Jeddo replied softly. "There are only five of us. It took six to get out and we had the element of surprise then. They'll be expecting us this time." Jeddo couldn't bring himself to also mention the simple fact that Thalassar might be dead.

"I am not going to run away and leave him to the torment of those *sadists*!" Ayra bellowed, pointing accusingly at the land behind them. Her other hand began drifting to the hilt of her sword. "If you won't take me there, I'll go there myself."

"Ayra, listen to me," Jeddo said, urgency creeping into his voice. "We're going to go back for him, I promise. But not yet. Our ship is still damaged and none of us have had time to properly recover. We're almost at Fort Vanguard. We'll warn the dwarves, resupply, get ourselves a new ship or repair this one. Maybe we can even bring an army of Pyradian Dwarves along with us. But if we go back now, we die, and that does nothing to help Thalassar. Ok?"

Jeddo could see the conflict in Ayra's eyes. They'd been through this before though, just after they pulled away from Volhad, and Jeddo felt sure she'd see reason. Still, that didn't make it any less painful to watch.

After a very tense minute, Ayra finally nodded, relaxing her arms at her sides. "Ok," she whispered. "Ok." All the strength and fury seemed to have flushed right out of the elf.

"Ok," Jeddo repeated, watching sadly as Ayra shuffled back down to the hold.

Anger began bubbling in the gnome's stomach. The Dark Elves had taken so much from Ayra. They had stolen her from her child, forced her to endure a hundred years of suffering, and now they had taken her husband from her just moments before they escaped. Ayra's outbursts were one of the hardest things for Jeddo to deal with. Seeing someone so strong brought low to such an emotionally devastating state...it filled Jeddo with a fury beyond anything he had felt before.

Jeddo vowed to keep his promise to Ayra, that they would go back to Vanaria with an army at their backs, rescue Thalassar, and stop whatever vile plot the Dark Elves were planning.

King Zarat was going to pay.

CHAPTER 30:
A QUEST FOR VENGEANCE

FINALLY, THE PAIN STOPPED. SILMANUS LAY THERE, gasping for breath, every muscle in his body screaming and robbed of strength. His mind ached as much as his body, vision blurred as he clawed desperately at the ground, trying with all his might to use what little strength he still possessed to drag himself out of the way, to move just a little farther so that whatever spell the Dark Elf had cast would miss, would crash against dirt and not Silmanus.

But it was useless. He was too weak and succeeded only in drawing a few faint lines in the dirt, shallow gashes that stood as his last imprint upon a world he was about to be rent from.

He heard it then, a powerful explosion that sent wisps of black cascading around his vision, blotting out his last sight of the world, stealing from him one last glimpse at the stars. There would be more pain and then silence, deep and eternal peace. Silmanus waited for it, shut his eyes and steeled his mind against the coming agony.

He waited. And he waited. And he waited. Ages seemed to pass as Silmanus waited for the waves of anguish to roll over his body, for his final death throes to seize him and send him writhing across the ground.

After an eternity of waiting, Silmanus wondered if he was already dead. He blinked open his eyes, struggling to see past the tears that had gathered there.

Around him, thirty-four Dark Elves lay dead, and as many humans alongside them. Blood stained the dark ground, visible only in the flickering light of the bonfire and blazing huts. Ivar and Helga stood stoically above several brutalized corpses, bleeding from dozens of scratches and a couple of deeper wounds. Linos was propped up against his trident, wiping sweat and blood from his brow as he panted. Anne and Norman lay dead in the dirt, several deep, long gashes lining their lifeless bodies, dull eyes wide and unseeing. Mara was on her knees, shedding silent tears and staring at Silmanus with wide, helpless eyes. And Cara...

Silmanus realized with horror that he was not dead, that the explosion he had heard was the sound of a spell breaking upon a wooden shield, which now lay in splinters around and across Silmanus, the targe's trademark iron spike sitting uselessly on the dirt, the metal rusted and warped.

Cara lay beside that spike, her breathing shallow, her arms splayed limply across the ground.

"Cara," Silmanus whispered, his voice husky and weak. "Cara."

The fierce Lochadian woman turned her head, locking her eyes with Silmanus. There was pain in those fiery brown orbs, but not regret. Her left arm, her shield arm, was black and rotted, the veins on the left side of her neck swollen and black as well. Cara gave a weak smile, her voice hoarse and grating as she spoke.

"Loch a thistle up th' erse," she said with a wince. "If eh'd knoon it woods hurt thes bad, eh'd hae lit th' damn elf kill ye. Waur than 'at bludy healin' speel yoo'd used."

"No, no, no," Silmanus protested. "No, this can't be happening."

"Och, suck it up, ye big pansy!" Cara snapped, wincing at the jolt of pain in sent through her chest. "Aam nae gonnae anywhaur! Nae if Ah can help it!" Cara winced again and her face blanched. "But Gods be damned, Ah don't ken if Ah can."

"Cara," Silmanus said weakly. "Thank you."

"Aw, sae yer cheers," Cara breathed, looking up at the stars above. "Jist gie me a damned medic an' a shot ay whisky." Cara looked back at Silmanus. "Don't ye daur die oan me, elf. Ah didn't tak' 'at damned speel jist fer ye tae die in th' end."

Silmanus nodded. "You hang in there, too, Cara," Silmanus replied, trying to fight back tears.

"Don't ye fash yerse abit me, laddie," Cara sighed, telling Silmanus not to worry. "If Ah die, weel, it's hoo Ah was meant tae gang. Jist gie ben thes fur me."

With that, Cara closed her eyes and looked once more to the stars, her face pale and empty. Silmanus wasn't sure if she was breathing anymore. If she was still alive.

Silmanus wanted to cry, wanted to break down and scream, but he simply couldn't. He didn't have a shred of energy left in his entire body, all his strength sapped away by the Dark Elf magic. All he could do was close his eyes and let the blackness swallow him whole.

Silmanus awoke to a pair of soft, chocolatey eyes staring down at him. A damp cloth was being wiped over his forehead and the air around him smelled of balsam and pine, as well as a sweet, woody fragrance that Silmanus couldn't quite place.

As his blurry vision shifted into focus, Silmanus recognized Nazim, the healer boy, as the owner of those youthful brown eyes. Three brass incense pots released smoke into the air around Silmanus, likely the source of the smells. Various herbs hung from the ceiling and an assortment of vials and bandages lined the walls. He was in the healer's hut.

Nazim noticed Silmanus' gaze land on the incense. "Myrrh, pine, and sandalwood," he said with a distinctive Hynari accent. "Where I come from, incense is good for healing."

Silmanus nodded. It was true too; burning various woods

released their magic and could help restore a person's vitality. The High Elf rested his head back. "How long have I been asleep?"

"Not long. One day, two nights."

Silmanus' whole body ached, although not nearly as bad as it had during the attack. His head throbbed as well and his vision swam a little bit.

"You are not ok yet," Nazim said in as stern of a voice as the little twelve-year-old could muster. "I will get Eleanor, she will help." Nazim rushed off, calling for Eleanor.

Silmanus closed his eyes, breathing deeply as he tried to fight away the headache. After a few minutes, Nazim returned with Eleanor. She gave Silmanus a warm smile.

"Good to see you awake, Silmanus," Eleanor said. "You saved a lot of lives the other night. This village owes you a tremendous debt."

"I'll count it repaid if you can get rid of this headache I've got," Silmanus grunted.

"Sadly, there's nothing I can do for that. I've already given you what painkillers I can, only time will heal the rest."

Silmanus let out a heavy sigh. "How much time?"

Eleanor shrugged. "I honestly have no idea. I've never healed someone from magical wounds before, so I couldn't tell you. Not too much longer though, I'm sure. You have a remarkable immune system."

"I'll take that as a compliment." Silmanus paused for a moment. "How?"

Eleanor blinked. "Sorry?"

"One day, two nights. Even for a wizard as powerful as myself, that's a remarkably quick time to recover from the kind of wounds I had," Silmanus explained. "How did you do it?"

Eleanor smiled slyly. "I learned from the best," she said with a wink.

It dawned on Silmanus as he noticed the empty vials and

frostpetal leaves lying next to him. The wizard grinned. "You used my tonics."

Eleanor put her hands on her hips. "*Your* tonics? I made those myself, I'll have you know."

"My apologies," Silmanus replied. "You are a very fast learner. I can see why Mara respects you so much."

"Speaking of whom, there's someone who would like to see you," Eleanor informed. "If you're up to it?"

Silmanus gave his best attempt at a casual wave. "Yeah, sure."

Mara stepped into the hut, looking at Silmanus with a mixture of relief and sadness. "I'll give you two some privacy," Eleanor said, leading Nazim out of the hut.

Mara rushed forward and wrapped Silmanus in a hug, which caught the elf totally off guard. He knew as well as anyone that Mara was not the hugging type. Feeling rather awkward, not to mention exhausted, Silmanus weakly patted Mara on the back.

"Ow, ok, please get off now," Silmanus winced, his sore body protesting painfully against Mara's embrace.

The young woman let go and stood straight again, nodding apologetically. "Thank you so much," she said. "If it hadn't been for you, so many more of my people would be dead, and probably me along with them. I don't know how I can repay you."

Silmanus shook his head. "You don't need to," he said with a smile. "All I ask is that you keep a promise of your own."

Mara frowned. "And what was that?"

"Help me find out what happened to my parents," Silmanus urged. "Mara, I can't explain why, but their disappearance and the Dark Elf attacks...I'm sure that they're linked. And don't you want to know what the Dark Elves are up to? Why they're going after you *now*, and not years ago?" Silmanus' eyes turned grim. "We need to go to Vanaria."

Mara bit her lip. "That's a suicide mission," she said at length. "Vanaria is the most secure kingdom in the world, except maybe for Pyradia. Still, you can't simply waltz in and steal something that they are likely guarding twice as diligently now. Not even my father could do it and he was one of the finest Rangers to have ever lived."

"And so are you," Silmanus said. "I have seen you do battle with Dark Elves time and time again and every single time, you outmatch them twofold. Dark Elves, Mara! The deadliest combatants on this planet! And do not forget, you'll have a wizard with you, and this time, I won't have any reason to hold back my most destructive spells. Not to mention Linos, who is a monster with that trident of his. You'll have Ivar and Helga, too, and I'm sure Cara..." Silmanus trailed off suddenly, his heart sinking as he remembered what had happened.

"Where's Cara?" Silmanus asked anxiously, trying to sit up.

Mara held him down gently. "She's ok," Mara told him. Silmanus felt relief wash over him like a warm ocean wave. "She's hurt, and badly, but Eleanor has managed to save her. With frostpetal, of all things." Mara shook her head with a smile, remembering her first encounter with Silmanus. "She's going to be ok. She just needs rest."

Silmanus nodded. "So, will you go? If not for me and my parents, then for your people, your father, for getting to the bottom of this mess."

After a few minutes that seemed like an eternity, Mara finally began nodding. "Alright," she agreed. "But *I* am in charge. You do everything I say. Got it?"

Silmanus grinned and nodded, although his neck did not thank him for the movement. "Got it," he said eagerly.

"Good. My first order is to stay there and rest. Don't even think about moving until Eleanor gives you the all-clear," Mara instructed sternly.

"You got it, Boss," Silmanus replied.

Mara sighed. "And don't call me 'Boss'."

"Whatever you say, Boss."

Mara shook her head and left, mumbling something about how much a pair of elf ears could fetch on the black market. Silmanus just grinned and closed his eyes again, anxious to get rested so he could get back at the Dark Elves who had brought so much pain and evil to this village.

It took a few days, but Silmanus was soon back on his feet, completely recovered from his physical injuries. His magic, however, was still healing, worms of dark energy still lingering in his soul like veins of ice. Silmanus knew his magic had been scarred, that an echo of the damage would remain there for the rest of his life, but, with time, his strength would return in full.

As Silmanus began rejoining the community, he was greeted by an endless flood of "thank yous" and "we are in your debts" by the grateful villagers. One little girl, no older than six and with a head of curly blonde hair, had given Silmanus a little kiss on the cheek, thanking him for saving her "momma and little brother." The gratifying gesture stuck with Silmanus for the rest of the day, a reminder of the innocence he was now fighting to protect.

Silmanus spent the day hidden away in his hut, studying his spells and hiding from the compliments and gifts he was being showered with. He didn't want any recognition for his acts and the attention was rather irritating.

That evening, Silmanus rose from bed to find Cara. He was directed to a hut near the one Silmanus had been recovering in.

Stooping into the doorway, Silmanus entered the warm, candlelit room. It was clearly a healer's hut as well, as evidenced by the various ointments and vials along some shelves along the wall, but Silmanus guessed it was more of an auxiliary hut, in case Eleanor's main one was occupied.

Three beds were laid in the centre of the hut, a person lying in each. Silmanus didn't recognize the first two, but the third held the unforgettable red hair and freckle face of Silmanus' wily Lochadian friend.

Cara noticed Silmanus enter. "Geid tae see ye oan yer feit, elf," she wheezed. Cara was still weak, her face paler than usual and a tired look in her eyes.

"Good to see you alive," Silmanus replied, smiling. "How's your arm?"

Cara gave a little shrug. "Hurts," she laughed. "But Eleanor says it will gie better. Don't suppose there's anythin' ye can dae fur it, is thaur?"

Silmanus shook his head. "Not yet. If you're desperate, I can later, but wait until you're stronger. You know better than anyone that it'll hurt."

Cara nodded. "Reit ye ur." There was a brief silence before Cara said, "Weel, doc says Ah need tae rest, sae yoo'd better scram afair she drags ye it by yer lugs."

"Yeah, you're probably right," Silmanus grinned. He turned to leave but hesitated and turned back. "I'm glad to see you're alive."

"Ye tay, elf," Cara replied with the warmest smile she could muster. "Noo gie it ay here."

Silmanus grinned again and left Cara in peace, meandering through the village back to his own hut, where he lay down for a good night's sleep.

A few more days passed, and Cara got stronger with each. Eleanor had mastered the frostpetal tonic remarkably quickly and had been using it to great effect to help heal Cara. Silmanus eventually used his excruciating healing spell to repair the last of the damage on Cara's arm. Before long, she was back on her feet and as lively as ever.

Monotony had a chance to set in for a couple days after that. The Dark Elf wizards had destroyed several huts and Silmanus had inadvertently burned down a few himself, so he spent his time helping with repairs. He took a few hours every day to meditate and exercise his magic, gradually pushing out the last of the dark magic.

Then, one morning, Mara approached Silmanus wearing a stuffed leather backpack. Her sword was slung across her back behind it. One of her knives was sheathed in her leather boot, the other on her belt opposite her hatchet. A quiver of arrows hung behind the knife and her bow was strapped to the side of her pack. Linos stood beside her, also carrying a backpack with his trident in hand.

"Get packed," Mara ordered. "We leave for Marrelnia in an hour."

Marrelnia was the Sea Elf kingdom, home to the merriest and most welcoming of the elves. Its capital city, Andorei, was situated at the end of the Elven Bay, making it the perfect place for a trading port. The dwarves of Thelegard and men of Lochadia traded goods with the Sea Elves and the captains of those ships were often willing to ferry passengers between the nations.

Silmanus wasted no time. He grabbed everything he had, books, blanket, and everything else, magically tying up the pack and slinging it across his back before belting his swords across his waist and grabbing his staff.

A loud cough came from the doorway of his hut. Silmanus whirled around to see Bredon standing there, the grumpy cook that had been so put off by Silmanus' presence at the village.

"I wanted to thank ye, elf," the man said in a low voice, eyes at the ground. "Yer shield saved me wife and little boy. So, I brought ye these." Bredon held out a silver coffee pot and a large leather bag, as well as an ornately carved mug, decorated with knots and designs typical of Lochadian craft.

Silmanus opened the leather bag, delighted to see it stuffed with coffee grinds. "Ye earned these," Bredon said, still not meeting Silmanus' eyes.

The wizard gave a grateful nod, placing a hand on one of Bredon's burly shoulders. "Thank you. You're a good man, Bredon. Your son is lucky to have you."

"Yer not so bad yerself, elf. Guess I was wrong about ye."

"Take care, Bredon. I'll miss your cooking." With that, Silmanus patted Bredon's shoulder and strode past him, eager to get on the road to Marrelnia, and from there, Vanaria.

Linos and Mara were waiting for him. Linos sat astride a muscled chestnut stallion, leather bag on his back, fearsome trident in his hand. Mara was armed with her sword and bow, wearing a backpack stuffed with travel essentials, and mounted on the most majestic creature Silmanus had ever seen.

Blackthorn had lived up to expectation. Her fur was sleek and glossy, a shade of black that Silmanus could not quite describe, powerful muscles rippling beneath. She had a flowing mane and tail, as well as a pair of magnificent black wings tucked at her sides. An intelligent light gleamed in her keen eyes, seeming to look straight at Silmanus with a curious expression.

"Whoa," was all Silmanus could manage, struggling to contain the childish giddiness rising up inside him.

His attention was soon torn from the captivating animal, however. Blizzard stood beside them, padding impatiently at the ground, fur like snow shimmering in the sunlight. Silmanus' horse gave a jealous whiny, silently scolding Silmanus for admiring a different equine creature.

Silmanus noticed with some surprise Ivar and Helga waiting with Linos and Mara as well, dressed in their customary furs, armed with their massive axes and carrying packs of their own. Silmanus noted with some amusement that they were mounted on identical black horses, feeling a pang of pity for the poor beasts having to bear such monstrous humans. They were massive, muscular horses though, so Silmanus figured they'd be alright.

Cara was there, too, grinning like an excited child on the back of her shaggy steed, wearing a tartan sash and simple brown clothing. She had been fashioned a new, spiked targe, which sat gleaming on her left arm, long dirk sheathed on her belt. Silmanus noticed she also carried an assortment of axes on her belt and leather backpack.

"I've made all the arrangements," Mara informed the wizard as he pulled himself into his saddle. "Reynard is in charge. He'll look after everyone."

Silmanus nodded grimly. He knew that Mara didn't just mean short-term arrangements; she had prepared for a permanent shift in leadership. The odds of the group returning from their quest were slim to none. Despite the probability of a painful death ahead, they paraded out of the village with their heads held high, the cheering of the villagers at their backs, the uncertainty of adventure before them. It was off to Vanaria, the land of Dark Elves.

It was off to their dooms.

Epilogue

KING ZARAT SLUMPED FORWARD IN HIS CHAIR, RESTING his elbows on his desk and his head in his hands, rubbing exhaustion from his eyes.

It had been ten days since the prisoners had escaped. Zarat seethed at the mere thought of that devastating day. The dwarves, vermin though they might have been, were his only chance at executing his plan, at liberating his people from the clutches of Vanaria.

Everything had been going according to plan, until the prisoners escaped. Not only had they slipped through Zarat's fingers, but they had killed his general, Mordasine, Zarat's finest warrior and most cunning tactician. Zarat's friend.

Attempts to recapture the prisoners had been frustratingly unsuccessful. They had taken Zarat's fastest ship and the Dark Elf doves, which were used as scouts and messengers, could not fly over the open water, nor could they fly fast enough to catch the stolen sloop.

Worse yet, the warriors he had sent north hadn't contacted him in a week. The wizards were supposed to keep a regular magical relay with him, and their prolonged silence likely meant something had gone wrong. That Ranger girl—damn her and her father— was a loose end Zarat could not afford to have, and it seemed that she, too, had escaped his grasp, and for a second time.

Zarat's plan had fallen to ruin.

A brief knock on Zarat's door startled the Dark Elf from his thoughts. He stood up suddenly, smoothing out his black clothing before answering, "Enter."

A Dark Elf woman pushed open the black door, bowing to Zarat as she entered his chambers. She was dressed in the black uniform of a Dark Elf soldier, but the silver dove wings embroidered on the shoulders of her jerkin revealed that she was not just a soldier, but a captain of the Dark Elf army.

Zarat knew this Dark Elf. He knew every Dark Elf in his kingdom. This was Azmarel, one of Zarat's most lethal captains, skilled both in swordplay and magic. She had been the one to capture Thalassar, one of the High Elf prisoners, and was one of the five captains in line to succeed Mordasine.

"Azmarel. What a pleasant surprise. What brings you here at this hour?" Zarat asked, speaking quietly. Sindra was asleep in their bed, and he did not want to wake her.

"My liege, we have been trying to break the High Elf for many days now, but he proves stubbornly resilient to all of our methods," Azmarel explained. Zarat noted that she spoke without any fear or hesitation, which Zarat admired; many of his other soldiers were frightened to bring Zarat bad news, on account of the king's temper.

"Get to your point, Azmarel," Zarat urged, knowing the captain never brought him news that wasn't without meaning.

"I believe that continuing to torment this High Elf is simply a waste of time. If he even knows where his allies are going, he will never reveal it," Azmarel stated plainly.

Zarat's heart dropped. Thalassar had been his last hope. "Then kill him," the king ordered coldly.

"Well, my lord, I believe there to be a better use for him," Azmarel replied.

"Do tell," Zarat said flatly.

Azmarel laid out her plan to Zarat, who nodded slowly. There was a reason this elf was a captain, and she was showing it.

"There is, however, a risk," Azmarel finished. "These dwarves and their allies are far more resourceful than we had anticipated, and the plan could fail. We need to prepare for Plan B."

Zarat straightened. Plan B was an intimidating and difficult option. It could result in an absolute annihilation of his entire army, and Zarat could not afford that. But what other choice did he have?

After a minute, Zarat finally nodded. "Very well," he said. "I will deal with the High Elf. Begin the preparations…General Azmarel."

Azmarel's chest swelled with pride and she grinned sinisterly. "As you wish, my lord," she answered, bowing low before leaving the room.

Zarat let out a deep breath. All was not lost yet. His plan could still come to fruition. The wheels of war were turning.

And soon, Zarat would burn the world.

As the Dark Elves laid in place the first steps for their new plan, a dark figure hundreds of deciums away watched through a black scrying stone. White chains, once enchanted with the most powerful magic to have ever been used, lay shattered on the dark, ragged floor around him. He was equal parts tangible and incorporeal, a malevolent collection of ancient power and dark magic, his body a twisted combination of shadow and flesh. Hellish red eyes burned with an evil, intense enough to drive a man to madness in a mere instant. His mouth was a void of soul-sucking blackness, a bottomless pit darker than anything else in the universe. Shadowy energy snaked off his body, seeping deep into the rock beneath his feet, filling the cavern with choking, sinister darkness.

Uzteus smiled at the sight of the plotting elves, his grip on their corrupted minds as strong as it ever was. The seeds for his second coming had been sown.

And this time, no one could stop his return.

Glossary and Pronunciations

Aeternium: *Ay-**ter**-nee-um*. Refers to some of the pivotal tales in the history of Aeternerras.

Places

Aeternerras: *Ay-**ter**-ner-ah*. The island continent upon which these lands and peoples dwell.

Andorei: *An-**dor**-ay*. The capital city of Marrelnia.

Arcantia: *Ar-**can**-tee-ah*. A fallen dwarven kingdom. Because it no longer exists, Arcantia is the only listed location that cannot be found on the map, but it used to lie within the Forgotten Mountains. Adjective form: Arcantian (*Ar-**can**-tee-in*).

Argenrros: *Ar-**jen**-roess*. The capital city of Faeryln.

Eiraland: ***Eer**-a-land*. One of the human kingdoms, found between Faeryln and the Northguard Mountains. Adjective form: Eiran (***Eer**-in*).

Esnia: ***Ez**-nee-ah*. A human kingdom in the middle of the west coast. Adjective form: Esnian (***Ez**-nee-in*).

Faeryln: *Fay-riln*. The nation of the High Elves. Adjective form: Faeryn (*Fay-rin*).

Fell Lands, The: The desolate lands south of the Fire Mountains where the forces of evil were banished.

Fort Vanguard: A massive fortress–city in Pyradia, designed to protect against Dark Elf invasion.

Gryzland: *Griz-land*. The kingdom of the gnomes. Adjective form: Gryzan (*Griz-in*).

Helvark: *Hell-vark*. The northernmost human kingdom. Adjective form: Helvan (*Hell-vin*).

Hynar, North/South: *Hi-nar*. The desert lands in the southwest of Aeternerras. Divided between the North and South. Adjective form: Hynari (*Hi-nar-ee*).

Island of Banishment: The fabled island where the Dark God, Uzteus, was imprisoned.

Lochadia: *Lah-kay-dee-ah*. A human kingdom found just west of the Iron Mountains. Adjective form: Lochadian (*Lah-kay-dee-in*).

Marrelnia: *Mah-rel-nee-ah*. The nation of the Sea Elves. Adjective form: Marrelnian (*Mah-rel-nee-in*).

Pyradia: *Pie-ray-dee-ah*. The nation of the Fire Dwarves. Adjective form: Pyradian (*Pie-ray-dee-an*).

Thelegard: *Thel-e-gard*. The nation of the Iron Dwarves. Adjective form: Thelegarn (*Thel-e-garn*).

Vanaria: *Vah-nare-ee-ah*. The kingdom and place of banishment of the Dark Elves. Adjective form: Vanarian (*Vah-nare-ee-in*).

Volhad: *Vole-had*. The capital city of Vanaria.

People

Amber: *Am-ber.* A dwarven warrior and adventurer, Jeddo's companion. One of the story's protagonists.

Anne: *An.* A human huntress, one of Mara's lead hunters. Sister to Norman.

Airic: *Ay-ric.* The former King of Lochadia. Deceased.

Ayra: *Ay-ruh.* A High Elf, imprisoned by the Dark Elves. Wife to Thalassar.

Azmarel: *Az-mar-el.* A fierce Dark Elf captain.

Bredon: *Bree-dun.* A human, Mara's chief cook.

Cara: *Car-ah.* A human warrior and seamstress, friend to Mara.

Cedric: *Se-dric.* Acting king (chieftain) of Lochadia.

Eleanor: *El-en-or.* A human physician, Mara's chief physician.

Evalyn: *Ev-ah-lin.* A human, imprisoned by the Dark Elves. Wife to Percival.

Guralyn: *Ger-uh-lin.* A dwarf, imprisoned by the Dark Elves. Wife to Harik.

Harik: *Har-ik.* A dwarf, imprisoned by the Dark Elves. Husband to Guralyn.

Helga: *Hel-guh.* A human warrior, one of Mara's guard captains. Twin sister to Ivar.

Ivar: *Eye-var.* A human warrior, one of Mara's guard captains. Twin brother to Helga.

Jeddo: *Je-doe.* A gnomish adventurer, Amber's companion. One of the story's protagonists.

Linos: *Lie-noess.* A human warrior, Mara's best friend.

Mara: **Mar**-*uh*. A human warrior, huntress, and the leader of her village. One of the story's protagonists.

Mordasine: **Mor**-*dah-zeen*. The General of the Dark Elf forces.

Nazim: *Nah-**zeem**.* A young human physician, apprenticed to Eleanor.

Norman: **Nor**-*min*. A human hunter, one of Mara's chief hunters. Brother to Anne.

Percival: **Per**-*si-vil*. A human merchant, imprisoned by the Dark Elves. Husband to Evalyn.

Reynard: **Ray**-*nard*. A human tradesman, Mara's chief of trade and storage.

Silmanus: **Sil**-*mun-us*. A High Elf wizard. One of the story's protagonists.

Sindra: **Sin**-*druh*. The Queen of the Dark Elves. Wife to Zarat.

Thalassar: **Thal**-*ah-sar*. A High Elf, imprisoned by the Dark Elves. Husband to Ayra.

Zarat: **Zare**-*at*. The King of the Dark Elves. Husband to Sindra.

Gods

Hutos: **Hew**-*toess*. The King of the Dwarven Gods.

Ilbus: **Il**-*bus*. The God of Eiran religion. Also recognized by Lochadia.

Sarissa: *Sa-**riss**-a*. High Elf goddess of elves and magic.

Uzteus: **Uz**-*tee-us*. The elven name for the Dark God. Also called Zakor (**Zay**-*kor*) and Fitis (**Fie**-*tis*) in some human religions.

MATERIALS

Arcanium: *Ar-**cane**-ee-um*. A substance made of pure magic, found often as a liquid or a crystal. Extremely unstable, but has many useful properties and potentials.

Mithril: [*Pronunciation varies.*] A very light and strong metal, found abundantly in the Iron Mountains.

Red Iron: A rare type of metal found only in the Fire Mountains. It is impervious to virtually any flame and offers its wearer extraordinary protection against heat.

Silversteel: A magical metal made by combining mithril with silver. Wards against dark magic. Very commonly used by High Elves.

Units

Castle: A unit of currency, made of gold. The largest unit of currency, worth 10 Shields and 100 Helms.

Decium: ***Dess**-ee-um*. A standard unit of distance. Equivalent to the distance a person can walk in ten minutes.

Helm: A unit of currency, made of copper. The smallest unit of currency, worth 0.1 Shields and 0.01 Castles.

Shields: A unit of currency, made of silver. The middle unit of currency, worth 10 Helms and 0.1 Castles.

Months/Dates

Resgal: ***Rez**-gull*. A Lochadian celebration meaning "Day of Renewal". Marks the coming of the warm weather and harvest season and occurs on the first day of Somaig.

Somaig: *So-mayg*. The fifth month in the Lochadian calendar, meaning "Near Summer". The High Elves call this month Floritha (*Flor-ith-ah*).

Acknowledgements

I DON'T THINK ANY BOOK HAS EVER BEEN THE RESULT OF just a single person's efforts. While the author might be the one to write the book, there are many more people involved in revising it, polishing it, and turning that terrifying stack of 8-by-11 paper into a beautiful, legitimate novel. Which is about as cliché as it gets, but that doesn't make it any less true.

Before taking this to publishers, I had to actually write and revise this book, and there are a number of people whose support and editorial assistance I have found absolutely invaluable. There is an endless list of teachers and friends and family who have encouraged me throughout this project—and continue to do so. In particular, I would like to thank Mila Knecht, Mikaila Kimball (who was also part of the inspiration behind Mara), Brook Hann, and Paris Fuzy, who have not only been huge supporters of my novel but each took the time to sit down with the earlier drafts and helped me whip them into shape. Of course, I also owe so much to my family, who have helped me with editing, finding a publisher, and more. Call me sentimental, but I truly could not have finished this book without all of you. So thank you.

I'd also like to extend a special thank you to Canadian author and family friend Terry Fallis. He took the time to give me some excellent advice on writing and publishing which really helped me figure out where to take this novel.

However, the publication process is rather difficult without a publishing company, so I would also like to thank FriesenPress for their tremendous role in this undertaking. More specifically, I would like to thank my Publishing Specialist Team, Jordan Rokosz, Diane Cameron, Liza Weppenaar, and Jessica Feser, for guiding me through this incredible process and answering all my many questions. I'd also like to thank my cover designer, Geoff Soch, for creating the stunning cover to this book. And of course, another huge thank you goes to FriesenPress Editor Catherine Rupko, both for her inspiring praise and her editing expertise. She really helped me bring this book to a whole new level.

And thank you, reader. I know this is also pretty sappy, but it truly does mean a lot knowing that there are people out there who have taken the time and interest to sit down with (and hopefully enjoy) my book. Never stop reading!

About the Author

A.G.V. MCPHERSON IS AN AVID reader of fantasy and player of fantasy games including Dungeons & Dragons. It is fitting, then, that he should write a novel in this beloved genre. Mr. McPherson has previously written many unpublished short stories and a novel and has also won academic awards for English on three occasions.

From Out of the Shadows is the first of four books in *The Aeternium Cycle* series. Born in Timmins, Ontario, A.G.V. McPherson now lives with his family in Corbeil, Ontario, surrounded by a myriad of trees and a plethora of pets, including a dog, a gecko, a rat, and some fish.